A History and Anthology of the Spanish Folktale, with Studies of Selected Texts

A HISTORY AND ANTHOLOGY OF THE SPANISH FOLKTALE, WITH STUDIES OF SELECTED TEXTS

Huw Aled Lewis

With a Foreword by
Patricia Odber de Baubeta

The Edwin Mellen Press
Lewiston•Queenston•Lampeter

Library of Congress Cataloging-in-Publication Data

Lewis, Huw Aled.
  A history and anthology of the Spanish folktale, with studies of selected texts /
Huw Aled Lewis ; with a foreword by Patricia Odber de Baubeta.
      p. cm.
  Includes bibliographical references and index.
  ISBN-13: 978-0-7734-5323-4
  ISBN-10: 0-7734-5323-7
  I. Title.

hors série.

A CIP catalog record for this book is available from the British Library.

The Edwin Mellen Press
Box 450
Lewiston, New York
USA 14092-0450

The Edwin Mellen Press
Box 67
Queenston, Ontario
CANADA L0S 1L0

The Edwin Mellen Press, Ltd.
Lampeter, Ceredigion, Wales
UNITED KINGDOM SA48 8LT

Printed in the United States of America

For my parents

TABLE OF CONTENTS

FOREWORD

This ground-breaking book achieves several objectives at one fell swoop. First and foremost, it makes available to the English-speaking reader, for the first time, fifteen folktales that do not appear in any other collection. The fact is, a disappointingly small number of Iberian folktales have appeared either in the original Spanish or in English translation over the last hundred or so years, and most of the latter are now out of print, out of date, or aimed at an exclusively juvenile readership. Thus we find Fernán Caballero's *Air built Castles* translated by Mrs Pauli (1887), a single folktale, 'The crafty farmer' published by Henry Thomas (1938), and *Spanish Fairy Tales* retold in English by John Marks with abundant illustrations but absolutely no indication of provenance (1957). Again, for children, Virginia Haviland's *Favorite Fairy Tales told in Spain* (1963). More recently, 64 Basque folktales and fables collected by José Miguel de Bandarián between 1900 and 1956 have been translated into English by Linda White (1991), and Robert Fedorchek has recently published English versions of fairy and wonder tales from the eighteenth and nineteenth centuries (1997, 2002), but his source texts are firmly located in the realm of the literary and therefore more refined than popular. Given this paucity of material, Dr Lewis's study is vitally important, making an invaluable contribution to scholarship by advancing knowledge and understanding of Spanish oral narrative and related areas, not only as studied in degree programmes, both undergraduate and

postgraduate, in universities in the USA and Europe, but equally as a point of reference and comparison for scholars of European folklore and cultural studies.

Dr Lewis's contextualisation and readings of Spanish folktales are manifestly informed by his earlier doctoral research which dealt, among other questions, with the Otherworld in popular medieval Spanish literature. This anthology, based on a thoroughgoing knowledge of the history and methodology of folktale research in Spain, comprises fifteen folktales, both the original Spanish texts and their English translations. Equally important, however, is the impeccably referenced introduction to the volume, virtually a monograph in its own right, which provides a history of the popular tale in Spain, broaches pertinent methodological considerations, considers at length the possible applications of those theories discussed, and opens up many new avenues of exploration for scholars.

The volume opens with an extremely useful introduction to Spanish folktales, indicating their purpose and the roles they fulfilled within communities and societies. Dr Lewis rightly points out that there has not been a great deal of attention paid to folktales in Spain. A number of Spanish genres have only been partially explored. The folktale is one of them, and it has not benefited from the kind of archaeological excavation undertaken for, say, the ballad, or, more recently, the proverb.

Through a comprehensive literature review, he draws our attention to the strongly regional bias of Spanish folklore studies, effectively providing the reader with a map of cultural recovery. Dr Lewis also takes the time and trouble to present a scheme of tale types that readers will be able to extend to their other readings. Indeed, he is at pains to guide the reader through the principal approaches to folklore analysis, namely the anthropological, structuralist and psychoanalytical, any of which the reader may choose to apply, in whole or in part, to the tales in this anthology. At every stage, he is at pains to set out the interpretative options available to the reader, always informing us about his own perspective and the reasons for adopting it.

It is worth singling out the lucid explanations of Freud and Jung, especially theories of the collective unconscious and archetypes. These may well be names and concepts that trip off the academic tongue, but they are not always adequately explained for the undergraduate or non-specialist reader. Increasingly, commentators use such terms, assuming the reader will immediately grasp their significance, failing to realize that readers may have a partial or faulty understanding of what are essential critical concepts or analytical tools.

It should also be noted that the folktales constitute a highly integrated mini-corpus. One of the principal selection criteria is commonality of theme, which has given rise to an unquestionable unity and cohesiveness within the anthology. Just about all of these stories show the drive towards adulthood, or rather how youth is being nudged towards adulthood and social integration. The folktales under discussion are all about growing up and taking responsibility, lessons no less relevant in the twenty-first century than when they were first recounted in oral narrative or recorded in writing. Something of a Darwinian ethos also permeates the tales; the underlying message of 'La princesa encantada' is summed up in the following terms: 'the weak and ailing will not succeed in this world for the dangers it presents, embodied in the serpent and giant, are real and great'.

Dr Lewis offers clear and convincing interpretations of the tales, breaking through their deceptive simplicity to demonstrate that they are immeasurably more complex than they first appear, and offering disconcertingly bold readings, as, for example, in 'Luisa y el dragón'. His illuminating commentaries are a good read in their own right, encouraging us, in turn, to read and reflect more widely, applying different theories and interpretations to other writings or, indeed, to human experience in general.

The author clearly delights in his subject matter, commenting on the 'very satisfying use of narrative triads', and emphasizing the artistry and symmetry that characterize the construction of the folktale. He singles out the stylistic and

psychological richness of the oral narrative, reminding us that there is infinitely more to folklore than primitive peoples sitting around the flickering flames in a shadowy cavern telling tales intended to amuse or even frighten one another. In these many-layered narratives, the emphasis is always on human society, and stories frequently enshrine a surprisingly dark view of parent-child relationships. Fathers lust after their daughters, mothers attempt to poison their sons, stepmothers are equally murderous towards their stepdaughters, and children must overcome or even (symbolically) kill their parents before they can assume their rightful place in adult society. Virtues and qualities such as gratitude and humility often bring their own rewards, yet deference to one's elders is not always a viable option.

Interestingly, 'El viaje maravilloso' stands out from the other tales because of the Christian elements that place it 'half-way to becoming a sermon'. These give the story a rather distinctive shape and texture, and also demonstrate how the stories can be appropriated for different purposes. In fact, they may be substantially altered or undermined with the deliberate overlaying of new meanings, a perhaps inevitable process over the course of time.

Dr Lewis sets out his criteria for editing and translating the folktales with admirable clarity. This work is characterized above all by a quest for authenticity and the avoidance of any unwarranted distortion or mediation of the original narratives. Translation can be a very personal act; Dr Lewis has made his translation process as transparent as possible, offering fluent, accurate renderings that do ample justice to the style and richness of the source texts. Moreover, the translator sensibly avoids the vexed question of the dialectal option. Translating into one British dialect in preference to another would have produced entirely the wrong resonances and connotations, mapping a social geography simply not present in the Spanish tales.

What is most remarkable about the tales that Dr Lewis has chosen to foreground? The way in which they bear witness to the continuity of human experience. I believe it is no exaggeration to suggest that focusing, as so many of

them do, on the passage from immaturity to maturity, the folktales may be viewed as the not-so-distant ancestors of the modern *Bildungsroman*, especially if we recall Jonathan Culler's (1975) discussion of cultural models and culturally significant actions, such as leaving home.

Dr Lewis brings to his task the analytical and linguistic skills that we would expect to find in any scholarly monograph or erudite article focusing on canonical literary texts, or quality translation. Nevertheless, we cannot help being struck by the author's almost intuitive understanding of these tales. There is as much relish in the retelling as in the translating and analysis: his commentaries are written with gusto, his translations hit the right note. This is not a dry and dusty account of folktales and their transmission, as we can see from vigorous lines such as 'Bullies, muscles and gung-ho heroes never ever triumph in these accounts'. Dr Lewis has done exactly what the reader or listener is supposed to do – he has responded by identifying with the underdog or inchoate hero.

In conclusion, Huw Lewis has become a new link in the storyteller's chain. He has made it possible for these Spanish folktales to traverse the boundaries of space, time and language. Thanks to his labour of love, they may now be read and appreciated by a new group of readers in the twenty-first century.

Dr Patricia Odber de Baubeta
Department of Hispanic Studies
The University of Birmingham

ACKNOWLEDGEMENTS

My thanks are due to the helpful comments and suggestions made by Professors Gareth Alban Davies, Ian Michael and Nicholas Round, and by Dr Patricia Odber de Baubeta. I am also grateful to the Biblioteca Nacional and the Consejo Superior de Investigaciones Científicas in Madrid for access to their resources, without which the current volume would not be possible.

INTRODUCTION

Since the dawn of civilization, mankind has attempted to make sense of the universe he inhabits by exploring its manifest workings and rules, as well as its riddles and hidden meanings. Science, religion and philosophy have helped to unravel some of these mysteries, as have myth and folktale, the strength of whose grip on the human mind, especially the subconscious, and particularly in pre-literate societies, is amply proven both by their currency in a wide array of societies and in a variety of languages, as well as by their enduring appeal and survival into modern times. This appeal continues unabated to the present day, in spite of the myriad alternative distractions and exhaustive sources of information available within contemporary society, as is shown by the popularity within genres such as literature, film and pantomime of stories whose debt to myths and folktales, either direct (for example, in the plots of pantomimes such as *Cinderella* or *Jack and the Beanstalk*) or indirect (for example, in the structures of novels and films such as *The Lord of the Rings* and *Harry Potter*) is clear for all to see. The enduring appeal of myth and folktale can be explained in part by their gripping plots, which deal with themes such as love, hate, treachery, death, triumph and disaster, all of which are topics which have fired the human imagination since time immemorial. However, another important factor that has contributed to their continuing relevance to societies throughout the ages is their metaphysical function as codes that explain, in imaginative and symbolic terms,

the workings of the cosmos and society. Myth, with its focus on superhuman beings, tends to focus on the former, while the folktale, whose protagonists are usually of more humble origins, predominantly explores the latter. Both, however, seek to provide their audience with an understanding of the world they inhabit and, especially in the case of the folktale, to provide them with patterns of behaviour that can, when appropriate, serve as warnings against, or guides for, their own endeavours.

All of this is reinforced, of course, by the highly communal nature of both myth and folktale. Originally transmitted by word of mouth, they evolved as a traditional form of literature,[1] subject to the usual modifications (both in terms of style and content) that are normally associated with oral culture, thus producing numerous variants, not only across linguistic divides, but within cohesive societal units also. They would also be recounted to groups (for example, the assembled village), not just from one individual to another, thus providing a focus for social gathering and the development of a single coherent worldview. Indeed, the goal of social cohesion lies at the very core of myth and folktale, whose symbolic framework is posited on providing a common understanding of society and the world, whose evolution is indebted to the endeavours of countless contributors, and whose delivery would bring the community together.

For all these reasons, myths and folktales have occupied, since their inception, a prominent position within popular culture, appealing to the conscious mind in the form of their intriguing plots, to the subconscious by dint of their symbolic resonances, and to the emotions through their generation of feelings of community. This, of course, is not to deny the value and importance of other forms of popular culture. Songs, too, from the lengthiest of epics to the

---

[1] For a discussion of traditional and popular literature, see Ramón Menéndez Pidal, *Poesía popular y poesía tradicional en la literatura española; conferencia leída en All Souls College el lunes, día 26 de junio de 1922* (Oxford: Clarendon Press, 1922). For a discussion of popular and elite culture, see C.W.E. Bigsby, ed., *Approaches to Popular Culture* (London: Edward Arnold, 1976).

simplest of lyric verse, would provide entertainment for the masses and bring them together in social gatherings. Some of these would also provide models of behaviour (for example, within Hispanic culture, the *Poem of the Cid*, where the protagonist is presented as the ideal Christian, warrior and father). In the realms of prose, exempla and other forms of popular tale would provide further means both to entertain and to instruct, but their didactic function is more explicit and often focused on the practical, pragmatic minutiae of social intercourse or spiritual development. Folktales, on the other hand, tend to explore grander social issues, such as the passage from childhood to adulthood, the responsibilities and problems of parenthood, or the relationship between the individual and the collective, their explorations of these themes being all the more effective because they are achieved through symbolic association rather than explicit exposition. By appealing to the subconscious as well as to the conscious mind, their emotive resonance is stronger and their grip on the human psyche is enhanced.

Given their associations and symbolic meanings, it is not surprising, therefore, that folktales should have achieved and retained such prominence in the popular imagination. Nor is it difficult to understand why they should also have been incorporated into more erudite literary forms in later centuries. As Chapter 1 shows, however, only in comparatively recent times have Spanish folktales been collected and studied in a systematic fashion. During the Middle Ages, much popular material was incorporated into the emerging literary genres, but relatively little of this was derived from the folktale *per se*. The greater part of this material is drawn from exempla and popular superstition, the former probably because of their very clear and explicit didactic function, the latter perhaps because of the human mind's understandable obsession with guarding against the unknown. Folktales, by contrast, are not explicitly didactic, nor do they offer any protection, irrational or otherwise, against life's vicissitudes, while the magical elements often contained within the tales might have attracted the disapproval of the Church. It is therefore understandable that they were

overlooked by early authors and scholars: regarded primarily as harmless entertainment, their deeper connotations and meanings went unnoticed, and the tales themselves unrecorded.

During the sixteenth and seventeenth centuries, when some collections of popular tales did begin to appear, folktales, with their marvellous and even supernatural elements, were again omitted in favour of more down-to-earth accounts which, while entertaining and even instructive, nevertheless fail do delve deeply, if at all, beneath the surface of the human mind. Even during the nineteenth century, when collections of authentic folktales began to emerge, there was also a taste for incorporating some of this material into contemporary literary genres, undermining much of its psychological resonance, as this relies heavily on the specific combination of a tale's structure and its symbolic connotations. If these are manipulated by a more conscious approach to literary creation, the folktale's impact is diluted, and it becomes increasingly difficult to identify its core meaning as a result of the modifications and additions made to it. As has been established above, folktales can only properly be understood as an expression of the collective; when an individual hand becomes too evident, or when they are placed in an inappropriate context, their role as an expression of popular culture and collective experience is undermined, and the point of the tale is lost.

From the above, it will be understood that a full appreciation of these folktales can only be achieved if they are reproduced as accurately as possible, with no form of stylistic or grammatical alteration or 'correction'. Naturally, something will always be lost in transcription: these tales are meant to be heard rather than read, and the performative dimension should not be forgotten. With this caveat in mind, this anthology faithfully reproduces the folktales as they appear in the original sources, with only a few modifications to paragraphing and punctuation. Spelling is unchanged and in many instances clearly reflects the spoken, rather than the written, word, for example, *güeno* for *bueno* 'good', *pa* for *para* 'in order to', *usté* for *usted* 'you'. Throughout, the oral background of

these accounts is reflected in their narrative style, in devices such as the repetition of the conjunction *y* 'and', the large amount of direct speech, and the occasional presence of the first-person narrator. Nevertheless, some of the tales undoubtedly betray a more conscious re-working, or the influence of the written word, such as in 'The Enchanted Forest', where the tale has been modified to address a more religious goal, in 'The Tambourine Made of Louse Skin', whose orthography is more standardized than in the other tales, and, to a lesser extent, in the reference to 'kind reader' at the end of 'The Sultan's Three Children'. These are included as examples of the type of influences that can affect folktales, and the results which such influences and modifications can produce. In all cases, the English translations attempt to reproduce the fluidity and natural expression of the original Spanish.

Chapter 2 outlines some of the main theoretical approaches to the study of myths and folktales, together with the main figures associated with those approaches. Chapter 3 provides an analysis of the folktales themselves. While any of the methods outlined in Chapter 2 could be adopted, for the purposes of the present study a predominantly Freudian psychoanalytical approach has been chosen, but this by no means precludes other modes of interpretation, which are equally as valid. The analyses represent one starting-point for an understanding of the tales' various resonances and implications, not a definitive interpretation. Indeed, the relatively simple narrative style of popular tales overlays a highly complex web of meaning and association which can be interpreted in a variety of ways and on several levels. It is the interrelation between this simplicity and this complexity that allows folktales to affect the human subconscious in such a lasting fashion, and makes them such a fascinating focus for research. This book is offered as a contribution to such an investigation in the field of Hispanic folktales.

PART I

The Spanish Folktale: Context and Analysis

CHAPTER 1

The History of The Popular Tale in Spain

The Middle Ages

Since the dawn of vernacular literature in the Iberian Peninsula, tales, anecdotes and *exempla* have been the meat and drink of so-called 'popular' and 'erudite' literature alike, providing material for works as diverse as the anonymous *Poema de Mío Cid* (*Poem of the Cid*),[2] Juan Ruiz's *Libro de buen amor* (*Book of Good Love*), and Berceo's *Milagros de Nuestra Señora* (*Miracles of Our Lady*). As well as being influenced by written sources, each of these very different texts also draws extensively on material from popular belief, superstition and folktale presenting (to a varying degree) conscious literary re-workings and crystallisations of situations and anecdotes already widely current in the popular oral traditions of their day. Nowhere is such written crystallisation of oral tales more noticeable than in the proliferation of vernacular collections of popular tales and exempla that began in Castile in the reign of Alfonso X, the Wise. The furthest origins of this material can be traced, in western tradition, to Aesop's fables and their Latin derivatives (especially the *Romulus*, of widespread popularity throughout Europe), and in oriental tradition to the *Panchatantra* and

---

[2] See Alan Deyermond, 'Folk-Motifs in the Medieval Spanish Epic', *Philological Quarterly*, 51, 1, (January 1972), 36-53.

other Indian fables. In these cases the means of transmission (as far as it is traceable) of the material is literary, but the origins of many of the tales are clearly rooted in the oral tradition. Entering Spain via north Africa, and eventually translated from Arabic to vernacular Spanish at the instance of Alfonso, the oriental stories, together with their western counterparts, offered preachers and moralists exemplary tales with which to instruct their congregations and audiences in graphic, entertaining and practical illustrations of the ethics and codes of behaviour being advocated or condemned from the pulpit. Thus these tales (commonly, though by no means exclusively stories about talking animals) came to be collected in manuals which preachers could use as sourcebooks for their sermons. From the twelfth century we have a veritable proliferation of such exemplum collections in the Peninsula, the earliest, Pedro Alfonso's Latin *Disciplina clericalis*, being followed from about the mid-thirteenth century by translations of other collections, such as, from oriental tradition, *Barlaam and Josaphat, Calila and Dimna, Libro de los gatos* (*Sendebar* or *The Book of Cats* [c. 1350]), and from Latin sources, the *Libro de los exemplos por a.b.c.* (*The Alphabetical Book of Exempla* [c. 1400-21]). The most notable literary production deriving from this genre was undoubtedly Don Juan Manuel's *El conde Lucanor* (*Count Lucanor* [1335]), where popular wisdom and tradition is combined with the conscious artistry of the literary craftsman. Designed, as they were, to exemplify certain modes of behaviour, the tales in these collections necessarily focus on such major themes and *topoi* as honesty, fidelity, wisdom and humility, all in concrete circumstances designed to illustrate how these qualities should be applied in everyday life and situations. Furthermore, although the morals illustrated by them are universally applicable and designed to instruct the commoner and the nobleman alike, it is noticeable that the many of these tales (particularly those from *El conde Lucanor*) deal with aristocratic characters, reflecting the clerical and didactic filtering process through which the tales have passed.

The Spanish Golden Age (sixteenth and seventeenth centuries)

Noticeable by their absence from collections such as those mentioned above are tales that, rather than dealing with concrete and specific moral dilemmas, depict *rîtes de passage*, tracing the major phases in human development (birth, puberty, marriage, death) and providing successive generations with norms against which to validate themselves as well as a means of exploring the complex and confusing issues which those vital stages inevitably generate. This certainly does not signify that such tales did not exist, of course. As I have already indicated, much material from such stories was included by medieval authors in their works, as references are to be found in troubadour compositions of the thirteenth and fourteenth centuries. Furthermore, since the fantastical contents of such tales bore no obvious relation to the practicalities of everyday living, and also focused primarily on the lower echelons of society, they were of less interest to the philosophers, theologians, and noblemen who provided the impulse for preserving such tales in writing. Not until the sixteenth century does Spain provide us with written compilations of such tales, and even then such production was limited to a few select works: Juan de Timoneda published four collections of tales: *El sobremesa y alivio de los caminantes* (*The After-Dinner Entertainer* [1563]), *El buen aviso* (*The Wise Warning* [1564]), *El patrañuelo* (*The Book of Tall Tales* [1566]), and *El sobremesa añadido* (*More After-Dinner Entertainment* [1569]),³ while in 1574 Melchor de Santa Cruz de Dueñas published his *Floresta española* (*Spanish Treasury*).⁴ As the titles of some of these collections clearly indicate, these collections were regarded primarily as

---

³ *Obras de Juan Timoneda* (Madrid: Sociedad de bibliófilos españoles, 1947-19480. See also J. Wesley Childers and John J. Reynolds, 'A Guide to the Motif-Index of Timoneda's Prose Fiction', *Kentucky Romance Quarterly*, 25 (1978), 399-412.

⁴ Ed. with a prologue and notes by María Pilar Cuartero and Maxime Chevalier, with a preliminary study by Maxime Chevalier (Barcelona: Crítica, 1997). For further information regarding the folktale during the Spanish Golden Age, see José María Pedrosa, *El cuento tradicional en los Siglos de Oro* (Madrid: Arcadia de las letras, 2005).

sources of light entertainment rather than as a means of gaining insight into the human psyche, and although they contain material which is oral and popular in origin, it is also significant that they still eschew the type of material that is of primary interest to us here, namely tales that focus mainly on the lower classes, containing fantastical elements, recounting events that are archetypally relevant to human rites of passage.

The Nineteenth Century

Not until the late nineteenth century does the serious and extensive study of popular traditions and folk literature make its appearance in the Iberian Peninsula.[5] This, of course, coincides with such study elsewhere in Europe, which had been prompted to a large extent by the Romantic interest in all forms of expression of 'primitive' ideas and modes. In Spain, this interest was soon to focus primarily on that most extensive and traditional of all indigenous popular verse forms, the ballad, but not before some important developments had taken place in the study of popular superstition, belief and tale. It is significant that this research seems to have been organized largely on a regional basis in Spain, with Catalonia and Andalusia being very much at its forefront. Individual collectors were extremely industrious in some other regions, for example Antonio de Trueba y la Quintana (Antón de los Cantares), who published some ten different anthologies of folktales collected from the Basque region between 1851 and 1910,[6] most of which ran to several editions. However, it was really in Catalonia,

---

[5] For a detailed account of folktale collection in Spain during the nineteenth century, see Alejandro Guichot y Sierra, *Noticia histórica del folklore. Orígenes en todos los países hasta 1890. Desarrollo en España hasta 1921* (Seville, 1922, repr. Junta de Andalucía, 1984).

[6] For example, *Cuentos campesinos* (Leipzig: F.A. Brockhaus, 1865); *Cuentos de varios colores* (Madrid: Centro general de administración, 1866); *Cuentos populares* (Madrid, Romero, 1909). For translations of some of his tales, see Robert M. Fedorchek, 'The Adventures of a Tailor', *Marvels & Tales*, 12, no 2 (1998), 351-63; *idem*, 'The King's Son-in-Law', *Marvels & Tales*, 15, no 2 (2001), 202-16; *idem*, *Stories of Enchantment from Nineteenth-century Spain* (Lewisburg, Pa: Bucknell University Press, 2002).

and to an even greater extent in Andalusia, that such research and publication began to be co-ordinated in a more systematic fashion. No-doubt this was due in part, at least, to the support of publishing houses such as Verdaguer, which seems to have been quite prolific in this field, producing various collections in the 1870s and 1880s. In Catalonia, not only did folklorists such as Mariano Aguiló y Fuster,[7] Francisco Pelayo Briz[8] and Francisco Maspons y Labrós[9] publish collections of tales, some with notes, but folklore material also began to be published in the Barcelona journals *La Gaya Ciencia* (*The Poesy* [1868]) and *El Renacimiento* (*The Renaissance* [1871]). Meanwhile, in Andalusia, literary figures such as Fernán Caballero (the pseudonym of Cecilia Francisca Josefa Böhl de Faber)[10] began reproducing folktales in their writings, although the literary air added to these stories make them largely unreliable as anything more than a general indicator of the type of material that was available in the region at the time.[11] Indeed, in a letter to Juan Eugenio Hartzenbusch, dated 11 April 1882, she states that, 'los cuentos no los compongo, y no hago sino anotar y borderlos' ('I do not invent these tales, I simply note and embroider them'). Unfortunately, it is precisely this embroidery that makes them unreliable as a focus for folklore

---

[7] *A la sombra del ciprés; cuentos y fantasías* (Palma: Imprenta de D.F. Guasp, 1863); *Recull de eximplis e miracles, gestes e faules e altres ligendes ordenades per A-B-C, tretes de un manuscrit en pergami del començament del segle XV* (Barcelona: A. Vergaduer, 1881).

[8] *Endevinallas populars catalanas: accompanyadas de variants y confrontaments ab endevinallas francesas, lituanas, vascas, gallegas, italianas, ribagorzanas, provensalas, alamanyas, anglesas, portuguesas, nearnesas, castellanas y senegambesas, seguidas de un aplech de endevinallas modernas* (Barcelona: Librería d'Edualt Puig, 1882).

[9] *Lo Rondallayre; quentos populars catalans* (Barcelona: Verdaguer, 1871-1872); *Lo Rondallayre; segona série* (Barcelona: Verdaguer, 1872); *Lo Rondallayre; tercera série* (Barcelona: Verdaguer, 1874).

[10] In some ways, Fernán Caballero was continuing in the footsteps of her father, Johan Nikolas Böhl von Faber who, in the sphere of Spanish literature, is known as the editor of a collection of early poems and of the theatre of Lope de Vega. For recent translations of some Spanish tales by Caballero, see Robert M. Fedorchek, 'The Devil's Mother-in-Law', *Marvels & Tales*, 15, no 2 (2001), 192-201; *idem*, 'The Bird of Truth', *Marvels & Tales*, 16, no 1 (2002), 73-83; *idem*, *Stories of Enchantment from Nineteenth-century Spain*; *idem*, 'The Souls in Purgatory', *Marvels & Tales*, 17, no 2 (2003), 258-61.

[11] See, for example, her *Cuentos y poesías populares andaluces: coleccionados* (Leipzig: F.A. Brockhaus, 1861).

research, though her alterations are less dramatic than those of Zorrilla who, in his *Leyendas* (*Legends*)[12] simply takes the kernel of various tales and legends, and then re-writes them in verse form. More illuminating and significant, however, are the numerous folklore journals that were founded in Andalusia from the second half of the century, and which have become known as the *Seville initiative*. In 1869, Federico de Castro y Fernández (a lawyer) and Antonio Machado y Núñez (a physicist) founded the *Revista Mensual de Filosofía, Literatura y Ciencias de Sevilla* (*Seville Monthly Journal of Philosophy, Literature and Science*) as a vehicle for publishing materials relating to the region, but the most significant single figure in the field of folklore research during this period is undoubtedly Antonio Machado y Álvarez who, in 1879, inaugurated a popular literature section in the Seville journal, *La Enciclopedia* (*The Encyclopaedia*), where a serious synchronic and diachronic study of popular literature was initiated. He was also the creator in 1881 of *El Folklore Español* (*Spanish Folklore*), which he envisaged as a society that, organized on a regional basis, would undertake the study of all aspects of popular local tradition and lore, and which had its counterpart in José María Sbarbi y Osuna's *La Academia Nacional de Letras Populares* (*National Academy of Popular Literature*), founded in January, 1882. Not surprisingly, Ramón Menéndez Pidal was also at the forefront of attempts to co-ordinate folklore research at the Universidad Central. As a first step in establishing his national organisation, Machado founded his own regional branch, *El Folklore Andaluz* (*The Folklore of Andalusia*), and its monthly journal (of the same name), in March 1882. This was precisely the impulse needed by other parts of Spain, which began founding their own regional branches of what was hoped would become a national organisation: *El Folklore Bético-Extremeño* (*The Folklore of Seville-Extremadura*) was founded in April, 1883, followed by *El Folklore Castellano* (*The Folklore of*

---

[12] José Zorrilla, *Leyendas* (Madrid: Cátedra, 2000).

Castile) in November, 1883, *El Folklore Vasco-Navarro* (*The Folklore of the Basque Country and Navarre*) in March, 1884, and *El Folklore Catalán* (*The Folklore of Catalonia*) in May, 1885. Unfortunately, although only Murcia, León, Aragón, Valencia, the Balearics and the Canaries failed to form a regional society at some point, Machado's initiative was painfully short-lived, the original *Folklore Andaluz* itself lasting less than a year. The reasons for this collapse are many and varied, but the failure of this attempt to co-ordinate folklore research on a national level did not signify a total end to the study of folklore within the various regions of Spain. Collections of tales and popular material continued to be published, the above-mentioned figures continuing to provide a lead in this respect. Antonio Machado y Álvarez published *Estudios sobre literatura popular* (*Studies on Popular Literature*),[13] a *Colección de enigmas y adivinanzas en forma de diccionario* (*Collection of Enigmas and Riddles in the Form of a Dictionary*)[14] and, in collaboration with Federico de Castro y Fernández, a collection of *Cuentos, leyendas y costumbres populares* (*Tales, Legends and Popular Customs*).[15] Indeed, in excess of twenty different anthologies and studies were published in the last quarter of the century alone, the most notable single production undoubtedly being the eleven-volume *Biblioteca de las tradiciones populares españolas* (*Library of Spanish Popular Traditions* [1883 – 1886]).[16] Clearly, therefore, there was considerable enthusiasm for the study of popular tradition and lore in Spain during the second half of the nineteenth century but, for reasons which are considered below, it proved impossible to sustain any form of co-ordination for these efforts, and so collections continued to be produced piecemeal with little regard to producing a global overview of the importance of popular tale and folklore within the Iberian Peninsula.

---

[13] Seville: A. Guichot and Company, 1884.

[14] Seville: Baldaraque, 1880.

[15] Seville: Gaditana, 1872.

[16] Ed. by Antonio Machado y Álvarez (Seville: A. Guichot and Company, and Madrid: Fernando Fé.

The Twentieth Century

The twentieth century has seen an enormous boom in the study of the popular cultures, traditions and tales of all nations, and this fact has inevitably brought with it a more methodical, reasoned and careful approach to the study of these phenomena, with the result that modern collections of tales appear to be more trustworthy and 'authentic' than their nineteenth-century predecessors. On an international level, several eminent scholars have made important contributions to our understanding of the various ways, and levels on which, myths, rituals and folktales function as they reflect and interact with their cultural surroundings, and some of their findings are discussed below in relation to the methodology of folktale analysis. The extensive field and theoretical research conducted by anthropologists such as Claude Lévi-Strauss has given us a fascinating insight not only into the way the myths and rituals of a given society reflect and explore the concerns and beliefs of the people to which it is endemic, but also into how a great many of the myths and rituals of different peoples, in spite of apparent superficial differences in detail among them, are, in fact, closely related to each other in terms of their subject-matter and world-view. Vladimir Propp's analysis of the structure of the folktale has shown us that many popular tales are also closely related in *form*, not merely in content, and as a result of these investigations invaluable research tools have been produced in the form of motif and tale-type indexes, the most significant of these on an international level being Stith Thompson's *Motif-Index of Folk Literature*,[17] and Antti Aarne and Stith Thompson's *The Types of the Folktale*.[18] These and their nation-specific counterparts (for example, the *Index of Spanish Folktales*,[19] the *Motif-Index of Spanish Exempla*,[20] *Tales from Spanish Picaresque Novels: A Motif-Index*,[21]

---

[17] 6 vols., 2nd edn., Copenhagen & Bloomington, 1955-8.
[18] Folklore Fellows' Communications N° 74 (Helsinki, 1928. 2nd edn, 1961).
[19] Ralph S. Boggs, Folklore Fellows' Communications, N° 90 (Helsinki, 1930).
[20] John Esten Keller, University of Tennessee Press, 1949.

Types and Motifs of Judeo-Spanish Folktales[22]) allow similar tales and even individual elements within tales to be traced from one text to another, and across national and linguistic boundaries, a procedure which can be helpful when attempting to decipher the meaning of obscure references, or even the possible sources of certain narrative devices, although there has also been considerable critical debate concerning the value of such indexes.[23]

In Spain, this more methodical approach to the study of folklore and the folktale began during the early 1920s when Aurelio M. Espinosa, a first-generation American of Spanish descent,[24] travelled through Spain collecting popular tales from all parts of the country, eventually publishing them in three volumes with extensive comparative notes during the period 1923-6.[25] Thanks to him, and to his equally enthusiastic son, of the same name,[26] as well as to other early collectors such as José A. Sánchez Pérez,[27] Antonio Machado y Álvarez, Aurelio de Llano Roza de Ampudia,[28] Constantino Cabal,[29] Marciano Curiel Merchán,[30] and others of similar verve and dedication, a substantial corpus of material was collected and preserved, a corpus that has been augmented and

---

[21] J. Wesley Childers, New York: State University of New York, 1977.

[22] Reginetta Haboucha, New York: Garland, 1992.

[23] See, for example, *Journal of Folklore Research*, 34, no. 3 (1997), which focuses on this issue, and Dan Ben-Amos, 'Are There Any Motifs in Folklore?' in Frank Trommler ed., *Thematics Reconsidered* (Amsterdam: Rodopi, 1995), 71-85.

[24] It may be significant in itself that this scholar, one of the foremost early collectors of the traditional, popular tale in Spain, was an American who did not normally reside in the Peninsula, as this meant that he was relatively unscathed by the rivalries that had disrupted the movement for decades.

[25] Aurelio M. Espinosa, *Cuentos populares españoles*, 3 vols. (Stanford University Press, 1923; 2nd edn., Madrid: CSIC, 1946-7); idem, *Cuentos populares de España*, 3 vols. (3rd edn., Madrid: CSIC, 1965).

[26] Aurelio M. Espinosa (hijo), *Cuentos populares de Castilla* (Buenos Aires: Espasa-Calpe, 1946).

[27] *Cien cuentos populares* (Madrid: Editorial Saeta, 1942; reprinted Barcelona: Biblioteca de Cuentos Maravillosos, 1992).

[28] *Cuentos asturianos. Recogidos de la tradición oral*. Archivo de Tradiciones Populares (Madrid: Caro Raggio, 1925).

[29] *Los cuentos tradicionales asturianos* (Madrid: Voluntad, 1924).

[30] *Cuentos extremeños* (Madrid: CSIC, 1944).

enhanced by the endeavours of more recent collectors[31] including, for the Basque region, José Miguel de Barandiarán and his nephew, Luis Barandiarán Irizar.[32] One of the regions which has proven most fruitful for research into popular culture and tradition has been Galicia.[33] As well as collections of tales taken from medieval[34] and more modern[35] sources, many critical studies of the traditions and the significance of Galician tales, beliefs and customs have also appeared,[36] such as Fermín Bouza Brey's *La mitología del agua en el noroeste hispánico* (*Water Mythology in North-eastern Spain*),[37] which explores the particular significance of water, a prominent feature of Galician folktales, and his *Etnografía y folklore de Galicia* (*Galician Ethnography and Folklore*),[38] which attempts to place Galician folklore more clearly within its cultural and social context. The crucial importance of attempting a synthesis such as this is, perhaps, best summarized by an even more recent student of Galician popular culture, María del Mar Llinares, in her monograph on the presentation of demons and apparitions in Galician folklore,[39] when she declares that the purpose of her study is to provide a general treatment of this subject, rather than focusing on individual instances, as had been the case in the past. It is precisely this global

---

[31] For a more detailed study of the state of folklore research prior to 1961, see Frances Gillmor, 'Folklore Study in Spain', *Journal of American Folklore*, 74 (1961), 336-43; Antonio Rodríguez Almodóvar, *Los cuentos maravillosos españoles* (2nd edn., Barcelona: Crítica, 1987), 13-19.

[32] José Miguel de Barandiarán, *Brujería y brujas en los relatos populares vascos* (San Sebastian: Txertoa, 1984); Luis Barandiarán Irizar (ed.), *A View from the Witch's Cave: Folktales of the Pyrenees.* Translated by Linda White (Reno: University of Nevada Press, 1991).

[33] Its rural communities, many of them comprised of relatively small nuclei of population, and its geographical position on the periphery of modern Spanish industry and commerce make the region ideally suited for the preservation of traditional cultural values, ideas and attitudes.

[34] Manuel C. Díaz y Díaz, *Visiones del más allá en Galicia durante la alta edad media.* Biblioteca de Galicia 26 (Santiago de Compostela: Bibliófilos Gallegos, 1985).

[35] X. M. González Reboredo, *Lendas galegas de tradición oral.* Biblioteca Básica da Cultura Galega (Vigo: Galaxia, 1983); Maruxa Barrio & Enrique Harguindey, *Contos populares.* Biblioteca Básica da Cultura Galega (Vigo: Galaxia, 1988).

[36] It should be noted that interpretative and classificatory work on Galician popular tales was begun as early as 1928: see González Reboredo, *Lendas galegas*, 9.

[37] Vigo: Real Academia Gallega, 1973.

[38] 2 vols., Vigo: Xerais, 1982.

vision which is only beginning to be addressed in folklore research in Spain in general, but which is slowly and painstakingly taking shape thanks to the sustained efforts of researchers in this field.

However, collections and studies of popular tales and traditions from other parts of Spain, as well as from Galicia, have been produced in recent years. From 1983 we have *Folklore de Asturias. Leyendas, cuentos y tradiciones* (*Asturian Folklore. Legends, Tales and Traditions*)[40] celebrating the centenary of folklore research in Asturias, accompanied by an overview of the history of folklore research in that region.[41] A similar, though more extensive and detailed study of the evolution of folklore research in Andalusia appeared in 1990,[42] indicating the growing interest during recent decades not only in folklore and popular culture themselves, but also in the history of their study and in the methods employed in their investigations by various researchers at different points in time. Again, it is significant that the author should conclude that folklore study in Spain in the nineteenth century foundered primarily due to the lack of support given to this type of investigation by the more traditional ranks of Spanish academia.[43] This disdain and wariness undoubtedly contributed to the movement's demise, but one should not be too quick to dismiss other important factors, such as the intense rivalry between the leading scholars in different areas of Spain, compounded by the fierce nationalism of the various Spanish regions, who at the time were more interested in asserting the distinctiveness of their own individual cultural identities than in seeking commonalities with other traditions. As opposition to folklore research grew, scholars turned their gaze towards the very important field of investigation into the Spanish ballad, which would prove

---

[39] *Mouros, ánimas, demonios. El imaginario popular gallego* (Madrid: Akal Universitaria, 1990), 5.

[40] María Josefa Canellada (Gijón: Ayalga Ediciones, 1983).

[41] José Luis Pérez de Castro, *Folklore de Asturias. Los estudios de folklore en Asturias* (Gijón: Ayalga Ediciones, 1983).

[42] Encarnación Aguilar Criado, *Cultura popular y folklore en Andalucía. (Los orígenes de la antropología)* (Sevilla: Diputación Provincial, 1990).

to be somewhat of a less hazardous endeavour because of the long-standing presence and prestige of the ballad in Spanish literary tradition, as well as the ideological nexus of epic-ballad and the Reconquest-Castilian hegemony.

It is therefore hardly surprising that co-ordinating serious folklore research on a national level in Spain should have proved practically impossible for so many decades. Nevertheless, many important strides have been taken in this direction. Of particular importance, perhaps, among these is the work of Antonio Rodríguez Almodóvar.[44] Selecting tales from Aurelio M. Espinosa's collection of the 1920s, Almodóvar proceeds to examine and to classify them according to Vladimir Propp's analysis in his *Morphology of the Folktale*. Preceding his edition of these texts with a précis of Propp's approach, a brief survey of Spanish folklore research, and an analysis of his chosen tales following Propp's definition of the various *functions* of the folktale, Almodóvar's monograph is of historical importance in that it *does* relate these tales to their wider, European context, so moving away from the previous tradition of viewing Spanish folktales in isolation or strictly within ethno-geographic boundaries. Another extremely productive researcher and author who has attempted to paint a broader picture of the traditions and popular culture of Spain and of its various regions is, of course, Julio Caro Baroja[45] whose wide-ranging investigations explore the folklore of many centuries and of numerous regions within Spain, though with particular emphasis on Castile and the Basque area. More recently still, new editions have begun to appear of those tales collected by the early-twentieth century Spanish folklorists mentioned on pages 17-18, such as that

---

[43] Aguilar Criado, *Cultura popular y folklore en Andalucía*, 332.

[44] *Los cuentos maravillosos españoles* (2nd edn, Barcelona: Crítica, 1998).

[45] His publications include, among others, *Algunos mitos españoles* (2nd edn., Madrid, 1944); *El carnaval: análisis histórico-cultural* (Madrid: Taurus, 1965); *Ensayo sobre la literatura de cordel* (Madrid: Ediciones de la Revista de Occidente, 1961); *Ritos y mitos equívocos* (Madrid, 1974); *La estación de amor: fiestas populares de mayo a San Juan* (Madrid: Taurus, 1979); *Ensayos sobre la cultura popular española* (Madrid: Dosbe, 1979); *Del viejo folklore castellano. Páginas sueltas* (Valladolid: Ambito, 1988).

edited by José A. Sánchez Pérez, with a prologue by Carmen Bravo-Villasante,[46] who indicates that this is to be but the first in a series of editions of Spanish popular tales. It is certainly to be hoped that those tales which are currently dispersed throughout Spain's regions will some day be co-ordinated and compiled in accessible and scholarly collections. In this respect, the Madrid Consejo Superior de Investigaciones Científicas (CSIC), together with its numerous other centres located throughout Spain, could play a crucial role since it already offers the researcher free and easy access to a valuable, large and constantly increasing database of traditional customs, tales and beliefs. Under its auspices, the *Revista de Dialectología y Tradiciones Populares* (*Journal of Dialectology and Popular Traditions*) was founded in 1944, and this continues to publish on a regular basis vital research into the folk customs of all parts of the Iberian Peninsula, thus providing a common focus for all those scholars engaged in the study of popular culture south of the Pyrenees.[47] Although much effort is still needed to extend its holdings to the widest possible extent, due acknowledgement should be given to the tremendous work that has already been done by the CSIC by way of the collection and organisation of its materials. In a similar vein, more research is needed to expand and to update the information contained in the *Index of Spanish Folktales*, which needs to be revised with attention to the growing number of regional tales from the Autonomous Regions which have been appearing since its publication, while the *Motif-Index of Spanish Exempla*, by its very nature, was never intended to be a complete motif-index covering all aspects of Spanish folklore from all ages, and as a result has a very limited application. This last study has already been complemented, in part, at least, by compilations such as Mª. Jesús Lacarra's *Cuentos de la Edad Media*

---

[46] *Cien cuentos populares españoles* (Barcelona: Biblioteca de Cuentos Maravillosos, 1992).

[47] In Portugal, one must also recognise the efforts of individuals such as the ethnographer and philologist, José Leite de Vasconcellos, who in 1964 published his *Contos populares e lendas* (Coimbra: Universidade de Coimbra, 1964) and, more recently, José Viale Moutinho's *Contos populares portugueses: antologia* (Porto: Familia 2000, 1978).

(*Tales from the Middle Ages*),[48] which contains a motif-index of those tales included in her text, and Maxime Chevalier has produced *Catálogo tipológico del cuento folklórico español* (*The Types of the Spanish Folktale*).[49]

So it will be seen that, while the whole field of folktale research continues to expand in Spain, there remains considerable scope for further development and collaboration, the most urgent need undoubtedly being the production of comprehensive tale-type and motif indexes that encompass the extensive popular material already available for scholarly study. In the meantime, the anthology offered in this volume is presented as an introduction to this fascinating area of study, which will best be appreciated from the basis of an understanding of the main methodologies and approaches to folktale research.

---

[48] Odres Nuevos (Madrid: Castalia, 1989).
[49] Madrid: Gredos, 1995.

CHAPTER 2

Methodology

The Structural Analysis of Folktales

In 1928 the Russian folklorist, Vladimir Propp, basing his analysis on 100 Russian marvellous tales, published his *Morphology of the Folktale*,[50] in which he sought to describe the basic structure of all such tales, using the same approaches and methods used by philologists in their study of language. As a result he produced an abstract model which has been of enormous influence in Europe and beyond, and which is of great value as we attempt to classify various tales and relate them to one another. According to Propp's method, folktales should be studied (and classified) according to the *functions* of the characters, rather than according to the specifics of their content. In this case, a character's *deeds* are the only thing of importance: *who* performs them, and *how* are only of secondary importance. In other words, if, in Tale *x*, the king gives an eagle to a brave soldier, and the eagle then carries the soldier to another kingdom, then this is analogous to Tale Y where a magician gives the hero a boat, and the boat then

---

[50] 2nd ed, revised and edited with a preface by Louis A. Wagner and a new Introduction by Alan Dundes (Austin, Texas: University of Texas Press, 1968); see also his *Theory and History of Folklore*, ed. with an introduction and notes by Anatoly Liberman (Manchester: Manchester University Press, 1984).

takes him to another kingdom. The individual details (king / magician; eagle / boat) are unimportant, since exactly the same *function* is performed in both cases: the protagonist is magically whisked away as the result of the gift bestowed upon him by a powerful ally. The following is a list of these basic *functions* (31 in total) as identified by Propp:

Initial situation

1. There is a *separation*. (This may be in the form of someone leaving his/her home, or even dying).

2. Some kind of *taboo* (interdiction/prohibition) is imposed on the hero.

3. The *taboo is broken*. Sometimes a new character (an enemy/aggressor) is introduced at this point.

4. The aggressor tries to *interrogate* for information.

5. The aggressor *obtains information* on his/her prospective victim.

6. The aggressor tries to *trick* his/her victim.

7. The victim is *deceived* by the aggressor.

8. The aggressor *injures* or otherwise causes distress to someone close to the hero (usually a member of his family).

8a. The aggressor steals something from a member of the hero's family, or that family member wants something (*lack*).

9. News of 8 or 8a is *revealed*, and everyone turns to the hero for help.

10. The hero *agrees* or *decides to help*.

At this point another phase in the tale begins, as the hero again ventures forth into the world, this time on a quest to aid another member of his family. The first phase in the tale creates a problem which has to be resolved. The second phase focuses on the steps undertaken to reach this resolution.

11. The hero *leaves home*.

12. The hero *undergoes a test* in preparation for receiving a magical object or helper.

13. The hero *reacts* to the actions of his future benefactor.

14. The hero receives the *magical object* or *helper*.

15. The hero is *led* or *transported* to the object of his quest.

16. The hero and the aggressor meet in *combat*.

17. The hero receives a *mark*.

18. The hero is *victorious*.

19. The original misdeed is *corrected*.

20. The hero *returns* (home).

21. The hero is *pursued*.

22. The hero is *helped*.

Many tales are comprised of two (or more) *series* of functions, known as *sequences*. At this point, therefore, a second sequence may begin with a second transgression, and the above functions can be repeated, eventually to be followed by the dénouement of the tale, which occurs in the following way:

23. The hero *arrives incognito* at his destination.

24. A *false hero* tries to persuade everyone of his authenticity.

25. The hero is set a *difficult task*.

26. The hero *accomplishes the task*.

27. The hero is *recognized*.

28. The false hero is *uncovered*.

29. The hero is *transformed*.

30. The false hero is *punished*.

31. The hero *marries* and becomes a king.

Not all the above functions need appear in a given tale, but however many are included or excluded, they always come in the same order, unless the tale has become corrupted in some way (some examples of such corruption will be found in this anthology).

By applying this model to our study of all popular tales, we can identify the group known as folktales (also called marvellous tales) as opposed to exempla, saints' legends, simple animal tales and a whole host of other possible sub-divisions of the vast corpus of traditional accounts and stories. Furthermore, within the body of marvellous tales themselves, the same model can be used to identify tales which belong to various different types of folktale. It would be a mistake, therefore, to think that all traditional stories are basically the same for, just as there are various types of literature (the novel, the play, the short story, poetry, etc.) so, too, there are various types of popular tale. And, just as some of these literary genres may be further sub-divided (the romantic novel, the adventure novel, etc.), so, too, may folktales be further sub-divided according to the structural patterns to which they adhere, all identified by applying the model proposed by Propp, and thanks to which we can compare like with like and so follow the most fruitful avenues for research.

In addition to identifying the functions which provide the basic structure for all marvellous tales, Propp also indicated that many of these functions tended to be grouped together in certain *spheres of action*, each of which, in turn, is centred around seven basic roles, or characters, as shown in the following table:

CHARACTER	SPHERE OF ACTION
1. Villain	misdeed (8); combat with hero (16); pursuit (21)
2. Donor	test of hero (12); provision of magical object (14)
3. Helper	transportation of hero (15); correction of misdeed (19); help (22); accomplishment of difficult task (26); transformation of hero (29)

4. Princess (object of desire) and her father	setting a difficult task (25); marking the hero (17); uncovering false hero (28); recognition of real hero (27); punishment of false hero (30); marriage (31)
5. Dispatcher	sending away of hero (11)
6. Hero	departure on quest (11); reaction to the actions of benefactor (13); marriage (31)
7. False hero	Departure on quest (11); reactions (usually negative) to actions of benefactor (13); deceit (24)

In each of these cases, the character(s) associated with each particular sphere of action is the instigator or primary cause of the sundry events listed in that particular sphere. Further analysis shows that these various characters can be grouped in pairs and threes that provide the mainspring for the development of the plot. Thus the hero is alternately obstructed by the villain, the princess and the false hero, and aided by the donor and helper, who provide the hero with the means to overcome the numerous difficulties placed in his path. It should be noted, of course, that some overlapping can occur in this respect; for instance, the princess may herself assume the role of the helper to aid in overcoming difficult tasks imposed by her father. In all cases, however, a delicate balance is set up so that the tale will constantly oscillate between triumph and reversal, defeat and climactic victory, and so from the very outset such tales can be seen to operate largely on the fundamental numerical principles of two and three. Certain sequences are repeated to form doublets, or even triplets; many tales feature two or three brothers who depart on similar quests; the hero often receives two or

three helpers as allies. Similarly, obvious pairings are formed by the hero/princess, the villain/helper, and the donor/false hero, so further underlining the simple binary combinations which are the building-blocks of so many marvellous tales, and which clearly illustrate the marked tendency of such popular material to work in simple patterns that nevertheless serve as a vehicle for the myriad complex concerns and issues that have occupied the human mind (particularly the subconscious) since earliest times.

However, it will be seen that there are obvious limitations to the structural analysis of folktales. Although this approach provides an invaluable starting-point by helping us to identify which particular tales we wish to study further, it can afford no insight whatsoever into the 'meaning' of such tales, their possible origins and their effect on the human psyche. This problem is addressed by Claude Lévi-Strauss, whose elucidation of the analogies between myth and language laid the theoretical and intellectual foundations for the study of myth and ritual as a series of units (or mythemes) which, while they may have universal resonance, are nevertheless contingent, deriving specific meaning only from the relation of mythemes to each other:

> The true constituent units of a myth are not the isolated relations but *bundles of such relations*, and it is only as bundles that these relations can be put to use and combined so as to produce a meaning.[51]

To be sure, identifying these mythemes is by no means an easy task, as he himself recognizes:

> The only method we can suggest at this stage is to proceed tentatively, by trial and error, using as a check the principles which serve as a basis for any kind of structural analysis: economy of explanation; unity of solution;

---

[51] Claude Lévi-Strauss, 'The Structural Study of Myth', in *Structural Anthropology*, trans. by Claire Jacobson and Brooke Schoepf (New York: Basic Books, 1963), 211.

and ability to reconstruct the whole from a fragment, as well as later stages from previous ones.[52]

Painstaking as this approach may have to be, it can produce some highly satisfying results, for by tabulating the mythemes it becomes possible to identify relationships between elements that occur at different points in a given story, but which nevertheless serve a similar purpose, a notion Lévi-Strauss explains via the example of the Oedipus myth, which he tabulates as follows:

Cadmos seeks his sister Europa, ravished by Zeus			
		Cadmos kills the dragon	
	The Spartoi kill one another		
			Labdacos (Laios' father) = *lame (?)*
	Oedipus kills his father, Laios		Laios (Oedipus' father) = *left-sided (?)*
		Oedipus kills the Sphinx	
			Oedipus = *swollen-foot (?)*
Oedipus marries his mother, Jocasta			

---

[52] Lévi-Strauss, 'The Structural Study of Myth', 211.

	Eteocles kills his brother, Polynices		
Antigone buries her brother, Polynices, despite prohibition			

The mythemes in each column share certain features: the overrating of blood relations, the underrating of blood relations, the denial of the autochthonous origin of man (the dragon is a chthonian being, while the Sphinx unwilling to allow men to live) and the persistence of the autochthonous origin of man (difficulty in walking is a characteristic of all new-borns).[53] Levi-Strauss shows how these reveal that the myth explores the inherent contradiction between a belief that mankind is autochthonous, 'and the knowledge that human beings are actually born from the union of man and woman'.[54] Essentially, it explores the mysteries of birth and existence.

Valuable as Lévi-Strauss' structural approach is as a method for elucidating meaning from myths and tales, it is by no means the only possible approach. Another source of illumination in this respect is psychoanalysis and the fascinating insights offered by pillars of the psychoanalytical approach such as Sigmund Freud and Carl Gustav Jung.

The Psychoanalytical Analysis of Folktales

It became apparent to researchers studying the hidden 'meaning' of folktales that these accounts were very similar to dreams in their symbolic framework, that the same images and motifs occurred in both these forms of human imagination

---

[53] Lévi-Strauss, 'The Structural Study of Myth', 215-16.

(monsters, for instance, are common in dreams and folktales alike, as is 'magical' transportation), and that their logic (which can seem disjointed and irrational to the conscious mind) and development were also analogous. Both dream and folktale explore the pictorial and magical nature of the images that they contain, rather than their rational associations and connotations. Gradually it was understood that these tales were not merely sources of entertainment and of childish distraction, but that they explored and revealed some of the hidden depths of the human subconscious. They represent, then, an attempt to confront and overcome some of the latent fears endemic to all individuals in all societies. It was realized, in effect, that understanding such tales could lead to a better understanding of ourselves, and so the methods developed in the new science of psychoanalysis began to be applied to their study.

The Freudian School

Sigmund Freud is, of course, generally regarded as the father of modern psychoanalysis, and so it is not surprising that his ideas should also have had great influence on the analysis of folktales.[55] His approach was essentially based on four basic tenets or theories:

1. *The theory of culture.* Freud maintained that there were no clear-cut links between the world of the child and the adult, between the primitive and the civilized, dream and the waking state. Each of these states is, to the conscious mind, self-contained and there is no formal means of dialogue between them. For Freud, therefore, folktales are like neurotic symptoms, the result of a compromise between different stages of psychological development, as the 'civilized' mind attempts to come to grips with the impulses and urges generated by the

---

[54] Lévi-Strauss, 'The Structural Study of Myth', 216.

[55] See, for instance, Sigmund Freud, *The Interpretation of Dreams* (Harmondsworth: Penguin, 1991).

'primitive' instinct. This, of course, is also true of dreams, where we see the mind covering raw urges with a symbolic veneer that maintains a certain propriety, and so avoids the necessity of confronting an unpleasant reality head-on.

2. *The theory of human personality.* The most important feature of human development from early childhood to adulthood was, for Freud, the development of various forms of sexuality. Not surprisingly, therefore, he saw in dreams and folktales an attempt to explore this development in a graphic form, since some of the most powerful urges that had to be dealt with in the progression from a primitive to a civilized state were the sexual ones.

3. *The theory of unconscious formations.* Freud further showed that in order to explore these primitive impulses, the mind indulges in fantasy – imagining a scenario where the subject is present, and which involves, in a twisted form, the carrying out of some desire. Such fantasy and role-play clearly plays a key part in folktales.

4. *The theory of the workings of dreams.* Freud also studied exactly how dreams (and therefore, for the purpose of our analysis, folktales) are formed, and identified several main processes of transformation as the initial ('real') scenario is changed to become the resultant dream or folktale:

> *Dramatisation*: a wish is replaced with a real image and an imaginary situation is created.
>
> *Reversal of values*: essential details become apparent accessories to the story, and incidental details are brought to the forefront. The real impulses are therefore masked further.
>
> *Condensation*: many diverse elements are condensed into one powerful symbol.

Representation by symbol: such symbols are never clear-cut representations of invariable elements – only the context can give the final meaning to such symbols and enable us to understand them, and one should not, therefore, over-indulge in generalisations. Nevertheless, Freud did indicate that some important symbols are frequently linked with the same concept (for example, long or sharp objects and weapons tend to represent masculine sexuality, while boxes, caves, vases etc. tend to symbolize female sexuality).

All of these ideas can be condensed into one basic tenet, which is the foundation stone of the Freudian school, namely that the repression of desire and the need to fulfil repressed wishes is at the core of the symbolism of dream and folktale. This is exactly why dream and folktale operate in the never-never world of magic and symbol (their manifest content), for they explore desires (their latent content) that the civilized mind, and society, cannot possibly condone or openly confront (an obvious example, frequently associated with Freudian analysis, being the oedipal desire). Such is the power of these desires, however, that they must find some form of expression, which becomes shrouded in symbol, metaphor and allegory that deflects attention away from their true goal. Nevertheless, by expressing such desire in symbolic fashion, the mind finds a valve which helps relieve the pressure from the unconscious on the conscious, and so retains the balance expected of a healthy individual. Only when such preoccupations are fully repressed, when they are not allowed to surface even in symbolic fashion, is there a danger of them seriously affecting the equilibrium of the conscious *ego*.

Jung

In stark contrast to Freud, Carl Gustav Jung saw dreams not as the neurotic workings of a sick mind, but as the expression of eternal human problems illustrated through the use of collective figures, symbols of universal currency drawn from the stock of humankind's collective unconscious.[56] He agreed that the sexual drive is of no mean importance in human motives, but also showed that in many cases other impulses, such as hunger, ambition, fanaticism, envy, revenge, or the devouring passion of the creative instinct and religious spirit are even more significant and powerful motivators. Rather than interpreting them as attempts to represent unfulfilled wishes (and so look back towards the cause or origin of the dream), he suggested looking more towards their end result, for he saw dreams as being intimately connected with the realization of the development of identity and personality. Rather than expressing illicit desires, dreams therefore represent an attempt to compensate for and to balance the lopsidedness of the conscious mind as it unfolds and develops, and they also have a prospective function, anticipating future conscious achievements, and preparing the individual for change and development. They therefore can perform a very positive function, helping the individual to discover and come to terms with new stages in his personal evolution, and they do not purely perform the largely negative function of fulfilling unsanctioned desires.

As well as identifying this more positive, and certainly more broad-ranging, function of dreams, Jung's other great contribution to dream analysis was to identify the two different parts of the unconscious, which he termed the *personal* and the *collective*. As the term implies, the personal unconscious is associated with someone's individual development and experiences, and is the source from which most of the concrete dream images are drawn. The collective

---

[56] These ideas are explored extensively in his writings: Carl Gustav Jung, *Collected Works* (Princeton: Princeton University Press, 1991).

unconscious, on the other hand, is that part of the human mind which is inherited and projects archetypal representations of well-known mythological motifs. Jung describes these archetypes as structures that pre-exist in the brain, but which can only manifest themselves in concrete examples, and uses the analogy of the crystal: the abstract notion of a crystalline structure can only manifest itself in the concrete, specific form of individual crystals, none of which are exactly identical in form, but all of which adhere to the same fundamental pattern. The specific symbol used for the archetype in each dream depends entirely on the personal unconscious of the individual concerned, and so it is impossible to generalize about such images: each has to be analysed separately and on its own merit. This is an important difference between Jung's approach and that of Freud, for, whereas the latter tends to attach fixed meanings to the images and symbols encountered in dreams (and folktales), Jung encourages a more pragmatic approach. This is a significant development, as it recognizes the frequently fluid nature of the significance of many dream-images, which can sometimes simultaneously be both positive and negative, and the view also fits in very well with Propp's observation that one character can sometimes perform several different functions within the structure of a marvellous tale. But, although the individual images are unique and need to be studied for their own individual merit, the archetypes which they represent are, of course, constant, and the four principal ones identified by Jung as having a particularly noticeable influence on the unconscious mind are:

> *the mother*: obviously an influential figure during the formative years of any child, the reactions to the mother can vary widely (ranging from a hypertrophy of the maternal element with the consequent exaggeration and appropriation thereof, to resistance to the mother), and also depends on the sex of the child.

rebirth: this category encompasses all forms of transformation, the passing from one state to another, growth and change.

spirit: often equated with the father-figure in fairy tales, the spirit is the unconscious voice of conscience and morality, and is often symbolized by old men, dwarves and wise animals – essentially, by anything that questions and challenges.

trickster: this is the archetype of malevolence, which can is also associated with stupidity, and is the adversary who must be overcome in order to triumph and succeed.

It will be seen that the above archetypes certainly do embody broad-ranging concepts of universal currency, and that they are also ones that can be clearly identified in folktales, where evil stepmothers, metamorphoses, helpers and advisers, and evil opponents all feature prominently. Indeed, all the above-mentioned ideas about the function of dreams can be applied quite effectively to myths and folktales. For, whereas dreams focus on the progress of the *individual* through various important phases in his life, folktales work their magic on the *collective* level of society as a whole, emphasising the normality of all change and progress (including such widely divergent phases as puberty and death), and warning against the very real perils of everyday life. For this reason, they use images and symbols that are both simple and easily recognizable (the witch, the dragon, the brave warrior or the beautiful princess), but at the same time warn against the danger of accepting everything, and everyone, at face value (hence the motif of the beast who is really an enchanted prince, or of the beautiful Siren that lures men to their doom). Their content may vary greatly, and they speak in metaphor for not all experiences are exactly the same; all individuals, however, do pass through similar phases of personal development, and must understand the dangers and pitfalls that may be encountered in life. The symbols and situations depicted in folktales therefore leave their imprint on minds that are

already receptive to the problems and ideas they explore in a metaphorical fashion, and as they do so, they delve to the unconscious levels of the mind and prepare the individual (who may well be a child in the process of becoming aware of the demands and responsibilities of adulthood, but may also be an adult faced with important decisions and change) for progression to a new phase in life.

Bettelheim

A further significant contribution to the analysis of folktales was made by Bruno Bettelheim, who focused his study on the effects produced by marvellous tales on children.[57] His analysis therefore eschewed Freud's attempt to trace the origins of the strange phenomena that appear in such accounts, and also concentrated Jung's abstract theories into a practical and concrete investigation of the tangible effects produced by folktales on malleable, developing minds; the results of his analysis are again illuminating. Surprisingly, perhaps, he concluded, for one thing, that folktales provided children with a greater sense of security: the witches, ogres and monsters that appear with such regularity in marvellous tales are, as Jung suggested, projections of human fears and anxieties but, far from traumatizing children, as one would expect, such projections can be reassuring in that they show that the individual's own violent fantasies are neither unique nor monstrous. While not encouraging or condoning such tendencies (it should be noted that the demon is invariably defeated), they do allow them to be placed within the wider social context, to be shared with others, and so made less intimidating, for only after fears have been projected onto external objects can the individual begin to come to terms with them, to understand them, and,

---

[57] Bruno Bettelheim, *The Uses of Enchantment: The Meaning and Importance of Fairy Tales* (Harmondsworth: Penguin, 1991).

ultimately, to overcome them. The first effect of marvellous tales, therefore, can be said to be a *socializing* one.

Another vital function of folktales, according to Bettelheim, is to help establish some basic concept of world (or social) order. They do not deceive or overly protect their audience by projecting the world as being a perfect place. On the contrary, the world portrayed in folktales is heavily flawed, and is constantly threatened by evil and impending doom. But they do not present the world in a totally negative light either, for, while they may present the reader or listener with images of extreme evil, they also depict the good helpers and advisers that are constantly on hand to guide the protagonist and help him or her in their fight against oppression. The world portrayed is therefore a balanced one, and closely mirrors, albeit in symbolic form, real adult experience. Furthermore, marvellous tales sometimes also seem to condone 'immoral' acts such as fraud and deception (depicting, for example, the youthful protagonist deceiving the ogre into parting with some prized possession). In such cases, these tales are again being realistic, for not all actions are depicted as good or bad, black or white; there exists a considerable grey area where the end, if it is for the common good, can very well justify the means. In such cases, folktales can once again be very reassuring, showing us all that the weak can sometimes triumph over the strong, that victory can often be snatched from the jaws of adversity. In all cases, however, it is important to note that good does always triumph over evil (although the struggle can be a very hard one indeed), and social order (by means of the establishment, or re-establishment of family bonds and peaceful co-existence) is restored, so once again calming any fears and pointing to the fact that normality can always be regained in spite of the influence of destabilizing elements.

Synthesis

Mutually exclusive as some of the approaches outlined above may seem, they can nevertheless be synthesized into a coherent, cohesive approach that allows us to study folktales with a degree of objectivity and understanding:

i. In the same way that the dreamer is the protagonist of his/her dream, so, too, the creator of the story is the protagonist of a folktale; but, in addition, the listener is similarly identified with the protagonist, allowing the whole of the audience to participate in the process of self-exploration and discovery. Dream is an individual phenomenon; folktale is a social one.

ii. The folktale is always located in time-out-of-time, in an unspecific, artificial world in which we can all temporarily live. As is the case with all forms of literature, it also has a coherence and significance normally lacking in real life, and so allows us to explore life's problems in a controlled environment. As a result, answers are more forthcoming, although they rarely make themselves immediately apparent to the conscious mind.

iii. Just as the structure of the folktale should be studied from the standpoint of its various *functions* (the deeds of the characters within a specific context), so, too, should its images and symbols be studied in their own contexts. Symbols do sometimes have common connotations, but these are by no means hard-and-fast or exclusive, and we should therefore beware of providing explanations that are too simplistic.

iv. The plots of folktales are 'magical' in nature; that is to say they do not follow the conventions of conscious thought and logic, but work as a

series of mental rituals through which participants bring about desires, dispel fear or guilt, and prepare themselves for change. These mental rituals are accessible to us all because they follow a determinate series of steps, a structure or form that is inborn and common to all individuals in all societies.

v. Folktales show a repeated concern with primal situations: relationships (which sometimes, although not always, may have sexual connotations), growth, and the major phases in human development. They also depict the world 'as it is', with no desire to conceal its flaws and dangers, but with the constant reassurance that through the application of wisdom, courage and constancy, the individual, and society as a whole, may still win through.

vi. Folktales may present a number of possible 'meanings' and interpretations. Reversal is, indeed, one of their common features, and by this I mean not only that elements from real life are often changed and inverted to conceal their true significance, but that even within a given tale, the significance of specific characters and symbols may vary according to the viewpoint taken. A princess may simultaneously be an object of desire and a clever and dangerous opponent; both interpretations may be simultaneously valid, and the combination of interpretations can even provide a more complete and rounded understanding of the meaning of the tale for, simple as they frequently seem at the surface level, marvellous tales provide us with a plethora of insights into the workings of the human mind and instincts, and rarely prove to be as straightforward as their basic plot suggests.

CHAPTER 3

Analysis of the Tales

Seven Sunbeams *(Siete Rayos de Sol)*

Belonging to the family of tales known as 'The Devil's Daughter' (type T313), this folktale is of particular interest in the Hispanic context since one version or another of this account may well have been the source of Cervantes' 'Tale of the Captive' ('Historia del cautivo') from Part I of his *Don Quixote*.[58] This tale type is certainly of ancient origin (folklorists have seen traces of it in the Classical legend of Jason and Medea),[59] but this particular version also provides us with some interesting variants from the standard model. From the structural point of view, this tale illustrates very well the way many such accounts are comprised of more than one sequence, but in this case two such sequences run in parallel, as we shall see. It also illustrates how a character that performs one function in one sequence, can perform a completely different role in another.

The hero of the first (and main) sequence of the tale is undoubtedly the prince whose gambling in the initial situation, and deception by the aggressor (here the devil himself), forces him to leave home and wrestle with a dangerous

---

[58] Maxime Chevalier, 'Para una arqueología de los cuentos tradicionales en Castilla y León', in Luis Díaz Viana, *Etnología y folklore en Castilla y León*. Colección de estudios de etnología y folklore 2 (Salamanca: Junta de Castilla y León, 1986), 197-202, at 198.

[59] Chevalier, 'Para una arqueología de los cuentos tradicionales en Castilla y León', 198.

and powerful opponent. He is aided in his struggle by the girl Seven Sunbeams (Siete Rayos), who helps him overcome the obstacles placed in his path, and who eventually becomes his consort, but who herself also becomes the heroine of another sequence within the tale. This begins when the prince's theft of her clothes forces her to help him in his quest, and progresses through various stages of vicissitude, including the usurping of her rightful place by a false heroine (the youth's new bride-to-be), until she is eventually recognized and rewarded with marital stability. These two plots may be mapped as follows:

THE PRINCE AS HERO	SEVEN SUNBEAMS AS HEROINE
INITIAL SITUATION	
7. The devil deceives the hero into entering into an agreement with him, as a result of which:	
11. The hero leaves home.	
12. The hero undergoes a test (having to follow the instructions regarding the bathing doves), and:	8a. Having had her clothes stolen by the prince (lack), Seven Sunbeams is forced to
14. Receives a magical object (the ring) and helper (Seven Sunbeams).	10. Help him in his quest.
15. She transports him to the object of his quest (the Devil's castle), where	
16. He meets the aggressor in combat. This takes the form of the multiple difficult tasks which he must accomplish in order to save his life.	16. In the course of her combat with her father (after all, it is Seven Sunbeams who actually accomplishes the tasks set), she
	17. Receives a mark (the missing fingertip), but is eventually

18. The hero is victorious, and at this point we have the mis-placed intrusion of his marriage, which should, according to all logic, be postponed until the end, and has undoubtedly been moved forward here to preserve propriety in the presentation of his relationship with Seven Sunbeams.

20. He returns home, but is

21. Pursued by the furious Devil, and

22. Helped, in spite of his foolishness in choosing the wrong horse, by Seven Sunbeams.

25. When the hero forgets Seven Sunbeams, he is set a difficult task (obtaining the stone and knife), which he

26. Accomplishes, and thanks to which he is

29. Transformed (his memory is restored).

18. Victorious. As with the sequence that focuses on the male hero, the marriage is mis-placed at this point.

21. Fleeing from her father's wrath, she is pursued by him and only manages to escape thanks to the

22. Help provided by the magical objects in her possession.

23. Separated from the prince, who forgets her, Seven Sunbeams is forced to arrive incognito at her new home, where she has been supplanted by a

24. False heroine – the prince's new bride-to-be.

27. When the prince's memory is restored, Seven Sunbeams is recognized, the

28. False heroine is uncovered, and

31. The happy marriage which was erroneously located earlier in the account, and which should logically occur here at the end, is now replaced by a joyful re-uniting of man and wife, who live happily ever after.

31. Happy reunion again replaces the marriage that should now be the culmination of the story.

As we can see, each sequence provides a different sphere of influence for the youth and Seven Sunbeams. In the first, the prince is the hero, Seven Sunbeams is his helper, and the Devil is the aggressor. In the second, Seven Sunbeams is the heroine and is presented with a series of aggressors: the prince, whose theft of her clothes coerces her into providing help; her father, who opposes her marriage; and the false heroine, who stands in the way of its happy fulfilment.

A noticeable feature of this, and many other folktales, is the way that the female protagonist (irrespective of whether we look at her in the role of helper or of heroine), is invariably wiser and more practical than her male counterpart. From the outset, the prince is presented as frivolous and foolish: he wastes his time gambling, thanks to which (and thanks also to his own arrogance and gullibility) he falls into the Devil's power; his incapacity to accomplish the tasks imposed by the Devil cause him to break down (hardly the reaction one would expect of a typical hero), and he also unwisely disregards the advice Seven Sunbeams gives him about which horse to choose for their flight. However, he does learn and develop as the plot unfolds. By heeding the advice given to him by the hermit early on in the tale, he shows that there is hope for him, and his forgetfulness at the end of the story is caused by circumstances beyond his control, since he does actually attempt to adhere to the instructions his wife has given him. Finally, he successfully accomplishes the task imposed by Seven Sunbeams thanks to his own diligence and commitment, so showing that he has now matured enough to be successfully integrated into adult (i.e. married) society. Seven Sunbeams, on the other hand, is sagacious and powerful from the

outset. Essentially, she is more mature, knowing the appropriate way to proceed in all given situations, and is capable of taking the initiative herself. In no way can she be regarded as the passive and dependent princess generally associated with fairy tales. Between them, therefore, these two protagonists address some very common social perceptions, and even overturn them to some extent. On the one hand, the youthful prince illustrates quite graphically how wisdom and maturity are rarely inborn, but that both can be acquired with help, good counsel and, just as importantly, experience (some of which can be very bitter indeed). He shows that mistakes are normal in the process of personal development, but that they are rarely irrevocable if they are used positively as part of the learning process. Between them, the prince and Seven Sunbeams underline how the weak can also triumph against the strong, that there are ways and means of overcoming seemingly insuperable problems.

As was mentioned above, this version of the folktale contains several motifs that deserve closer scrutiny, as they present us with interesting variations from the more standard form of the tale. The first of these comes at the very beginning, when we are told the circumstances in which the childless monarchs are given a son:

> Este era un rey que no tenía hijo y echó una promesa pa que su mujé la reina tuviera un hijo. Y Dios le dio un hijo tan hermoso que no había en to el mundo otro más hermoso que él.

> [There was once a king who had no children, and he wished for his wife the queen to have a son. And God gave him such a beautiful son that there was none more beautiful than he in the whole world.]

Immediately, we must ask ourselves: what is the promise the king has made, and what has this got to do with the rest of the tale? For an answer, we must look to other versions of the same story, where this promise is spelled out and where it is intimately linked with the unfolding of the plot. In a version from Soria, we are told the following:

Estos eran un ray y una raina que se casaron y estuvieron mucho tiempo casaos sin tener fruto de bendición. Y cogió ese ray y esa raina y se fueron a vivir a un monte a matar fieras el ray. Y se fue el ray al campo y vido tantas fieras ai que le dijo a su mujer que iba a ir a cazar fieras todos los días. Y cazaba tantas fieras que un día vino y le dijo a su mujer: —el primer fruto de bendición se lo prometo al demonio.

Y al poco tiempo la raina tuvo un niño con un letrero en las costillas que dicía que a los quince años era del demonio.[60]

[There was once a king and a queen who got married and were married for a long time without having any fruit from their union. And this king and this queen got up and went to live in the mountains so that the king could kill wild beasts. And the king went out into the fields and saw so many wild beasts there that he told his wife that he was going to hunt wild beasts every day. And he hunted so many wild beasts that one day he came and told his wife: 'I promise the first fruit of our union to the devil.'

And a little while later the queen had a boy with a sign on his ribs saying that once he was fifteen he would belong to the devil.]

Here, we are given answers to some of our questions, although others are also raised, as is discussed below. For a society that judges all conjugal relations on the basis of their fruitfulness, the failure to produce a child is a serious shortcoming. This lack is exacerbated in the folktale where the childless couple are a king and queen, who are always in the public eye, and on whose descendants will depend the future security of the realm. A (male) child must therefore be produced at all costs. The monarchs' retreat to the countryside stresses the importance of the basic, biological functions that are the focus of this initial part of the tale, and the proliferation of the animals around them brings

---

[60] Aurelio M. Espinosa, *Cuentos populares españoles*, 3 vols (Stanford University Press, 1923; 2nd edn, Madrid: CSIC, 1946-47), 248.

their own barrenness into sharp relief. In a last, desperate attempt to overcome this obstacle, the king makes a pact with the Devil, and it is precisely when this contract comes to fruition that the main part of the story will begin, when the son has to attempt to extricate himself from the predicament and danger in which he has been placed thanks to the rash promise of his father.

As well as this social function of underlining the importance of reproduction, continuity and stability, this part of the tale has many other psychological ramifications. The son's entry into adulthood (he is 15 when the Devil claims him) is made problematic because of the earlier deeds of his parents (or, more specifically, of his father). His life-or-death struggle to overcome the destiny imposed on him by his parents is, in fact, a dramatization of the struggle of all young adults to assert their own individuality and free themselves from the identity and constraints that have been placed on them from above; it is symbolic of the struggle for independence and of the search for personal identity. The fact that the father is the person specifically named as having entered into the pact is also significant, as the clash of identity and struggle for supremacy are normally much more pronounced between parents and offspring of the same sex. Significantly, therefore, the son leaves home when he comes of age, and will only return at the end of the tale when he has established his own identity.

Evidently, the beginning of our version of the folktale has become confused although, as mentioned above, the Soria version raises its own set of problems. Foremost amongst these is the king's promise to give his first-born child to the Devil. If the purpose of the pact is to produce offspring, it seems self-defeating to give that offspring away. It may be, therefore, that the Soria version also omits important details, perhaps in an attempt to avoid over-plotting and provide a crisper start to the tale, but with the result that some unexpected links are made within the narrative. The motif of hunting is also an interesting additional detail. On the one hand, in traditional tales and legends hunting is an activity which very often heralds contact with the supernatural: away from the sphere of normal social control and expectation, the protagonist finds himself out

in the wilds, on the threshold between this world and the supernatural realms. The hunt is also a quest that can symbolize the love-chase (this is certainly true of the Spanish ballads[61]), a fact which fits in very well with the situation at the beginning of this tale, where the king and queen are in desperate need of a child. Conversely, however, the hunt is also pre-eminently a masculine pursuit that takes the hunter away from wife and family, therefore making reproduction more difficult, and so can also be regarded as a symbol of abandonment. What is clear from the Soria version, however, is that the desire for offspring is central to this tale, and that at some stage a promise is made in order to precipitate the birth of a child. Returning to our version of the story, we remember that we are told that a child is born as a result of a promise, but the specifics of the promise are omitted, as they will have no function in the development of this account. Furthermore, the promise now seems to be made to God, rather than to the Devil, a logical change in a community that might be keen to avoid any suggestion of blasphemy or diabolism, and one which provides us with another logical explanation for excluding the specific terms of the promise, as it would certainly not be seemly to depict God as cruelly depriving this couple of their beloved son just as he is entering adulthood. It also provides us with another tantalising possibility namely that an earlier version of this tale might have involved two promises being made: one to the Devil (perhaps by the father), and one to God (perhaps by the mother). With the passage of time, these separate strands of the tale might have become intertwined, and produced the version we now have before us. This hypothesis fits in very well with the tale's symmetry, where we have: two promises; two versions of the protagonist (discussed below); two narrations of testing; and two brides, who are eventually resolved into one at the end of the narrative, providing a happy conclusion as two (duality and confusion) become one (unity and clarity). This opening motif therefore provides us with an

---

[61] See E. Rogers, 'The Hunt in the *Romancero* and Other Traditional Ballads', *Hispanic Review*, 42 (1974), 133-171; 'The Perilous Hunt: Symbols in Hispanic and European Balladry', *Studies in Romance Languages*, 22 (Lexington: Kentucky University Press, 1980).

excellent example of the cross-fertilisation that often takes place in such accounts (as with the ballad and all other forms of oral literature), of the transformations that can take place over time and in order to satisfy local requirements such as morality (as when the prince's marriage to Seven Sunbeams is brought forward) and religious orthodoxy, and of the sundry changes that can take place through simple forgetfulness or confusion.

At this point in our tale, we are introduced to the motif of the prince's gambling, which is a starting-point for numerous other versions of the same account, and is the means by which he is entrapped by the Devil. Of course, the association between the Devil and gambling is found in many exempla, miracle tales, ecclesiastical prescriptions and canon law. However, even this common feature shows some intriguing differences from the norm. In other variants of the tale, the prince usually encounters a disguised Devil, who lures him into a sense of false security by initially losing every contest. The stakes increase with every round, until finally they play for the prince's life; he loses, and consequently must endeavour to save himself from the fate to which he has foolishly condemned himself. The first curious deviation from this usual development is the motif of the prince's hat, which then takes the form of a dove, and which turns out to be the Devil in disguise. It is certainly not uncommon for the Devil to appear in the form of a charming and beautiful creature such as the dove in this tale, a clear example of the way folktales often warn against the dangers of accepting things at face value; but the motif of the hat is quite unusual, although it, too, can be explained if we examine its possible psychological connotations. Our point of departure here must be the fact that the hat is a part of the prince's own attire, and presumably of some visual import as a symbol of rank and status. Having played and won against everyone else around him, therefore, the prince begins to play and gamble against himself, placing his hat on the opposite side of the table as a symbolic other self. One feature which further suggests that this really is the case is the fact that this symbolic other self wins; previously, it had been impossible to defeat the prince, as the skill far outmatched that of his

sundry other opponents. Now, however, he is faced with an opponent of at least equal stature (himself) and who, if this other self is in fact the demon inside, is certainly a more skilful gambler than the prince now that he has been stripped of his incisive ruthlessness. Both parts of this hypothesis are borne out by the development of the tale: the hat/dove is a demon, and the prince does lose. The notion that the prince is actually playing against himself here also helps to explain why he does not win the initial encounters, as happens in other variants of the same tale: in fact, in a way, he does win, since his opponent is merely an extension of his own ego. He finds himself in a classic paradox, playing a game which he can neither win nor lose, as he is continually playing against himself. It is this paradox, however, that provides us with the link to the other possible scenario for the beginning of the tale, described above, where the prince must overcome the obstacles placed in his path by his parents, represented by the pact with the Devil. By trying to extricate himself from this contract, the prince is actually wrestling with that part of his persona that has been placed on him from the outside, the part of his ego that is the result of his parents' nurture. Similarly, when he plays against the part of himself symbolized by the hat, he is playing against a part of his identity that is not integral to him, one which is outside him, but is still a part of his whole being (perhaps a symbol of his future self), and which is simultaneously therefore both familiar and alien. In conjunction with this, it should be remembered that the head (especially the royal head, as represented on coinage or in the notion of the king as the Head of State), is usually linked to the notion of the individual being authentically present in the world, whereas the hat is a symbol rather gratuitously associated with the individual due to its association with the head. In this tale, perhaps the hat performs the added function of symbolising the protagonist's immaturity at this point in the story; later, when he has overcome his youthful impetuousness, the hat will be exchanged for the more fitting and regal crown. In all events, the prince is essentially always struggling with himself, striving to come to terms with different, and often contradictory aspects of his evolving ego and, as I have

already mentioned, it is this growth and development of the persona that is depicted and explored throughout the course of this tale.

Earlier in this discussion we saw that the numbers two and three are very common features of the structure of folktales, and we have already seen, also, that in 'Seven Sunbeams' doubling (in the form of parallel structures, the principal pair formed by the prince and Seven Sunbeams herself, etc.) is important. Here, we now have two examples of a triplet in the increasing stakes for which the prince and the dove play: first they bet all their money, then their clothes (where it is not the expense of the garments which is at stake, but their value as a symbol of the prince himself and their protective function), and finally their lives. Such incremental echoing therefore builds up to the fateful climax, where we now see the prince bet his life three times, the repetition now serving an emphatic purpose, stressing the fact that it will not be easy for him to extricate himself from his predicament. These triplets will be further echoed later in the story, as the prince has to accomplish the three tasks imposed on him by the Devil, and will have to win his life back a total of three times: by accomplishing the tasks, by fleeing with Seven Sunbeams, and finally by regaining his memory of her. So we see once more that folktales are by no means haphazard constructions arrived at by the random combination of disparate elements: although some confusion and corruption do occur with the passage of time, they have very highly-wrought structures that explore many different combinations and possibilities, but always do so with balance and close attention to detail.

Another triplet is presented to us in the three doves/daughters that bathe in the river every day. As when the prince repeatedly gambled his life with the Devil, this triplet has an emphatic effect, stressing the dual nature of the Devil's daughters, who partake of both bird and human qualities, the former indicating their close association with the Devil as his offspring, the latter showing that they also belong to the world of mortals, and that there is therefore some hope of their sympathizing with the prince's plight. Not surprisingly, the youngest daughter is to be the prince's target, and will prove to be his invaluable ally. Her astuteness

is immediately brought to the fore when she initially refuses to undress, being the only one of the sisters to realize that they are being watched; at the same time, her sympathetic nature is also indicated when she does eventually yield to her sister's pleas, although she knows that this may compromise her own person. We see, therefore, that she is insightful but accommodating, the one who lives closest to the boundary of the two worlds (natural and supernatural), and consequently the one who will be successful in crossing it freely; clearly, she is a good choice as a helper. This presentation of the youngest sister being superior to her siblings has many parallels in other folktales, where the youngest offspring is almost invariably the wisest and most courageous. Again, this has deep psychological repercussions, as it overturns the expected norm of family life, where the eldest sibling is usually placed in the position of greatest responsibility, and expected to care for the interests of the younger ones, while the youngest brother or sister is given the least responsibility, and is powerless to influence his or her elders. But, as a corollary to the way the protagonist of a folktale is usually depicted as overcoming superior odds thanks to guile and courage, so too is the younger sibling frequently presented in a more positive light than his/her elders, and frequently surpasses them in achievement: the disempowered in real life are brought to the forefront of folktales, and are presented as positive role-models that provide hope for change and a better future.

The three tasks the prince is set have a clear symbolic value. First, he must clear a rocky mountainside, plant it with saplings, and return with the fruit of the trees by the following day. The sexual connotations are self-evident: in a very short space of time, something which is barren must be made fertile, a feat which was not achieved by the protagonist's father for a long time; we immediately have a symbol here of the protagonist striving to surpass his father. We also remember, of course, that the prince is himself in the process of entering (fertile) adulthood, and so he now takes a symbolic step closer to maturity with, significantly, the help of Seven Sunbeams. Similarly, the mill which he must construct as his second task is associated with sustenance and life; it is a place

where the fruits of the soil may be turned into edible produce; but, unlike the hillside of the first task, it is a human construct, designed for social, rather than individual, purposes. This is clearly a very different challenge from the solitary one of the gaming table at the beginning of the tale. It therefore effectively symbolizes a further step forward in the prince's development: not only has he reached sexual maturity (task 1), but he has successfully integrated this aspect of his personality with the expectations of civilized society. Finally, the search for the ring in the third task is an obvious prelude to the marriage that quickly follows, and also echoes (in yet another doublet) the ring Seven Sunbeams had given the prince at the river, and which has been his constant link with her throughout these ordeals. The personal commitment made at their first encounter thus becomes sanctioned by parental approval, and will eventually be confirmed by their wedding (a triple approval, once more).

The triple failure of the Devil to enter the couple's bedroom (deceived by the speaking spittle left behind by his daughter) is soon followed by his pursuit of them. By this time, of course, the prince has failed to heed Seven Sunbeams' advice, and has again acted foolishly by judging the two horses by their appearance: as we have already seen, a pleasant outward appearance can conceal weakness and corruption, and vice versa. Furthermore, while the notion that the apparently frail horse of thought is fleeter of foot than the robust horse of the wind may seem somewhat philosophical in tenor, it in fact coincides extremely well with all that we have seen to date, where the seemingly inferior prince and Seven Sunbeams, through cunning and good judgement (i.e. the power of thought) constantly overcome the threatening postures of their powerful opponent. It is worth stressing once more, therefore, that folktales always tend to show how the physically weaker party may overcome the stronger one by the use of that most valuable of assets, the mind. Bullies, muscles and gung-ho heroes never ever triumph in these accounts.

A great many transformations, of one kind or another, take place during the course of this folktale, such as: hat – dove – Devil – monster (during the

pursuit); Seven Sunbeams – dove; and the numerous transformations that take place in order to complete the tasks and to flee from the Devil, not to mention the change that takes place in the prince when he forgets about his bride. All of these can be interpreted as constant reminders that this whole tale is concerned with change and with the passing from one state (immaturity) to another (maturity), a process which necessarily involves marriage as a means of integration into and perpetuation of society. They are a constant reminder that the whole of life is a continual process of evolution, and that stability is a relative state, not an immutable one, fixed in stone. They recur with such frequency precisely because they are symbolic echoes of this fact, for their power and influence are derived precisely from their repetition and consequent imprint on the human mind. As we have seen, the whole tale is constructed on this principle of repetition and echo, as each individual element acquires greater force and significance every time it recurs, eventually forcing the subconscious to recognize and absorb its meaning and be comforted, reassured, and strengthened by it.

The Three Dresses (Los tres trajes) and The Girl with No Arms (La niña sin brazos)

Although, at first sight, these two tales seem quite dissimilar, they nevertheless contain many common elements and a comparative analysis can yield many insights into their true meaning and significance. Conversely, from the outset it is obvious that 'The Three Dresses' ('Los tres trajes') is comparable in structure to the classic tale of Cinderella and, indeed, it belongs to that family of tales, as can be seen from the following table[62]:

---

[62] Perhaps the best-known version of 'The Three Dresses' is Charles Perrault's 'Donkey Skin': Charles Perrault and Christine Angot, *Peau d'âne* (Paris, Stock, 2003); for translations of this and other tales by Perrault, see Charles Perrault, *Complete Fairy Tailes*, translated from the French by A.E. Johnson and others (London: Constable, 1962).

CINDERELLA	*LOS TRES TRAJES*
After the death of her father, a beautiful girl is left in the care of her stepmother and two stepsisters.	After the death of her mother, a beautiful girl is left in the care of her father.
The stepsisters mistreat her and make her their servant.	The father falls in love with her and decides to marry her.
	She asks a neighbour for advice, who suggests that she impose certain conditions on the marriage (the three dresses).
	The father acquires the dresses, and the girl must run away to evade his advances.
	She begins to work as a servant in the prince's palace.
A prince holds a ball and invites all the principal figures from the community.	The prince holds a huge celebration (three balls) so that he may find a wife.
While she is alone, a fairy godmother appears and supplies Cinderella with all the things she needs to go to the ball (a dress, a coach and horses).	
At the ball, Cinderella meets the prince and he falls in love with her.	Donning her special dresses, the girl goes to the balls and the prince falls in love with her.
Before the end of the ball, Cinderella runs away, but loses one of her shoes in the process.	The girl flees before the end of every ball, but receives a token of the prince's love (a ring).

The prince searches for his loved-one, and recognizes her by means of the shoe.	The prince falls ill (with love), but is restored to good health when he recognizes the girl by means of the ring.
Cinderella marries the prince.	The girl marries the prince.

The Spanish version of the tale, however, provides us with additional information at the beginning of the story that helps to explain later events, for we are told that the father falls in love with his daughter, and attempts to marry her, a clear statement of his incestuous intent and a strong incentive for her to leave home when she fails to thwart his advances. This incestuous motif has been heavily obscured in the story of Cinderella, but elements of it survive in the extreme jealousy shown by the ugly sisters and their mother towards Cinderella, who is described as young and beautiful; some sexual connotations are retained, therefore, as the heroine is shown to be far more desirable than her stepsisters and stepmother, a fact which is reinforced when the prince eventually rejects them in favour of Cinderella herself. However, whereas at least part of the purpose of 'The Three Dresses' is to warn against the impropriety and social unacceptability of incest, a circumstance which provides the protagonist with a strong incentive for setting out on her travels, in Cinderella we have a tale aimed primarily at exploring the jealousy and rivalry that develop between siblings, and between parent and child, as the latter approaches maturity.

At this point, it is worth considering the presentation of all stepmothers in folktales, as they are invariably cast as jealous of their adoptive daughters, and severe in their treatment of them. However, this jealousy and severity may manifest themselves under two different circumstances. In the first of these, the stepmother is simply jealous of the daughter's youth and beauty, and feels resentful as a result, eventually taking steps to remove her from the parental home. This normally involves attempting to kill her, but is most famously exemplified in the story of Snow White, where the enchanted apple is used as a

symbol of death. In such tales, the stepmother's real motive is clear: it is not the abstract notion of the daughter's youth and beauty she resents, but the very concrete threat this poses to her own marriage. It should be remembered that, in primitive societies, incest was not uncommon, and so the stepmother fears that she will be rejected by her husband in favour of the beautiful daughter, eventually taking steps to prevent this from happening. It should also be noted that the jealous party in such tales is never the daughter's *natural* mother, as it was obviously deemed inappropriate that her own flesh and blood should feel such animosity towards her, and act with such ruthlessness. These tales are designed to warn against the inappropriateness of all intensive and destructive feelings in a 'civilized' society, but try to avoid undermining basic familial ties in the process by abstracting these feelings from the real self and real parents or siblings, and locating them in the implausible step-relatives. In addition, due consideration should be given to Freud's observation that projection and role-reversal both play a major role in dreams and folktales alike, and in which case we must also consider the other side of the coin, whereby the daughter is really the jealous party, but projects these feelings onto the intruding stepmother. Again, this is a valid interpretation of the scenario: a fundamental prerequisite of this folktale (as well as of a great many others) is the fact that the daughter is now reaching sexual maturity, entering the phase in her life when she is attractive to the opposite sex and when, by extrapolation, she also becomes sexually aware herself. As the father is the male with whom she is in closest and constant contact, it is natural that her feelings should initially be directed towards him, but these are thwarted by the presence of the stepmother, who occupies the desired position as the father's consort. Jealousy therefore causes the stepmother to be perceived as evil and as being the girl's natural enemy. All these are incestuous feelings that must be exorcized and re-directed towards more acceptable goals, such as marriage with the prince, and the tale therefore develops in a manner that guides its intended audience in the right direction.

The second common circumstance in which the stepmother manifests her jealousy and animosity is after the birth of her own, natural children. In this case, two major factors come into play: the stepmother's personal envy, and also her legitimate fears for the future fate of her own offspring. She understandably wishes that they should be the father's beneficiaries, and receive all the emotional attention and material wealth that are in danger of being monopolized by the elder daughter. On the other hand, if we consider this to be another case of projection, we may say that the elder daughter is really the jealous party, afraid that attention will be lavished on the new arrivals at her expense, and so she projects herself into a situation where she is the 'servant', and they her masters. In both these scenarios, both interpretations (that of the truly jealous stepmother, and that of the envious daughter who projects her feelings onto others) are equally valid and by no means mutually exclusive: folktales often do work on a variety of levels, pointing simultaneously in different directions, and by doing so they encourage each individual to find their own interpretation, to seek out the meaning that most readily conforms to their own experiences in life, and which provides them with the answers or reassurances they need.

When the father makes his desires (sexual union) known to his daughter in 'The Three Dresses', she immediately responds in the manner society would expect, by rejecting his advances. He is still her father, however, and so she is initially reluctant to reject all contact with him. Consequently, she remains at home and imposes a condition which must be fulfilled before their relationship may be taken any further, namely that he obtain three special dresses, which we can immediately identify as symbols of purity and chastity (these being the common connotations of the heavenly bodies with which the three dresses are associated), and as clear indications to her father that his desires are inappropriate: she goes to pains to put obstacles in his path, and to emphasize her own purity, which will be soiled if he is successful. It is highly unfortunate for her that he overcomes these obstacles by obtaining the goods requested by her, and his success in this respect must be interpreted as a symbol of his successful

sexual conquest of his daughter: she uses her innocence as a defence against him, but he acquires control of this innocence, of the chastity embodied in the sun, moon and star dresses, and the only way she can save herself from further violation is to flee from home, taking the dresses with her. Significantly, as she does so, she exchanges them for impoverished rags at the earliest opportunity, the implication of which is clear: her purity has been compromised and cannot be paraded in public, and so the dresses are wrapped up, hidden from general view, to be replaced by an image of lesser purity, the off-white dress. The celestial dresses will only emerge again for the three balls which will be the means by which she will be re-integrated with society, and receive its sanction and support. The three balls obviously function as a triplet, designed to emphasize her slow but steady return to social acceptance, and even the dramatic elevation of her status, which will be achieved when she is united in marriage with the prince, whose successive gifts to her (a bracelet, a ring and earrings) testify to his dedication and commitment. Interestingly, it is possible that the order of the presentation of these gifts has been confused in the tale we have here. Logically, one would expect the ring (a symbol of marriage and sexual union) to be the last of the gifts, rather than the earrings, a hypothesis supported by the fact that the prince is presented with the ring and earrings simultaneously, in recognition of the importance of the ring as the most symbolic gift of all. Folktales, as all forms of oral literature, become confused over time.

Returning to the father in this tale, it is noticeable that he continues to be an obstacle to the protagonist's social integration even though she has removed herself from his home, for she provides two reasons for turning down the prince's repeated offers of marriage: her youth (an indication that she is still not quite mature enough to undertake this serious commitment), and the objection of her father, whose shadow still looms large. The illness provoked by the prince's love for her proves to be the decisive factor, however, and by means of the triplet of cakes each of which contains one of the gifts he had given to her as a token of

his love, she eventually makes herself known to him, bringing about his recovery and her acceptance as a fully integrated member of society.

Similar remarks can be made if we regard the young girl's predicament as being caused by a projection of her own incestuous desires onto her father. As she begins to awaken sexually, she reacts to the only male in her immediate environment, namely her father, in which case the mother's death may be fictitious, a repressed wish to remove her as an obstacle. This, of course, is also true of the first scenario, where the mother need not necessarily really be dead in order for the father to covet his own daughter. Troubled by her instinctive urges, which she knows to be wrong and misdirected, the daughter seeks counsel in the form of the neighbour, whom we may regard as an embodiment or projection of the heroine's conscience, and who reminds her of propriety by means of the three dresses that are graphic representations of the expectations of society and of morality. But this attempt to deflect her impulses by means of a reminder of conventional values is unsuccessful, and so the girl must remove herself from the parental home until her desires may be directed towards a legitimate target, here represented by the prince. It is noticeable, however, that her entrance into the prince's household is by no means a complete break from the past and from her infantile urges, for the prince is himself a symbol of power and love, as was her father, and she will not be totally free of her earlier complexes until she can rid herself of all feelings of domination and subservience. Consequently, when she attends the three balls and gradually approaches maturity, she is unable to accept the prince's proposal of marriage as she is still in a weak and dependent position. Only afterwards, when the prince falls ill and so confirms that he loves her as much as she him, and she is able to act in a relatively dominant fashion by making him well again, can she agree to marriage. Now that the prince has seen her for what she really is, and has accepted her for it, she can likewise accept herself and there is no longer any need to repress desire and hide from public view: her inclinations are now all legitimate, she has been accepted, and she is

free to enter adult life and normal social intercourse, the ghosts of her formative years having been fully exorcized.

The numerous religious references in 'The Girl with No Arms' ('La niña sin brazos') illustrate the way in which so many tales have been changed over the course of time due to Christian influences, for the references to the Devil, to Saint Peter and to the reason for the girl's dismemberment (so that she can no longer make the sign of the cross and so ward off the Devil) are presumably designed both to deflect from the tale's scandalous repercussions, and to make it conform more closely to the expectations of a Catholic society. This provides us with an excellent example of the way storytellers of each age and environment work with elements from their own social experience and belief-systems. In spite of this, the tale's essential elements are all still present, albeit in a heavily disguised form, and there are a variety of clues, both internal and external, that allow us to untangle its highly complex web of associations and implications. The Devil, here as elsewhere, is associated with evil, corruption and immorality, and it is obvious from the outset that his encounter with the girl's father is not a chance one: he has his own, personal agenda that we soon discover to be that of abducting the daughter, undoubtedly with the aim of violating her and so defiling her chastity. This hypothesis is supported by the girl's dismemberment, a well-known motif which Propp interprets as an amplification of the motif of the cut or missing finger (which occurs in other tales, such as that of 'Seven Sunbeams' ('Siete Rayos de Sol', discussed earlier), and which itself echoes a traditional initiation ritual in some primitive societies, when a finger (usually the little one), is cut after circumcision. Such dismemberment is therefore part and parcel of entry into adult life, and is a corollary of sexual maturity, a notion which is certainly consistent with the motif of the missing finger in 'Seven Sunbeams', where the eponymous heroine loses her finger when the hero spills a drop of her blood, an image with obvious sexual connotations. It is also of no mean importance that the hero later recognizes Siete Rayos precisely because of this 'deformity': essentially, he here recognizes the sexual partner to whom he is now

committed. So, in 'The Girl with No Arms', we have an extreme example of this motif, where the Devil's violation of the abducted girl is symbolically represented by the amputation of her arms. Two further considerations give added weight to this interpretation. In the first place, there is the reference to the daughter's habit of making the sign of the cross whenever a visitor comes to her home. What is the significance of this? Why does she act in this way when there is a knock at the door? Her reaction makes very little sense as a habitual, general response. It only becomes part of a logical pattern if we regard it as an attempt on her part to emphasize her innocence and purity when these are threatened, the cross, of course, traditionally having great power in the context of a potential threat. In other words, her reaction has the same symbolic value as the request for the three dresses in 'The Three Dresses': it is an attempt to ward off the fear of violation by stressing purity and propriety. When all water (with all its cleansing, purifying connotations) is thrown out of the house, her defences are removed in the same way as are those of the protagonist of 'The Three Dresses' when the symbolic dresses fall into her father's power. That this removal of all form of protection leads to sexual violation is indicated by the fact that the front door is eventually opened to allow the Devil to enter. Previously, the girl's resistance had maintained her virginity intact, but the Devil's successful penetration into the house at the third attempt could be a symbolic parallel of his sexual penetration. Finally, we should also note that the prince's parents object to their son's marriage to the strange girl on the grounds that '. . . it was a dishonour to marry a girl with no arms . . .'. Her objections in this respect are certainly very feeble if we take them at face value, and they are soon dismissed by the prince; they make much more sense, however, if we consider that the parents are really talking about the dishonour (*deshonra*) of the girl having already lost her virginity before ever coming to the palace. Her sexual violation, not her physical disability, is the real stumbling-block to marital joy.

At this point, due consideration should also be given to the role of the father, who seems to stand idly by as his daughter is abducted from her bed. On

one level, we could regard the tale as being about comic and venal negligence. In his desire to acquire greater wealth, the father fails to recognize the signs of who the stranger is, and fails to protect his daughter properly: is a reminder of the duty of care a parent owes to their child. The father is conspicuous by his absence when the Devil visits their home for the third time, when the girl is asleep, and one might be tempted to assume that the Devil has simply taken advantage of the fact that the father has left home (perhaps to go to work cutting wood) in order to abduct the daughter. This, however, does not make any sense as it does not conform to the two previous visits, when the Devil specifically arranges to call when the father is at home with his daughter. If the Devil's intention is to abduct her, why on earth should he complicate matters by arranging for her father to be present, and later change his mind? One rational interpretation is if we regard the Devil here as representing, symbolically, the darker side of the father himself, as he wrestles with his incestuous feelings towards his maturing daughter. On the first two occasions the Devil (the father's incestuous desires) is kept firmly outside the door by the daughter's chastity and propriety, in the same way that the daughter's request for the three dresses had symbolized her successful resistance in the previous tale; on the third occasion, however, the Devil usurps all control of the father (hence the apparent absence of the latter during the third visit, for in reality he and the Devil are one and the same person), and takes advantage of the girl's vulnerability as she sleeps in her bed, the sexual implications of which require no elucidation. Resist as she might, she can no longer protect herself and she is abandoned to her fate, the amputation of her arms providing graphic proof of the loss of her virginity, reinforced by the comic double-entendre of the girl now crossing her legs in order to make the sign of the cross.

As in 'The Three Dresses', the remainder of the tale therefore tracks her gradual re-integration into society and her attempt to rid herself of the stigma forced on her by her father's actions. However, her return to grace will be an arduous one indeed, and her deflowering will have still further consequences

before its infamy may be exorcized. This comes in the form of the prince's apparent rejection of her and of her sons when he is deceived into believing that she has given birth to two mice instead of two babies. In other versions of the same tale the sons are referred to as two monsters, but in both cases the connotations are easy to trace: primitive belief frequently maintains that monstrous creatures are born from an incestuous relationship, and the girl's apparent conception of inhuman offspring confirms all the worst fears of everyone concerned, and presents the prince with a situation that is doubly problematic: not only does it seem that she has been conducting an incestuous (i.e. totally unacceptable) relationship with her father, but severe doubt is also cast over the paternity of the two boys. It is precisely for this reason that the girl reacts in such a calm, resigned fashion when she receives the forged letter in which the prince seems to order her to kill the two babies. She is neither outraged nor incredulous, for she fully recognizes the reasons behind such a harsh condemnation: she thinks that the prince believes them to be the spawn of an incestuous union, and so understands why he might want to be rid of them.

At this point, the girl is still mutilated, and we can take this as a symbol of the fact that her past continues to dominate her present. This does change, however, and her limbs are restored to her when she enters the house of the kindly ascetic, here identified as *San Pedro* (St Peter). Up to this point, her rejection by society has been complete: forced to flee from her father's house, she is first opposed by her future parents-in-law; then she believes herself to be rejected by her husband; and finally all passers-by turn their backs on her, refusing to help or to show any charity towards her. She has been completely ostracized by an uncaring society that seems to scorn the victim even more than the perpetrator of the crime, and her growing thirst at this point in the tale not only effectively highlights her abandonment as she is left to wither under the weight of social disapproval, but also reminds us of the Devil's second visit to her home, when all the water was cast out. Just as the expulsion of the water had been used as a symbol of her increasing vulnerability and of the soiling of her

purity, so it is used here as a symbol both of continuing vulnerability, and also of the beginning of her return to grace. When she is accepted into St Peter's house, she is offered water, and her arms are restored to her; this offer of protection and of acceptance puts her firmly on the road to social rehabilitation, and will culminate in her reunion with the prince. In rational terms, it is once more very difficult to accept that the prince does not recognize her simply because her arms have now been restored. It is much more logical to interpret this motif as a symbol of his refusal to believe her innocence, and to accept the truth regarding the paternity of his sons, whom he similarly refuses to recognize, even though they constantly address him as *papá*. At first he is totally unwilling to accept that he really is their natural father, but their insistence eventually forces him to face the truth, and to believe in them and in his wife, his ecstatic reaction marking the girl's full reintegration and return to social acceptance.

Another element which requires comment is the return of the character of the girl's father (the prince's father-in-law) at this point in the story. On the one hand, it acts as a further reminder to the audience of the incest motif which seems so central to this tale. However, it is also closely related to another narrative thread, which appears from the outset, about prohibitions, charms and protection against evil. We recall the motif of the sign of the cross that the girl used so effectively to ward off the Devil during the early part of the story. The father, however, had clearly pledged himself to the Devil, and he returns here as a reminder that there is always a price to pay for such a pact. Although he succeeds in getting past the girl's first line of defence (the invocation of Jesus, Mary and Joseph, which is effective in preventing the Devil from entering the house), he cannot escape the power of the curse that is directed at him, and is destroyed. This second narrative thread therefore reinforces superstitious belief in methods for warding off evil, and reminds us of the need to avoid evil in the first place.

So we see that these two tales, although they seem to bear little or no resemblance to one another in terms of their manifest content, actually deal with

very similar situations, fears and dilemmas, and their latent content is therefore very closely related. In this respect, 'The Girl with No Arms' can be seen to delve a little deeper than 'The Three Dresses', as it exposes many social ills and injustices beyond the taboo of incestuous liaison, for the girl's problems in this tale are severely compounded by the reaction of society as a whole, which refuses to support and to protect her in her hour of need. Indeed, were it not for the kindly intervention of the character referred to as St Peter (perhaps a symbol of a 'good father', contrasted with the 'bad father' of the earlier episodes, as well as a figure whose heavenly associations offer a means of escaping the Devil and entering Paradise), her future would seem very bleak indeed, but his help and comfort are all that is needed to expel the ghosts of the past and bring her peace of mind. As well as condemning all incestuous desires as destructive and unnatural, therefore, this tale also makes an incisive critique of the lack of support that is often to be found from society as a whole in such circumstances. We notice that the girl is effectively abandoned twice (after the rape and after the birth of her sons, which effectively gives us two stories in one), and that the community around her turn their backs on her. But things need not necessarily develop in this fashion, and in St Peter's intervention we are given a positive example of the way society really should deal with its weaker and more vulnerable members, not by disenfranchising them, but by offering them the protection and support that will allow them to be healed and to contribute to normal social development. In conjunction with this, it should also be borne in mind that these two tales, as well as the others discussed in this collection, can be interpreted in ways other than the purely psychoanalytical. Both stories deal with situations whereby women are shown to bring to marriage something which is mysteriously unacceptable (represented here by poverty and misfortune). This can be interpreted either as a destructive sexuality (which incorporates the incest motif elucidated above, and also encompasses other forms of illicit desire and unbridled emotion), or as a disturbing 'otherness', the dominant factor here being, of course, their ability to give birth. The motif of the girl with no arms apparently

giving birth to two mice instead of two human children itself suggests a questioning and exploration of parenthood, of women's capacity to bear children, and of the relationship between these offspring and their parents, especially the father. The sympathetic reaction of both the prince and his mother to the apparent birth of two monstrosities underlines this view, as it highlights an awareness of the mystery of the processes of Nature, and in particular of procreation. As well as reinforcing some deep-rooted taboos in the human psyche, therefore, these tales also help to elucidate and reinforce social attitudes to superstition, marriage, parenthood, and the dangers of evil influences. They work on a variety of levels, and appeal precisely because of this fact: each time a tale is heard (or, more recently, read), it conjures up new connotations and new meanings which manifest themselves, as appropriate, according to the listener's needs and latent preoccupations. Never static in their meaning, popular tales evolve and grow hand-in-hand with their audience.

The Castle of Nevercomeback (El castillo de irás y no volverás)

This classic folktale is replete with familiar motifs or situations, and also presents us with numerous possibilities for variations and modifications. Our text focuses on the fate of three brothers, but other versions feature only two (the number two commonly being used to emphasize contrast in modes of behaviour, whereas the number three usually highlights development and progression). The very first line of our tale presents us with an apparent conundrum, as it mentions seven sons who never re-appear and play absolutely no role in the development of the plot. As we have seen happen elsewhere, some confusion has obviously crept in here, and the seven-headed serpent, which makes its appearance later on as the elder brother's adversary, finds an echo in this early slip. Nor is this surprising, since the number seven is also a significant number, along with two and three, in many myths, folktales, and systems of belief. Not only is it a prime

number, but there are, for instance, seven days in creation, and consequently seven days in the week; there are seven graces; the seventh son of a seventh son is believed to be endowed with special powers, and in the biblical story of Jacob we see that the protagonist is the youngest of seven brothers. It is of little wonder, therefore, that this aberrant motif should have crept into the beginning of our tale, especially if the father's profession as a fisherman stimulated an unconscious association with biblical tradition. What is clear, however, is that the reference to the seven sons is a redundant motif here, although by pre-figuring the seven-headed serpent, it does provide a certain stylistic balance and narrative unity to the tale, which essentially consists of three separate stories: that of the fisherman and the miraculous fish, that of the three brothers' quest, and the mystery of the Castle of Nevercomeback.

The first significant motif in this story, therefore, is that of the speaking fish which promises the fisherman an abundant catch if he is set free, a promise which he duly keeps. The fish has a symbolic value in a great many cultures and traditions, some of which is certainly of great relevance here: in general, the fish is sexually ambivalent, representing both the male and the female,[63] but in both cases it is a symbol of fecundity, and may also symbolize abundance, wealth, and regeneration.[64] These connotations are evidently in play here, where the fish provides his captor with an abundant catch that increases his prosperity, and is later presented as the source of the three sons. Furthermore, medieval bestiaries present the fish as a symbol of compassion and love, this being another of its features here, as it shows no sign of bitterness or anger even when it is about to be killed and eaten: it is understanding and offers good help and counsel.

Triple repetition is again in evidence: the fisherman catches the strange fish three times; three sons/dogs/colts/lances are born; the castle is visited three times. The elements one would expect of a marvellous tale are present: the separation, the donor (the fish, which is later converted into the magical objects

---

[63] J.C. Cooper, *Symbolic & Mythological Animals* (London: Aquarian Press, 1992), 100.

[64] Cooper, *Symbolic & Mythological Animals*, 102.

it donates: the dog, colt, and lance), the combat with the aggressor (the serpent), the false hero (the coalman), and the eventual marriage of the hero (eldest son) with the princess. At this point we are given a third tale in the form of the conundrum of the Castle of Nevercomeback, which again contains the expected elements of separation, combat with the aggressor (the witch) where the youngest son will now be victorious, and general marriage, and which can be seen in part to be a doublet of the first sequence, but which also introduces some important new lessons. Whereas the serpent had been defeated by dint of courage and physical strength (the domain of the elder brother), the riddle of the castle will only be solved through caution and cunning, which are the prerogative of the youngest. Here, therefore, the middle brother serves only to emphasize further the danger inherent in visiting the castle as well as the difficulty of escaping from it and, as I have already mentioned, other versions of the same tale present us with only two brothers. Of course, this does not imply that folktales aim to disenfranchise middle-order siblings by suggesting that they contribute nothing to social stability; rather, it should be regarded as an example of the way folktales do tend to present a picture of a polarized society: the protagonists are either royalty or paupers (as here), the eldest or the youngest, male or female. No middle ground is ever suggested in these respects. In the case of social class, this partly reflects the reality of life when these accounts first came into being, in an age when the notion of the middle classes had never even been conceived; but this is only part of the reason, for it is noticeable that when a tale focuses on the nobility, it concentrates on its very upper echelons, while the peasants portrayed are ones who, like the fisherman in this tale, are on the verge of starvation. This undoubtedly occurs because folktales tend to deal predominantly in extremes: characters are either incredibly beautiful or hideously ugly, selflessly courageous or pathetically cowardly, immensely insightful or the epitome of stupidity. The bold symbolism needed to drive their message home through oral transmission can tolerate nothing less than such stark contrast, and in a very similar way the juxtaposition of the two closely-linked stories (that of the first-born, and that of

his younger twin) in this one folktale serves to highlight that both physical and mental maturity and strength are necessary in order to become fully integrated into civilized society.

Another seemingly curious feature of folktales such as this one is the way they seem to condone social *mobility*, in spite of the fact that a very important aspect of their educational function is to promote a return to normal interaction and relations, and hence to *stability*. Here, it is vital that we distinguish between two different types of stability. On one level we have inter-personal relations, family ties, sexual union and integration into expected social order. These are the values folktales seek to extol and foster in their audience, showing that equilibrium and the maintenance of the *status quo* are beneficial to the individual as well as to society as a whole. They are in evidence in a motif which, by analogy with other folktales that deal with similar situations, one would expect to find in the second half of this account: strictly speaking, the two younger siblings should respect the princess' marital status by placing their lance between themselves and her in bed, so preventing any sexual contact and symbolizing their chastity and fidelity to their elder twin. The relative complexity of this folktale, however, where separate stories are closely intertwined, makes the omission understandable. Furthermore, it could be argued that these are very clearly magical brothers, born out of the dispositions of a magical fish. They are also preternaturally close to one another through their telepathic water-bottles and might be regarded as one and the same person, an interpretation that fits in well with the sense of progression from one brother to the next, each one representing a more mature and wise incarnation of the previous. On a second level, we have the values of self-improvement, the acquisition of wealth and personal comfort by means of one's own merits, which certainly brings with it the possibility of change, as lowly peasants are raised to the rank of princes and monarchs. So we see that psychological and emotional stability are promoted alongside the sanctioning of mobility within social hierarchy, a mobility which is

mirrored graphically in the physical journeys peasant heroes must undertake before they reach the object of their quest.

The brothers' transformation into animals at the hands of the witch is readily understandable, and is a motif which is paralleled in many myths and legends, the most familiar of which is probably Circe's enchantment of Odysseus' men when she turns them into pigs. Here, the brothers are transformed into a dog and a wolf respectively, the canine association of both transformations indicating quite clearly that the second enchantment is a doublet of the first. As with the pigs in the *Odyssey*, the dog and wolf here symbolize man's base animal instinct, the raw, primitive urges that have brought the two brothers to this sorry state, and from which they cannot be freed until 'the beast' (here a lion, and which is itself a doublet of the monstrous serpent of the first half of the tale), has been tamed and killed. When the younger brother finally achieves this end, all three may return home and be fully integrated with society and its conventions. Marriages ensue, and everyone can live happily ever after.

The Palace of Enchantments (El palacio de los encantos) and The Enchanted Forest (La selva encantada)

These two tales will be studied together as they offer us an excellent example of the way the same structure can be manipulated and brought to life with different points of detail, and made to appeal to different sectors of society as a result. We can see that in both cases, the story is essentially the same:

1. A poor peasant is in love with someone rich or powerful, who returns the same love.
2. In order to avoid an undesirable marriage, the rich/powerful parents banish their offspring to a distant retreat of difficult access.

3.   The poor peasant goes in search of his/her beloved, and receives help to reach the object of his/her quest.

4.   The peasant must overcome a series of obstacles, which (s)he accomplishes thanks to magical objects or helpers.

5.   The rich/powerful lover is disenchanted, they marry and live happily ever after.

The differences in detail do, however, create subtle differences of direction and significance in the two versions, not least of which are those brought about by the difference in sex of the protagonist: in 'The Palace of Enchantments' ('El palacio de los encantos'), the peasant who sets out on this difficult quest is female, in 'The Enchanted Forest' ('La selva encantada'), the same character is male, and the obstacles placed in their path, as well as their means of overcoming them, are decidedly different. In her search for the missing prince, the heroine of 'The Palace' is aided by two old women who, in accordance with the psychological patterns identified by Jung, are undoubtedly embodiments of the protective and caring mother, as they show concern for the girl's safety and welfare, and very obligingly agree to deceive their sons and help her in her quest. This is interesting as we notice that the prince's mother is never mentioned at any point, and it is the king (male) that insists that his son be imprisoned in the enchanted palace. Similarly, the North-West Wind (*Aire Gallego*) and East Wind (*Aire Solano*) are presented as dangerous (male) adversaries who will stop, and even devour, the shepherdess if they discover her. The core of this tale therefore presents us with the male and female principles in direct conflict. The only sympathetic male character is the prince himself, and even his credentials are dubious. For one thing, his physical presence in the tale is so fleeting as to make it impossible to analyse him in any great depth, his only active function being to give the shepherdess the iron shoes and some directions on how to go about finding the enchanted palace. Otherwise, he is completely passive: he submits to his father's will, becomes the imprisoned object of the shepherdess' quest, and when she finds him, he spends most of his time asleep. It is also noticeable that

his two guardians in the enchanted palace are themselves female, a further suggestion, perhaps, that the prince should not be held up as a paragon of maturity, for male children in privileged households were usually reared by and among women until they reached a certain stage in their personal development. It is this immature state that the king seeks to prolong, while the girl's task is to give her lover his maturity.

'The Enchanted Forest' ('La selva encantada'), on the other hand, presents us with a different scenario altogether. The daughter who is the object of the poor peasant's desire has both a mother and a father, and her banishment to the enchanted forest comes about by accident rather than by design when, in a hasty fit of temper, her parents wish that she be whisked away rather than marry someone below her station. This is a scenario paralleled in many folktales, where a rash and impulsive desire is fulfilled, eventually to cause the wisher to regret his foolish words, one example of which was provided in 'Seven Sunbeams', when the father made an unwise pact with the Devil. Such situations in folktales are designed to show that impulsiveness and haste can cause much damage and distress, so underlining the value of acting wisely and with restraint. Having realized their mistake, the parents now enrol the help of the poor peasant to rescue their daughter, and act as donors, providing him with a horse, sword and money to help him on his quest. Immediately, we see that this tale does not present us with a polarization of the male and female principle, a fact confirmed when we see that, although our hero is further helped by three hermits (which we may here equate with the spirit archetype that provides help and advice, and which Jung identifies with the father-figure in folktales), he is also obstructed by a giant and innumerable warriors, as well as by an old hag. Both sexes are to be found on both sides of the fence in this tale therefore, helping the hero as well as opposing him, although there is also a marked predominance of male characters throughout, as compared with the more equal distribution in the number of male and female characters in 'The Palace'. The latter therefore presents us with a highly polarized, but roughly balanced, society, while 'The Forest' presents us

with a male-dominated society, but where male and female attitudes are shown to be roughly similar. The fact that 'The Forest' is a male-oriented tale is also evident in the way in which the hero overcomes the obstacles placed in his path; invariably, he chooses direct confrontation, and with the aid of his animal helpers (all of which are symbols of power and ferocity) defeats his opponents by dint of brute force. The heroine of 'The Palace', on the other hand, achieves her goals through trickery and the use of astute ploys. In fact, in most respects 'The Forest' seems an inferior production: the three hermits fail to underwrite any specific devotional point, nor do they provide the advice they promise. The helpful animals are a trite and rather gratuitous device, and neither lover actually learns very much on any level. There is a mild reversal of social fortunes, but little else to make this more than an adventure tale, which is in stark contrast to the richly resonant and tense storytelling of 'The Palace'. By altering the narrative focus and presenting us with a society overwhelmingly dominated by the masculine principle, 'The Forest' has lost much of its potential impact.

An Adventure Story (Un cuento de aventuras)

Although the beginning of this tale is reminiscent of that of 'The Palace of Enchantments' and 'The Enchanted Forest', with the imprisonment of the three princesses in an enchanted castle and their rescue by three lowly peasants, its development is radically different, as the following outline illustrates:

1. The princesses are abducted (separation).
11. The hero leaves home in search of them.
16. The hero and the aggressor (the anonymous abductor) meet in 'combat' (the rescue).
18. The hero is victorious.

22. The hero is helped in the form of the ring the youngest princess gives him (a ring which we immediately recognize as being analogous in properties and symbolic value to that in *Siete Rayos*).

23. The hero arrives incognito at the palace, disguised as a servant.

24. The false heroes (the elder brothers) persuade everyone that they have rescued the princesses themselves.

25. The hero is twice set a difficult task: that of obtaining the lion's milk, and that of defeating a powerful enemy.

26. The hero accomplishes these tasks.

27. The hero is recognized.

28. The false heroes are uncovered.

30. The false heroes are punished.

We see that, structurally, this tale is much more complex and involved than the two previous ones, and that the hero must overcome a great many more difficulties before he can realize his goal of marrying the princess and being accepted at court. The motif of the three princesses and three brothers offers the possibility of triple sequences which is not exploited in this story, but the tale does offer one doublet in the two tasks he must accomplish in the second part of the tale (and which forms a triplet when combined with the rescue of the princesses themselves). Being the youngest of the three brothers, it is not surprising that the hero overcomes all obstacles through his cleverness: while the elder brothers vainly try to take the castle by force, he uses stealth and cunning to free the princesses, and the other two tasks are accomplished thanks to the aid of the princess' ring (and we have already seen that, just like the younger brother, the female in folktales is normally associated with guile and wisdom). Significantly, although the rescue of the princesses is recounted at greatest length, the three tasks accomplished by our hero actually increase in value and importance as the tale develops: first, he saves the princesses, who are the king's daughters and therefore an embodiment of the future of the realm; then he saves

the ruler himself, the king (without whom the land would be without a leader); and, finally, he saves the kingdom itself, thwarting the invasion that is about to take advantage of the king's weakness. The latter task, which is the most vital of them all, is the one which is given least narrative attention, and so this tale clearly exemplifies the proven tendency of dreams and folktales to marginalize the most important, essential elements, and bring more trivial details to the forefront. Thus, our hero's most important deed will be that of saving the realm, and it is for that reason that he will ultimately be rewarded by marriage to the princess. Meanwhile, the apparent courage of the elder brothers in attacking the castle is also shown to be a sham, for they shy away from undertaking the dangerous tasks that they must accomplish if they are to save the king and the realm. Physical courage, therefore, is shown to be shallow and transitory, wisdom and guile being the primary qualities required of a successful ruler. This suggestion is reinforced by the king's own predicament. From the outset he is presented as weak: his health is poor, as a result of which he loses his daughters and almost loses his kingdom. His weakness nearly brings about everyone's downfall, and so it is shown that moral fortitude and sharp-wittedness are the essential requirements for any good ruler, both of which the youngest brother possesses in ample measure. By exercising these qualities, he restores the stability of the realm and assures its future. By analogy, we can also say that the individual, when he successfully integrates himself with adult society, assures its future and continuing good health.

The Tambourine made of Louse Skin (El pandero de piel de piojo)

The longest of all the tales contained in this collection, 'The Tambourine made of Louse Skin' ('El pandero de piel de piojo') is also the most literary in style and the most heavily influenced by literary sources, although the tale itself is traditional and many popular variants are known. The most obvious suggestion

of corruption from literary sources is probably the identification of the strongman as Hercules, a logical development as his name is synonymous with superhuman strength throughout the western world, but an equation which is completely out of keeping with the normal procedure in folktales: in other versions of the tale the strongman is identified merely as a giant, or by some other generic form that describes his capabilities (an Asturian version of the tale identifies him as Unified Strength [*Fuerzas-Unidas*]), in the same way that the other human helpers have names that describe their talents: Dead-Shot, Sharp-Ears and Swift-as-the-Wind. In fact, anonymity is a usual characteristic of all helpers and donors, unless they are also a prominent figure in the tale in question; they are referred to as a hermit, an old woman, a magician or even as a passer-by, but they are patently not given proper names. The reason for this is straightforward when we consider their psychological functions, for they always represent or donate skills and qualities the hero will need in order to overcome the difficulties ahead, and as such are really external projections of attributes that already exist in the protagonist. Thus, when the hero of a tale receives a magical ring, a flying carpet or a helper that is as strong as a hundred men, he is not really being given an unfair advantage through the intervention of some powerful ally; rather, these aids are symbols of the way the hero digs deep within himself to produce those skills that he needs most urgently, and so they also act as a symbol of his growing maturity and self-awareness, as his character develops and he realizes that the means to overcome all difficulties are to be found within himself. Helpers and donors are therefore not named, because they are all parts of the hero himself, and have no separate identity of their own, except as exterior projections of various parts of his character and personality.

A further indication of the confusion and corruption of this particular tale is the fact that Dead-Shot seems to play a very marginal role indeed: excluded from playing any part in untangling the riddle of the tambourine, in accomplishing the various tasks imposed on the hero, or in thwarting the marriage with the false hero (the prince who has usurped the protagonist's

rightful place at the altar), his presence is only justified through the rather awkward inclusion at the end of the tale, when all obstacles have been overcome and the marriage has taken place, of the motif of the wicked witch who wishes to avenge her son's humiliation (although it is important to note that the form she assumes in order to reap revenge, that of the owl, is commonly a portent of death in folktales, and so the motif itself is not unexpected: it has merely been misplaced). Logically, Dead-Shot should be called upon at the same time as the other helpers and animals, when the hero needs to accomplish the difficult tasks he has been set. A Castilian variant, for example, relates how Swift-as-the-Wind is bewitched and falls asleep while fetching the water from the Pure Spring, but is woken when the marksman fires a shot at the wheels tied to his feet, enabling him to return to the palace by the stipulated deadline; in this way, Dead-Shot plays an important role in the hero's success, but his displacement in our story indicates that his original function has been forgotten, to be replaced by a marginal one that is intended as a justification for his existence.

The third feature that indicates the literary influence on this tale is its very style, which is certainly more conscious than one would normally expect to find in a purely oral account. This is evident primarily in the added detail which it contains, such as the conversations between the hero and the animals, as he initially objects to their company, and the relatively long and highly unusual section at the end of the tale when we are told of the specific rewards accorded to each of the hero's helpers, including the animals. All these features give the tale added colour, but contribute nothing to its structure or to its psychological connotations, and so must be regarded as later additions included for curiosity's sake. So we see how traditional tales can be elaborated in a very self-conscious fashion to produce accounts which, while they adhere in essence to their original form, exhibit contents that are more varied and meticulous than one would normally expect.

Finally, it is interesting to note that this is the first of the tales studied by us in which the human and animal worlds clearly interact. We have seen

transformations elsewhere, of course, but the animals depicted here are not in any way magical, and have no unusual gifts except the ability to speak, which is merely used as the simplest way of incorporating them into the tale. Significantly, only the ant participates in completing the difficult tasks set for the hero, and this is hardly surprising as the ant is universally regarded as a symbol of industry and is used as such here, as a projection of that particular quality in the hero himself. But, though the other animals have no specific symbolic value in this tale, they do each behave according to their natural inclination and capabilities, the beetle entering the prince's mouth, and the mouse the princess' clothing, in order to disrupt their wedding. In each case they also act as a voice of conscience, and are therefore to a certain extent symbolic in that they represent the hero himself and argue his case before the people who are seeking to deny him his deserved reward. None of these animals should be placed in the same category as the mythical or magical animals encountered elsewhere, and which invariably represent fears and psychoses that need to be overcome and tamed. On the contrary, these animals are very positive projections of the hero, and also serve to highlight the important link between humanity and nature. They serve to stress the importance of maintaining a respect for the natural equilibrium of the world, and of maintaining a balance between the primitive and the civilized, one which the princess has herself been threatening to destroy. For we can see in the louse and fennel which she uses as materials for her singular tambourine an image of the way civilization has become distanced from nature in her court and of the way, by analogy, a rift has been wrought between the primitive and the civilized, between instinct and reason, between the conscious state and the darker recesses of the mind. The louse and the fennel are presented as grotesque and distorted examples of their kind, but is this a true reflection of how they really are, or a comment on the princess' perception of them? She removes both from their natural environment, and kills them in order to produce an artificial object for her own amusement. The primary task of the hero in this tale, therefore, must be to restore the balance and heal the ills caused by the complete suppression of all

instinctual and 'natural' behaviour. Hence the important inclusion of the three animals as his helpers, each of which behaves 'naturally', and two of which act as the voice of conscience that will force the princess to accept the shepherd in marriage. Human society and Nature are reconciled, the balance of world order is restored, and normality can therefore be resumed.

Luisa and the Dragon (Luisa y el dragón)

The key to interpreting this tale lies in understanding the relationship between Luisa and the dragon (*dragón*), whose name suggests that he is some hideous monster, but who we are told '. . . era un terrible hombre que tenía atemorizada a toda la comarca, porque se comía a todos los niños de los contornos' ('. . . was a terrible man who terrorized the whole neighbourhood, because he ate the children from all the lands around.'). He is a man, therefore, but his actions are so monstrous that he is given a beastly name and becomes the bogey man of the entire community, terrorizing young and old alike. His relationship with Luisa, however, is very strange, for it is a remarkable coincidence that his daughter should bear the same name, and that the two girls should be so physically alike that the cowherd is unable to distinguish between them. Undoubtedly, this is more than a case of mere happenstance, and our suspicions are aroused even further when the heroine kills the daughter of the *dragón*, yet is still able to deceive the goatherd into believing that she is the same daughter when she returns to the *dragón*'s estate for the second time later in the tale. Finally, we notice that the *dragón*'s wife is a very willing accomplice in the early stages of the tale, even though she must be aware of the heroine's implication in her daughter's murder: why does she continue to act in such a kind and supportive way? The only satisfactory way of making any sense of these contradictory details is to conclude that Luisa is herself really the *dragón*'s daughter, and that the latter is only killed in a symbolic sense, her death being used as a metaphor

for her removal from her father's household and from her dependence on him. This is why both girls bear the same name, why they are physically alike (for they are one and the same person), why the *dragón*'s wife is so supportive, and why Luisa continues to be recognized as the *dragón*'s daughter by his servants: his daughter has not really died, and they have no reason to distrust the word of their employer's child. They therefore follow her orders, and Luisa is able to abscond with some of her father's most prized possessions.

Unlike other tales we have examined to date, this particular story begins when the protagonist has already left home and is already attempting to make her own way in life. Nevertheless, she does return to her place of origin on three separate occasions, and each time we see that she takes a significant step forward toward independence and, eventually, to dominance over her parents. As elsewhere, we see that marriage plays an important role in this process of self-realization, but here it is only one part of a much more general evolution that will culminate in the death of both parents. The repeated request that one of her employers' sons should marry one of her sisters (and eventually that the youngest son should marry Luisa herself) is obviously a triplet used for cumulative effect, for the real, objective existence of these sisters is very doubtful: they only ever appear as appendages to Luisa, and are never presented as performing any actions of their own, however minor and insignificant. Effectively, there really are no such sisters, and the first two marriages act by way of a prelude to Luisa's own nuptials. They also provide her with an excuse to return to her father's home, in order to acquire the dowry that must be presented before any such union can take place, the motif of the dowry being itself yet another clue to the fact that Luisa (and the two sisters that are merely amplifications and extensions of her own identity) is the daughter of the *dragón*. The two elder sisters have a late parallel in the *dragón*'s other two daughters, killed by Luisa when she comes for the sword, and which are yet another echo that strongly suggests that our heroine and the daughter of the *dragón* are one and the same.

Luisa's material acquisitions are symbols of her repeated success and culminate in the appropriation of the remarkable sword that proves to be so difficult to purloin, and which leads to the death of the *dragón*'s wife (who, according to the interpretation given above, may be Luisa's own mother) and almost to her own. In each theft we can see a steady transfer of wealth (and therefore of power) from the *dragón* to Luisa, the implication being that, as she matures and her parents grow older, control of the parental estate gradually passes from the older to the younger generation. But this process is never a simple one; as in real life, there is a resistance to relinquishing control and to investing the child with the authority and independence it craves, a situation imaginatively conveyed in the above quote, which presents the *dragón* as a 'child-eater'. Such trust and freedom are therefore very hard to come by, and require all of Luisa's guile and cunning to obtain. In fact, total freedom from parental influence can only be attained with the latter's death, at which point the child now fully usurps their role, and the whole process can begin again with the participation of a new generation of offspring. The first death is that of the *dragón*'s real daughter (Luisa's double), who is killed by Luisa herself, symbolizing the death of childhood and the beginning of adulthood, a process which is explored in this tale and which reaches its next significant milestone in the death of the mother, which occurs when the third object, the sword, is stolen. The event is highly symbolic and extremely logical. The sword (an obvious phallic symbol in this case, especially as its theft is so closely associated with the *dragón*'s retirement to bed) is the object that will secure Luisa's marriage. Her marriage, however, itself symbolizes Luisa's incorporation into the adult world, at which point she assumes all the responsibilities concomitant with her new status, but which had previously been the exclusive domain of her mother. Her mother must be ousted, therefore, and symbolically leave a 'vacant position' in the adult world before Luisa can seal her own marriage. So it is highly significant that the prelude to this death should be Luisa's attempt to steal her father's sword, with all its Freudian connotations. It is noticeable that this is the

only point when the mother is openly hostile and resistant to Luisa, when she realizes that her own position is threatened by Luisa's attempt to capture the phallus that she had previously dominated. The mother's insecurity in this respect is underlined in the ruse Luisa uses to free herself from imprisonment: she persuades her mother to loosen her bonds so that she may remove a louse that is disfiguring the latter's face, the motif of physical disfigurement perhaps being an image of the ravage the years have caused her. She knows that she is ageing and slipping from her previous position of (sexual) domination and power, and desperately tries to resist by restraining the daughter that is threatening to usurp her place. When Luisa kills her mother and successfully absconds with her father's sword, we see that she has now taken over her mother's place in the social hierarchy, but there is also a strong suggestion that the *dragón*'s own sexual potency has been compromised as a result. He, too, is ageing, and it will not be long before he is similarly removed from this world, leaving his estate and all his power exclusively in his daughter's hands. When Luisa contrives to seal the *dragón* in a coffin and cremate him, she removes the last stumbling-block to her full integration into the adult world: the 'monster' is removed, and the cycle of life may begin again. The story emphasizes the need to break prohibitions and expectations in order to grow and flourish, a fact alluded to in the anti-moralistic and humorous punch line that refers to Luisa's lack of kindness (*poca bondad*) towards the *dragón* and his wife. This is a story that legitimizes rebellion rather than conformity as a prerequisite for social renewal.

The Enchanted Princess (La princesa encantada)

This tale presents us with a rite of passage of a type that will be quite familiar to anyone conversant with myth or medieval romance, for here the hero must frequently traverse some aquatic barrier in order to reach a strange land where the normal laws of the real world do not apply, and where he must accomplish

some notable feat in order to prove his worth. Evidently, the time has come for the hero of this tale to establish himself in the adult world and, in spite of his father's resistance, he is eventually allowed to go fishing, and hence to participate in the daily toil which is his family's livelihood. This represents his first step towards manhood, as he is allowed to share the responsibility of earning the day's food. This process proceeds apace when he follows the trout to the depths of the lake, and is led to an unfamiliar land where he will be tested and where he will learn some valuable lessons before achieving social integration. We have already seen that fish have many associations in traditional lore and belief, but the motif of the trout is of particular interest as this fish is commonly associated with health and fertility in European tradition, and both these elements are in evidence when the youth enters the enchanted castle. The various rooms he enters all provide him with some form of sustenance or protection in the form of heat, food, drink, clothing and rest, and so stress the importance of strength and good health as a prerequisite to facing the challenges of adult life: the weak and ailing will not succeed in this world for the dangers it presents, embodied in the serpent and giant, are real and great.

The trout's function as a symbol of fertility is developed in the image of the enchanted princess, whom the youth must rescue if he is to prove his sexual maturity and readiness to enter adult life. Achieving this goal, however, will require a variety of skills, not least of which is showing the willingness to face danger and honour a commitment. The youth has already begun to show his maturity in this respect, of course, for he was courageous enough to follow the trout into the deep waters, and to pursue his quest even when his destination has taken on very unexpected and potentially deadly dimensions. He continues to show this bravery and commitment, however, by undertaking to disenchant the princess, and by participating in the wild animals' dispute over their prey. In this he acts both courageously and wisely, and receives a precious reward as a result. In our analysis of 'The Tambourine Made of Louse-Skin', we saw that animals may be used as embodiments of certain desirable qualities that any hero must

possess in order to be successful. This is clearly the case here, where each creature (a lion, greyhound, eagle and ant) provides the youth with a token that will allow him to take advantage of each of their unique qualities and talents should the need ever arise. These will later be used to good effect by the hero as he tackles the various challenges that must be completed if the princess is to be freed, but let there be no mistake — it is really the hero himself that triumphs on each occasion, not an animal substitute, for the qualities he must display in order to succeed are all ones that can be translated into very human terms, qualities such as strength, courage, speed, cunning and stealth.

Unusually, perhaps, the first of the challenges seems to be the hardest to complete, although other tales have shown us the danger of making rash evaluations. In fact, we can see that several triplets are used here to reinforce the image of the hero's evolution from boyhood to manhood. The serpent is fought three times before it is defeated, and a total of three animals are engaged in some form of combat (the serpent, as well as the doe and dove, where the competition is one of speed rather than of strength). It is noticeable that, in order to defeat the serpent, the hero/lion must be furnished with food, drink and a kiss, references which take us back to the enchanted palace and the hero's entry into this magical realm. There, we saw that the trout's symbolic value as an image of health and fertility had been expanded in great measure, and here we find that these values are reinforced, so stressing the importance of physical as well as spiritual sustenance in order to overcome these challenges, and also pointing once more toward their true meaning: only by succeeding in the tasks set before him can the hero prove that he is sufficiently developed, both physically and mentally, to enter adult life.

The hero's appearance outside the princess's bedroom takes us back to a motif we first encountered in 'Luisa and the dragon', when the evil *dragón*, or in this case the giant, is thrice awoken when the protagonist attempts to make off with its most treasured possession. In *Luisa*, the object in question was a sword;

here it is the princess, but the sexual parallel is clear for the princess, as the giant's enchanted consort, is as much a function and symbol of his sexual potency as was the *dragón*'s sword. Furthermore, just as the theft of the sword was a prelude to the *dragón*'s death, so the hero's abduction of the princess is associated with the giant's death in this tale. In both cases, if the younger generation is to thrive, then the older one must perish, and there could scarcely be a more effective way of symbolizing this situation than to present the golden egg as the instrument of the giant's death. The egg, which is symbolic of birth, youth and fertility, kills the giant, and the old is therefore unequivocally forced to give way to the new.

This story provides us with an excellent example of the genre. It makes very satisfying use of narrative triads, as well as of other numerical sequences: we have one protagonist and one princess; two shepherds' daughters; four animals; five episodic units (the young fisherman, the enchanted princess, the grateful beasts, the quest at Mt Sinai, the disenchantment of the princess); six rooms; seven things that are 'for' the protagonist (the six rooms plus the princess), so incorporating all the numbers from one to seven. It combines a clear thematic focus with rich formal elaboration of the tale, which itself shows some attractive variation in the tone of storytelling, so highlighting the stylistic as well as psychological richness of the oral tale.

The Three Oranges of Love (Las tres naranjas del amor)

The motif of the prince (or princess) who does not laugh, and which is the starting-point of this tale, is of widespread currency throughout world myth and folklore, and its significance must be appreciated if we are to make sense of its inclusion in this account. Many traditions insist that the land of the dead is bereft of all laughter, and some tales recount how a hero who enters the land of the

dead must refrain from laughing lest he give away the fact that he is still alive.[65] Conversely, entrance into life (be it birth, re-birth, or a ritualistic rite of passage) is accompanied by laughter, and several folktales speak of laughter as causing plants to flower and grow.[66] In brief, therefore, we can see that laughter is generally associated with fertility and life, while its absence is a corollary of stagnation and death, so this folktale immediately presents us with the tragic and potentially disastrous situation of a prince (the leader and symbol of his land and people) who is sterile, without an heir and without any prospect of engendering any descendants.

On closer examination of the tale, however, we are immediately presented with a plethora of perplexing elements. For one thing, we notice that the prince is effectively presented as being sad twice over: he begins as the 'prince who never laughed', but a spell is later cast on him by the witch that he should never laugh until he find the three oranges of love, at which point 'the prince became sad'. How could he possibly become more downcast than he already is? In fact, comparison with the motif of 'the prince who never laughed' as it appears in other tales shows us that two distinct elements have become wildly confused here. One version of the motif presents us with a sad prince (or princess) whose hand in marriage is offered to the first person who succeeds in making them laugh. In this variant, the sexual connotations of laughter are self-evident, since the phenomenon is explicitly associated with marriage and, logically, with reproduction. The second format for the motif describes a prince (or princess) who unwisely laughs at the misfortune of a sorcerer (or sorceress), who condemns them to a life devoid of laughter until some special condition be fulfilled. These two variations of the motif may have become confused here: the beautiful maiden who elicits the prince's laughter (and so wins his hand in marriage) is replaced by the sorceress here, who actually does succeed in her

---

[65] For details regarding this and other aspect of laughing in myth and folktales, see 'Ritual Laughter in Folklore', in Propp, *Theory and History of Folklore*, 124-46.

[66] Propp, 'Ritual Laughter in Folklore', 137.

objective (as does her more eligible counterpart in the motif's original form), but crowns this achievement, not by marrying the prince, but by placing a taboo on him as punishment for his ridicule. Thus, both possible narrative lines are forced together, and this union is echoed in the way the whole tale itself seems to be comprised of two separate accounts, the first focusing on the prince's quest for the oranges of love, and the second on his wife's quest for acceptance at court.

The association of laughter with fertility and procreation has certainly not been ousted from our tale, however. In fact, if we associate laughter with sexual initiation, then a possible reading of the story is as a depiction of two forms of sexual initiation: the first graceless and perfunctory, the second dignified by a questing process and associated with beauty. The prince's problem is to disentangle the two and to implement the right choices consequent upon this. It is therefore significant that the witch should insist that he find the oranges of *love* before he may laugh again, and that the third of these should present him with a beautiful maiden whom he marries and who later becomes the mother of his son. His task in seeking out the symbolic oranges is to acquire the maturity and wisdom he will need in order to fulfil his role as husband and father. In the triplet of the oranges we witness his development in this respect: he is unprepared for what awaits him when he opens the first casket, and so he fails; he is too impatient when he opens the second, and is again unsuccessful; on the third occasion, however, he is calm and ready, and the symbol of the flowing water is again indicative of the sexual associations of this quest, and a son is born barely a year later. Thus, this part of the tale seems to provide an encouraging sense that sexual maturity can be achieved, and the right choices can be made.

At this point, the second plot begins to unfold, and the tale takes on a new direction. The first half of the tale had contained several structural complexities: the prince is both the victim and the hero of the story, the witch is both the aggressor and the helper. The second plot is much simpler in structure, although it does present us with several parallels and reversals of the first half of the story, as well as many similarities with other tales examined in this study. The princess

now becomes the protagonist of the tale, so providing us with another example of the way some folktales choose to explore their theme from both the male and the female point of view. Like the prince, she is both the victim and the heroine of her story, but the witch now fulfils the much more consistent roles of aggressor and false hero, usurping the princess' position at court, and reaping all the benefits this entails. Earlier, I mentioned that in one version of the motif, the prince's sadness comes about when he unwisely laughs at the plight of a sorcerer, and this motif is frequently echoed in this part of the tale, when the princess laughs at the witch's foolish belief that the beautiful reflection in the water is her own. It is normally the princess' mockery that provokes the witch's wrath, therefore, leading her to bewitch her and to take her place. Our condensed version of the tale omits this particular aspect, but it preserves the woman's intense rivalry and jealousy, which is itself a direct parallel of the wicked stepmother motif that we have identified elsewhere. Her desire to change places with the young and desirable princess is similar to the stepmother's wish to repress the attractive stepdaughter, and both characters achieve their goal by casting a spell that, temporarily at least, removes this upstart rival from the picture. It is also interesting to note how the narcissistic tendencies of both the younger and older pairs are similarly portrayed in both accounts. The stepmother in Snow White admires herself in the mirror in the same way as the witch of 'The Three Oranges of Love' preens herself in the fountain, and both are angered when they realize that they are not the outstanding beauty they first thought. The mirror/fountain episode might also imply some risk of merged identities between the witch (and, by implication, her kind of sexuality) and the princess herself, highlighting the fact that the latter has not yet reached the desired state of being. Thus, both Snow White and the princess bring about their own downfall through their self-indulgence; Snow White cannot resist the temptation of the apple, whose sexual connotations are of widespread currency in popular tradition, and are by no means limited to Christian doctrine, while the princess is herself undone by her desire to 'look good', and whose sharp penetration by the hairpin

also has sexual implications. Undone by her own foolishness, as was the prince in the first half of the tale, she, too, must show patience and fortitude if she is to be reinstated and a mature, balanced partnership is to be achieved.

The Three Riddles (Los tres acertijos)

In one respect, this tale presents us with a reversal of the situation in 'The Tambourine Made of Louse-Skin'. In the latter, the princess herself was the author of a puzzle (the unusual tambourine) that her future husband had to solve. Here, it is the prospective groom himself who must defeat the princess with an insoluble riddle, but in both cases the motif performs exactly the same function, for the princess will only marry someone who proves himself to be her equal (or superior) in cunning and intellect, and a suitor must therefore prove his intellectual prowess as a first step to winning her hand. However, whereas in 'The Tambourine' the princess then proceeded to test some of the hero's other (physical) qualities (such as his strength, speed and industry), here the focus remains on his mental skills, which he uses to trick the maid, the queen and the princess into sleeping with him, therefore placing himself in a position to defeat the final challenge of filling a sack with truths. In accordance with the egalitarian tendency of folktales, therefore, this story serves to show how the humblest peasant can defeat the loftiest of adversaries.

Evidently, marriage is a central theme in this tale as it is the prize that tempts the hero to leave home in the first place. It may seem strange that his own mother should attempt to poison him at this stage, and certainly her reason for doing this, namely that she would prefer for her son to die by her hand rather than by the king's ('. . . she preferred for her son to die on the waay, rather than be hanged by order of the king') is misleading. In fact, what we have here is another version of the motif of the parent who resists the child's entry into adult life. Her attempt to kill him is an attempt to make him stay a child forever, and

this interpretation helps to explain the hero's rather blasé reaction when he discovers his mother's treachery; he bears no rancour because he knows that this is not really an 'assassination' attempt, but a manifestation (albeit a somewhat warped one to our eyes!) of her over-protectiveness. By avoiding death at this point, he overcomes the first obstacle, but many more await him including, significantly, overcoming the opposition of the princess' parents, whom he also defeats (by tricking the queen into sleeping with him, and by meeting the king's challenge to fill a sack with truths). As elsewhere, therefore, we see that the older generation must be overcome in order to be allowed to enter into adult society.

Finally, we see that the sexual dimension of the tale is highlighted in the sequence when the hero guards the rabbits. Rabbits are themselves very traditional symbols of fertility, and this aspect is developed further in the triplet of the attempts by the maiden, queen and princess to steal one of them. The challenge itself is highly symbolic: the hero is supposed to guard the rabbits (symbols of fertility) for a period of one year. If he loses even one of them, this will be a sign of his own sexual immaturity. Not only does he accomplish this task, however, but he also sleeps with three different women, culminating in the princess herself, and so shows that he is fully capable of accepting the demands and responsibilities of adult life.

The Enchanted Monkey (La mona encantada)

In 'The Three Riddles' we were given an inkling of the dangers of judging things and people at face value, as the humble (and, according to his mother, idiotic) shepherd proved to be more than a match for the princess, the king and all their royal advisers. Here, the same idea is developed in much greater detail, where the triplet of the ugly trough, rag and monkey, which turn out to be exceptionally beautiful acquisitions, remind us that a surface reading is never adequate, that one should always delve deeper in order to identify and recognize the true value

of the things around us, a principle which is true of folktales themselves, of course, whose manifest content covers a much more profound psychological significance.

The quest on which the three brothers are engaged in this tale is, ultimately, entry into manhood, here symbolized by accession to the throne, together with all the power and influence it entails. As elsewhere, the younger brother will be the one who successfully accomplishes the set tasks, although his achievements are not presented in quite the triumphant terms of other folktales. Certainly, he shows more diligence than his brothers, who content themselves with fulfilling their quests close to home, not venturing as far afield as their younger sibling. Also, he shows integrity in accepting the objects and wife given to him in the enchanted house: he neither disdains to receive them (in spite of his reluctance), nor does he discard them on the way home; in this, he shows respect for those that had kindly given him shelter, and so proves himself worthy of receiving gifts of greater value. This is a theme which occurs in different guises in a number of different folktales, including the next tale in this collection, 'The Marvellous Journey' ('El viaje maravilloso'), and another, analogous one, 'The Three Golden Orbs' ('Las tres bolas de oro'),[67] where a beautiful maiden gives each of three brothers, in turn, a golden orb, with instructions on how to use it to good effect. The first two brothers are so enamoured with the gift, however, that they forget even to thank the maiden for her generosity, and soon lose their orbs as a result. The youngest brother, however, graphically shows his gratitude by crying with joy, and is rewarded accordingly. Respect and gratitude, therefore, are qualities that are advocated and positively encouraged in many folktales, including this one, where the younger brother behaves politely and with decorum, for which he is ultimately rewarded with the crown.

Nevertheless, there is a certain fortuity about the protagonist's good luck in this tale, which undoubtedly has wider implications. The horse, which refuses

---

[67] An example of this tale may be found in Constantino Cabal, *Los cuentos tradicionales asturianos* (Madrid: Voluntad, 1924), 49-54.

to take any other road than the one that leads to the enchanted house, could be regarded as a projection of the hero's subconscious, which leads him in the right direction in spite of his apparent determination to take another route. It could, on the other hand, be seen as the hand of fate, an interpretation which throws life's trials and tribulations into sharp relief. Certainly, strength of character, integrity, maturity, and all the other qualities advocated in folktales are to be commended and striven for, but other, unpredictable, factors also contribute to a person's destiny, and every individual must accept that, sometimes, things are simply beyond their control. This is a lesson latent in many other tales, where the heroine's enchantment, or the hero's obstruction, seems completely gratuitous. Adverse, as well as good, fortune can affect the development of a tale, and the protagonist must accept such reversals with equanimity. After all luck, in one form or another, is an attribute of any hero in any genre, so the hero of this tale accepts his apparent failure with suitably good humour, and reaps the rewards.

The motif of the enchanted monkey, who turns out to be a beautiful maiden who becomes the hero's bride, has obvious parallels with well-known tales such as *Beauty and the Beast*, and *The Frog Prince*, except that the female is the enchanted party in our tale. Her disenchantment is never presented as a goal in this tale, not even a secondary one, but it is nevertheless achieved, and its importance should not be under-estimated. In fact, we have here yet another example of two parallel plots being developed within the one tale: in the one, the prince is on a quest for sovereignty (or adulthood), which he achieves through the magical objects acquired in the enchanted house; in the second, the enchanted monkey (a beautiful maiden) seeks to be disenchanted and integrated into human society. This is achieved in a manner that directly parallels the disenchantment of the beast and of the frog prince in the aforementioned tales: the beast becomes human when his beloved *chooses* to return to his side and become his wife; the frog prince becomes human when he is kissed (with the usual connotations of sexual union, marriage, etc.); in our tale, the enchanted monkey becomes human when the hero agrees to take her with him to court, the

implication (which is already contained in the king's test that the sons should seek out a beautiful fiancée) being that once at court, they will be married. In each case, the willing acceptance of marital union causes a drastic transformation that allows the enchanted character to return to human form and become part of human society once more, and so this tale really presents us with the path followed by two characters to attain maturity and recognition, all of which culminates in the marriage with which the tale inexorably ends.

The Marvellous Journey (El viaje maravilloso)

The theme of gratitude and humility plays an important part in the first half of this tale, where the magical donkey that provides its owner with all sorts of goods and riches is a direct parallel to the golden orbs in 'The Three Golden Orbs', described above. Although they do acquire a certain amount of wealth and status, the two elder brothers in this tale both lose the donkey given to them by the strange gentleman, and so fail to attain even greater riches. Their failure is due to two main causes: their ingratitude, as they fail to give proper thanks and recognition to the generous donor; and their greed, symbolized by their gluttony, and which causes them to be slothful and unwilling to follow the donkey when it enters the river. Their greed and ingratitude are then emphasized by their refusal even to recognize, let alone help, their poor relations when they pass them in the street. These faults are singularly absent from the youngest brother who, in accordance with folktale tradition, shows himself to be wise and thoughtful in all his actions, showing gratitude to his benefactor and contenting himself with fulfilling his barest needs, rather than allowing himself to be dominated by greed and ostentation.

The motif of the ass as the magical means of acquiring wealth is indeed unusual, as the animal is traditionally associated with stupidity and stubbornness. Nevertheless, it does make some sense if we remember that stupidity is one of

the causes of the elder brothers' downfall, as they fail to recognize and make proper use of the wondrous gift that they have been accorded. The younger brother shows wisdom in controlling the ass wisely, and by thinking of others, giving his father all that he needs to live a life of comfort and repose. Again, this is a sharp contrast with the actions of the elder brothers, who had markedly turned their backs on all family ties.

At this point, the tale takes a markedly religious turn as it begins a new sequence that involves the hero's journey to a fantastical other world abode. The first half of the tale had conformed very closely to traditional lines, where the only unusual feature of any significance is the way the elder brothers are seen to prosper; analogy with 'The Three Golden Orbs', for instance, indicates that the brothers should really lose the donkey before they are able to obtain any riches. In fact, we can see that the religious orientation of the second half of the tale has infiltrated and affected this particular development. The sights our hero sees as he travels through this land are recognizable motifs from myth, folklore and religion. Medieval Mariology frequently presents the Virgin Mary as a fertile meadow through which several rivers (commonly associated with the Christian virtues) flow. It is not surprising that on this journey through the other world, which will culminate in the hero's encounter with the Virgin herself, should come across fields of several types, although their presentation does differ somewhat from the expected. Here, the fertile meadow provides no physical sustenance, while the sandy ground sustains a great many beasts, and the rivers are comprised of tears, milk and blood. This presentation is entirely consistent with biblical tradition, however, and is further combined with motifs that we have already encountered in our analyses of folktales in this collection. The rock faces which we later learn are the hero's hard-hearted elder brothers are remarkably similar in nature to the rocks which entrap the brothers in 'The Sultan's Three Sons' ('Los tres hijos del sultán', discussed below), while the motif of the missing finger, which was elucidated in detail in our discussion of 'The Girl with No Arms', is associated with circumcision and sexual maturity, a

96

connotation which is retained here as the brother loses the tip of his finger when he touches a bed. Later, we are told that these beds are located in the palace of Hell, and that they await the arrival of the two elder brothers, but this is clearly a gloss that has been put on a much earlier motif. Indeed, the whole motif of the enchanted palace has been transformed here so that it represents the afterlife, a role which it was never originally intended to fulfil, and the function of the beds and missing fingertip, which one would expect to be associated with the hero's sexual maturity, have similarly been altered.

When the protagonist eventually returns to his home, he is shocked to discover that 200 years have elapsed since he left, and that he and his family are now the stuff of legend. This motif of the miraculous passage of time (a very close analogy of which appears in Alfonso X, the Wise's *Songs of the Virgin Mary* [*Cantigas de Santa María*[68]], no. CIII, where 300 years fly by as a monk listens to the sweet song of a bird of paradise) is quite unusual in folktales, although its many versions are common enough in myth, legend and medieval romance. The myth of Creation itself could be regarded as one form of this motif, for the creation of the universe, which modern science maintains took billions of years to accomplish, is presented in the Bible as having taken place in a mere six days. Medieval romance frequently presents us with an inverse version of this motif, when a knight of great renown seems to spend a considerable length of time in an other world realm, but returns home to find that hardly any time has passed at all. The most famous parallel of this in Spanish tradition is probably Don Juan Manuel's tale in *Count Lucanor* of Don Yllán and the Dean of Santiago, the former being a necromancer who tests the latter by making it seem as if a whole lifetime has elapsed, when only a few minutes have really elapsed. In all these cases, the magical passage of time is in some way instructive. Sometimes, it simply marks a hiatus as a hero undergoes some formative experience or other; on other occasions, it teaches us that time, and life, have a

---

[68] Walter Metmann (ed.), Alfonso X, *Cantigas de Santa María* 3 vols, (Madrid: Castalia, 1986-89).

frighteningly fleeting quality, and that it is dangerous and foolhardy to waste any of them. This is true of our tale, where the vain, wasteful endeavours of the elder brothers and their like are shown to be ultimately futile.

This tale exemplifies the way in which many such accounts may be adapted and accommodated to suit new circumstances and a changing environment. The first half of the tale adheres fairly closely to expected structures and ideas, but the second part, which depicts the hero's journey through a marvellous realm, re-combines motifs in an unusual and unexpected fashion, and explains them in terms of traditional Christian belief and doctrine. The tale is thus diverted from its original function of illustrating the qualities required to engage successfully in adult society, and instead illuminates those qualities that are desired of a good Christian, and show the fate of those who disregard the proper modes of behaviour. Indeed, the story is half-way to becoming a sermon, as allegory and its exposition as a form of revealed knowledge are the decisive vehicles of meaning here, the heavy and overt didacticism carrying the tale somewhat outside the tradition and the creative ambivalence proper to it. Again, we have an example of how traditional tales can be undermined by the deliberate overlaying of new meanings. In both cases, however, the tale is still basically concerned with transformation, as a human passes from one phase in life to another, and learns what is expected of him in the process. Only if he lives up to the ideals expounded by the tale, will he be accepted and assimilated into the new state.

The Sultan's Three Children (Los tres hijos del Sultán)

Finally, we come to 'The Sultan's Three Children' ('Los tres hijos del Sultán'), which combines a number of the motifs and ideas we have already explored in the course of our analysis, but which presents some of them in confused fashion,

or out of context, and provides us with a last example of how folktales frequently do become confused as a result of the passage of time.

The themes of wisdom and gratitude are in evidence from the outset. The two elder sisters are unwise in their choice of husbands, but further compound their foolishness by being jealous of their younger sister, and undermining her by stealing her children. By doing so, not only do they show the evils of envy, but also of ingratitude, for the Sultan has made their wishes come true by marrying them to the baker and fisherman respectively. Here, however, we can also see the traditional motif of the jealous sisters at play as they attempt to repress the younger sister who, presumably, is more attractive and more desirable than they.

The elder sisters try to undermine the Sultan's wife by replacing her new-born children with a dog, a lion and a piece of rotten meat, all of which the Sultan accepts with remarkable calmness and aplomb. We have already come across a similar situation in 'The Girl with No Arms', of course, where we saw that giving birth to bestial offspring was regarded in primitive belief as a sign of incestuous union, and where the king was comparably resigned and unperturbed at the news. We might conjecture, therefore, that here the motif is also meant to represent an incestuous relationship which the Sultan suspects, and which has possibly been suggested to him by the jealous sisters. He does not reject his wife, but his belief in the ill-will directed at him causes a rift which will not be healed until all suspicion has been washed away.

This is achieved symbolically in the children's quest for the magical tree, bird and water, a quest which, as in so many other cases, will only be successfully completed by the most unlikely candidate: the younger sister, who shows the wisdom and fortitude required to complete the tests and obstacles placed before her. The lie regarding her mother's incestuous liaison begins to be dissipated when she uses the water to clean her brothers, now transformed into black rocks. The purifying quality of the water immediately begins to cleanse them of all guilt and stain, and is a necessary prelude to their being visited by their father, the Sultan. He, too, begins to benefit from the special attributes of

the water, although a much more logical development would be for his wife to be washed by the water, and so regain her purity (in the same way as her arms are restored to 'The Girl with No Arms'). When this purity is restored, and the Sultan hears the truth from the magical tree and bird, the family may be re-united, normality restored, and the evil sisters dealt with in appropriate fashion. Here, they are flung into the depths of a river, where water will once more, it is presumed, endeavour to work its cleansing miracle and rid the sisters of their evil ways. The characters all receive their just desserts, and everyone lives happily ever after. . .

Conclusion

From the above analyses, it will be clear that, while there may be clear differences in the apparent content of folktales, their themes are very unified, focusing on reinforcing society's values and integrating the individual into that society. However, they are never totally clear-cut in doing so, and the variations encountered reveal how these tales form part of a spectrum of storytelling possibilities, achieving different ends within different contexts. Some tales are deliberately ambiguous, and certainly very malleable, small changes in detail leading to quite distinct outcomes, sometimes focusing on sibling rivalry, sometimes on the struggle for supremacy between parent and child, other times on the difficulties of dealing with increased maturity and sexual awareness. However, while the tales may seem to be directed primarily at children going through these problematic phases in life, one should not disregard their value for adults, acting as they do as reminders of the parent or older sibling's duty to comprehend the changes the young child is currently undergoing, and the need to allow the child the appropriate space in which to come to terms with its constantly shifting place within the social environment. It is not by chance or mere fancy that the enemies faced by the protagonists of these tales are often

giants, ogres or demons, for these are clear symbols of the way a young child may regard its environment as being hostile: when it is still relatively weak and vulnerable, for the child adults assume gigantic proportions and their actions can indeed seem cruel and malicious, while the world seems a vast and dangerous place, filled with hitherto unknown threats. As the child develops, however, the world seems to stabilize, distances become smaller, giants appear more benign, frogs become princes, and a successful transition from childhood to adulthood has been achieved.

PART II

The Tales

CHAPTER 4

Texts and Translations

The tales in this volume come from a variety of collections published in the first half of the twentieth century, representing the traditions of different parts of Spain. Many have been very meticulously preserved by their original collectors, with indications of their provenance (including, in some cases, the name of the story-teller), along with an attempt to reproduce the spoken word as accurately as possible (thus there are examples of *güeno* for *bueno*, 'good', *pa* for *para*, 'in order to', *to* for *todo*, 'all', *pu* for *pues*, 'then', *acabao* for *acabado*, 'ended', and so forth). All available source details are given in the footnotes at the beginning of each story. Every tale has been reproduced here exactly as it is found in the source text (with the exception of punctuation, and accentuation, which have both been modernized), with no form of stylistic or grammatical alteration or 'correction'.

Throughout, the oral background of these accounts is reflected in their narrative style, in devices such as the repetition of the conjunction *y* 'and', the large amount of direct speech, and the occasional presence of the first-person narrator, who sometimes addresses the listener/reader directly, and occasionally presents him/herself as a witness to the events described. Nevertheless, some of the tales undoubtedly betray a more conscious re-working to reflect changing social and religious ideas, and in some cases show the influence of the written

word. An example of the former may be found in 'The Enchanted Forest', which appears to have been modified to address a more religious goal, while the reference to 'kind reader' at the end of 'The Sultan's Three Children' reflects an increasing awareness of the tale as a written artefact, intended for private reading as opposed to oral delivery. Some tales, such as 'The Tambourine Made of Louse Skin', show less attention to the need for accuracy and authenticity in the reproduction process, and exemplify how external sources (particularly literary ones) can corrupt and confuse traditional narratives.

Naturally, something will always be lost in transcription: these tales are meant to be heard rather than read, and the performative dimension should not be forgotten. A skilled story-teller can enliven any tale through the use of different voices, intonation, and action, the consequent appeal and effect being quite different from that generated by a story read silently to oneself, as the delivery can have a marked effect on the interpretation of the narrative. In addition, even when a tale has been meticulously recorded by a field researcher, this represents the reproduction of just one particular performance of the story; another story-teller might provide a slightly different rendition, and even the same performer is unlikely to recount a tale in exactly the same way, word for word, emphasis for emphasis, every time it is told. Each performance of a tale is therefore itself an act of re-creation, and can be modified to target specific audiences at specific times; this fact no-doubt contributes to the vibrancy of the genre, as each telling is fresh and new.[69]

This anthology seeks to reflect some of the richness and diversity of the genre. However, in spite of the differences between the tales, there are strong points of contact, also. While no two stories here are exactly the same in terms of content, they do share similar themes, a major one being the progression from

---

[69] For more on the performance of folktales and other forms of oral narrative, see Albert Bates Lord, *The Singer of Tales* (Cambridge, Mass.: Harvard University Press, 1960); Richard Bauman, *Story, Performance and Event: Contextual Studies of Oral Narrative* (Cambridge: Cambridge University Press, 1986); John Miles Foley, *The Singer of Tales in Performance* (Bloomington: Indiana University Press, 1995).

childhood to adulthood and integration into the adult world and into society Through these tales, we can see the diverse ways in which the challenges and problems of growing up can be explored and elucidated in a popular and entertaining manner. It should be remembered, however, that an alternative interpretation of the tales might see them as comments on the challenges that face all members of society, not just its children, which is why they can be enjoyed by audiences of different ages, and from various walks of life, as issues regarding social conformity and inter-personal relations affect us all. Stark warnings about the dangers and problems of the real world underpin the fantastical and fanciful surface content of the tales, but there is also reassurance regarding the ability of the individual to overcome life's obstacles. Ultimately, these stories are meant to comfort and reassure their audience, not frighten them, and their lessons remain as relevant today as they ever were; in this, too, we have another reason for the continuing popularity of the genre and its derivatives.

In all cases, the English translations attempt to reproduce the fluidity and natural expression of the original Spanish, without attempting to mirror the dialectal forms found in some of these tales; rather, the translations are intended to reflect the general style and tone of the original Spanish in a manner that will make them accessible to all. At the same time, however, those familiar with Spanish and its regional variations will be able to recognize dialectal forms in many of the source texts, which reflect the language and traditions of various parts of the Iberian Peninsula.

Perhaps the single most important factor in selecting the tales for the current volume has been their inherent appeal and potential value to a variety of different readers. It is hoped, therefore, that the stories in this collection will be of interest and use to a range of users, and that they will be enjoyed by all, proving once more their ubiquitous appeal and their ability to engage with different audiences in different ways.

A. Siete Rayos de Sol [70]

Éste era un rey que no tenía hijos y echó una promesa pa que su mujé la reina tuviera un hijo. Y Dios le dio un hijo tan hermoso que no había en to el mundo otro más hermoso que él. Y además era tan jugaor que siempre staba jugando y a to el mundo le ganaba. Y cuando les había ganao a toos y ya no le quedaba nel mundo con quien jugá puso su sombrero a un lao e la mesa y él se sentó al otro lao y se puso a jugá con su sombrero.

Pero vamo, que al dale las cartas su sombrero se gorvió una paloma que empezó a jugá con él. Y le ganó la paloma too sus intereses y too su dinero. Y entonce es cuando dijo él: 'Pu, güeno, ya m'has ganao toos mis intereses y mi dinero ahora vamo a jugá los vetidos.' Conque empezaron otra vez a jugá y le ganó la paloma los vetidos. Y dijo entonce él: 'Pu güeno, ya que m'has ganao los intereses y los vetidos vamo ahora a jugá mi vida.' Y otra vez jugaron y ganó la paloma otra vez. Y va la paloma y le dice entonce: 'Mira, ya que t'he ganao la vida la vamo a gorvé a jugá.' Y jugaron otra vez la vida y otra vez se la gorvió a ganá la paloma. Pu entonce le dice la paloma: 'Ya me voy. Quéate viendo por onde yo me voy y me sigues depués y llegarás al Castillo de Siete Rayos de Sol, qu'es onde yo vivo. Si no, vengo yo a buscarte y sacarte d'aquí y despedazarte.' Y en eso dio un güelo y se fue.

Y va entonce el muchacho y le cuenta al rey su padre lo que l' ha pasao. Y el padre le dice: 'Pu na, hijo mío: no hay más que cojas un güen caballo y te vayas a buscá el Castillo de Siete Rayos de Sol.' Y cogió él el mejó caballo que tenía su padre y se marchó. Y en el camino onde iba se encontró con una almita y se apeó y ató el caballo y vido a un almitaño que le daba la barba al estogamo. Y le dijo en seguía: 'Mal te quieren los que te envían aquí. Ya sé que vienes a buscá

---

[70] A tale from Granada in the province of Granada. Espinosa, *Cuentos populares españoles*, 240-5.

A. Seven Sunbeams

There was once a king who had no children, and he wished for his wife the queen to have a son. And God gave him such a beautiful son that there was none more beautiful in the whole world. But he was also so fond of gambling that he was always playing cards with everyone and beating them all. And when he had beaten everyone and there was no one to play with in the whole wide world, he took off his hat and put it on one side of the table and he sat down on the other and began to play against his hat.

But, as he dealt the cards to his hat it became a dove and began to play cards with him. And the dove won all his belongings and all his money. And so he said, 'Well, then, now that you've taken all my belongings and all my money, let's play for my clothes.' So they began to play again and the dove won all his clothes. And then the lad said, 'Fine; now that you've taken all my belongings and all my money and all my clothes, let's play for my life.' Again they played and again the dove won. Then the dove said to him, 'Look, now that I've won your life once, let's play for it one more time.' They played for his life again, and again the dove won and said, 'It's time I left. Watch where I go and follow me later, and you'll come to the Castle of Seven Sunbeams, which is where I live. If you don't follow me, I'll come to look for you and take you away in little pieces.' And then it flew away.

So the lad went and told his father the king all that had happened. And his father said, 'Well, my son: you must take a good horse and go in search of the Castle of Seven Sunbeams.' So he took his father's best horse and left. On the way he came across a hermitage, where he got off the horse and tied it up and saw a hermit with a long beard down to his stomach, who exclaimed straight away, 'Whoever sent you here wishes you no good. I know that you've come in search of the Castle of Seven Sunbeams. It's nearby, and three doves come from

el Castillo de Siete Rayos de Sol. Aquí está cerca y vienen tres paloma too los días a bañarse al río. Hoy van a vení y las dos mayores entrarán en seguía y la menó no va a queré entrá. Pero por fin entrará y tú vas y te escondes en una junquera y cuando la menó entre a bañarse vas y le quitas sus vetidos. Y esa, la menó, es Siete Rayos de Sol, la princesa menó de las tres hijas del diablo, que es el rey del Castillo de Siete Rayos de Sol.'

Conque vamo que fue el muchacho y se escondió en una junquera qu' estaba ai cerca el río. Y vido que llegaron las tres palomas. Y al llegar a la orilla del río se gorvieron tres hermosas princesas. Y en seguía las dos mayores se desvistieron. Y fue primero la mayó y dijo: 'Yo, mujé,' y se tiró en el agua. Y entonce fue la segunda y dijo: 'Yo, mujé,' y se tiró tamié en el agua. Y las dos entonce es cuando le dijieron a la menó: 'Vamo, ¿que tu no entras en el agua?' Y ella dijo: 'No pueo ahora porque vengo retentaílla de un dolol.' Y era que sabía que aquél estaba allí escondío, y tenía miedo que le robara la ropa. Y ya le dice la mayó: 'Pero siempre vienes con nosotras. No sé por qué hoy no quieres.' Y ya dijo ella: 'Güeno, pu pa no dales a utes un digusto vi a entrá.' Y al momento que se quitó las ropas y entró en el agua salió aquél y le robó sus vetidos.

Depué salieron las dos mayores y se vistieron y se gorvieron palomas y se fueron volando pa su casa. Y la menó salió y le dijo al muchacho: 'Dame mis ropas. Ya sé que vienes en busca del castillo de mi padre. Toma este anillo.' Y el joven entonce le dio sus vetidos y se vistió ella y se gorvió paloma y le dijo: 'Móntame y vamo ahora mismo al castillo.'

Y llegaron al castillo y salió el diablo, que era la paloma qu'había jugao con él y le había ganao la vida, y el muchacho lo saluda y le dice: 'Dios guarde a sté. Ya stoy yo aquí.' Y el diablo le contesta: 'Hombre, m'alegro, que ya staba poniéndome el calzao pa i a buscarte.' Y ya lo coge aparte y le dice: 'Pu na; te vi a quitar la vida porque te la he ganao. Pero, mira te la perdono si haces una cosa. Toma este azadón y estas varillas. Vas ahora a aquella sierra de piedra y plantas toas las varillas y pa medio día me traes frutas de toos esos álboles.'

there to bathe in the river every day. They'll come again today, and the two oldest ones will enter the water straight away, but the youngest will not want to go in. She'll enter in the end, though, and you should go and hide in the reeds and steal her clothes when she enters the river to bathe. She is called Seven Sunbeams, and is the youngest of the three princesses, daughters of the Devil, who is king of the Castle of Seven Sunbeams.'

So the lad went and hid in the reeds close to the river, and he saw three doves approaching. They became three beautiful princesses as they reached the river bank, and the two oldest ones undressed straight away. First the eldest said, 'I'm a woman', and dived into the water; then the second said, 'I'm a woman', and dived in too. Then the two said to the youngest, 'Come on, why don't you come into the water?' to which she replied, 'I can't just now because I'm not feeling very well.' But really she knew that the prince was hiding nearby, and she was afraid that he'd steal her clothes. The eldest said, 'But you always come in with us. I don't understand why you don't want to today.' So she replied, 'Very well, then; I'll come in so as not to offend you.' But the instant she undressed and entered the water, the prince jumped out from his hiding-place and stole her clothes.

Soon, the two eldest came out of the water, became doves again and flew off home. The youngest came out and said to the lad, 'Give me my clothes. I know that you're looking for my father's castle, so take this ring.' So the youth returned her the clothes and she got dressed and became a dove and said, 'Climb on my back and we'll go straight to the castle.'

They arrived at the castle and the Devil, who was the dove who had won the lad's life at cards, came out, and the youth greeted him and said, 'God be with you, here I am.' The Devil answered, 'Well, I'm glad to see it, because I was just putting on my shoes to come after you.' Then he took him to one side and said, 'Well, I'm going to take your life because I've won it from you, but I'll let you go if you do one thing for me. Take this hoe and these twigs and go to

Conque coge el pobre muchacho las varillas y el azadón y se va a la sierra y al vela toa de piedra se pone a llorá. Y asina llorando como stába se restregó los ojos con el anillo y se acordó de Siete Rayos y dijo: 'Siete Rayos de Sol, ayúdame.' Y se le presentó al momento Siete Rayos y le preguntó qué le pasaba. Y el le dijo: '¡Qué m'ha de pasá! Que tu padre m'ha dao este azadón y estas varillas y m'ha mandao que vaya y las plante en aquella sierra de piedra y que pa medio día le lleve las frutas de los álboles.' Y le dice ella: 'Échate en mi falda y no te apures.' Y s' echó en su falda y se durmió, y cuando ispertó ya staban los álboles en la sierra de piedra llenos de fruta. Y cogió él la fruta y se la llevó al diablo y le dijo: 'Señó, aquí stá la fruta ya.' Y el diablo al verla le dijo: 'Güeno, hombre, está bien. Pero máteme Dios si mi hija Siete Rayos no anda en esto.' Y él le dijo: 'Yo no conozoo a su hija ni a sté, y a mi casa me voy.'

Pero el diablo le dijo entonce: 'Güeno; eso está mu bien. Pero ahora tienes que haceme un molino con siete piedras moliendo a la pal, que al ruido de las piedras me ispierte yo de la siesta. Si haces eso tienes perdoná la vida.' Conque otra vez salió el pobre muchacho llorando. Y se restregó otra vez con la mano y se acordó de Siete Rayos al ver el anillo y dijo: 'Siete Rayos de Sol, ayúdame.' Y en seguía se presentó Siete Rayos y le dijo: 'Pero ahora, ¿por qué lloras? ¿Qué te pasa?' '¡Qué m'ha de pasá!' dice el muchacho. 'Le he llevao a tu padre las frutas y ahora dice que tengo que hacele un molino con siete piedras moliendo a la pal y que al ruido de las piedras se ispierte él de la siesta.' Y le dijo ella: 'Toma estas cenizas y vas y las echas por ai y verás como saldrá el molino.' Y cogió él las cenizas y las echó por ai cerca del diablo y en seguía salió un molino con siete piedras moliendo a la pal. Y tanto era el ruido qu'hacían las piedras que se ispertó el diablo de su siesta. Y el muchacho le dijo: 'Señó, aquí tiene uté el molino con las siete pridras moliendo a la pal.' Y dijo el diablo: 'Está mu bien. Pero máteme Dios si mi hija Siete Rayos no anda en esto.' Y él le dijo: 'Ya l'he dicho a sté que yo no conozco a su hija ni a sté, y a mi casa me voy. Pero el diablo le dijo: 'No, señó, que tavía farta lo prencipá. Una vez que pasaron

that rocky mountain and plant all the twigs and bring me fruit from them all by midday.'

So the poor lad took the twigs and the hoe and went to the mountain and when he saw that it was all rocky he began to cry. As he was crying, he rubbed his eyes with the ring and remembered Seven Sunbeams and said, 'Seven Sunbeams, help me'; she immediately appeared and asked him what was wrong, to which he replied, 'What do you think is wrong? Your father has given me this hoe and these twigs and told me to plant them on that rocky mountain and bring him fruit from them all by midday.' She replied, 'Lie down in my lap and don't worry.' So he lay down in her lap and fell asleep, and when he woke up the trees on the rocky mountain were all full of fruit. So he took the fruit to the Devil and said, 'Sir, here is the fruit.' When the Devil saw it he said, 'Well done, my lad. But may God strike me dead if my daughter Seven Sunbeams doesn't have a hand in this', to which he replied, 'I don't know you or your daughter, and I'm going home.'

But the Devil then said, 'That's all well and good, but now I want you to build me a mill with seven stones grinding together so that the noise will wake me from my nap. If you do that, I'll spare your life.' So the poor lad once again left in tears, and he rubbed his eyes again and remembered Seven Sunbeams when he saw the ring and said, 'Seven Sunbeams, help me.' Seven Sunbeams appeared straight away and asked, 'Why are you crying now? What's wrong?' 'What do you think is wrong?', said the youth. 'I took the fruit to your father and now he wants me to build him a mill with seven stones grinding together so that the noise will wake him from his nap.' She replied, 'Take these ashes and scatter them over there and you'll see how the mill springs up.' So he took the ashes and scattered them close to the Devil and immediately a mill with seven stones grinding together appeared. The noise was so loud that the stones made that they woke the Devil from his nap, and the lad said to him, 'Sir, here's the mill with seven stones grinding together.' And the Devil replied, 'Very good. But may God

mis tataragüelos por el estrecho e Gibrartá se les cayó en el mar una sortija, y quiero ahora que vaya uté y la saque y me la traiga.'

Se salió el joven entonce del palacio y dijo: 'Ahora sí m'ha cogío. Porque ¿cómo voy a sacá el anillo del mar?' Y se restregó una mijilla y vido el anillo y se acordó de Siete Rayos y dijo: 'Siete Rayos de Sol, ayúdame.' Y llegó en seguía Siete Rayos y le dijo: '¿Qué te pasa ahora?' '¿Qué m'ha de pasá!' dice él. Ahora m'ha dicho tu padre que tengo que sacá del mar y llevale un anillo que se les cayó a sus tataragüelos cuando pasaban por el estrecho e Gibrartá. Y ella le dijo entonce: 'Pu, toma este puñal y me matas y coges bien toa la sangre y me echas en el mar.' Y él le dijo: 'Pero yo ¿cómo te voy a matá?' Y ella le dijo que si él no la mataba el diablo los mataría a los dos, y que cuando él la echara al mar ella saldría con la sortija del fondo del mar. Y va él y coge el puñal y la mata y la echa en el mar. Pero se le cayó una gota e sangre en la tierra. Y en unos momentos salió ella viva y con el anillo. Y si hermosa estaba antes más hermosa salió del fondo del mar. Pero como se le había caío una gota e sangre salió ella manca de un deo.

Pu güeno; se fue el muchacho y le entregó al diablo el anillo. Y el diablo le dijo: 'Mu güeno, mu güeno, hombre. Pero máteme Dios si mi hija Siete Rayos no anda en esto.' Y él le dijo: 'Ya l'he dicho que no conozco a su hija ni a sté, y que a mi casa me voy.' Pero el diablo le dijo: 'Ahora te vas a casá con una de mis hijas.' Y quería casalo con una pa matalo. Y fue y lo llevó al palacio y les mandó a sus tres hijas que metieran un deo por debajo e la puerta y que él escogiera una pa que se casara con él. Y Siete Rayos metió el deo que tenía manco y asina la conoció él. '¿Quién es?' preguntó el diablo. 'Siete Rayos.' 'Ya yo mu bien lo sabía.' Conque arreglaron las bodas y se casaron el joven y Siete Rayos. Y esa noche el diablo tenía intención de matalos a los dos.

Se fueron a acostar y Siete Rayos le dijo a su marío: 'Mi padre nos quiere matá. Ahora vas tú a la cuadra y verás dos caballos. El más flaco es el del pensamiento y ese traes y nos vamos. No vayas a escogé el gordo, que ése es el

strike me dead if my daughter Seven Sunbeams doesn't have a hand in this', to which he replied, 'I've already told you that I don't know you or your daughter, and I'm going home.' But the Devil replied, 'Oh, no, not yet. You haven't done the main task yet. Once, when my great-great-grandparents came across the Straits of Gibraltar, they dropped a ring into the sea, and I want you to find it and bring it to me.'

So the lad left the palace and said, 'He's got me now, because how on earth am I going to find that ring in the sea?' And he rubbed his cheek and saw the ring and remembered Seven Sunbeams and said, 'Seven Sunbeams, help me.' Seven Sunbeams immediately appeared and said, 'What's wrong now?' 'What do you think is wrong?' he replied. 'Now your father has told me to find a ring that your great-great-grandparents dropped in the sea as they crossed the Straits of Gibraltar, and bring it to him.' So she said to him, 'Take this knife and kill me and collect all my blood and throw me into the sea.' 'What do you mean, kill you?' he replied. But she told him that if he didn't kill her, the Devil would kill them both, and that when he threw her into the water she would appear with the ring from the sea bed. So he took the knife and killed her and threw her into the sea, but he spilt a drop of blood on the ground. A few minutes later she re-appeared alive and bearing the ring. If she was beautiful before, she was even more beautiful now, but the tip of one finger was missing because of the spilt drop of blood.

So the lad went and gave the Devil the ring, and the Devil said, 'Very good; very good indeed. But may God strike me dead if my daughter Seven Sunbeams doesn't have a hand in this', to which he replied, 'I've already told you that I don't know you or your daughter, and I'm going home.' But the Devil said, 'Now you must marry one of my daughters.' The real reason he wanted him to marry was so that he could kill him. So the Devil took him to the palace and told his three daughters to stick one finger out from underneath the door so that the lad could choose one of them to marry. And Seven Sunbeams stuck out the

del viento.' Y mientras él fue por el caballo echó ella tres salivazos en un vaso pa que hablaran cuando se fueran. Y subió él con el caballo gordo, y le dice ella: '¡Ay, Dios mío! ¿Qué has hecho? Ahora semos perdíos! Pero vamo pronto.' Y se montaron en el caballo y echaron a corré.

Y el padre dijo: 'Ya aquellos estarán dormíos. Voy ahora a matarlos.' Y llegó a la puerta y dijo: '¡Siete Rayos! ¡Siete Rayos!' Y uno de los salivazos contestó: 'Mande uté, padre.' Y se retiró el y dijo: 'Caramba, que tavía stán ispiertos.' Y poco depués llegó otra vez a la puerta a vé si staban dormios y dijo: '¡Siete Rayos! ¡Siete Rayos!' Y el segundo salivazo ya poco seco contestó en voz baja: 'Mande uté, padre.' Y dijo él: 'Ya se van durmiendo,' y se retiró. Y ya a la media noche llegó otra vez y llamó: '¡Siete Rayos! ¡Siete Rayos!' Y entonce el tercer salivazo que ya staba casi too seco dijo, que apenas se oía: 'Mande uté, padre.' Y él dijo: 'Ya stán casi bien dormíos.' Y entró en la habitación y no encontró a naide, y dijo: 'Ya me lo figuraba. Ya s'han escapao. Pero los seguiré y los mataré.' Y fue y se subió en el caballo del pensamiento y se marchó a alcanzalos.

Y cuando ya iba alcanzándolos se gorvió un bicho pa matalos. Y gorvió el muchacho la cara y lo vido venir y le dijo a Siete Rayos: '¡Mira, allá viene una fiera que nos agarra!' Y tiró ella un peine y se vio un montarral de peines que se tardó mucho tiempo pa pasá. Y poco depués gorvió el muchacho la cara otra vez y vido venir otra vez a la fiera y dijo: '¡Allá viene una fiera que nos agarra!' Y le dijo ella entonce: 'Toma esta navaja y tírala por la cola del caballo.' Y la tiró él y se vio un montarral de navajas que el pobre diablo salió hecho peazos de heridas que llevaba. Pero tavía iba siguiéndolos y cuando ya se acercaba lo vido el muchacho y dijo a Siete Rayos: '¡Allá viene una fiera que nos agarra!' Y le dio ella un puñao e sal y le dijo: 'Tira esa por la cola el caballo.' Y la tiró y se gorvió un montarral de sal y al pasar se le metió al diablo en toas las heridas y daba unos gritos que temblaba la tierra. Pero tavía iba siguiéndolos. Y cuando ya los iba alcanzando otra vez lo vido otra vez el joven y le dijo a Siete Rayos: '¡Allá viene

finger with the missing tip so that he recognized her. 'Which one are you?' asked the Devil. 'Seven Sunbeams.' 'I knew it!' So the wedding was arranged and the youth and Seven Sunbeams were married, but the Devil planned to kill them both that night.

They went to bed and Seven Sunbeams told her husband, 'My father wants to kill us. Go to the yard and you'll find two horses. Bring the scrawniest of the two, which is Thought, and we'll leave. Don't bring the fatter one, which is Wind.' While he went for the horse, she put three drops of saliva in a glass so that they would talk after the two of them had left. He came back with the fatter horse, and she said, 'My God! What have you done? We're done for! But let's leave straight away.' So they mounted the horse and rode off at a gallop.

Her father said to himself, 'The two of them will be asleep by now, so I'll go and kill them.' On reaching their door he called, 'Seven Sunbeams! Seven Sunbeams!', and one of the drops of saliva answered, 'At your service, father.' So he left saying, 'Goodness me, they're still awake.' A short time later he went back to their door to see if they were asleep, and called, 'Seven Sunbeams! Seven Sunbeams!' And the second drop of saliva, which had already begun to dry out, whispered back, 'At your service, father', and he said to himself, 'They're starting to fall asleep', and he left. At midnight he went back once more and called, 'Seven Sunbeams! Seven Sunbeams!' The third drop of saliva, which had now almost completely dried out, answered in a voice that could hardly be heard, 'At your service, father.' And he thought, 'Now they're almost sound asleep', and he entered the bedroom and when he didn't find anyone he said, 'I thought as much. They've already escaped. But I'll follow them and kill them.' So he went and mounted the horse called Thought and rode after them.

When he'd nearly caught up with them he turned himself into a bull to kill them. The young lad turned around and saw him coming and said to Seven Sunbeams, 'Look: a beast is coming to grab us!' So she threw a comb behind them and it became a forest of combs that took him a long time to pass through.

una fiera que nos agarra!' Y le dio ella entonce un sombrero y le dijo que lo tirara por la cola el caballo. Y lo tiró y se gorvió una sima y allí cayo el diablo y ya no pudo salir. Y se marcharon ellos y él le gritó a Siete Rayos: '¡Premita Dios que te orvide tu marío!'

Y ya llegaron al pueblo onde vivía el joven y la dejó a ella en una fuente y el llegó primero. Y ella le dijo: 'Que no te abrace naide porque si arguno te abraza me orvidas.' Y llegó y salieron sus padres y les dijo él: 'No me abrace naide. Apañá las carrozas que voy por mi mujé.' Y en esa media llega la agüela y corre y dice: '¡Ay, nieto mío!' Y le abrazó y al momento orvidó a su mujé. Le dio el sueño e San Juan y no se gorvió ya a acordar de ella.

Conque ya Siete Rayos cansá de esperar se dio cuenta de lo que pasaba y les dijo a las criás del palacio que iban a la fuente que preguntaran si querían una criá en el palacio. Y fueron las criás y le dijieron al rey qu'había una moza en la fuente que quería serví, y él le dijo que viniera. Y se puso a serví en el mismo palacio onde staba su marío pero el ni se acordaba de ella.

Y ya con el tiempo fue él y se echó una novia y echaron torneos pa casase. Y era la costumbre en esos tiempos regalales anguna cosa a los criaos del palacio el que se casaba. Y a too les daba lo que pedían. Y ya le preguntó el prencipe a Siete Rayos: 'A ti, ¿qué quieres que te regale?' Y ella le dijo: 'A mí una piedra de tusón y un cuchillo sin honor.'

Conque ya estaba pa casase el prencipe cuando hizo un viaje a una capitar pa comprar too los regalos. Y too encontró menos los regalos pa Siete Rayos. Y andando y buscando llegó ande staba un viejo y le dice: 'Diga uté señó, ¿tiene uté pa vendé una piedra de tusón y un cuchillo sin honor?' Y le contesta el viejo: 'Me quedan los úrtimos.' Y se los compró y se fue pa su palacio. Y llegó y les dio a toos sus regalitos.

Y como no comprendía pa qué quería aquella criá la piedra de tusón y el cuchillo sin honor, dijo: 'Cuando le dé a la criá aquella sus regalos me voy a escondé pa vé que hace con ellos.' Y fue y la llamó y le dio sus regalos y se hizo

A little later the lad turned around again and saw the beast catching up with them once more. 'A beast is coming to grab us!' he cried. So she then said, 'Take this knife and throw it behind us.' So he threw the knife behind them and it became a forest of knives that chopped the Devil full of cuts, but he still chased after them and when he was catching them up once more the youth saw him and said to Seven Sunbeams, 'A beast is coming to grab us!' She gave him a handful of salt and said, 'Throw this behind us.' So he threw it behind him and it became a forest of salt that worked its way into all the Devil's wounds as he tried to pass through it, making him scream so loudly that the earth shook. But still he chased after them, and when he had almost caught them the youth saw him again and said to Seven Sunbeams, 'A beast is coming to grab us!' So she then gave him a hat and told him to throw it behind them. He did so and it became a chasm and the Devil fell into it and was trapped. So they went on their way and the Devil shouted to Seven Sunbeams, 'I hope to God your husband forgets you.'

Soon they arrived at the youth's village and he left his wife by a fountain so that he could go first, but she warned him, 'Don't let anyone kiss you, because if they do you'll forget me.' He entered the village and his parents came out to greet him, but he said, 'Don't kiss me. Decorate the carriages and I'll go and fetch my wife.' But just then his grandmother ran up to him crying, 'My dear grandson!' and kissed him, making him forget his wife in an instant. He fell into St John's sleep and remembered her no more.

Tired of waiting, Seven Sunbeams realized what had happened and told the palace maids (who used to come to the fountain) to ask if they needed another servant. They told the king that there was a girl by the fountain who wanted to enter his service, and he said that she should come to the palace. So she became a servant in her husband's palace, but he remembered nothing about her.

After some time he was betrothed and tournaments were arranged for his wedding. It was also the custom at that time for the groom to give a present to each of the palace servants, and the prince gave everyone what they asked for.

el que s'iba pero se metió detrás de la puerta. Y vido que cogió ella los dos regalos y los puso en la mesa. Y entonce es cuando le dijo a la piedra: 'Piedra de tusón, ¿no fui yo quien plantó las varillas en la sierra de piedra que salieron logo los álboles pa que llevara el prencipe la fruta a mi padre pa medio día?' Y la piedra contestó: 'Sí, sí, tú fuiste.' Y entonces ya aquél comenzaba a recordá argo. Y dijo entonces Siete Rayos: 'Piedra de tusón, ¿no fui yo quien hizo un molino de siete piedras moliendo a la pal que del ruido que hacían se isperto el rey, mi padre?' Y la piedra contestó: 'Sí, sí; tú fuiste.' Y ya aquel ya iba recordando. Y dijo entonces Siete Rayos: 'Piedra de tusón, ¿no fui yo quien sacó el anillo del mar depués de que el prencipe me mató y m'echó en el mar?' Y la piedra contestó 'Sí, sí, tú fuiste.' Y el prencipe ya iba recordando too, y dijo: '¡Dimoño, si eso m'ha pasao a mí!' Y entonce dijo Siete Rayos: 'Cuchillo sin honor, ¿qué me merezco yo?' Y el cuchillo le contestó: 'Que te des la muerte conmigo, Siete Rayos.' Y al oi el el nombre de ella se acordó de too. Y entonce es cuando ella cogió el cuchillo y se iba a dar la muerte con él cuando salió él de onde staba escondío y la sujetó y le dijo: 'Siete Rayos, perdóname, que yo soy tu marío y t'había orvidao.' Y entonce salió y les dijo a toos que Siete Rayos era su mujé. Y la otra novia se quedó con el rabillo arzao y él se quedó con su mujé.

When the prince asked Seven Sunbeams, 'What should I give you?', she answered, 'A fleece stone and a knife without honour.'

When the prince was on the verge of getting married, he went to the city to buy all the presents, and he found them all except the ones for Seven Sunbeams. While he was searching, he came across an old man and asked him, 'Excuse me, sir. Do you have a fleece stone and a knife without honour for sale?', to which the old man replied, 'These are my last ones.' So he bought them and returned to the palace to give everyone their presents.

As he didn't understand why that particular maid wanted a fleece stone and a knife without honour, he thought, 'When I give that servant her presents, I'll hide to see what she does with them.' So he called her and gave her the presents and pretended to leave, but really he hid behind the door, and saw her take both the presents and put them on the table. Then she said to the stone, 'Fleece stone, wasn't I the one who planted the twigs on the rocky mountain that then grew into trees so that the prince could take their fruit to my father by midday?', and the stone answered, 'Yes, it was you.' And then the prince began to remember. Next Seven Sunbeams said, 'Fleece stone, wasn't I the one who built the mill with seven stones grinding together making a noise that woke the king, my father?', and the stone answered, 'Yes, it was you.' And the prince remembered more. Finally, Seven Sunbeams said, 'Fleece stone, wasn't I the one who fetched the ring from the water after the prince had killed me and thrown me into the sea?', and the stone answered, 'Yes, it was you', and the prince remembered nearly everything and cried, 'Heavens, all of that happened to me!' Then Seven Sunbeams said, 'Knife without honour, what fate do I deserve?', and the knife answered, 'To die by my blade, Seven Sunbeams.' When the prince heard her name, he remembered everything, and when she took the knife and prepared to kill herself he jumped out from his hiding-place, grabbed her and said, 'Forgive me, Seven Sunbeams. I'm your husband and I forgot you.' So then

he went outside and told everyone that Seven Sunbeams was his wife, and his wife-to-be was left high and dry, and he stayed with Seven Sunbeams.

B. Los tres trajes [71]

Este era un matrimonio que eran ya muy ancianos y no habían tenido familia. Y fue la esposa y le rogó a San Antonio que le diera una hija de tres colores, blanca, negra y colorá; lo blanco pa la cara, lo negro pal pelo y lo colorao pa la hermosura. Y les dio San Antonio la hija, pero al dar a luz la madre murió y quedó viudo el anciano.

Y al morir la esposa le había dicho a su marido que se casara sólo con una joven que se pareciera a ella, y como la hija fue la que llegó a parecerse a ella dijo el padre que con ella se casaría. Y ya el padre estaba tan enamorao de su hija que la dijo que tenía que ser su mujer. Y fue la niña y se lo contó a una vecina y ésta la dijo: 'Dile a tu padre que te casas con el si te trae tres vestidos, uno de sol, otro de luna y otro de estrellas.'

Y se fue el padre en busca de los tres vestidos y en Roma los halló y se los trajo a su hija. Y fue luego la hija y se lo contó todo a una vieja hechicera y la hechicera la dijo que doblara los vestidos y se marchara por esos mundos a ganar la vida. Y se marchó la niña con sus tres vestidos por los mundos. Y cuando ya había caminao un día y una noche se encontró en el monte a la misma vieja hechicera que la dio un vestido de pelincanito y la dijo: 'Toma este traje de pelincanito[72] y póntelo y vete a aquel campo y ponte allí en aquella fuente por donde ha de pasar el rey cuando vaya de caza. No te hará daño. Cuando llegue déjate coger por él.'

---

[71] From Jaraíz de la Vera in the province of Cáceres. Espinosa, *Cuentos populares españoles*, 207-9.

[72] The exact meaning of 'pelincanito' is not entirely clear, but it is probably a combination of 'pelín' (a familliar expression meaning 'a little'), 'cano' (white), and the diminutive suffix '-ito'. Thus, the word is probably meant to convey the idea of something that is a little bit white, or 'whiteish', or, as rendered here, 'off-white'. Alternatively, the word could be a dialectal form of 'pelicanito', meaning white- or grey-haired. In either case, the meaning ties in very well with the notion of compromised purity that is so important in this tale.

B. The Three Dresses

Once there was a an old couple who had no children. And the wife went and asked Saint Anthony to give her a daughter made up of three colours, white, black, and red; white for her skin, black for her hair and red for beauty. And Saint Anthony gave them the daughter, but her mother died while giving birth and the man was left a widower.

On her death bed the wife told her husband that he should only marry a young woman who looked exactly like her, and because the daughter grew up to look like her mother, the father said that they should marry. And the father was so in love with his daughter that he insisted that she became his wife. And the girl went and told a neighbour who said to her: 'Tell your father that you will marry him if he brings you three dresses, a sun dress, a moon dress and a star dress.'

And the father went in search of the three dresses and found them in Rome and brought them to his daughter. And so the daughter went and told an old witch about it all and the witch told her to take the dresses and set off to seek her fortune in the world. And so she left with the three dresses and wandered the world. And when she had walked for a day and a night she came across the same old witch in the mountains, who gave her an off-white dress[73] and said: 'Take this off-white dress, put it on, and go to that field over there and go into that spring because the king will pass by when he goes out hunting. He won't hurt you. When he comes let him take you.' The girl went there and before long the king passed by with his huntsmen. And they took the girl in the little white dress and took her to the palace.

The king's son was by now ready to get married, and his mother told him to marry. And he told her that he would look for a bride soon enough, that there

---

[73] See footnote 72.

Fue allí la niña y pasó a poco el rey con sus soldaos de caza. Y cogieron al pelincanito y se lo llevaron al palacio.

Y el hijo del rey ya estaba en disposición de poderse casar, y le dijo la madre que se casara. Y el la dijo que ya buscaría novia, que no tenía prisa. Y ya fue la madre y le dijo: "Pon baile una de estas noches desde la una hasta las tres pa que vengan mozas y escojas una pa que sea tu esposa." Y dijo el hijo que estaba güeno, y arreglaron el baile. Y cuando ya se había ido el hijo del rey al baile dijo el pelincanito que si le dejaban ir al baile. Y la madre le dijo que fuera si quería. Y fue el pelincanito y se quitó el traje de pelincanito y se puso el de sol y se fue al baile. Y al llegar al baile todos salieron a recibir a la niña que estaba muy guapa con su traje de sol. El hijo del rey no la conoció y fue y la sacó a bailar y comenzó a hablar con ella y la dijo que si se casaba con el. Y ella le decía que no, que era muy joven y que no quería su papá. Y estuvo bailando con ella toda la noche y la dio una pulsera. Y ya antes de acabarse el baile dijo ella que la molestaba el aire de una ventana, y en lo que el fue a correr la ventana se escapó ella y se fue a casa sin que la vieran. Y salió el hijo del rey preguntando por onde se había escapao pero nadie lo supo decir.

Y el pelincanito fue y la contó a la reina madre todo lo que había pasao en el baile. La contó que había ido al baile niña moza vestida de un traje de sol que no había otra en el mundo de guapa y que el rey había bailao toda la noche con ella y la había regalao una pulsera. Y cuando llegó el rey su madre le preguntó si era verdá lo que decía el pelincanito y el la dijo que sí y que la noche siguiente quería dar otro baile pa ver si iba otra vez esa moza.

Y la segunda noche fue el pelincanito otra vez, esta vez vestido del traje de luna, y estaba la niña más guapa que la noche anterior. Y otra vez bailó el rey toda la noche con ella y la dijo que si se quería casar con él. Pero ella le dijo otra vez que no, que no podía ser porque era muy joven y no quería su papá. Y la preguntó el rey si sabía cantar y dijo ella que sí. Y todos la rogaron que cantara y cantó y más enamorao quedó el rey de ella de lo bien que cantaba. Y esta vez la

was no hurry. And his mother told him: 'Arrange a dance some night from one until three o'clock so that young girls come and you can choose one to be your wife.' And the son agreed, and they arranged the dance. And when the king's son had gone off to the ball the girl in the little off-white dress asked if she might go to the dance. And the mother said that she should go could go if she wanted. So the girl took off the little white dress and put on the sun dress and went to the ball. When she arrived at the ball everyone came out to greet the girl who was so beautiful in her sun dress. The king's son didn't recognize her and he danced with her and began to speak with her and asked her to marry him. But she refused, saying that she was very young and that her father didn't want her to marry. He danced with her all night and gave her a bracelet. Before the dance ended she said that the breeze from a window bothered her, and while he went to shut the window she escaped and returned home without being seen. And the king's son asked where she had gone but no-one knew.

And the girl in the little off-white dress went and told the queen mother everything that had happened at the ball. She told her that a young girl had gone to the ball wearing a sun dress and that no-one in the world was more beautiful and that the king had danced with her all night and given her a bracelet. And when the king came his mother asked him if what the girl had said was true and he said that it was and that he wanted to hold another ball the following night to see if the young girl came again.

And on the second night the girl went again, wearing the moon dress this time, and she was even more beautiful than the night before. And again the king danced with her all night and asked her if she would marry him. But she refused again, saying that she couldn't because she was very young and her father didn't wish it. And the king asked her if she could sing and she said she could. So everyone asked her to sing and when she sang the king fell even more in love with her because she sang so beautifully. This time the king gave her a gold ring. But before the dance ended the girl said she wanted to go outside for a moment

regaló el rey un anillo de oro. Y ya antes de que se acabara el baile dijo la niña que quería salir afuera un momento y salió a la huerta y se desapareció sin que la vieran. Y salieron todos en busca de ella y viendo ella que ya se acercaban se puso su traje de pelincanito y se puso en la escalera. Y ai la vio el rey y le dio una patada y le dijo que se fuera a casa porque creyó que era el pelincanito que andaba ai molestando. Y se fueron a palacio y el pelincanito le contó a la reina todo lo que había pasao esa noche. La contó que había ido otra vez la moza, esta vez vestida de un traje de luna y más guapa que antes, y que el rey había bailao toda la noche con ella y la había regalao un anillo de oro. Y el rey dispuso otro baile pa la noche siguiente.

Y la tercera noche la niña se quitó el traje de pelincanito y se puso el de estrellas que era el más bonito de todos y estaba más reguapa que nunca. Y fue al baile y estuvo toda la noche bailando con el rey. Y otra vez la dijo que se casara con él, pero ella le decía siempre que no, que no podía ser porque era muy joven y su papá no quería. Y esa noche el rey la regaló unos pendientes muy preciosos. Y cuando ya se acababa el baile dijo la niña: "Ya me voy, ya me voy, que ya suenan los esquelitos del coche y si mi padre lo sabe que estoy aquí a deshoras me pega." Y salió y se fue. Y otra vez llegó el pelincanito y le contó a la reina madre lo que halbia pasao en el baile. La contó que había ido la moza vestida de un traje de estrellas mucho más bonito que los dos otros trajes y que el rey había bailao con ella toda la noche y la había regalao unos pendientes.

Y el rey ya que no la volvió a ver se puso malito en la cama y ni quería comer. Y ya fue el pelincanito y hizo tres pasteles y en cada uno puso uno de los regalos del rey y fue y se lo dio a la reina pa que se lo diera a su hijo. Y fue ella y le dio primero el de la pulsera. Y al partirlo el vio la pulsera y se alegró y la dijo a su madre: 'Madre, ¿quién ha hecho este pastel?' Y la madre le contestó que el pelincanito lo había hecho pa que comiera y que había hecho dos pasteles más. Y el la dijo: 'Tráigalos.' Y le trajo los otros dos y al partirlos halló el rey en ellos el anillo y los pendientes. Y gritó entonces: '¡Esto me da la vida, madre! ¡Dígale

and she went into the garden and disappeared without anyone seeing her. They all went to look for her and seeing that they were coming close she put on the little off-white dress and stood on the stairs. The king saw her there and gave her a kick, telling her to go home because he thought that the girl was being a nuisance. And they all went back to the palace and the girl told the queen everything that had happened that night. She told how the young girl had appeared again, wearing a moon dress this time, and even more beautiful than before, and that the king had danced with her all night and given her a gold ring. And the king arranged another dance for the following night.

On the third night the girl took off her little white dress and put on the star dress which was the prettiest of all and she was even more beautiful than ever. She went to the ball and danced all night with the king. Again he asked her to marry him, but she continued to refuse, saying that she was very young and the father didn't wish it. That night the king gave her some exquisite earrings. When the ball was nearly finished the girl said: 'I'm leaving, I'm leaving, I can hear my coach bells and if my father finds out that I'm here late at night he'll hit me.' And she left. Again the girl told the queen mother everything that had happened at the ball. She said how the young girl had appeared wearing a star dress which was much more beautiful than the others and that the king had danced with her all night and given her some earrings.

When he didn't see her again the king became ill in bed and refused to eat. So the girl in the little off-white dress made three cakes and put one of the king's presents in each one and gave them to the queen to give to her son. First she gave him the cake with the bracelet. And when he cut it he saw the bracelet and was filled with joy and said to his mother: 'Mother, who made this cake?' And his mother answered him that the girl in the little white dress had made it for him to eat and that she had made two other cakes and he replied: 'Bring them to me.' So she brought the other two and on cutting them open the king found the ring and the earrings. And he cried: 'This brings me back to life, Mother! Tell the

uste al pelincanito que venga en seguida!' Y cuando la madre salió a llamarla ya la niña venía vestida con el traje de estrellas. Y al momento él la reconoció y la dijo a su madre que esa sería su esposa.

Y se casaron y fueron muy felices y comieron perdices. Y a mí no me dieron nada porque no les dio la gana.

girl in the little off-white dress to come here straight away!' And when the mother called her the girl came wearing the star dress. He recognized her straight away and told his mother that she would be his wife.

And they married and were very happy and ate partridges. And they didn't give me anything, because they didn't want to.

C. La niña sin brazos [74]

Era un padre que tenía una hija y pa mantenerla tenía que ir todos los días al monte a por leña, si llovía porque tronaba y si tronaba porque llovía.

Y un día que fue al monte a por leña le salió un hombre de una encina y le dijo: 'Diga usté. ¿Cómo viene uste hoy al monte a cortar leña?' Y el hombre le contesta: 'Pues vengo porque tengo una hija que mantener.' Y ya le dijo el hombre de la encina, que era el diablo: 'Pues mire que yo le daré a usté todo el dinero que le haga falta. Tenga ustí.' Y diciendo esto le dio un talegón lleno de monedas de oro y plata. Y luego le dice: 'Vayase usté a su casa con su dinero y esta noche aguárdeme en su casa.' Y se fue el pobre leñero pa su casa muy contento.

Y llegó y le contó a su hija lo que le había pasao y le entregó el talegón de dinero y le dijo que iba a hacerles una visita el señor que le había dao el dinero. Y la muchacha era muy cristiana y siempre que llegaba alguno a su casa hacía le señal de la cruz. Y le dijo a su padre: 'Pero, quién será ese señor?' 'Esta noche cuando venga se lo preguntaremos,' le contestó el padre. Y en estas estaban cuando llegó el diablo y llamó en la puerta: '¡Tran, tran!' Y al momento la muchacha hizo la señal de la cruz y salió a ver quién era. Pero ya no encontró a nadie. El diablo se había desaparecido al hacer ella la señal de la cruz.

Conque al otro día fue el hombre otra vez a por leña al monte y le salió otra vez el diablo. Y el leñador le dice: '¿Cómo no fue uste anoche a mi casa?' Y el diablo le contesta: 'He tenido el tiempo ocupao y no he podido. Pero mire, coja este saco de dinero y lléveselo a su casa. Y esta noche si me espera en su casa, que ya iré. Y una cosa le ruego y es que mande a su hija tirar toda el agua que haiga en la casa.'

---

[74] From Zamora in the province of Zamora. Espinosa, *Cuentos populares españoles*, 179-82.

C. The Girl with No Arms

Once, a man had a daughter and in order to look after her he had to go to the mountains for wood every day, come rain or come shine. One day, when he went to the mountains for wood a man appeared from an oak tree and said: 'Tell me how is it that you come for wood to the mountains today?' And the man answered: 'I come because I have a daughter to bring up.' And the man from the oak tree, who was the Devil, said to him: 'Look, I'll give you all the money you need. Here you are.' And saying this he gave him a purse full of gold and silver coins. Then he said: 'Go home with your money and wait for me tonight at home.' And the poor woodcutter went home very happy.

He went and told his daughter what had happened to him and gave her the purse full of money and said that they would be visited by the man who had given him the money. The girl was very devout and every time someone came to the house she would make the sign of the cross. And she said to her father: 'But, who is this man?' 'We'll ask him tonight when he comes', answered her father. They were still talking when the Devil arrived and knocked on the door: 'Bang, bang!' Straight away the girl crossed herself and went to see who it was. But she didn't find anyone because the Devil had disappeared when she made the sign of the cross.

So the following day the man again went to the mountains for some wood and the Devil appeared before him again. And the woodcutter asked: 'Why didn't you come to my house last night?' And the Devil answered: 'I was very busy and I couldn't make it. But look, take this bag of money and go home. And tonight if you wait for me at home I'll come. The one thing that I ask you is that you tell your daughter to throw out all the water from the house.' So the man went home and gave his daughter the bag of money and told her what the man from the oak tree had said. Because the girl was so devout she said to her father: 'But if I

Y fue el hombre y llegó a su casa y le entregó a su hija el saco de dinero y le dijo lo que había dicho el señor de la encina. Y la muchacha como era tan buena cristiana le dijo a su padre: 'Pero si tiro a la calle toda el agua que hay en la casa no podré hacer la señal de la cruz.' Y el padre le dijo: 'Tírala toda, que no hace falta.' Y ella la tiró toda. Y apenas la había acabao de tirar a la calle cuando va llegando el diablo y llama en la puerta: '¡Tran, tran!' Y la muchacha como no había agua en la casa se mojó los dedos con saliva y hizo la señal de la cruz. Y salió a abrir la puerta pero no halló a nadie. El diablo se había desaparecido otra vez al hacer ella la señal de la cruz.

Y al otro día fue el leñador al monte otra vez y salió el diablo. Y el leñador le preguntó: '¿Cómo no ha ido usté anoche?' Y el diablo le contestó: 'Es que estoy siempre ocupao. No he podido.' Y ya le dice al leñador: '¿Tienen ustedes corral delante de su casa?' Y el leñador le dice: 'Sí.' '¿Y suele su hija echar la siesta allí por la tarde?' 'Sí.' '¿A qué hora suele ella echar la siesta?' 'A las dos.' Y después de esta conversación le dio el diablo otro saco de dinero y le dijo: 'Váyase uste a su casa con este saco de dinero y cuando le haga falta más venga por más.' Y se fue el leñador pa su casa con otro saco de dinero.

Y ya el diablo determinó robarse a la muchacha. Y a las dos del día siguiente llegó a la casa del leñador cuando la muchacha estaba echando la siesta. Y dormida como estaba la cogió y la subió en su caballo y salió corriendo con ella. Y de repente despertó la niña y levantó un brazo pa hacer la señal de la cruz. Y el diablo cogió un cuchillo grande y le cortó el brazo. Y ya iba a levantar la niña el otro pa hacer la señal de la cruz cuando córtaselo también el diablo con el cuchillo. Y entonces la niña como pudo hizo la señal de la cruz con las piernas. Y cuando hacía la señal de la cruz con las piernas el diablo la cogió y la dejó colgada del pelo de un árbol muy alto y se desapareció en su caballo.

Y ai se quedó la niña colgada del pelo del árbol y sin brazos onde el diablo la dejó. Y cerca del árbol había un palacio onde vivían un rey y una reina que tenían un hijo. Y los perros del rey subían todos los días al árbol onde estaba

throw out all the water from the house I won't be able to cross myself. Her father answered: 'No matter: throw it all out.' So she threw it all out. No sooner had she thrown it out than the Devil arrived and knocked on the door: 'Bang, bang!' Because there was no water in the house the girl wet her fingers with spit and crossed herself. The she went to open the door, but didn't find anyone. The Devil had again disappeared when she made the sign of the cross.

The following day the woodcutter went to the mountains again and once more the Devil appeared. And the woodcutter asked him: 'Why didn't you come last night? And the Devil answered: 'It's because I'm always busy. I couldn't make it.' Then he asked the woodcutter: 'Do you have a yard in front of your house?' And the woodcutter answered: 'Yes.' 'And does your daughter normally have a nap in the afternoon?' 'Yes.' 'At what time does she normally have a nap?' 'At two o'clock.' After this conversation the Devil gave him another bag of money and said: 'Go home with this bag of money and when you need more come to me.' So the woodcutter went home with another bag of money.

Then the Devil decided to kidnap the girl. And at two o'clock the following day he came to the woodcutter's house when the daughter was having a nap. He grabbed her while she was asleep, put her on his horse and galloped away. Suddenly the girl woke up and lifted an arm to cross herself. The Devil took a big knife and cut off her arm. The girl was about to raise the other arm to cross herself when the Devil cut it off with the knife, too. Then the girl crossed herself as best she could with her legs. And when she made the sign of the cross with her legs the Devil hung her by her hair from a very tall tree and disappeared on his horse.

The girl was left hanging by her hair from the tree where the Devil had left her, and without arms. Not far from the tree there was a palace where a king and queen lived with their son. Every day the king's dogs went to the tree where the girl was hanging and took her the food that was given to them at the palace. Because they gave her their food every day the dogs became thinner and thinner.

colgada la niña y le llevaban pa comer lo que les daban en el palacio. Y de darle la comida a la niña los perros se iban quedando cada día más secos. Y el rey al verlos tan secos dijo: '¿Pero por qué es que mis perros se van quedando cada día más secos? ¿Que los criaos no les dan de comer?' Y dio en reñir con los criaos. Y los criaos dijon que no, que siempre les daban lo de siempre. Y ya dijo el rey: 'Pues acechar a los perros a ver qué hacen con la comida.' Y acecharon los perros y vieron que subían siempre con la comida y se la daban a una hermosa dama que estaba colgada del árbol. Y la dama era tan guapa que el hijo del rey dijo que la bajaran del árbol. Y fueron los criaos del rey y la bajaron, y la llevaron al palacio.

Cuando ya la niña estaba en el palacio el hijo del rey se enamoró de ella y les dijo a sus padres que se quería casar con ella. Y sus padres le dijon que era una deshonra casarse con una mujer sin brazos, que no podría criar a sus hijos ni nada. Y él les dijo que no le importaba que no tuviera brazos, que habiendo dinero y teniendo criaos todo era fácil. Y se casaron el hijo del rey y la niña sin brazos. Y a los pocos meses de estar casaos se murió el rey y el hijo quedó de rey y la niña sin brazos de reina.

Y pronto tuvo que marcharse el rey a reinar a otro reinao y dejo a la niña sin brazos encinta. Y en ese medio tiempo tuvo ella mellizos y se lo enviaron a decir al rey. Y el diablo cogió la carta y puso otra onde le decía al rey que la reina su mujer había dao a luz dos ratones. Y contestó el rey con otra carta onde decía: 'Pues si ha dao a luz mi mujer dos ratones que los críe hasta que yo vuelva.' Y otra vez cogió el diablo la carta y puso otra onde decía: 'Coge a esos dos niños que has dao a luz y degüellalos. Si no, eres tú vitima.'

Y cuando llegó la carta la coge ella y se echa a llorar y dice que a sus hijos no los mata ni por todo lo que hay en el mundo. Y la agüela empezó también a llorar y le dijo a la niña: '¿Qué vamos a hacer?' Y dijo la niña: 'Pues nada. Hágame usté unas alforjas pa echar a uno por delante y a otro por detrás y marcharme sola yo con ellos.' Y la agüela le mandó hacer las alforjas y se

Seeing them so thin the king asked: 'Why are my dogs getting thinner every day? Don't the servants give them any food?' And he began to scold the servants. The servants said no, they were giving them as much as ever. So the king said: 'Then watch the dogs to see what they do with the food.' They watched the dogs and saw that they always took the food and gave it to a beautiful lady who was hanging from the tree. And the lady was so beautiful that the king's son told them to get her down from the tree. The king's servants got her down, and took her to the palace.

When the girl was in the palace the king's son fell in love with her and told his parents that he wanted to marry her. His parents told him that it was shameful to marry a girl with no arms, because she couldn't bring up his sons or anything. He told them that he didn't care that she had no arms, because with money and servants this was no problem. So the king's son and the girl with no arms married. Within a few months of their marriage the king died and the son became king and the girl with no arms became queen.

Soon the king had to go to rule another kingdom and left when the girl with no arms was expecting a child. While he was away she had twins and they sent a message to tell the king. The Devil intercepted the letter and replaced it with another which said that the queen had given birth to two mice. The king answered with another letter which said: 'If my wife has given birth to two mice let her bring them up until I return home.' Again the Devil intercepted the letter and replaced it with anoher which said: 'Take the two children you've produced and slit their throats. If you don't do it, you'll be next.'

When the letter arrived she read it and began to cry and said that she wouldn't kill her sons for anything in the world. Their grandmother also began to cry and asked the girl: 'What are we going to do?' The girl answered: 'Nothing. Make me some saddlebags so that I can put one in front of me and one behind and I'll leave with my sons.' The grandmother ordered the saddlebags to be made and the girl with no arms set off into the world with the twins in the saddlebags.

marchó la niña sin brazos por el mundo alante con sus dos mellizos en las alforjas.

Y caminando, caminando, ya llegó a una fuente con hambre y sé. Y nadie le daba una limosna ni agua pa beber. Y al llegar a la fuente dijo: 'Tengo sé. Pero si bajo a la fuente no podré subir.' Y se fue camino alante muerta de sé y hambre hasta que allá muy lejos vio a una señora que estaba lavando en unas filas muy majas y le dijo: 'Señora, ¿me hará usté el favor de unos bocaditos de agua? Porque si bajo a beber no podré subir, y si no bajo me muero de sé.' Y la señora le contestó: 'Mira, vete y llama en aquellas puertas blancas que ves allá lejos, muy lejos. Y te saldrán a recibir y te darán todo lo que te haga falta.'

Y fue la niña y llamó y salió a recibirla San Pedro y la dijo que qué se le ofrecía. Y ella le dijo: 'Quiero que me haga usté el favor de un poquito de agua que ya me muero de sé. Si bajo por ella a la fuente no podré subir, y si no bajo me muero de sé.' Y ya le dio San Pedro un vaso de agua y le dijo: 'Si usté nos obedece le vamos a dar todo lo que le haga falta y le pondremos sus brazos pa que pueda criar a sus niños.' Y dijo ella que obedecería. Y San Pedro le puso sus brazos y la llevó a una montería onde nada les faltaba a ella y a sus niños. Y allí en la montería tenía una casa y muchos criaos. Y la dijo San Pedro que no almitiera a nadie en su casa sin que dijera antes tres veces, 'Jesús, María y José.'

Y ya volvió el rey de reinar por otras partes. Y cuando llegó a su palacio le preguntó a su madre por la reina y ya le contó ella lo que había pasao. Y cuando supo el rey la verdá y el engaño de las cartas sospechó que el diablo era el de la culpa de todo y empezó a maldecirle. Y se le apareció el diablo y le dijo que no se apurara que él le ayudaría a buscar a su mujer. Y es que el diablo quería cogerlos a los dos. Y se marchó el rey con el diablo y el suegro a buscar a su mujer. Y el suegro estaba tentao del diablo porque le había mandao a su hija que tirara a la calle toda el agua de la casa.

Y caminando el rey por la montería se les hizo de noche y vieron la luz de la casa de su mujer. Y se dirigieron allí sin saber quién vivía y llamaron en la

After walking for some time she came, hungry and thirsty, to a spring. No-one gave her any charity or water to drink. Coming to the fountain she thought: 'I'm thirsty. But if I go down to the spring I won't be able to climb back up again.' So she carried on walking, dying of thirst and hunger, until in the distance she saw a lady who was washing at some very fine waters and said: 'Madam, would you be kind enough to give me some swigs of water? Because if I go down there to drink I won't be able to climb back up again, and if I don't go down I'll die of thirst.' The lady answered: 'Look, go and knock on those white doors way off in the distance. They'll greet you and give you everything you need.'

So the girl went and knocked on the door and Saint Peter greeted her and asked her what she wanted. She replied: 'I'd be very grateful for some water because I'm dying of thirst. If I go down to the spring for some water I won't be able to climb back up, and if I don't go down I'll die of thirst. So Saint Peter gave her a glass of water and said: 'If you do as we say we'll give you everything you need and restore your arms so that you can bring up your children.' She said that she would obey. So Saint Peter restored her arms and took her to a mountain where she and the children wanted for nothing. There in the mountains she had a house and many servants. And Saint Peter told her not to let anyone in the house without first having them say 'Jesus, Mary and Joseph' three times.

The king returned home from ruling elsewhere. And when he came to his palace he asked his mother about the queen and she told him everything that had happened. When the king found out the truth and the trick that had been played with the letters he suspected that the Devil was to blame for everything and began to curse him. And the Devil appeared before him and told him not to worry because he would help him find his wife. This was because the Devil wanted to trap them both. So the king left with the Devil and his father-in-law to look for his wife. His father-in-law had already been tempted by the Devil because he'd told his daughter to throw all of the water from the house.

puerta. Y salió la niña a recibirles y les dijo que entraran, pero que todos los que entraran tenían que decir tres veces, 'Jesús, María y José.' Y el rey dijo tres veces, 'Jesús, María y José,' y entró. Y el suegro aunque estaba tentao del diablo también lo dijo y entró. Pero el diablo como no pudo decirlo no entró. Y allí fuera, onde estaba, quería decir 'Jesús, María y José,' pa entrar a hacer de las suyas, pero no pudo. Todo lo que decía era, 'Tudu, tududu, tudu.' Y ya que todos estaban dentro el diablo tuvo que marcharse.

Y pusieron la cena y se sentaron a la mesa y el rey miraba y remiraba a aquella mujer tan guapa y decía: '¿Si será esta mujer mi esposa?' Y la miraba y la remiraba y ya le iba a preguntar, pero decía: 'No, no puede ser porque mi mujer no tenía brazos y esta tiene brazos.' Y como hacía frío los criaos puson un brasero cerca de la mesa pa que el rey se calentara. Y cuando ya iban a comenzar a cenar la niña echó la bendición: 'En el nombre del Padre y del Hijo y del Espíritu Santo. El que esté tentao del diablo que dé un estampido y se salga.' Y el padre de la niña, que estaba tentao del diablo, se volvió cenizas y se desapareció. Y todos quedaron muy elevaos, pero el rey no dijo nada.

Y ya se puson a cenar. Y el rey como estaba cerca del brasero se le comenzó a quemar la capa. Y los niños que por guapos y ricos el rey no dejaba de mirar le dijeron: 'Papá, que se le quema la capa.' Y el rey los miraba y los remiraba pero no decía nada. Pero se lo dijon tantas veces que por fin le dijo el rey a la niña: '¿Sabes que no puedo cenar porque me dicen estos niños, 'Papá, que se le quema la capa?'' Y en este momento fue cuando ella le echó los brazos y le dijo: 'Sí, esposo mío, estos son tus hijos y yo soy tu esposa.' Y ya le contó todo lo que había pasao y cómo ella había venido a vivir allí. Y el rey se abrazó a ella y abrazó a sus dos hijos loco de alegría.

Y se los llevó a su palacio donde todos vivieron muchos años muy felices, y comieron muchas perdices. Y a i no me dieron nada porque no les dio la gana.

As they were journeying through the mountains night came and they saw the light from the king's wife's house. So they headed there without knowing who lived there and knocked on the door. The girl greeted them and invited them in, but insisted that all who came in had to say, 'Jesus, Mary and Joseph' three times. The king said 'Jesus, Mary and Joseph' three times, and went in. Although he'd been tempted by the Devil the father-in-law also said it and went in. But because the Devil couldn't say it he didn't go inside. There outside he wanted to say, 'Jesus, Mary and Joseph' to go inside and do his worst, but he couldn't. All that he said was 'Toodoo, Toodoo, Toodoo.' Because they were all inside the Devil had to leave.

They made dinner and sat at the table and the king kept on staring at the beautiful woman, saying: 'Is it possible that this woman is my wife?' He kept on staring at her and was about to ask her, but said to himself: 'No, it can't be because my wife had no arms and this woman has arms.' And because it was cold the servants put a stove next to the table so that the king could warm himself. When they were about to eat the girl gave the blessing: 'In the name of the Father and of the Son and of the Holy Spirit. Let those that have been tainted by the Devil scream and leave.' The girl's father, who'd been tempted by the Devil, turned to ashes and disappeared. And they were all surprised, but the king said nothing.

They began to eat. Because the king was close to the stove his cloak began to catch fire. And the children, who the king couldn't stop staring at because they were so fine and handsome, said to him: 'Father, your cloak is on fire.' And the king stared at them but said nothing. But they repeated this so many times that at last the king said to the girl: 'Do you realize that I can't eat because these children keep on saying "Father your cloak is on fire"?' And it was then that she threw her arms around him and said: 'Yes, my husband, these are your sons and I'm your wife.' And she told him everything that had happened

and how she had come to live there. And the king, mad with joy, kissed her and his two sons.

He took them home where they all lived very happily for many years and ate partridges. And they didn't give me any because they didn't want to.

D. El castillo de irás y no volverás [75]

Éste era un pescador. Tenía siete hijos. No tenía más que la pesca. Y volvía un día, y salían los hijos: 'Padre, ¿qué ha cogido ustez? ¿Trae ustez algo?' '¡No, hijos! . . . Unas mermejillas que no pesan más que un cuarterón . . .'

Al otro día iba a pescar y le sucedía lo mismo. 'Bueno . . ., ¡esto es terrible! No sé cómo podré vivir.'

Al otro día se marchó bastante más allá que de costumbre. Le prepararon la comida — unos torreznos, su barril de vino. Y ya, según estaba pescando, desesperado, dijo: '¡No vuelvo a pescar más en mi vida!' De pronto va a tirar de la caña y, como no podía con ella, dice: 'Pues, ¿ves? Tras de no sacar nada, se me enreda todo, y voy a perder la caña.' Y ya va tirando tirando, y por fin pudo orillar un pescado muy grande. Y le dijo el pecezón: 'Pescador, pescadorcito, suéltame, y tendrás toda la pesca que tú quieras.' '¡Bien, hombre! . . . Conque una vez que he cogido un poco de fortuna, ¿la voy a desperdiciar? No te suelto.' 'Suéltame, y te daré lo que tu quieras. Podrás venir con un carro a por peces.' 'Bueno, te voy a soltar. Pero me vas a dar todo lo que me has prometido.'

Pues, le soltó el pescador, asustado de ver un bicho tan grandón. Llegó a casa, se preparó, y le pregunta la mujer: '¿Adónde vas?' '¡Mira! . . . Voy a por el burro y la rede, que he cogido muchos peces.' Y la mujer se llenó de alegría. Y se fue el pescador, trao la rede y fue al sitio donde pescó el pez. Pues, se asoma el pecezón y le dice: '¡Echa la rede, echa!' Echó el pescador la rede y la sacó llena. Vuelve a tirar otra vez, y saca más. Carga el burro de peces y se va a casa tan contento el hombre. Salieron todos los hijos a recibirle como de costumbre. 'Padre, ¿trae ustez muchos?' '¡Sí, hijos! ¡Hoy traigo! ¡Bien podéis llevarlos a vender!' Se acercan los chicos y ven que es verdaz. Bailaban de alegría todos. '¡Padre, por Dios! Pues, ¿qué ha hecho ustez, padre? ¿Cómo ha

---

[75] From Peñafiel in Valladolid. Espinosa (hijo), *Cuentos populares de Castilla*, 105-12.

D. The Castle of Nevercomeback

Once, there was a fisherman. He had seven sons. Fishing was his only livelihood. One day he was coming home, and his sons came to meet him: 'Father, what have you caught? Do you have anything?' 'No, my sons. Just some smallfry that hardly weighs a quarter of a pound.' The following day he went fishing and the same thing happened. 'Well . . . , this is terrible! I don't know how I can survive.' The following day he went quite a bit further than usual. They prepared lunch for him — some rashers of bacon, and a cask of wine. And now, as he was desperately fishing, he said: 'I'll never fish again in my life!' Suddenly, he began to reel in his line and, since it wouldn't move, he said: 'Do you see? On top of not catching anything, everything has become tangled, and I'm going to lose the rod.' He tugged and tugged, and at last managed to land a very large fish. And the fish said to him: 'Fisherman, my dear fisherman, let me go and you'll have all the fish you want.' 'Well, now! . . . So, once I've had a bit of luck, shall I waste it? I won't let you go.' 'Let me go, and I'll give you whatever you want. You can bring a wagon for the fish.' 'Alright, I'll let you go. But you must give me everything you've promised.' So the fisherman let it go, astounded to have seen such a large creature.

He arrived home, got ready, and his wife asked him: 'Where are you going?' 'Look! . . . I'm going to fetch the donkey and my net, because I've caught a lot of fish.' And his wife was very happy. The fisherman went and got the net and went to the place where he'd caught the fish. Then the huge fish appeared and said: 'Cast your net, cast it out!' The fisherman cast the net and pulled it out full of fish. He cast it again, and caught even more. He loaded his donkey with fish and he went home very happy. All his sons came out to meet him as usual. 'Father, have you brought many fish?' 'Yes, my sons! Today I have a lot of fish! You can take some to sell!' The boys approached and saw that it

sacado tantos peces?' 'Pues, ¡hala hijos! ¡Corriendo a venderlos, que he enconrao una fortuna en el río!'

Bueno, ya vendieron los peces. Y al otro día fue y volvió con otros tantos. Claro, ya los vendieron lo mismo. Hicieron mucho dinero, compraron una casita y compraron ropa. Y ya no les faltaba nada. Y la mujer le dice: '¿En qué consiste esto que te has encontrao?' 'Chica, no te lo digo, que sois unas parlonas las mujeres.' 'Pues, me lo tienes que decir, o, si no, no te voy a dejar en paz.' 'Pues, no te lo digo,' le dijo él.

Bueno, pues al otro día fue con un carro —pues se compró un carro— para traer la pesca. Pues, la mujer estaba embarazada, y todos los dias le daba guerra para que la dijera en qué consistía la fortuna ésa. 'Bueno, chica, ya que te empeñas, te lo voy a decir. He sacao un pez muy grande, el rey de los peces, y me ha prometido, si lo soltaba, darme toda la pesca que yo quisiera. Y ahí está la fortuna.' 'Bueno . . . Pues, mira . . . Si le vuelves a coger otra vez, no te vengas sin él. Porque esto es un capricho mío. Ya ves que ya tenemos casa . . ., ya tenemos todo. Así que, ¿me vas a dar gusto, o no?' 'Sí . . . Si le vuelvo a coger, te prometo traerle.'

Bien, a los dos días vuelve a ir a pescar y le coge. Y entonces le empieza a decir: 'Suéltame, que no te engañé, que te volveré a dar mucho más de lo que te di.' 'Es verdaz que no me engañastes; pero ahora se trata de un capricho de mi mujer, y no puedo soltarte.' 'Bueno . . . Pues, bien . . . Ya que te empeñas, te voy a decir una cosa —cómo me ties que matar, lo que ties que hacer conmigo. La cabeza se la das a la perra, la cola a la yegua, el cuerpo para tu mujer, y las tripas las entierras en el corral.' 'Te podría vender y sacaría mucho dinero de ti.' '¡No! ¡Haz como te digo!' 'Bien. Así se hará.'

Pues, llegó a su casa con el pezcón, y la mujer, loca de alegría, llamó a todo el pueblo. ¡Todo el mundo asombrao de ver aquel pez tan grande! Y dijo el marido a la mujer: 'Pero esto no se vende. Mira, te voy a decir lo que me ha dicho que hagamos con él: la cabeza se la das a la perra, la cola a la yegua, el

was true. They all danced for joy. 'My God! What did you do, father? How did you catch so many fish?' 'Off you go! Run and sell them, because I've found a fortune in the river!' So they sold the fish.

The following day he went out and brought back just as many fish. Of course, they sold them all again. They made a lot of money, bought a house and bought clothes. Now they wanted for nothing. And his wife asked him: 'What is it you've found?' 'I won't tell you, my dear, because women are fond of gossip.' 'You must tell me because, if you don't, I won't leave you in peace.' 'I won't tell you' he answered.

And the following day he took a wagon with him (because he had bought himself a wagon) to bring home his catch. His wife was pregnant, and nagged him every day to tell her the reason for their good fortune. 'Alright, since you insist, I'll tell you. I caught an enormous fish, the king of fish, and it promised me that if I freed it, it would give me all the fish I wanted. That's the reason for our good fortune.' 'Very well . . . Look . . . If you catch it again, don't come home without it. I would like to see it. We already have a house . . ., we have everything we need. So, will you please me or not?' 'Yes . . . If I catch it again, I promise to bring it to you.'

A couple of days later he went fishing again and caught it. It began to say: 'Let me go, I didn't deceive you, and I'll give you much more than I've given you already.' 'It's true that you didn't deceive me; but now my wife wants to see you, and I can't let you go.' 'Very well. Fine. Since you insist I'll tell me how you should kill me and what you should do with me. Give my head to your dog, my tail to your mare, my body to your wife, and bury my guts in your yard.' 'I could sell you and get a lot of money for you.' 'No! Do as I say!' 'Very well. I'll do as you ask.'

So he arrived home with the enormous fish, and his wife, deliriously happy, called all the townsfolk. Everyone was astounded to see such a large fish! And the husband told his wife: 'But this fish is not for sale. Look, I'll tell you

cuerpo para ti, y las tripas se enterrarán en el corral.' Y así se hizo. A los tres meses nacieron tres perritos rubios, tres yeguas también rubitas y tres niños. Y en el corral, tres lanzas. Y los niños tan guapos y tan iguales.

Y llegaron a ser mocitos ya los tres niños y dijeron: 'Mire ustez, padre . . . Nos marchamos. ¡Qué hacemos aquí los tres?' 'Bueno, hijos, ya que os empeñáis. O voy a dar un recuerdo de vuestro padre. Tomaz cada uno una lanza, un perro y un caballo.' Y a todos les dio lo mismo. Y se dispusion todos a salir. Al despedirse de su padre y darle la mano y todo, el padre les dio a cada uno una botella de agua clara y les dijo: 'Cuando se enturbie esta agua, es que os pasa algo.'

Tomaron cada uno su dirección. Después de caminar mucho . . ., mucho . . ., entra uno en un pueblo, y están todas las mujeres llorando. Y les preguntó: '¿Qué les pasa, mujeres? ¿Por qué llorais?' 'Pues, mire ustez . . . Porque una serpiente de siete cabezas se presenta todos los años . . . Sortean a una moza para entregársela. Y este año la ha tocao a la hija del rey, que es muy guapa. Y no hay salvación para ella.' Y dice el hombre: '¡Pues, yo la mato!' '¡Ay, Dios mío! ¡Pues, inmediatamente decírselo al rey, que se casa con ustez la hija, y le da riquezas y todo lo que ustez quiera!' Y decía otra: '¡Ay, por Dios! Pero, ¿ustez tiene seguridaz, porque es una serpiente de siete cabezas?' '¡Sí, sí! ¡La tengo! ¡Me comprometo a matarla! Pues, ¿donde es el sitio?' 'Venga ustez, que se lo enseñaremos.'

Llegaron al sitio donde estaba la hija del rey. Y al verla tan hermosa como era, tuvo mas interés todavía. Y le dijo la hija del rey: '¿Dónde va ustez, joven? ¡Márchese de aquí!' 'Vengo a salvarla, señorita.' '¡Márchese, que la serpiente le devorará, que es una serpiente con siete cabezas!' Según estaba diciendo esto, a los pocos momentos llegó la serpiente con unos rugidos terribles. '¡Apártate, apártate!' le dice la serpiente. '¡Que te devoro y hago lo mismo que con la hija del rey!' '¡Que te va a matar! ¡Márchate!' dice la princesa, y se desmaya. Y dice él: '¡Aquí mi perro, mi lanza y mi caballo!' Y el perro empezó a

what it told me to do with it: give its head to the dog, its tail to the mare, take its body yourself, and bury its guts in the yard.' And so they did. Three months later three golden puppies, three golden foals and three children were born, and three lances grew in the yard. The children were beautiful and were all identical.

Soon the three boys became young men and said: 'Look, father . . . We're leaving. What can the three of us do here?' 'Very well, my sons, since you insist. I'll give you something to remember me by. Take a lance, a dog and a horse each;' and he gave each of them the same. They prepared to leave. As they said farewell to their father and hugged, he gave each one of them a bottle of crystal-clear water and said: 'When this water becomes cloudy, it means that one of you is in danger.'

Each one went off in a different direction. After travelling for a long, long time one of them came to a village, and all the women were crying. He asked them: 'What's the matter with you? Why are you crying?' 'Look . . . It's because every year a seven-headed serpent appears . . . They choose a girl by lottery to sacrifice to it. This year it's fallen to the daughter of the king, who is very beautiful. There's no hope of saving her.' The man said: 'I'll kill it!' 'My Lord! Tell the king immediately, so that you can marry his daughter and he will give you all the riches you may want!' And another said: 'But, good God! Are you sure, because it's a seven-headed serpent?' 'Yes, yes! I'm certain! I promise to kill it! Where should I go?' 'Come, and we'll show you.'

They came to the place where the king's daughter was waiting. Seeing her so beautiful, he became even more keen. The king's daughter said to him: 'Where are you going, young man? Leave here!' 'I've come to save you, my lady.' 'Leave, because the serpent will devour you, because it's a seven-headed serpent!' As she was saying this, the serpent arrived with some terrible roars. 'Go away, go away!' said the serpent. 'I'll devour you and I'll do the same to the king's daughter!' 'It'll kill you!' said the princess, and fainted. And he said: 'Come to me, my dog, my lance and my horse!' And the dog began to bite the

mordiscos, y él, en la yegua, se abalanzó sobre la serpiente. Él la dio con la lanza y la mató. Entonces sacó un pañuelo del bolsillo y la cortó las siete lenguas y las envolvió y las guardó. Y se marchó camino adelante.

Y comenzaron las mujeres a decir que se había salvao la hija del rey. Y empezaron a tocar las campanas, y todo el mundo comenzó a gritar de alegría. Y dijo el rey: 'Pero, ¿qué pasa?' '¡Su hija está salvada!' 'Pues, ¿qué ha pasao?' dijo el rey. 'Pues, que vayan por su hija, que un señorito la ha salvao.' Pues, fueron por ella. Y al llegar a palacio, dieron una fiesta en honor de ella.

Pero pasó por allí un carbonero —¿sabe?— y cortó las siete cabezas. Se presentó en palacio: 'Señor, vengo a casarme con su hija, como prometió ustez.' 'Pues, ¿qué ha pasao?' 'Pues que he matao la serpiente de las siete cabezas, y, para demostrárselo, aquí traigo las siete cabezas.' Y una vez que se repuso la hija, dijo ella que era mentira, que aquel hombre no era el que la había salvao. Decía el carbonero que era incierto, que sólo porque era carbonero, y feo, no querían cumplir lo que habían dicho. Bueno, pues decía una que sí, y otro que no. Y ya, convencido el rey, dijo que la palabra de rey tenía que cumplirse.

Y ya iban a celebrar las bodas. Pero, a todo esto, decidió el joven a volver a ver a la princesa. Llama y dice que quiere hablar con su majestaz. Le admiten, y dice: 'Vengo a ver qué ta está su hija que la salvé.' 'Pero, ¡hombre!' dice 'Es que la ha salvao un carbonero.' Y dice el joven: 'Pues, ¿cómo lo sabe ustez? ¡Si la he matao yo!' Y dice el rey: 'Pues, ya se va a casar con el carbonero, porque ha traido las siete cabezas de la serpiente.' 'Pues, ustez verá lo que falta en esas siete cabezas.' '¡Hombre! ¡No falta nada!' 'Mire ustez si tienen lenguas.' Efectivamente, van a mirarlas, y faltan las lenguas. 'Pues, mírelas ustez.' Saca el pañuelo y le presenta las siete lenguas. 'Entonces, ¿quién ha sido quien la ha matao?' Y claro, dijo la hija del rey que había sido él. 'Pues, entonces, ¡mandar prender a ese hombre por embustero!' Y entonces la princesa se casó con el otro, y celebraron las bodas con toda la alegría del mundo.

serpent, and he pounced on it on his mare. He ran it through with his lance and killed it. Then he took a handkerchief from his pocket and cut its seven tongues, wrapped them up and kept them. And he went on his way. The women began to shout that the king's daughter had been saved. They began to ring the town bells, and everyone began to shout with joy. And the king said: 'But, what's happening?' 'Your daughter has been saved!' 'So, what happened?' asked the king. 'Let them fetch your daughter, because a young man has saved her.' So they fetched her. And when she arrived at the palace they held a banquet in her honour.

But a coal merchant —you know?— passed by and cut off the serpent's seven heads. He came to the palace: 'Your Majesty, I have come to marry your daughter as you promised.' 'How's that?' 'I killed the seven-headed serpent and, to prove it, here are the seven heads.' Once the daughter came around she said that it was a lie, that this was not the man who had saved her. The coal merchant said that she was wrong, and that they refused to keep their word simply because he was an ugly coal merchant. So they continued arguing. But the king believed him and said that his word must be kept.

They were about to celebrate the wedding. But then, the young man decided to return to see the princess. He knocked on the door and said that he wished to speak to the king. They let him in, and he said: 'I've come to see how your daughter is, since I saved her.' 'But', said the king, 'a coal merchant saved her.' And the young man answered: 'How do you know this? Because I killed the serpent!' The king said: 'She's going to marry the coal merchant, because he brought me the serpent's seven heads.' 'Look and see what's missing from those heads.' 'Well! There's nothing missing!' 'See if they have any tongues.' So they went to look, and found the tongues were missing. 'Look, here they are.' He pulled out his handkerchief and showed the seven tongues. 'So who really killed it?' Of course, the king's daughter said that it was the young man himself.

Una vez estaban en la galería del palacio, y dice el joven: 'Oye, ¿qué es aquello que ves allí?' 'El Castillo de Irás y No Volverás. Y no te se ocurra nunca ir por allí, porque no vuelves.' 'Pues, tengo que ir un día de caza.' 'Pues, todo el que va queda allí.' Y él, por no disgustar a su mujer, calló. Pero fue. Un día se le antojó marchar. Cogió su yegua, su perra y la lanza y se marchó al Castillo de Irás y No Volverás. Subió con dirección a él hasta que llegó allí. Y había allí un arbolado muy espeso y puertas grandes, con argollas de hierro. Llama y no le responden. Vuelve a llamar otra vez más fuerte, y aparece una vieja: '¿Qué deseas, hijo?' 'Pues, mire ustez: quería ver este castillo.' 'Pero, ¿cómo vas a verle con la yegua?' '¿Dónde voy a dejarla? No tengo con qué atarla.' 'Pues, toma un pelo de mi cabeza para atarla.' Y el se echó a reír. '¡No! ¡No te rías! Tan pronto como le cojas, se volverá una maroma.' Bueno . . . En efecto, así fue. La ató, bajó, y fue a ver el castillo. Y allí quedó encantao. Quedó encantao como un perro, pues todos quedaban como animales en aquel castillo. Se volvieron a cerrar las puertas en la misma forma.

La princesa estaba llena de pena porque suponía que habia quedado en el castillo aquél. Pues, a todo esto, la botella del otro hermano se puso muy turbia. Cada día que pasaba, más turbia estaba la botella. El hermano decia: '¿Qué le pasará a mi hermano, que cada vez se pone más turbia mi botella? Algo le pasa a mi hermano. Hay que irle a buscar.' Bueno, echó andando, andando, hasta que llegó al pueblo donde estaba casao su hermano con la princesa. Y al llegar en el pueblo, notó el hermano que decían: '¡Viva el príncipe!' 'Calla, pues ¿qué pasará? Pues, mi hermano, ¿será rey, o qué sera? ¿Por qué dicen ustedes eso?' 'Pues, hace quince días que faltaba ustez, y estaba tan intranquila la princesa.' Y dice entonces él: 'Bueno . . . Se trata de mi hermano.' Y fue al palacio. Y al entrar, bajaron a recibirle todos. Y le dice la princesa: 'Por dónde has estao, hombre, que nos has tenido intranquilos? Ya te dije que no irías al Castillo de Irás y No Volverás. ¿No te lo decía?' Y él no decía nada. Y cenaron y se acostaron.

'Arrest that other man for his lies and deceit!' And the princess married the young man, and a joyous wedding took place.

One day they were on the palace balcony, and the young man said: 'Listen, what is that in the distance?' 'It's The Castle of Nevercomeback. And don't even think of ever going there, because you won't come back.' 'But I'd like to go hunting one of these days.' 'Everyone who goes there stays there.' So, in order not to upset his wife, he kept quiet. But he went there. One day he decided to go. He took his mare, his dog and his lance and went to the Castle of Nevercomeback. He headed towards it until he arrived. There was a thick wood and large gates, with iron door knockers there. He knocks and no-one answeres. He knocks again, and an old woman appears: 'What do you want, young man?' 'Look: I'd like to see the castle.' 'But how can you see it on your mare?' 'Where shall I leave her? I don't have a rope to tie her with.' 'Take a hair from my head to tie her.' And he began to laugh. 'No! Don't laugh! As soon as you take one, it'll become a rope.' Well . . . And so it happened. He tied the mare, got off it, and went to see the castle. And he became enchanted there. He was turned into a dog, because everyone became animals in that castle. And the gates shut as before.

The princess was very sad because she suspected that he'd been trapped in the castle. As a result of this, the next brother's bottle became very cloudy. As each day passed it became cloudier. The brother wondered: 'What must have happened to my brother, since my bottle gets cloudier every day? Something must be wrong. I must go and look for him.' So he set off and journeyed until the came to the village where his brother was married to the princess. Entering at the village, the brother noticed that they all said: 'Long live the prince!' 'Well, what can this be? Can my brother be the king, or what? Why do you all say this?' 'Well, a fortnight ago you went missing, and the princess was terribly worried.' So then he says: 'Yes . . . It's my brother.' And he went to the palace. As he entered, everyone came out to greet him. And the princess said: 'Where have you

Y a los pocos días vuelven a salir a la misma galería, y la vuelve a hacer la misma pregunta que su hermano: '¿Qué es aquel castillo?' 'Oye pues, ¿no te lo dije hace días? ¿No has estado en él, el Castillo de Irás y No Volverás? ¿Dónde has estado de caza hace pocos días, que nos has tenido tan intranquilos?' Y él, claro, ya cayó en la cuenta. 'Pues, ¡date! Allí estará mi hermano, pues la botella está cada vez más turbia.' Y cuando pudo, se marchó en dirección al castillo. Y hizo lo mismo que el otro. Llegó allá, llamó a la puerta, salió la misma vieja: '¿Qué deseas, hijo?' 'Pues mire ustez, venía a ver el castillo.' 'Pero, ¿Cómo vas a verle con la yegua?' '¿Dónde voy a dejarla? No tengo con qué atarla.' Y le dijo lo mismo que antes — lo del pelo. Y le dio el pelo. Bajó y quedó encantado él como un lobo — pues todos qudaban como animales en aquel castillo. Y, con todo esto, la botella cada vez más turbia . . . Y la mujer más intranquila . . .

Y el otro hermano vio que su botella se ponía cada vez más turbia. Y salió en busca de sus hermanos. Llegó, por fin, al pueblo donde estaba casao su hermano. Y le pasó lo mismo que a su hermano. '¡Viva el príncipe!' Y así se dio cuenta. '¿Qué pasara ¿Que si mi hermano sería rey? ¿Qué pasará aquí? Hasta que preguntó, como el otro: 'Pero, ¡hombre! . . . Ha faltao ya dos temporadas, y estábamos, muy intranquilos.' 'Pues ya estoy yo aquí.' Y decía él: 'Pues ya veremos lo que pasa aquí.' Y se dirige al palacio. Y le dice la reina: '¡Qué no te vuelva a ocurrir eso! Desde ahora en adelante me voy a ir contigo siempre. La primera vez me faltaste ocho días, y ahora van quince. No quiero que pase otra vez.'

Pues, ¡claro!, después de varios días salen a la galería, y vuelve a preguntar otra vez lo del castillo. 'Pero, ¡hombre! ¡Qué tonto eres! Has estado dos veces y no te acuerdas de cómo se llama. Y no vuelvas a ir, que hemos estado intranquilos todos en el pueblo.' Pues, como era más vivo que sus hermanos, se dio cuenta en seguida. Y como su botella se ponía cada vez más turbia, pues al día siguiente se marchó — pues se daba cuenta, de lo que decían todos, que sus hermanos tenían que estar en ese castillo. Y hizo como los otros:

been, because we've been terribly worried? I told you not to go to the Castle of Nevercomeback, didn't I?' And he said nothing. They had dinner and went to bed.

A few days later they're on the same balcony, and he asks her the same question as his brother: 'What's that castle?' 'Look, didn't I tell you a few days ago? Haven't you already been there, to the Castle of Nevercomeback? Where were you hunting a few days ago, making us all so worried?' He, of course, now realized what had happened. 'Very well! My brother must be there, since the bottle is getting cloudier every day.' When he could, he set off for the castle. And he did the same as his brother. He arrived, knocked on the door, and the same old woman appeared: 'What do you want, young man?' 'Look, I have come to see the castle.' 'But how can you see it on your mare?' 'Where can I leave her? I have nothing to tie her with.' And she said the same as before (about the hair). And she gave him the hair. He got down and was turned into a wolf: because everyone became an animal in that castle. And the bottle became cloudier, and the wife more worried.

The third brother saw that his bottle was getting cloudier. So he set off to find his brothers. At last, he arrived at the village where his brother was married and the same thing happened to him as to his brother. 'Long live the prince!' And so he realized what was happening. 'What's going on? Can my brother be the king? What's going on here?' Until he asked some people, as his brother had done. 'But, you've been missing twice and we were very worried.' 'Well I'm here now.' He said: 'We'll soon find out what's going on here.' He headed for the palace, and the queen said: 'This won't happen to you again! From now on I'll go with you wherever you go. The first time you were gone for a week, and now you've been missing a fortnight. I don't want it to happen again.'

Of course, a few days later they went out on to the balcony, and he asks her about the castle again. 'But, what an idiot you are! You've been there twice and don't even remember what it's called. Don't go there again, because we've

cogió el perro, la yegua y la lanza, y llegó allá. Y llamó como los otros. Abrieron la puerta, y aparece la vieja. '¿Qué quería?' 'Ver el castillo y sacar dos hermanos que tengo aquí metidos.' Y dice la vieja: 'Es mentira, hijo. Aquí no hay nadie. Ate el caballo y baje ustez.' 'No ato el caballo. Aquí paso con caballo y todo.' Se abalanza sobre ella y dice: '¡Ahora mismo tienes que decir dónde están mis hermanos, o si no, te mato!' Se abalanza sobre ella con el caballo, el perro y la lanza. 'No me mates.. . Yo te diré de qué forma están encantados.' 'Pues dime de qué forma están encantados.' 'El uno está de perro, y el otro de lobo.' 'Pues dime qué hay que hacer para desencantarlos.' 'Bien, hijo, no me mates, y yo te lo diré. Allí abajo hay un león que te enseñaré, que tiene un ojo abierto. Con esta flecha que tengo aquí, hay que darle en el ojo que tiene abierto.' El joven hizo como ella decía. Mató el león, y se desencantaron sus hermanos y todos los personajes que había allí.

Volvieron al palacio, donde los recibieron con grandes alegrías. Se casaron los dos hermanos, y colorín colorao, este cuento se ha acabao.

all been worried in the village.' Since he was brighter than his brothers, he realized what had happened straight away. And because his bottle was becoming even more cloudy, the following day he set off; because he realized, from what everyone had said, that his brothers must be in that castle. And he did like the others: he took his dog, his mare and his lance, and arrived at the castle. He knocked as the others had done. They opened the door, and the old woman appears. 'What do you want?' 'To see the castle and rescue my two brothers that are trapped here.' And the old woman says: 'It's a lie, young man. There's no-one here. Tie your horse and get down off it.' 'I won't tie my horse. I'll come in horse and all.' He pounces on her and says: 'You'll tell me right now where my brothers are, or I'll kill you!' He rushes at her on his horse with his dog and lance. 'Don't kill me. I'll tell you how they have been enchanted.' 'So tell me how they're enchanted.' 'One has been turned into a dog, the other into a wolf.' 'Tell me how to disenchant them.' Very well, don't kill me, I'll tell you. Down below there's a lion which I'll show you, which has one eye open. You must shoot him in his open eye with this arrow I have here. The young man did as she told him. He killed the lion, and his brothers and everyone else that was there were disenchanted.

They went back to the palace where they were greeted with great joy. The two brothers were married, and reddish red, this story's ended.

E. El palacio de los encantos [76]

El hijo de un rey se enamoró de la pobre hija de un pastor y la quería como si fuera una princesa. Ella también le quería a él, pero reconociéndose pobre y que no la correspondía ser la novia de un príncipe, así se lo decía y que la olvidase, ya que no podrían casarse, como era el deseo de ambos; pero tanto la visitaba y tales pruebas de cariño la daba, que al fin consintió en que la visitase como novio. Llegó a enterarse el rey, y quiso quitarle esa idea; pero no pudo conseguirlo, a pesar de usar amenazas y consejos. Visto que no le obedecía, le amenazó con llevarle al Palacio de los Encantos. El príncipe se lo dijo a su novia, y que como él no renunciaba a su cariño, tendría que ir al Palacio de los Encantos y que cuando él estuviera allá, fuera también ella para pasarlo juntos, donde serían felices si ella lograba encontrar ese palacio. 'Toma estos zapatos de hierro' la dijo; 'te los pones, te vas a la cañada del valle; allí verás tres encinas, de ellas sale una vereda, sigue por el norte y no dejes de andar, por trabajos que pases. Pregunta por el Palacio de los Encantos.'

Así lo hizo la joven, y a los tres días de andar llegó a un palacio ruinoso, en el que vivía una pobre viejecita. Al llegar, la dijo: 'Buenas tardes, abuelita.' Al ver a la joven, dijo la vieja: '¡Oh, joven desgraciada; dónde vas por aquí, si por aquí no pasan más que los pajarillos!'. 'Haga usted el favor de recogerme esta noche' dijo la joven. 'De muy buena gana' dijo la anciana; 'pero tengo a mi hijo, el *Aire Gallego*, que te devorará en cuanto llegue, y está al llegar.' Pero la joven la replicó: 'Abuelita, yo me volveré una escobita, me colocaré detrás de la puerta y no será posible que me vea. Cuando estén comiendo, pregunta usted a su hijo que dónde está el Palacio de los Encantos, que luego yo la daré a usted el pago.' Se volvió escoba, y al poco rato entró el *Aire Gallego*, quien pidió la cena

---

[76] Told by Domingo Barrado Avila from Madroñera in Cáceres. Curiel Merchán, *Cuentos extremeños*, 122-5.

E. The Palace of Enchantments

A king's son fell in love with the daughter of a shepherd and loved her as though she were a princess. She also loved him but, realising that she was poor and not suitable as the bride of a prince, she told him to forget her because they couldn't marry, as was their wish; but he visited her so much and gave her so many signs of his affection that at last she agreed to his visiting her as his betrothed. The king found out, and wanted to make son forget this idea; but he couldn't, in spite of his threats and advice. Seeing that the prince wouldn't obey him, he threatened to take him to the Palace of Enchantments. The prince told his beloved that he would have to go to the Palace of Enchantments because he refused to deny his love, but that when he was there, she should come too so that they could be together and they would be happy, if only she could find that palace. 'Take these iron boots' he said. 'Put them on and go to the bottom of the valley; there you'll see three oak trees: a path leads from them; head north and don't stop walking whatever difficulties you may find. Ask for the Palace of Enchantments.'

The young girl did as she was told, and after three days' walk she arrived at a ruined palace where a poor old woman lived. When she arrived she said: 'Good afternoon, old woman.' Seeing the young girl the old woman said: 'Poor, unfortunate girl! Where are you going, because only birds come this way?' 'Please be kind enough to give me shelter tonight', said the young girl. 'Gladly', said the old woman. 'But my son, the North-West Wind, will devour you as soon as he arrives, and he's about to arrive.' But the young girl answered: 'Old woman, I'll become a broom and hide behind the door so it won't be possible for him to see me. When you're eating ask your son where the Palace of Enchantments is and then I'll give you a reward.' She became a broom, and the North-West Wind came home and asked his mother for dinner, because he was very hungry. While they were eating his mother asked him if he knew where the

a su madre, pues tenía mucha hambre. Cuando cenaban, le preguntó la madre si sabía dónde estaba el Palacio de los Encantos, y él, bramando, dijo: 'A carne humana me huele a mí ¿Quién la ha preguntado a usted eso?' 'Los pajarillos que, cantando, decían que iban al Palacio de los Encantos, y yo, por curiosidad, te lo pregunto, hijo mío' dijo la madre. 'Ese palacio' dijo el *Aire* 'está muy lejos de aquí. Eso mi amigo *Aire Solano* es el que lo tiene que saber, que anda más que yo.'

Por la mañana se levantó la abuela, y la joven se presentó a ella, refiriéndola cuanto su hijo la había dicho. Dio la joven como pago una bolsa de oro a la vieja, y siguió su marcha, pasando trabajos y fríos. Anduvo tres días con sus noches, y llegó a otro palacio muy lóbrego. Salió a recibirla a la puerta otra ancianita, quien la preguntó que dónde iba, cuando por allí sólo transitaban los pájaros. La joven contestó: 'Voy al Palacio de los Encantos. ¿Sabe usted dónde está, abuelita?' 'No' dijo ésta. '¿No tiene usted ningún hijo?' 'Sí, tengo uno: el *Aire Solano*.' 'Pues su hijo debe saberlo.' 'Ten cuidado, pues si viene, te traga.' 'No se apure, abuelita; yo me vuelvo una aldaba si viene. Usted se lo pregunta, y yo la daré a usted pago.'

Cuando llegó la noche, entró su hijo dando bramidos y diciendo: 'Madre, ¿a quién tiene usted aquí, que a carne humana me huele?' 'Aquí no hay nadie, hijo mío, puedes verlo' dijo la ancianita. 'Siéntate, que vamos a cenar, que ya tendrás hambre; pero antes te voy a hacer una pregunta: ¿Sabes dónde está el Palacio de los Encantos?' '¿Quién se lo ha preguntado a usted?' dijo el *Aire*. 'Los pajarillos que, cantando, decían que iban al Palacio de los Encantos, y yo, por curiosidad, te lo pregunto, hijo mío' dijo la madre. 'Ese palacio, madre, está retirado de aquí, y para ir a él hay que pasar tres ríos, y en cada uno hay que echar una cucharada de lo que yo como.' Cuando esto oyó la vieja, al comer la sopa del cocido fue apartando cucharadas con que para el gato y eran para guardarlas; luego apartó de los garbanzos y después del tocino. Se marchó el *Aire*, y la

Palace of Enchantments was and, bellowing, he said: 'I smell human flesh. Who asked you that?' 'The birds who said in their song that they were going to the Palace of Enchantments, and I'm asking you out of curiosity, my son', said his mother. 'That palace', said the North-West Wind, 'is very far from here. My friend, the East Wind, is the one who would know, because he travels more than I do.'

The old woman got up in the morning, and the young girl came to see her, and she told her what her son had said. The young girl gave the old woman a bag of gold in payment, and continued on the journey, suffering many hardships. She walked for three days and nights, and came to another very lugubrious palace. Another old woman met her at the door and asked her where she was going, because only birds passed that way. The young girl answered: 'I'm going to the Palace of Enchantments. Do you know where it is, old woman?' 'No', she said. 'Do you have a son?' 'Yes, I have one: the East Wind.' 'Your son should know.' 'Be careful, because when he comes, he'll swallow you whole.' 'Don't worry, old woman; I'll turn into a door knocker if he comes. Ask him, and I'll repay you.' When night came, her son arrived bellowing and saying: 'Mother, who's here, because I can smell human flesh?' 'There's no-one here, my son, as you can see', said the old woman. 'Sit down and we'll have dinner, because you must be hungry; but first I want to ask you a question: do you know where the Palace of Enchantments is?' 'Who asked you that?' said the East Wind. 'The birds who said in their song that they were going to the Palace of Enchantments, and I'm asking you out of curiosity, my son', said his mother. 'That Palace, mother, is far from here, and you must cross three rivers to get there, throwing a spoonful of my food into each one.' When the old woman heard this she began to save some spoonfuls of his stew saying they were for the cat; then she did the same with his chick peas and then with his bacon. The East Wind left, and the old woman told the young girl what he had said, giving her the spoonsful of food she'd saved from his meal.

anciana dijo a la joven cuanto la había dicho su hijo, dándola las cucharadas de la comida que había apartado de lo que su hijo comía.

Siguió la joven su camino, y andar, andar varios días y noches, llegó al primer río, echando la cucharada de sopa, se formó el primer puente y pasó; llegó al segundo puente, echó la cucharada de garbanzos y pasó, y en el tercero echó el tocino y sucedió igual. A los dos días de andar vio un palacio con las tejas doradas, y observó que sus zapatos iban yo rozados, por lo que se puso muy contenta. Llegó por fin al palacio, y en él moraban una anciana, con su hija moza, quienes le recibieron cariñosamente; y sacando la joven una rueca de oro con el huso de plata que llevaba, como recuerdo del príncipe, se puso a hilar. Al ver la rueca la joven del palacio, dijo a su madre: 'Mira qué rueca tan preciosa. Di a esta joven si nos la quiere vender.' Se lo preguntó la anciana, y ella contestó: 'Yo te la regalo, siempre que me dejéis dormir en el cuarto donde está el hijo del rey.' Ni la madre ni la hija quisieron concederla lo que pidió; pero como eran tan grandes sus deseos de poseer la rueca, dijo la hija: 'Madre, déjela usted que entre, pues echaremos adormideras para que el príncipe no se despierte.'

De modo que la joven entró en el cuarto del príncipe, y toda la noche estuvo llorando y gritando: 'Por ti me volví escobita por ti me volví aldabita; toma tus zapatos de hierro, tómalos, que ya no las quiero.' Pero el príncipe no despertó, por el efecto que en él hacían las adormideras que le habían dado. Salió la joven por la mañana muy triste, y se puso a devanar en una devanadera de plata con el huso de oro. Se enamoró también de la devanadera la hija de la casa, y preguntó si se la vendía, y la joven la contestó que se la regalaba si la dejaba dormir una noche en el cuarto del príncipe. Madre e hija, por coger la devanadera, aunque de muy mala gana, la dejaron que durmiera otra noche en el cuarto del príncipe, dándole a éste otras adormideras para que no despertara. Repitió la joven lo mismo que la noche anterior; pero esta noche, como llevaba tanto tiempo dormido, por fin despertó el príncipe. Con gran alegría al verse juntos, se abrazaron, y ella le contó todo lo que había pasado hasta encontrarle, y

The young girl continued on her way, and after walking for several days and nights she came to the first river; when she threw in the spoonful of stew, a bridge appeared and she crossed; she came to the second bridge, threw in the spoonful of chick peas and crossed, and when she threw the bacon into the third river the same thing happened. After two days' walk she saw a palace with golden tiles, and noticed that her boots were now worn, which made her very happy. At last she arrived at the palace, where an old woman and her young daughter lived; they greeted her warmly and the young girl produced a golden spinning wheel with a silver spindle which she had brought with her as a reminder of the prince, and began to spin. When she saw the spinning wheel the young woman from the palace said to her mother: 'Look, what a beautiful spinning wheel. Ask that young girl if she wants to sell it.' The old woman asked, and she answered: 'I'll give it to you as long as you let me sleep in the same room as the king's son.' Neither the mother nor the daughter wanted to agree to this; but since they wanted the spinning wheel so much, the daughter said: 'Mother, let her go in there, and we'll give the prince a potion so that he doesn't wake up.'

So the young girl went into the prince's bedroom, and cried and shouted all night: 'I became a broom and a door knocker for you; take your iron boots, I don't want them any more.' But the prince didn't wake up because of the sleeping potion that he had been given. The young girl left very sad in the morning and began to reel on a silver spool with a gold spindle. The daughter of the house was captivated by the spool, too, and asked if she would sell it to her, and the young girl answered that she would give it to her if she allowed her to spend a night in the prince's room. So that they could have the spool, the mother and daughter allowed her, though grudgingly, to spend another night in the prince's bedroom, giving him some more sleeping potion so that he wouldn't wake up. The young girl repeated the words she had said the night before; but this night, because he'd been asleep for so long, the prince at last woke up. They

a la mañana siguiente salieron juntos al patio. Al ver esto, la madre y la hija, que estaban puestas por el rey como guardianas del príncipe, lloraban amargamente, temiendo el castigo del rey; pero el príncipe, muy contento, las dijo: 'No temáis, que ésta es la que me tenía que desencantar. Vosotras seguiréis en este palacio, a nuestro lado.'

Se casaron el príncipe y la pastora, y cuentan que fueron todo lo felices y tuvieron muchos hijos. Y colorín colorao.[77]

---

[77] Although the formulaic ending is incomplete, it is understood by the audience that 'Colorín colorao, este cuento se ha acabao' ('Reddish red, this tale has ended') is meant.

hugged, overjoyed that they were together again, and she told him everything that had happened before she found him, and the following morning they went out into the courtyard together. When they saw this the mother and daughter, who the king had made the prince's guardians, began to cry bitterly, fearing the king's punishment; but the prince said to them, contentedly: 'Don't be afraid, because this was the one who was destined to break the enchantment put on me. You'll stay in this palace at our side.'

The prince and the shepherdess married, and it's said they were happy and had many children. And reddish red.

F. La selva encantada [78]

Este era un matrimonio muy feliz: con fortuna, con honra y con salud; con una niña tan linda que hechizaba los ojos el mirarla; todos los que pasaban por su lado lo notaban con asombro: '¡Oh, Dios mío, qué linda!' Y quien lo notaba más y con asombro mayor era un gallardo mancebo, que desde que la vio se convirtió en esclavo suyo. Y como era tan gallardo, la niña le tomó mucho cariño; pero el mancebo era pobre, y los padres de la niña se enteraron de estos amores con disgusto, y cuando él se presentó para pedírsela en matrimonio, le respondieron así: '¡Ay, no! . . . ¡Por nosotros, nunca! . . .' Y al ver a la niña tan triste, la dijeron: 'Antes que te cases con él, permita Dios que te lleven a la selva!'

¿Cómo fue? ¿Cómo no fue? ¡Nadie pudo jamás averiguarlo! A la mañana siguiente la cama de la niña se halló intacta, y por mucho que sus padres la buscaron, y por mucho que lloraron de desesperación y de arrepentimiento, la niña no pareció y el corazón de los padres no vio una lucecilla de esperanza.

Entonces llamaron al galán. Le entregaron un caballo, una espada y una bolsa y le prometieron la niña si se marchaba a buscarla por el mundo. Y aquí tenéis que aceptó y que salió camino de la selva, que se extendía interminablemente a unas leguas del lugar. En el fondo de esta selva se levantaba un palacio; pero eran los senderos tan difíciles y tan grandes los peligros que en ellos se encontraban, que jamás ni la osadía ni el valor se acercaban a sus pórticos. Mas aquí tenéis que se acercó el amor, porque el galán se entró selva adelante y a poco encontró una ermita. Se adelantó el ermitaño a recibirle, llevando tras sí un león como si fuera un perrillo cariñoso. El ermitaño le estrechó las manos y le dijo: 'No temas, que yo te esperaba!' Y le ofreció de cenar, y cenaron juntos. El ermitaño continuó: 'Ya sé a lo que vienes, y te ayudaré. Mañana, cuando desaparezca el sol, encontrarás otro ermitaño,

---

[78] Cabal, *Los cuentos tradicionales asturianos*, 72-6.

F. The Enchanted Forest

Once, there was a very happy couple: they had fortune, honour and health; they had a daughter who was so beautiful that she enchanted everyone who laid eyes on her; everyone she met noticed this with astonishment: 'Oh my Lord, how beautiful she is!' The person who noticed this the most and with the greatest astonishment was a gallant lad, who became her slave from the moment he saw her. And since he was so gallant, the girl became very fond of him; but the lad was poor, and the girl's parents were not pleased to hear of their love, and when the lad came to ask for her hand in marriage, they answered him like this: 'Ah, no! . . . Over our dead bodies! . . .' And seeing the girl so sad they said to her: 'May God take you to the forest before you marry this youth!'

How did it happen? How indeed? No-one ever found out! The following morning the girl's bed was found empty, and no matter how much her parents looked for her, and cried desperately and repented, the girl didn't appear and her parents could see no chink of hope.

Then they called the lad. They gave him a horse, a sword and a bag of money and promised him their daughter's hand if he went to look for her. So he accepted and headed off for the forest, which stretched off into the distance a few leagues from their village. There was a palace at the far end of this forest; but the paths were so difficult and their dangers so great that neither daring nor courage had ever approached its gates. But love did approach them, because the lad headed into the forest and soon found a hermitage. The hermit came out to greet him, followed by a lion as tame as an affectionate dog. The hermit took his hands and said: 'Don't be afraid, because I was expecting you!' He offered him food, and they had dinner together. The hermit continued: 'I know why you've come, and I'll help you. Tomorrow, at sunset, you'll meet another hermit, my brother; you must do what he says, because I promise that he'll help you too.' And he

Hermano mío; has de hacer lo que te diga, porque te prometo que también te ayudará.' Y le echó su bendición, y le dijo al león a la hora de partir: 'Vete con él, y defiéndele!'

A la caída del sol, el camino los condujo a la otra ermita; se adelantó el ermitaño a recibirlos, y tras él marchaba un tigre como si fuera un perrrillo cariñoso. Y el ermitaño le dijo al galán: '¡No temas, que yo te esperaba!' Y después de la cena, continuó: 'Ya sé a lo que vienes, y te ayudaré. Mañana, cuando desaparezca el sol, encontrarás otro ermitaño, hermano mío; has de hacer lo que te diga, porque te prometo que también te ayudará.' Y le echó su bendición, y a la hora de partir le dijo al tigre: '¡Vete con él, y defiéndele!'

A la caída del sol, el camino los condujo a la otra ermita; se adelantó el ermitaño a recibirlos, y tras él marchaba un oso como si fuera un perrillo. El ermitaño le dijo al galán: '¡Gracias a Dios que por fin llegaste! Sé a lo que vienes, y te ayudaré de todo corazón si te encomiendas a Dios.' Y al oso le dijo así: '¡Vete con él, y defiéndele!'

Y aquí tenéis que el galán, el león, el tigre y el oso llegaron a un puentecillo que guardaba un gigante. Era el gigante feroz, tan grande como una montaña y con unos ojos que parecían echar fuego y con una boca que parecía quererse comer a medio mundo. En una mano tenía una maza como una torre, y a la cintura una honda como una serpiente. En cuanto vio al mancebillo fue hacia él, lo examinó con desprecio y le preguntó con rabia: '¿Adónde vas?' '¡A pasar!' '¡No se puede!' '¡Sí se puede, con la ayuda de Dios!' El gigante levantó la maza, pero antes de que la descargara sobre el mancebillo, éste le clavó su espada en un costado y pudo pasar el puente. El gigante dio un bramido, sacó la honda y le arrojó varios peñascos terribles; pero los animales se echaron sobre él, lo tiraron al suelo y lo mataron a mordiscos.

El mancebillo siguió y encontró una vieja; hilaba copos de cáñamo, y en cuanto le vio llegar dejó la rueca y salió a preguntarle: '¿Adónde vas?' '¡Al palacio!' '¡No se puede!' '¡Sí se puede, con la ayuda de Dios!' Silbó entonces la

gave him his blessing, and said to the lion as he left: 'Go with him and defend him!'

At sunset, the road led them to another hermitage; the hermit came out to greet them, followed by a tiger as tame as an affectionate dog. And the hermit said to the lad: 'Don't be afraid, because I was expecting you!' And after dinner he continued: 'I know why you've come and I'll help you. Tomorrow, at sunset, you'll find another hermit, my brother; you must do what he says, because I promise that he'll help you too.' And he gave him his blessing, and as he was leaving he said to the tiger: 'Go with him and defend him!'

At sunset, the road led them to another hermitage; the hermit came out to greet them, followed by a bear as tame as a dog. The hermit said to the lad: 'Thank God that you've arrived at last! I know why you've come, and I'll help you with all my heart if you place yourself in God's hands.' And he said to the bear: 'Go with him and defend him!'

So the lad, the lion, the tiger and the bear came to a small bridge guarded by a giant. The giant was ferocious, as big as a mountain, with eyes that seemed to shoot fire and a mouth capable of devouring half the world. In one hand he had a mace as large as a tower, and a sling hung like a serpent from his belt. When he saw the young man he went towards him, examined him with scorn and asked him angrily: 'Where are you going?' 'Across the bridge!' 'Impossible!' 'Yes it's possible, with God's help!' The giant raised his mace, but before he could strike the young man, the lad stabbed him in his side with his sword and crossed the bridge. The giant gave a roar, took out the sling and launched some terrible boulders at him; but the animals pounced on him, dragged him to the ground and mauled him to death.

The young man continued on his way and met an old woman; she was spinning tufts of hemp, and when she saw him approach she left the spinning wheel and came to ask him: 'Where are you going?' 'To the palace!' 'That's impossible!' 'Yes it's possible, with God's help!' Then the old woman, who was

vieja, que era la bruja más mala de todo el país, y salieron de la selva muchos toros, muchos carneros, muchos perros. Los animales que el mancebo llevaba se arrojaron sobre ellos y los mataron en un tris, a pesar de los aullidos de la bruja, que murió también en el zipizape de un abrazo del oso.

El mancebilló siguió y encontró el palacio. En un balcón aguardaba la niña, resplandeciente de hermosura; pero los guardias que cuidaban la puerta le pararon también: '¿Adónde vas?' '¡Adentro!' '¡No se puede!' '¡Sí se puede, con la ayuda de Dios!' Llegaron los animales, y los guardias entraron en la casa, se detuvieron en un salón y de repente sonó una corneta. El salón se llenó de guerreros, y entre los animales y los guerreros se inició una lucha mortal. El mancebillo aprovechó el momento para correr a la niña, y no hizo más que tocarla, y en el instante cesaron los clamores y los ruidos y desaparecieron los guerreros, los animales y el palacio. Se encontraron en un campo, y la hermosura del campo y la fatiga les cerraron los ojos y los hicieron dormir. Soñaron que estaban en misa y que recibían la bendición de Dios. Al despertar se encontraron en la casa de la niña, rodeados de sus padres, de sus amigos y de sus criados.

En seguida se casaron y fueron felices, y a mí, que fui y vine, no me dieron nada.

the most evil witch in all the land, whistled and a lot of bulls, rams, and dogs came out of the forest. The animals that accompanied the young man attacked them and killed them in a thrice, in spite of the witch's cries, and she was killed too, crushed by the bear's hug.

The young man continued on his way and found the palace. The girl was waiting on a balcony, as beautiful as ever; but the guards at the gate stopped him too: 'Where are you going?' 'Inside!' 'That's impossible!' 'Yes it's possible, with God's help!' The animals arrived, and the guards went inside to one of the rooms and suddenly a trumpet sounded. The room was filled with warriors, and a deadly battle began between the animals and the warriors. The young man took his chance to run to the girl, and hardly had he touched her when the shouts and noises stopped and the warriors, animals and palace disappeared. They found themselves in a field, whose beauty together with their tiredness made them close their eyes and fall asleep. They dreamed that they were at mass and were receiving God's blessing. When they woke up they found themselves in the girl's house, surrounded by her parents, their friends and servants.

They got married straight away and lived happily ever after, but they gave me nothing, even though I went there and back.

G. Un cuento de aventuras [79]

Pues señor, en este reino desaparecieron las tres princesas en la misma noche, y el reino se llenó de consternación. El rey, cuya salud era muy débil, creyó morir de pesar, y prometió la mano de sus hijas a los tres caballeros que las libertasen. Súpose que las princesas habían sido llevadas a un castillo bajo el poder de un encanto, y que más que de valor, los caballeros que las libertasen necesitarían de la astucia; y eran muchos los hombres de valor en los dominios del rey; pero, desgraciadamente, los de astucia eran muy pocos.

Tres hermanos que supieron la noticia se lanzaron a la empresa; los dos mayores se vistieron la armadura, se ciñeron la espada y partieron a caballo. El menor juntó clavos, buscó pitas y salió solo y a pie. Cuando divisó el castillo, vio que estaban sus hermanos acometiendo inútilmente a los portones. El encanto del castillo estaba precisamente en los portones, y todos los esfuerzos por abrirlos, derribarlos o romperlos resultaban estériles. El hermano menor cogió sus clavos, los fue metiendo en el muro, fue componiendo con ellos una escala y llegó al interior; las tres princesas le recibieron enloquecidas de alegría, y por el mismo camino consiguieron la libertad.

Los hermanos mayores se percataron con envidia de la hazaña del pequeño, y mientras él ascendía por el interior del muro, quitaron del exterior rodos los clavos. El pequeño los vio alejarse desde las almenas, llevándose las princesas como premio de la infamia que cometían con él. Y vio que la menor de las princesas, con gesto desfallecido, se volvía muchas veces a mirarle. La menor de las princesas le había dado una sortija en el momento de coger la escala y le había advertido así 'Cuando quieras obtener alguna cosa, pídesela a la sortija.' Y le pidió un caballo volador que le llevara a la corte; y se apareció el caballo, montó en él, cruzó los aires y le dejó el caballo en el campo, junto a la quinta del

---

[79] Cabal, *Los cuentos tradicionales asturianos*, 142- 7.

G. An Adventure Story

Well then, sir, the three princesses disappeared from this kingdom on the same night, and the kingdom was filled with sadness. The king, whose health was very poor, thought he would die of grief, and promised his daughters' hands to the three knights who would free them. It became known that the princesses had been taken to an enchanted castle, and that more than courage, the knights who freed them would need cunning; there were many courageous men in the king's lands but, unfortunately, there were few cunning ones.

Three brothers heard the news and undertook the task; the two oldest put on their armour and swords and set off on horseback. The youngest one gathered some nails, looked for pitons and set off alone and on foot. When he saw the castle, he saw that his brothers were making a useless attack on its gates. The castle's enchantment was focused on its gates, and every effort to open them, knock them down or break them was pointless. The youngest brother took his nails and started to place than in the wall to make a ladder and he got inside; the princesses were overjoyed to see him, and gained their freedom along the same path.

The older brothers were jealous of the younger one's success, and while he was climbing up the inside of the wall, they took out all the nails from the outside. The youngest brother saw them riding off from the ramparts, taking the princesses as a prize for the infamous deed. And he noticed that the youngest princess, almost fainting, kept looking back at him. The youngest princess had given him a ring as she climbed the ladder and told him: 'When you want something, ask the ring for it.' And he asked for a flying horse that would take him to court. The horse appeared, he mounted, flew through the air and left the horse in the field next to the king's estate and close to a small hut. In the hut he swapped clothes with a labourer and went to the estate so that they would employ

rey y al pie de una chozuela. En la chozuela cambió la ropa con un gañán y se presentó en la quinta para que le tomaran de criado. Le tomaron, en efecto, y allí se enteró de que sus hermanos se habían casado con las dos princesas mayores y de que la princesa menor estaba muy triste. Como regalo de boda el rey les había dado a sus hermanos dos bolas de oro de extraordinario valor.

Pero he aquí que la tristeza de la princesita la llevaba a buscar la soledad en los jardines del rey, e iba a los de la quinta a cada paso. Vio en ella al criado nuevo, y a pesar del disfraz le conoció. Pasearon a la sombra de los árboles, él le contó su aventura y ella le expuso su plan: 'Veré a mi padre' le dijo 'y le contaré toda la historia.' Pero por consejo de él desistió de contársela, y fue a su padre y comenzó a gemir. 'Hija mía, ¿qué te ocurre?' le preguntó su padre, que era muy bueno y la quería muchísimo. 'Que estoy enamorada de un criado, y si tú te opones a que se case conmigo, me voy a morir de pena.'

El rey se escandalizó, dijo que nones y riñó a su hija. Pero la pena de su hija se le quedó clavada en el corazón y acabó por enfermarse. Se reunieron los médicos, y uno muy ancianito, muy famoso, el más hábil y más sabio, dijo así: 'El rey se morirá en esta semana si no le dan la leche de leona.' ¡Qué atrocidad! ¡La leche de leona! Andaba una leona por el monte seguida de los cachorros; pero ¿quién iba a ordeñarla? Los dos yernos del rey cambiaron impresiones y acordaron engañarle con una comedia. Dijeron, pues, que se arrojaban a la gran aventura. Pero en el caminito del monte encontraron a su hermano de regreso con un cántaro de leche; pasmaron de asombro, mas se hicieron los desentendidos y le abrazaron, y le pidieron noticias de su hazaña . . . El temió de su intención y les ocultó la verdad, y era la verdad que le había dicho a la sortija: 'Quiero que en cuanto me vea se amanse la leona de tal modo, que me permita ordeñarla sin peligro.' Y mansa había encontrado a la leona.

Los hermanos dijeron: 'Si nos cedieras la leche te daríamos las bolas de oro que el rey nos regaló.' Hicieron el cambio y el rey bebió la leche y recobró al momento la salud. Pero quiso un rey vecino aprovechar la ocasión para invadir

him as a servant. They did indeed employ him, and he discovered that his brothers had married the two older princesses and that the youngest princess was very sad. As a wedding present the king had given his brothers two golden balls of extraordinary value.

But the little princess' sadness caused her to seek solitude in the king's gardens, and she went to the gardens of the estate at every opportunity. She saw the new servant there, and recognized him in spite of his disguise. They walked in the shade of the trees, he told her about his adventure and she told him her plan: 'I'll see my father', she said, 'and I'll tell him everything.' But at his request she didn't do this, and went to her father and began to moan. 'What's the matter with you, my daughter?' asked her father, who was very kind and loved her very much. 'I'm in love with a servant and if you oppose our marriage, I'll die of grief.'

The king was appalled, said no and scolded his daughter. But his daughter's grief penetrated deep into his heart and he became ill. All the doctors came together, and a very old and famous one, who was the most able and wise, said: 'The king will die this week if he does not drink some lion's milk.' How awful! Lion's milk! A lioness was roaming the mountains followed by her cubs; but who would milk her? The king's two sons-in-law discussed the matter and agreed to trick him with a ruse. Therefore they said that they would go on this great adventure. But on the way to the mountain they met their brother coming back with a jar of milk; they paled with surprise, but they played dumb and hugged him, and asked him to tell them of his deed . . . He was afraid of their motives and hid the truth, the truth being that he had said to the ring: 'When she sees me I want the lion to become so tame that she allows me to milk her without danger.' And the lion had been tame.

The brothers said: 'If you give us the milk we'll give you the golden balls that the king gave us.' They made the swap and the king drank the milk and immediately got better. But a neighbouring king took the opportunity to invade

sus estados y exigirle tributos; se juntaron los ministros en consejo y los dos yernos del rey creyeron de su deber el ponerse a la cabeza de las tropas. Llegaron a una llanura y allí se enteraron de que el enemigo avanzaba contra ellos; hicieron que las tropas acamparan y salieron los dos de exploración. Pero he aquí que en el camino encontraron a su hermano, que volvía de acabar al enemigo y llevaba sus banderas. Pasmaron de asombro, pero se hicieron los desentendidos; le abrazaron y le pidieron noticias de la hazaña. El temió de su intención y les ocultó la verdad, y era la verdad que le había dicho a la sortija: 'Quiero que infundas el pánico en el ejército que viene contra el rey y que él mismo se destroce.' Y así fue.

Los hermanos le dijeron: 'Si nos cedieras las banderas te daríamos todo lo que se te antojara.' Y él respondió: 'Se me antoja marcaros con un hierro candente.' 'Pero ¿y por qué?' 'Por capricho.' Los hermanos accedieron al capricho, él les cedió las banderas y ellos se las presentaron al rey atribuyéndose la victoria.

La princesita menor volvió a su padre: 'Padre' le dijo, 'me es imposible olvidarme de mi amor, y si vuelves a oponerte a que me case con él, me dejaré morir.' El rey se resignó; se hizo la boda y se celebró un banquete. ¡Había que ver qué banquete! ¡Qué de aves! ¡Qué de dulces! ¡Qué de licore! La princesita se sentó junto a su padre, reclinó contra su pecho la cabeza y díjole con ternura: 'Te han engañado, padre mío. Quien destrozó el ejército invasor no fueron mis cuñados, fue mi esposo.' '¿Tienes una prueba?' 'Sí . . . La marca de hierro candente que llevan mis cuñados en la espalda . . .' El rey mandó que les descubrieran la espalda, y se convenció de que la princesita no mentía. 'Pero, al menos' dijo el rey, 'ellos me devolvieron la salud con la leche de leona . . .' '¡Te engañaron también! . . . Quien te buscó la leche de leona fue mi esposo . . .' '¿Tienes una prueba? . . .' 'Sí . . . Las bolas de oro que les diste tú cuando se casaron con mis hermanas, y que ellos le entregaron a mi esposo a cambio de la leche . . .' Y puso sobre le mesa las dos bolas. 'Pero, al menos' dijo el rey, 'ellos

his lands and exact tribute; the ministers came together in council and the king's two sons-in-law thought it was their duty to be at the head of the troops. They came to a plain and saw that the enemy was advancing on them; they told the troops to set up camp and they went out to investigate. But on the way they met their brother who had just defeated the enemy and carried their banners. They paled with surprise, but they played dumb; they hugged and asked him to tell them of his deed. He was suspicious of their motives and hid the truth, the truth being be that he had said to the ring: 'I want you to spread panic in the army that is attacking the king and for it to destroy itself.' And so it had happened.

The brothers said: 'If you gave us the banners we will give you anything you want.' And he answered: 'I want to mark you with a burning iron.' 'But why?' 'Just a whim.' The brothers agreed to the whim, he gave them the banners and they presented them to the king, taking credit for the victory themselves.

The youngest princess turned to her father: 'Father', she said, 'I can't forget my love, and if you continue to oppose our marriage, I'll die.' The king resigned himself; the marriage took place and a banquet was held. The banquet had to be seen to be believed! What poultry! What sweets! What liqueurs! The little princess sat down next to her father, laid her head on his breast and said to him with affection: 'They've tricked you, father. It was not my brothers-in-law who defeated the invading army, but my husband.' 'Do you have any proof?' 'Yes . . . The brands that my brothers-in-law have on their shoulders . . .' The king ordered them to show their shoulders, and was convinced that the little princess was not lying. 'But', said the king, 'at least they gave me my health with the lion's milk . . .' 'They also tricked you then . . . It was my husband who got the lion's milk for you . . .' 'Do you have any proof? . . .' 'Yes . . . The golden balls that you gave them when they married my sisters, and that they gave my husband in exchange for the milk . . .' And she put the balls on the table. 'But', said the king, 'at least they freed you from the castle . . .' 'They also tricked you on that! . . . It was my husband who rescued us from the castle.'

te libertaron del castillo . . .' '¡Te engañaron también! . . . Quien nos sacó del castillo fue mi esposo.'

Y el rey ya no pidió prueba, y mandó que entregaran al verdugo a los hermanos mayores; por fortuna para ellos, el influjo del menor los libró de la cuchilla, pero fueron arrojados del palacio y perdieron el amor de sus princesas, sus amigos, y su rey . . .

The king didn't ask for any further proof, and ordered that the older brothers be given to the executioner; fortunately for them, their younger brother's influence saved them from the blade, but they were thrown from the palace and lost the love of their princesses, their friends and the king . . .

H. El pandero de piel de piojo [80]

Érase un rey que tenía una hija de quince años. Un día, estaba la princesita paseando por el jardín con su doncella, cuando vio una planta desconocida. Y preguntó, curiosa: '¿Qué es esto?' 'Una matita de hinojo, Alteza.' 'Cuidémosla, a ver lo que crece' dijo la princesa. Otro día, la doncella encontró un piojo. Y la princesa propuso: 'Cuidémoslo, a ver lo que crece.' Y lo metieron en una tinaja. Pasó el tiempo. La matita se convirtió en un árbol y el piojo engordó tanto, que al cabo de nueve meses, ya no cabía en la tinaja. El rey, después de consultar a su hija, publió un bando diciendo que la princesa estaba en edad de casarse, pero que lo haría con el más listo del país. Para ello se le ocurrió hacer un pandero con la piel del piojo, construyéndose el cerco del mismo con madera de hinojo. Luego hizo colocar en todas las esquinas de las casas del reino un nuevo bando, diciendo: 'La princesita se casará con el que acierte de qué material está hecho el pandero. A los pretendientes a su mano se les dará tres días de plazo para acertarlo. Quien no lo hiciere en este tiempo será condenado a muerte.'

A palacio acudieron condes, duques y marqueses, así como muchachos riquísimos, que ansiaban casarse con la princesita, pero ninguno adivinó de qué materia estaba fabricado el pandero y murieron todos al tercer día. Un pastor, que había leído el bando, dijo a su madre: 'Prepárame las alforjas que voy a probar suerte. Conozco las pieles de todos los bichos del campo y la madera de todos los árboles del bosque.' Después de discutir un rato con la madre, que temía le sucediera lo mismo que a tantos otros pretendientes a la mano de la princesa, el pastor logró convencer a su progenitora y emprendió el camino hacia la corte. En las afueras de un pueblo encontróse con un gigante que estaba sujetando un peñasco como una montaña y le preguntó: '¿Qué haces ahí, muchacho?' 'Sujeto

---

[80] From H.C. Granch, *Cuentos maravillosos y de hadas españoles* (Barcelona: Maucci, 1945), 36-44.

H. The Tambourine Made of Louse Skin

Once, there was a king who had a fifteen-year-old daughter. One day, the princess was walking in the garden with her maid when she saw an unfamiliar plant. And, curious, she asked: 'What's that?' 'A clump of fennel, your Highness.' 'Let's look after it, to see how it grows', said the princess. On another day, the maid found a louse. And the princess suggested: 'Let's look after it, to see how it grows.' And they put it in a jar. Time passed. The shrub became a tree and the louse became so fat that after nine months it no longer fitted in the jar. Having talked to his daughter, the king made it public that the princess was of marrying age, but that she would only marry the cleverest man in the land. In order to test this he thought of making a tambourine with the skin of the louse, making the frame from fennel wood. Then he ordered that the announcement be placed on the corner of every house in the land, saying: 'The princess will marry whoever guesses what the tambourine is made of. All suitors will be given three days to guess this. Whoever doesn't succeed during this time will be put to death.'

Counts, dukes and marquises, as well as rich young men, came to the palace, because they wanted to marry the princess, but none of them guessed what the tambourine was made of and they all died on the third day. A shepherd, who had read the announcement, said to his mother: 'Pack my bags, because I'm going to try my luck. I know the skins of all the creatures of the field and the wood of all the trees in the forest.' After arguing for a while with his mother, who was afraid that the same thing would happen to him as had happened to so many other of the princess' suitors, the shepherd managed to convince her and set off for the court. On the outskirts of a village he met a giant who was holding up a boulder as large as a mountain and asked him: 'What are you doing there, friend?' 'I'm holding up this pebble so that it doesn't fall and destroy the village.' 'What's your name?' 'Hercules.' 'You'd be better off leaving that and

esta piedrecita para que no caiga y destroce el pueblo.' 'Cómo te llamas?' 'Hércules.' 'Mejor dejas eso y te vienes conmigo; llevo un negocio entre manos y si me sale bien algo te tocará a ti. ¡Anda, ven!' Hércules echó a rodar la piedra en dirección contraria al pueblo, arrasando los bosques en una extensión de cinco kilómetros, y se marcho con el pastor.

Llegaron a otro pueblo y vieron a un hombre que apuntaba con una escopeta al cielo. '¿Qué haces ahí?' preguntóle el pastor. Y el cazador contestó: 'Encima dc aquella nube vuela una bandada de gavilanes. Por cada uno que mato me dan diez céntimos.' '¿Cómo te llamas?' 'Bala-Certera.' 'Mejor dejas eso y te vienes con nosotros; llevo un negocio entre manos y si me sale bien algo te tocará a ti. Anda, vente con nosotros.' Y Bala-Certera se unió al pastor y a Hércules.

A la salida de otro pueblo vieron junto al camino a un hombre que estaba con el oido pegado al suelo. El pastor le preguntó: 'Qué haces ahí?' 'Oigo crecer la hierba.' '¿Cómo te llamas?' 'Oídos-Finos.' 'Vente con nosotros; con esos oídois puedes prestarnos buenos servicios.' Y Oídos-Finos se marchó con el pastor, Hércules y Bala-Certera.

Llevaban andando un buen rato, cuando vieron a un hombre atado a un árbol, con sendas ruedas de molino a los pies. El pastor le preguntó: '¿Qué haces aquí?' 'He hecho que me aten, porque suelto me corro el mundo entero en un minuto.' '¿Cómo te llamas?' 'Veloz-como-el-Rayo.' 'Ya somos cuatro' dijo el pastor. 'No admitimos más socios. Vendrás con nosotros.' Desataron a Veloz-como-el-Rayo y éste dijo a sus compañeros que se colocaran sobre las ruedas de molino, asegurándoles que los conduciría adonde quisieran ir con la velocidad del rayo.

Mientras se colocaban todos, acercóse una hormiga que dijo: 'Pastor, llévame en el zurrón.' 'No quiéro, porque vas a picotear la tortilla que llevo para la merienda.' 'Llévame contigo, pastor, que tengo de prestarte buenos servicios.' El pastor metió la hormiga en el zurrón y en esto se acerca un escarabajo que le

coming with me; I have some business in hand and if it works out well you can have your share. Come on, come with me!' Hercules sent the stone rolling away from the village, flattening the woods for five kilometres around, and set off with the shepherd.

They came to another village and saw another man who was aiming a rifle at the sky. 'What are you doing there?' asked the shepherd. And the huntsman answered: 'A flock of sparrowhawks is flying above that cloud. They'll give me ten cents for every one I kill.' 'What's your name?' 'Sure-Shot.' 'You'd be better off leaving that and coming with us; I have some business in hand and if it works out well you can have your share. Come on, come with us.' And Sure-Shot joined the shepherd and Hercules.

As they were leaving another village they saw a man by the side of the road, his ear pressed to the ground. The shepherd asked him: 'What are you doing there?' 'I'm listening to the grass grow.' 'What's your name?' 'Sharp-Ears.' 'Come with us; with your hearing you can be of excellent service to us.' And Sharp-Ears set off with the shepherd, Hercules and Sure-Shot.

They had been walking for a good while, when they saw a man tied to a tree, with the wheels of a mill tied to his feet. The shepherd asked him: 'What are you doing there?' 'I've made them tie me up, because when I'm free I run around the whole world in a minute.' 'What's your name?' 'Swift-as-the-Wind.' 'Now we're four', said the shepherd. 'We won't take on more companions. You'ill come with us.' They untied Swift-as-the-Wind and he told his companions to sit on the mill wheels, promising to take them wherever they wanted to go with in a flash.

As they sat down, an ant approached and said: 'Shepherd, take me in your pouch.' 'No, because you'll eat the omelette that I've brought for my tea.' 'Take me with you, shepherd, because I'll be of good service to you.' The shepherd placed the ant in his pouch and then a beetle approached and said: 'Shepherd, take me in your pouch.' 'No, because you'll spoil an omelette that I have for tea.'

dice. 'Pastor, llévame en el zurrón.' 'No quiero, porque vas a estropearme una tortilla que llevo para la merienda.' 'Llévame, hombre, que tengo de prestarte buenos servicios.' El pastor metió el escarabajo en el zurrón, y en esto se acerca un ratón que le dice: 'Pastor, llévame en el zurrón.' 'No quiero que estropees la tortilla que llevo para la merienda.' 'No te la estropearé, que anoche llovió y tengo el hocico limpio. Llévame contigo, que tengo de prestarte buenos servicios.' El pastor lo metió en el zurrón.

Emprendieron todos la marcha montados en las ruedas de molino y sin darse cuenta llegaron a palacio. Alojáronse todos en un mesón que había frente al palacio, donde el pastor dejó a Hércules, a Bala-Certera, a Oídos-finos y a Veloz-como-el-Rayo, para ir a ver a la princesa. Cuando le enseñaron el pandero, dijo: 'Esto es de piel de cabrito y madera de cornicabra.' 'Te has equivocado' dijo el rey. 'Tienes tres días para pensarlo. Si no lo aciertas, morirás.' El pastor, desconsolado, volvió al mesón, y Oídos-Finos, el que oía crecer la hierba, le preguntó la causa de su tristeza. Contóle el pastor lo ocurrido y Oídos-Finos dijo: 'No te aflijas. Averiguaré lo que te interesa saber y te lo diré.'

Al día siguiente, se marchó al jardín donde paseaba la princesa con su doncella. Pegó el oído al suelo y oyó decir a la doncella: '¿No es lástima ver cómo matan a vuestros pretendientes, Alteza?' 'Sí, desde luego; pero estarán muriendo hasta que alguno acierte que el pandero está hecho de piel de piojo y madera de hinojo.' 'No lo acertará nadie.' Oídos-Finos no esperó más; volvió corriendo al mesón. 'Ya sé de qué es la piel del pandero' dijo a sus compañeros. 'De piel de piojo y madera de hinojo. Acabo de oírselo a la doncella de la princesa.'

Lleno de alegría, el pastor se dirigió a palacio y pidió ver al rey. El monarca le dijo: '¿No sabes que el que no acierta la segunda vez de qué es la piel del pandero, tiene pena de la vida?' 'Sí que lo sé, Majestad. Venga el pandero.' El pastor cogió el pandero, lo miró un momento y dijo: 'La piel de este pandero es de un animal que se mata así.' Y al decir esto, apretó una contra otra las uñas

'Take me with you, because I'll be of good service to you.' The shepherd placed the beetle in his pouch, and then a mouse approached and said: 'Shepherd, take me in your pouch.' 'I don't want you to spoil the omelette that I have for tea.' 'I won't spoil it, because it rained last night and my snout is clean. Take me with you, because I'll be of good service to you.' The shepherd put him in the pouch.

They all set off mounted on the mill wheels and before they knew it they were at the palace. They took up lodgings at an inn opposite the palace, where the shepherd left Hercules, Sure-Shot, Sharp-Ears and Swift-as-the-Wind, to go and see the princess. When they showed him the tambourine, he said: 'It's made of kid leather and the wood of goat's horn.' 'You're wrong', said the king. 'You have three days to think about it. If you don't guess correctly, you'll die.' The shepherd went back to the inn distraught, and Sharp-Ears, who could hear the grass grow, asked him why he was sad. The shepherd told him what had happened and Sharp-Ears said: 'Don't worry. I'll find out what you want to know and tell you.'

The following day, he went to the garden where the princess and her maid walked. He placed his ear to the ground and heard the maid say: 'Isn't it a shame to see how they're killing your suitors, your Highness?' 'Yes, of course; but they'll carry on dying until someone guesses that the tambourine is made of louse skin and fennel wood.' 'No-one will guess it.' Sharp-Ears didn't wait any longer; he ran back to the inn. 'I know what the skin of the tambourine is', he said to his companions. 'It's made of louse skin and the wood of fennel. I've just heard the princess' maid say so.'

The shepherd set off for the palace full of joy and asked to see the king. The monarch said: 'Don't you know that whoever doesn't guess correctly the second time what the skin of the tambourine, must pay with his life?' 'Yes I do know, your Majesty. Show me the tambourine.' The shepherd took the tambourine, looked at it for a moment and said: 'The skin of this tambourine is from an animal that you kill thus.' And saying this he squeezed his thumbnails

de sus pulgares. El rey miró para su hija. Y ésta preguntó al pastor: '¿De qué es la piel? Dilo pronto.' '¿De qué es la piel? ¡Ja, ja ja! La piel es de piojo.' 'Acertaste' dijo el rey.

El monarca reunió acto seguido a la Corte, para anunciar que el pastor había acertado y que se casaría con la princesa; pero ésta dijo que con un pastor no se casaba de ninguna manera. 'Un rey' dijo su padre 'no tiene más que una palabra. Tienes que casarte.' 'Bien' respondió la muchacha. 'Lo haré cuando me cumple tres condiciones: la primera es que me traiga antes de que se ponga el sol una botella de agua de la Fuente Blanca . . .' '¡Pero hija mía! La Fuente Blanca está a cien leguas de aquí.' 'Ya lo sé. No podrá hacerlo; pero por si acaso habrá de realizar otras dos pruebas: separar en una noche un montón de diez fanegas de maíz, poniendo a un lado el bueno, al otro el mediano y al otro el malo; y luego habrá de llevar en un solo viaje dos arcones llenos de onzas de oro desde el palacio al pabellón de caza.'

Marchóse el pastor a la posada, tan afligido como el día anterior, y refirió a sus compañeros las condiciones que, para casarse, le imponía la princesa. Veloz-como-el-Rayo, el que corría el mundo entero en un minuto, dijo: 'Por la botella de agua de la Fuente Blanca, que está a cien leguas de aquí, no te apures. Dame una botella y la traeré llena de agua en un abrir y cerrar de ojos.' En un santiamén regresó con la botella de agua. Hércules afirmó: 'Los arcones los transportaré yo, a donde quieras.' Y la hormiga asomó la cabecita por un agujero del zurrón y añadió: 'Llévame a la habitación donde está el maíz y te lo separaré en una noche.'

Al poco rato se presentó el pastor en palacio con la botella de agua y la hormiga en el bolsillo. Entregó la botella y pidió que le pusieran una cama en la habitación del maíz, ya que le sobraría tiempo para dormir. A la mañana siguiente, mientras el rey y la princesa estaban viendo el maíz, ya separado en tres montones, fue Hércules y trasladó los dos arcones al pabellón de caza. Pero la princesita se puso muy rabiosa y afirmó que no se casaría con el pastor

together. The king looked at his daughter. And she asked the shepherd: 'What's the skin? Speak now.' 'What's the skin? Ha, ha, ha! It's louse skin.' 'You're right', said the king.

The king immediately called the Court together, to announce that the shepherd had guessed correctly and that he would marry the princess; but she said that she would not marry a shepherd on any account. 'A king', said her father, 'must keep his word. You must marry.' 'Very well', answered the girl. 'I will do so on three conditions: first that he brings me a bottle of water from the Pure Spring before sunset . . .' 'But, my dear daughter! The Pure Spring is a hundred leagues from here.' 'I know. He won't be able to do it; but in case he does he must pass two other tests: he must separate out ten bushels of maize in one night, putting the good maize in one place, the mediocre in another and the bad elsewhere; then he must carry two chests full of gold bars from the palace to the hunting lodge in one journey.'

The shepherd went to his lodgings, as unhappy as the previous day, and he told his companions the conditions that the princess had set on their marriage. Swift-as-the-Wind, who could run around the world in a minute, said: 'Don't worry about the bottle of water from the Pure Spring, which is a hundred leagues from here. Give me a bottle and I'll bring it back full of water in the blink of an eye.' In a thrice he returned with the bottle of water. Hercules assured: 'I'll carry the chests to wherever you want.' And the ant stuck its head out from a hole in the pouch and added: 'Take me to the room where the maize is and I'll separate it in one night.'

A short time later the shepherd went to the palace with the bottle of water and with the ant in his pocket. He handed over the bottle and asked them to put a bed in the room with the maize, because he'd have plenty of time to sleep. The following morning, while the king and princess were inspecting the maize, now separated into three heaps, Hercules went and carried the two chests to the hunting lodge. But the little princess became very angry and said that she

aunque la mataran, presentando a la corte inmediatamente como su futuro esposo a un príncipe vecino muy guapo y arrogante. El pastor, compungido, abandonó el palacio. Una vez en la posada, contó a sus compañeros lo que había ocurrido, a lo cual dijo el ratón, asmoando el hociquito por un bolsillo: 'El día de la boda, el escarabajo y yo te vengaremos.'

Llegó el día de la boda. El pastor se presentó en palacio y dejó el ratón y el escarabajo en la habitación destinada al novio, marchándose luego a la posada a esperar los acontecimientos. Cuando el novio entró a acicalarse para la ceremonia, el ratón se le metió en el bolsillo de la casaca, mientras que el escarabajo se escondía en una de las amplias solapas. Fueron los novios hacia el altar, acompañados de los padrinos, entre nutrida y escogida concurrencia. Cuando el sacerdote preguntó al novio si aceptaba por esposa a la princesa, el escarabajo, de un salto, se le metió en la boca, con lo que el infeliz no pudo pronunciar palabra, sino que sintió una angustia horrible. Entretanto, el ratón salió del bolsillo y se metió por entre las ropas de la princesa, dándola un mordisco tan atroz en la rodilla que por poco se muere del susto. Novio y novia echaron a correr como locos hacia la puerta del templo, seguidos de los invitados, que no sabían lo que les pasaba.

Cuando hubieron regresado a palacio, el novio abrió la boca para excusar su conducta, pero el escarabajo se agitó de nuevo y tuvo que cerrarla más que de prisa, mientras que el ratón propinó a la princesa un nuevo mordisco y la obligó a refugiarse en su habitación para huir de lo que todavía ignoraba lo que era. Sola en su alcoba, la princesa se quitó el traje de novia y empezó a sollozar. 'Princesita,' dijo el ratón 'no descansarás un instante hasta que rompas con el príncipe y te cases con el pastor.' '¿Quién me está hablando?' preguntó la princesa espantada. 'La voz de tu propia conciencia' aseguró el simpático roedor.

Entretanto, el príncipe se esforzaba en matar el escarabajo haciendo gárgaras; pero el bicho se le metía en las narices hasta que pasaba el chaparrón, consiguiendo que estornudara sin parar, con tal fuerza que se daba con la

wouldn't marry the shepherd even if they killed her, and introduced a very handsome and arrogant neighbouring prince to the court as her future husband. The shepherd left the palace indignantly. When he was back in his lodgings, he told his companions what had happened, to which the mouse, sticking its snout out of a pocket, said: 'The day of the wedding, the beetle and I will avenge you.'

The day of the wedding arrived. The shepherd went to the palace and left the mouse and the beetle in the room assigned to the groom, and then returned to his lodgings to wait for things to develop. When the groom entered to prepare himself for the ceremony, the mouse jumped into his coat pocket, while the beetle hid himself in one of the large lapels. The bride and groom, accompanied by their best man and maid of honour, approached the altar through the large and select congregation. When the priest asked the groom if he accepted the princess as his wife, the beetle leapt into his mouth, so that the poor man couldn't say a word, but felt terribly sick. In the meantime, the mouse came out of the pocket and went into the princess's clothes, biting her so hard on the knee that she almost died of fright. Bride and groom began to run like madmen towards the church door, followed by the guests who didn't know what was happening.

When they returned to the palace, the groom opened his mouth to apologize for his behaviour, but the beetle moved again and he had to shut his mouth very quickly, while the mouse bit the princess again and forced her to retire to her room to flee from what she still couldn't see. Alone in her bedroom, the princess took off her bridal gown and began to sob. 'Princess', said the mouse, 'you won't rest for an instant until you break off your engagement with the prince and marry the shepherd.' 'Who's speaking?' asked the frightened princess. 'The voice of your conscience', said the kindly rodent.

Meanwhile, the prince was trying to kill the beetle by gargling; but the creature hid in his nose until the shower passed, making him sneeze continually, and with such force that he hit his head against the furniture. 'Aren't you going to leave me in peace, you wretched creature?' he roared angrily. 'I'll torment you

cabeza contra los muebles. '¿Es que no me vas a dejar tranquilo, miserable bicho?' rugió encolerizado. 'Hasta que no salgas de aquí te atormentaré sin cesar, día y noche.' El príncipe, al oír estas palabras, salió despavorido, no parando de correr hasta llegar a su reino. El escarabajo, cuando le vio cruzar el umbral de palacio se dejó caer y fue a reunirse con el ratón. 'Vamos en busca del pastor' dijo el ratón. 'Tengo la seguridad de que ahora la princesa se casará con él.' Fueron a la posada, contaron al pastor lo sucedido y cuando éste se presentó en palacio fue muy bien acogido por la princesa, que se colgó de su brazo y, acompañados por el rey y los altos dignatarios, volvieron a la iglesia, celebrándose la ceremonia con toda pompa y esplendor. Luego hubo un baile magnífico, en que bailaron Hércules, Veloz-como-el-Rayo y Oídos-Finos, mientras Bala-Certera se quedaba de centinela en la puerta de palacio. A medianoche, la madrina del príncipe desdeñado, una bruja horrible con muy malas intenciones, vino disfrazada de buho a matar al pastor, pero Bala-Certera, de un solo disparo, la envió al infierno.

Después del baile hubo un banquete monstruo, al que acudieron los reyes y los pastores de todos los países colindantes. Los compañeros del pastor se quedaron a vivir para siempre en palacio. Hércules, el gigante, fue nombrado mayordomo; Oídos-Finos, el que oía crecer la hierba, jefe de policía; Veloz-como-el-Rayo, el que corría el mundo en un minuto, correo real; y Bala-Certera, el cazador, capitán de la guardia. La hormiguita, el ratoncito y el escarabajo fueron debidamente recompensados. A la hormiguita le reservaron unos terrenos donde había toda clase de granos y golosinas apreciados por ella, y con el tiempo formó un pobladísimo hormiguero que todos los súbditos respetaban, pues se pregonó que se castigaría con la pena de muerte al que hollara aquel espacio. El ratoncito recibió un queso del tamaño de un pajar, para que hiciera en él su morada, prometiéndole otro igual cuando le hiciera goteras. El escarabajo recibió una hermosísima pelota de terciopelo verde y amarillo, con la que el

continually, day and night, until you leave here.' On hearing this, the prince fled, terrified, and didn't stop running until he reached his own realm. When he saw him cross the threshold of the palace the beetle dropped out of his mouth and went to join the mouse. 'Let's go and find the shepherd', said the mouse. 'I'm sure that the princess will marry him now.' They went to the inn, told the shepherd what had happened and when he went to the palace he was very well received by the princess who took his arm and, accompanied by the king and other dignitaries, they returned to the church and celebrated the ceremony with much pomp and splendour. Then there was a magnificent ball where Hercules, Swift-as-the-Wind and Sharp-Ears danced, while Sure-Shot stayed on guard at the palace gate. At midnight, the rejected prince's godmother, who was a horrible witch with evil intentions, came to kill the shepherd, disguised as an owl, but Sure-Shot sent her to hell with one bullet.

After the ball there was a huge banquet, attended by all the kings and shepherds from the neighbouring lands. The shepherd's companions stayed to live in the palace forever. Hercules, the giant, was made butler; Sharp-Ears, who could hear the grass grow, was made chief of police; Swift-as-the-Wind, who could run around the world in a minute, was made the royal postman; and Sure-Shot, the huntsman, was made captain of the guard. The ant, the mouse and the beetle were duly rewarded. The ant was given some lands where there were all sorts of grains and other delicacies that it liked, and in time it made a well populated ant hill which all the king's subjects respected, because it was announced that anyone who defiled that place would be punished by death. The mouse was given a cheese as big as a loft, so that he could make his home it, and was promised another when there were holes in it. The beetle was given a very beautiful ball of green and yellow velvet, with which the clever little animal performed marvels, rolling it from one end to the other of the garden given exclusively to it.

And they all lived happily ever after. And reddish red, this story's ended.

avispado animalito hacía verdaderas maravillas, rodándola de un extremo a otro del trozo del jardín destinado a él exclusivamente.

Y todos vivieron felices. Y colorín, colorado, este cuento se ha acabado.

I. Luisa y el dragón

I. Luisa y el dragón [81]

Esto habían de ser tres hermanas muy pobres, que salieron en busca de casa donde servir. Llegaron a una y preguntaron si necesitaban tres criadas, contestándolas el ama: 'Sí, sí; necesitamos tres criadas, pues las tres que teníamos se han marchado esta mañana.' Y se quedaron, de cocinera, la una; de lavandera, la otra, y de peinadora, la más pequeña, llamada Luisa. Esta un día, peinando al ama, se dejó caer una lágrima, y el ama, al verla tan desconsolada, la preguntó que por qué lloraba. Luisa, que sabía que su ama tenía tres hijos mozos y todos guapos mancebos, la contestó: '*Miristé* (mire usted), ama, bien se podía casar su hijo mayor con mi hermana la cocinera.' '¡Ah!, se lo diremos a él, a ver lo que dice' dijo el ama. De modo es, que se lo dijeron al mozo, y contestó éste: 'Para que yo me case con tu hermana, me tienes que traer la *vacá* del dragón.' (El dragón era un terrible hombre que tenía atemorizada toda la comarca, porque se comía a todos los niños de los contornos.) 'Anda, sí, sí, la traigo' dijo Luisa.

De modo es que fue Luisa en busca del dragón. Tenía éste una hija llamada también Luisa, de la misma edad y muy parecida a ésta. La mujer del dragón, al ver a Luisa, se compadeció de ella y la dijo: 'Mal negocio traes. Te meteré debajo de la cama, para que mi marido no te vea, y guárdate este pelo, que te servirá de mucho.' Así lo hizo Luisa, y a media noche, mató a la hija del dragón, se puso sus ropas, salió de casa por la mañana temprano y se fue al campo en busca de la *vacá* del dragón, diciendo al vaquero: 'Que dice mi *paire* que vaya usted allá.' El vaquero, como creyó que efectivamente era la hija del dragón, se marchó a casa de éste y le preguntó qué le quería. 'Yo, nada. ¿Quién te ha mandado venir?' le dijo el dragón. 'Su hija la chica' dijo el vaquero, 'que ha ido a llamarme de parte de usted.' 'Ya estamos perdidos' dijo el dragón;

---

[81] Told by Mª Alfonsa García Gil from Madroñera in Cáceres. Curiel Merchán, *Cuentos extremeños*, 161-4.

I. Luisa and the Dragon

There were three very poor sisters, who went out to look for work as serving girls. They came to a house and asked if they needed three maids, and the lady of the house answered: 'Yes, yes; we need three maids, because the three that we had left this morning.' And so they stayed, one as the cook; one as the laundry woman; and the smallest, who was called Luisa, as the hairdresser. One day, as she was combing her mistress's hair, Luisa let a tear fall, and the mistress, seeing her so sad, asked why she was crying. Luisa, who knew that her mistress had three young sons and that all of them were handsome youths, answered: 'Look, mistress, your oldest son could easily marry my sister the cook.' 'Ah!, we'll mention it to him to see what he says', said her mistress. So they mentioned it to the youth, and he answered: 'If I'm to marry your sister, you must bring me the dragon's cow.' (The dragon was a terrible man who terrorized the whole neighbourhood, because he ate the children from all the lands around.) 'Yes, of course, I'll bring it to you', said Luisa.

So Luisa went in search of the dragon. He had a daughter who was also called Luisa, of the same age and similar appearance. Seeing Luisa, the dragon's wife felt sorry for her and said: 'You come on dangerous business. I'll put you under the bed so that my husband doesn't see you, and take this hair, which will be very useful to you.' Luisa did as she was told and, at midnight, she killed the dragon's daughter, put on her clothes, left the house early in the morning and went to the fields in search of the dragon's cow, telling the cowherd: 'My father says that you should go and see him.' The cowherd, who believed that she really was the dragon's daughter, went to the house and the dragon asked him what he wanted. 'I don't want anything.' 'Who asked you to come?' said the dragon. 'Your youngest daughter', said the cowherd, 'who came to call me on your behalf.' 'We're all lost', said the dragon; 'my cow has been stolen.' He

'ya se llevó mi *vacá*.' Entró en la habitación, vio a su hija muerta y bramando de rabia se asomó al balcón por ver si veía a Luisa, para que le pagase lo que le había hecho; pero Luisa iba ya lejos con las vacas, y el dragón amenazándola con los puños, se conformó con decirla: 'Me mataste a mi hijita, te llevaste mi *vacá*, dejaste Luisota mala, que tú me las pagarás; déjate, que tú volverás.' 'Volveré o no; me cogerás o no' dijo Luisa, y siguió con sus vacas. Al llegar con ellas al río, echó Luisa al agua el pelo que la mujer del dragón la había dado, y se formó un puente por el que las vacas y ella pasaron; cuando ella hubo pasado se *esfarató* el puente. Llegó con las vacas a casa de su ama, la contó lo pasado, y el ama, al ver que la *vacá* del dragón valía tanto, dejó a su hijo casarse con la cocinera hermana de Luisa.

Pasó algún tiempo, y peinando un día a su ama, se dejó caer Luisa otra lágrima, y la señora la dijo que por qué lloraba. '*Miristé*, ama' dijo Luisa, 'lloro porque ya que se ha casado mi hermana mayor con su hijo mayor, ¿por qué no se casa mi hermana la mediana con vuestro hijo el mediano?' 'Se lo diremos a él' dijo el ama. 'Para que yo me case' dijo el mozo, 'me tienes que traer la *cabrá* del dragón.' No se asustó Luisa, porque ya conocía la casa del dragón y dónde estaba la *cabrá*. Así es que fue a ésta, y dijo al cabrero: 'Dice mi padre el dragón, que vaya usted allá.' Se presentó el cabrero al dragón, y extrañado éste de que hubiese dejado solas las cabras, le preguntó: '¿Quién te ha mandado venir aquí?' 'Su hija la chica' contestó el cabrero. 'Ya estamos perdidos, ya se llevó mi *cabrá*' dijo el dragón. Y cuando salía de casa, vio que Luisa iba pasando ya el río por el puente que había hecho como la vez anterior, y rabiando de disgusto, la dijo: 'Me mataste a mi hija, me robaste mi *vacá*, ahora te llevas mi *cabrá*, déjate, déjate, que tú volverás, y me las pagarás.' 'Volveré o no; me cogerás o no' dijo Luisa, y siguió con sus cabras. Al ver el ama que llegaba con aquella *cabrá* tan grande, se puso muy contenta y en seguida se celebró la boda de su hijo con la hermana mediana de Luisa.

entered into the bedroom, saw his dead daughter and, roaring with rage, he went out onto the balcony to see if he could see Luisa, to pay her back for what she had done; but Luisa was already a long way away with the cows and, threatening her with his fists, the dragon settled for saying: 'You killed my daughter, you took my cow, you left little Luisa in a bad state and you will pay for it; never mind, you'll be back.' 'I may or may not come back; you may or may not catch me', said Luisa and continued on her way with the cows. On arriving at the river with them Luisa threw the hair that the dragon's wife had given her into the water, and a bridge appeared for her and the cows to cross; when she had crossed, the bridge disappeared. She reached her mistress's house with the cows, told her what had happened and, seeing that the dragon's cow was so valuable, the mistress allowed her son to marry the cook who was Luisa's sister.

Some time passed, and while she was combing her mistress's hair one day, Luisa let another tear fall, and her mistress asked her why she was crying. 'Look, mistress', said Luisa, 'I'm crying because my oldest sister has married your oldest son, so why not have my middle sister marry your middle son?' 'We'll mention it to him', said her mistress. 'If I'm to marry', said the youth, 'you must bring me the dragon's goat.' Luisa was not afraid, because she already knew the dragon's house and knew where the goat was. So she went there, and said to the goatherd: 'My father the dragon says that you should go and see him.' The goatherd went to the dragon and, surprised that he had left the goats on their own, the dragon asked him: 'Who told you to come here?' 'Your youngest daughter', answered the goatherd. 'We're lost, because my goat has been stolen', said the dragon. And as he left the house, he saw Luisa crossing the river on the bridge that she had made in the same way as before, and frustrated with anger, he said: 'You killed my daughter, you stole my cow, and now you're taking my goat; never mind, you'll be back and you'll pay for it.' 'I may or may not come back; you may or may not catch me', said Luisa, and continued on her way with

Cuando hacía ya medio año que la hermana mediana estaba ya casada, un día, peinando Luisa a su ama, se dejó caer una lágrima, y como las veces anteriores, la preguntó el ama que por qué lloraba, y contestó Luisa: '*Miristé*, ama, ya que se han casado mis dos hermanas, podía yo también casarme con su hijo el chico.' 'Se lo diremos a él' contestó el ama. 'Para que yo me case contigo' contestó el mozo, 'quiero que me traigas el puñal del dragón que habla.' 'Lo traeré' dijo Luisa.

Salió al palacio del dragón, y cuando estaban dormidos, entró por el balcón, se fue derecha a la cama donde dormían las hijas del dragón y mató a las dos. Luego fue a coger el puñal del dragón, pero como éste hablaba, empezó a gritar, diciendo: '¡Que me llevan, que me llevan!' Despertó el dragón a las voces y dijo: '¿Quién anda por ahí?' 'Aquí no hay nadie más que nosotros' dijo la mujer. Cuando Luisa vio que el dragón y su mujer estaban otra vez dormidos, cogió de nuevo el puñal; pero éste volvió a gritar: '¡Que me llevan, que me llevan!' El dragón entonces dijo: 'Sí, sí, aquí anda alguien.' Encendió la luz y vio a Luisa, más muerta que viva, a quien dijo: '¿No decías que no te iba a coger nunca? Pues ya te cogí. Ahora voy a llamar a mis amigos para comerte en *frite*.' La ató bien atada, mandó a su mujer que pusiera una caldera de aceite a calentar, y cuando estuvo puesta, fue la mujer a ver a Luisa. Al verla ésta, la dijo: '*Miristé, miristé*, qué piojo más gordo la va por la carrera; me desate usted estos dos dedos que se lo quite.' La desató los dos dedos, y Luisa se desató toda la mano, agarró del pelo a la pobre mujer del dragón, la entró en la caldera, la tapó, cogió el puñal y se marchó. Cuando iba por el camino, se asomó el dragón, la vio con el puñal y la dijo: 'Me matastes mis hijitas, te llevaste mi *vacá*, me robaste mi *cabrá*, me mataste mi mujer, y te llevaste mi puñal; déjalo, déjalo, que tú me las pagarás.' 'Ya no te las pago, porque no vuelvo más' dijo Luisa. Llegó Luisa con el puñal a casa del ama y se casó con su hijo.

Estaban todos tan contentos, cuando un día se presentó el dragón en el pueblo donde Luisa y sus hermanas vivían. Luisa le conoció en seguida, y como

the goat. Seeing that she had such a large goat, her mistress was very happy and her son's marriage with Luisa's middle sister took place straight away.

When the middle sister had been married for half a year, one day, when she was combing her mistress's hair, Luisa let a tear fall and, as on the other occasions, her mistress asked her why she was crying, and Luisa answered: 'Look, mistress, now that my two sisters are now married, I too could marry your youngest son.' 'We'll mention it to him', answered her mistress. 'If I'm to marry you', answered the youth, 'I want you to bring me the dragon's talking knife. 'I'll bring it to you', said Luisa.

She left for the dragon's palace, and when they were asleep, she entered via the balcony, went straight to the bed where the dragon's daughters slept and killed them both. Then she went to steal the dragon's knife, but since it talked, it began to shout, saying: 'They're stealing me, they're stealing me!' The dragon was woken by the shouts and said: 'Who's there?' 'There's no-one here but us', said his wife. When Luisa saw that the dragon and his wife were asleep once more, she grabbed the knife again; but it began to shout again: 'They're stealing me, they're stealing me!' Then the dragon said: 'Yes, there's someone here.' He put on the light and saw Luisa, who was more dead than alive, and said to her: 'Didn't you say that I'd never catch you? Well I've caught you. Now I'm going to call my friends to fry you and eat you up.' He tied her well, ordered his wife to heat a cauldron of oil, and when this was done, his wife went to see Luisa. On seeing her, Luisa said: 'Look, look: an enormous louse is crawling across your face; untie these two fingers so that I can flick it off.' She untied two fingers, and Luisa freed her whole hand, grabbed the poor dragon's wife by the hair, threw her into the cauldron, covered it, snatched the knife and left. On her way home, the dragon appeared, saw her with his knife and said: 'You killed my daughters, you took my cow, you stole my goat, you killed my wife, and you took my knife; never mind, you'll pay for it.' 'I won't pay for it, because I'll never come back',

era lista, fue a contárselo a sus hermanas. Casualmente había muerto un hombre muy alto, casi un gigante, y para probar si le estaría bien la caja que le habían hecho, rogaron al dragón que se entrase en ella, pues era de alto igual que el muerto. Cuando el dragón estuvo dentro, taparon la caja, hicieron con ella una hoguera y la quemaron, muriendo dentro el *infeliz* dragón, víctima de la listeza y poca bondad de Luisa.

said Luisa. She arrived at her mistress's house with the knife and married her son.

They were all very happy, when one day the dragon came to the village where Luisa and her sisters lived. Luisa recognized him straight away, and since she was clever, went to tell her sisters. By chance a very tall man, who was almost a giant, had just died, and to test whether his coffin was big enough, they asked the dragon to climb inside, because he was as tall as the dead man. As soon as the dragon was inside they covered the coffin, made a bonfire and burnt it, killing the wretched dragon, who was the victim of Luisa's cleverness and little kindness.

J. La princesa encantada [82]

Era un pescador y tenía un hijo. Y no le quería dejar ir a pescar con el. Y el chico daba guerra porque quería ir con su padre. Y un día su madre le soltó al chico para que fuera con su padre, y se marchó. Y al llegar al río, extendieron la rede para pescar y vieron una trucha. Y le dijo el hijo al padre que si quería que se metiera por ella. Y el padre le dijo que bueno que se metiera. Y ei chico se metió y fue detrás de la trucha. Y la trucha se metió en un hoyo, y el chico detrás de ella. Y cayó el chico a un jardín. Y en el jardín vio un hermoso palacio. Entró el chico por una puerta y, al entrar, vio una habitación que tenía en la puerta un letrero que decía: 'Caliéntate, que pa ti está puesto.' El chico entró y se calentó. Y dice: 'Voy a ver qué hay allí más alante.'

Y se marchó a otra habitación. Y en la puerta había otro letrero que decía: 'Come, que pa ti está puesto.' Y entró y comió el chico. Y después de comer se marchó a otra habitación. Y miró otro letrero que decía: 'Bebe, que pa ti está puesto.' Y después de beber se fue a otra habitación. Y en la puerta había otro letrero que decía: 'Vístete, que pa ti está puesto.' Y entró y se vistió. Y después de vestirse se marchó a otra habitación que tenía en la puerta un letrero que decía: 'Duerme, que pa ti está puesto.' Y el chico entró y se echó a dormir.

Y le despertó una princesa encantada, y le dijo: '¡Márchate, que aquí hay un gigante, que cuando venga, te matará!' Y el chico la dijo: '¿Qué haría yo a ti para salvarte?' 'No puede ser' dice 'porque tendrás que ir al Monte Sinaí, y allí tendrás que coger una serpiente; la tendrás que abrir, y saldrá una corza corriendo; la cogerás, la tendrás que abrir, y saldrá una paloma blanca volando; la cogerás, la abrirás, saldrá un huevo de oro; y me le traerás, y esa es la salvación mía.'

---

[82] From Vega de Valdetronico in Valladolid. Espinosa (hijo), *Cuentos populares de Castilla*, 99-105.

J. The Enchanted Princess

There was a fisherman who had a son, and he didn't want his son to go fishing with him. But his son protested because he wanted to go with is father. So one day his mother allowed him to go with his father, and so he went. When they arrived at the river, they cast their net to fish and saw a trout. The son asked his father if he wanted him to dive in after the trout. The father said that he did want him to dive in. The son dived in and went after the trout. The trout swam into a hole and the lad followed. And the lad fell into a garden. There was a beautiful palace in the garden. The lad went in through the gate and, when he entered, he saw a room with a door which had a sign saying: 'Warm yourself, for this has been prepared for you.' The lad went in and warmed himself. And he said: 'I'm going to see what's further on.'

So he went to another room. And on the door there was another sign that said: 'Eat, for this has been prepared for you.' So the lad entered and ate. And after eating he went to another room. And he saw another sign that said: 'Drink, for this has been prepared for you.' And after drinking he went to another room. On the door there was another sign that said: 'Put on these clothes, for they have been prepared for you.' So he went in and got dressed. And after getting dressed he went to another room which had a sign on the door that said: 'Sleep, for this has been prepared for you.' So the lad went in and went to sleep. An enchanted princess woke him and said: 'Leave, because there's a giant here, and he'll kill you when he comes!' And the lad said to her: 'What should I do to save you?' 'It can't be done,' she answered, 'because you'll have to go to Mount Sinai and catch a serpent there; you must cut it open, and a doe will run out; you must catch it and cut it open, and a white dove will fly out; you must catch it and cut it open, and a golden egg will fall out; and to rescue me, you must bring it to me.'

Y el chico ya marchó de camino. Y al llegar a la mitaz del camino, se encontró con un león, un galgo, una aguilica y una hormiga. Y le dijeron que si les quería repartir una res muerta que tenían. Y les dijo que sí, que se lo haría. Cortó la cabeza de la res y se la dio a la hormiga, diciendo: 'Aquí tiene ustez esta cabeza para que no pase ustez frío este invierno y coma bien.' Y luego dice: 'Para el galgo, los huesos . . . Para el león, la carne magra . . . Para el águila, las tripas, para que vuele mejor.' Y terminó, y dijeron los animales que estaba bien. Y el chico se marchó otra vez de camino. Y cuando había andado una milla o así, le volvieron a llamar. La dijeron los otros animales al águila: 'Tú que aguantas más, que le alcanzas más pronto, ve a decirle que no le hemos dado las gracias, que se vuelva.'

Y cuando le alcanzó el águila, le dijo que se volviera, que no le habían dado las gracias, que les llamaría sinvergüenzas. Y el chico la contestó que era igual, que no se volvía. Y dijo el águila que sí, que se tenía que volver. Y ya volvió otra vez para atrás. Según iba por el camino, iba diciendo el chico: 'Ahora que han terminao con la res, empezarán conmigo.' Y iba con miedo. Y al llegar allí le dijo el león: 'No le hemos dado las gracias. Queremos darle algo en recompensa de lo que nos ha hecho. Yo, como león . . . ¡Tenga ustez un pelo!' Y se arrancó un pelo del hocico y se le dio. '¡Tenga ustez! Cuando diga ustez, '¡Dios y león!,' se vuelve ustez un león.' El galgo le dijo: '¡Tenga un pelo!' Se arrancó un pelo del hocico. 'Cuando diga usted, '¡Dios y galgo!,' se vuelve ustez un galgo.' Y el aguilica se arrancó una pluma y se la dio. 'Cuando diga ustez, '¡Dios y aguilica!,' se vuelve ustez un águila.' Y la hormiga le dijo: 'Yo no tengo nada que darle, pero le daré una patita aunque me quede cojita. Cuando diga, '¡Dios y hormiguica!,' se vuelve ustez una hormiguita.'

El chico les dio las gracias, se despidió de ellos y se fue otra vez de camino. Y cuando llegó al Monte Sinaí, dijo: '¡Dios y león!' Y se volvió un león. Y dijo: '¡Dios y hombre!' Y se volvió un hombre. Y dijo: '¡Dios y galgo!' Y se volvió un galgo. Y dijo: '¡Dios y hombre!' Y se volvió otra vez hombre. Y

So the lad set out. Half way there, he met a lion, a greyhound, a little eagle and an ant. They asked him to divide a dead cow between them, and said yes he'd do it. He cut off the cow's head and gave it to the ant, saying: 'Here's the head so that you're not cold in winter and you can eat well.' Then he says: 'The bones are for the greyhound . . ., the lean meat for the lion . . ., and the guts for the eagle, so that it can fly better.' He finished, and the animals said that they were pleased. The lad set out again, and when he'd walked a mile or so, they called out to him again. The other animals told the eagle: 'You're faster and can reach him first: tell him to come back so that we can thank him.'

When the eagle caught up with him, he told him to come back for them to thank him in case he thought them rude. The lad answered that it didn't matter, and that he'd not go back. But the eagle insisted that he must turn back. So he went back and, as he was walking, the lad said to himself: 'Now that they've finished off the cow, they'll start on me.' And he was afraid. When he arrived the lion said: 'We haven't thanked you. We'd like to give you something in return for what you've done. I, as a lion, . . . Here's one of my hairs.' He plucked a hair from his snout and gave it to him: 'Here you are! Whenever you say, 'Pray God, a lion!', you'll become a lion.' The greyhound said: 'Here's one of my hairs!' He plucked a hair from his snout and gave it to him. 'Whenever you say, 'Pray God, a greyhound!', you'll become a greyhound.' The eagle plucked out a feather and gave it to him. 'Whenever you say, 'Pray God, an eagle!', you'll become an eagle.' And the ant said: 'I have nothing to give you, but I'll give you one of my legs even though this will leave me lame. Whenever you say, 'Pray God, an ant!', you'll become an ant.

The youth thanked them, said goodbye and went on his way again. When he reached Mount Sinai, he said: 'Pray God, a lion!' And he became a lion. And then he said: 'Pray God, a man!' And he became a man. And then he said: 'Pray God, a greyhound!' And he became a greyhound. And then he said: Pray God, a man!' And he became a man again. And then he said: 'Pray God, an eagle!' And

dijo: '¡Dios y águila!' Y se volvió un águila. Dijo: '¡Dios y hombre!' Y se volvió otra vez un hombre. Y dijo: '¡Dios y hormiga!' Y se volvió una hormiga. Y dijo: '¡Dios y hombre!' Y se volvió otra vez un hombre. Y volvió a decir: '¡Dios y aguilica!' Y se volvió águila y se fue volando hasta el pueblo más próximo. Y al llegar allí dijo: '¡Dios y hombre!' Y se volvió otra vez un hombre.

Y fue a pedir posada en casa de un pastor. Y le preguntó el pastor que qué andaba haciendo por ahí. Y le dijo que se encontraba sin trabajo. Y le dijo el pastor si se quería poner a servir en su casa. Le contestó el chico que sí. Y le dijo el amo —el pastor— que no tenía que ir por el Monte Sinaí, que allí había una serpiente que le cogería y le mataría. Como era la que el buscaba, al dia siguiente se marchó al Monte Sinaí. Y al llegar al monte, metió las ovejas en la hierba verde. Y ya, cuando se llenaron la barriga las ovejas, las iba dirigiendo para casa. Y se encontró con la serpiente. Y dijo: '¡Dios y león!' Y se volvió un león. Y empezaron a luchar. Y ya rendidos, dice la serpiente:

> Si yo tuviera un pan caliente
> y una copa de aguardiente
> ¡yo te daría a ti la muerte,
> león valiente!

Y contestó el león:

> Si yo tuviera un pan caliente
> y una copa de aguardiente
> y el beso de una doncella
> ¡yo te daría a ti la muerte,
> serpiente fiera!

Y ya, cansados de estar luchando, cada uno se retiró a un lado. Y dijo: '¡Dios y hombre!' Y se convirtió otra vez en hombre. Y al llegar en casa del pastor le preguntó que dónde había estado con las ovejas. Y le dijo el chico que metía las ovejas entre el trigo — y comían la hierba y dejaban el trigo. Y ya, después de encerrarlas, se acostó.

he became an eagle. And then he said: 'Pray God, a man!' And he became a man
again. And then he said: 'Pray God, an ant!' And he became an ant. And then he
said: 'Pray God, a man!' And he became a man again. And then he said once:
'Pray God, an eagle!' And he became an eagle and flew to the nearest village.
When he arrived, he said: 'Pray God, a man!' And he became a man once more.

He asked for lodging in a shepherd's house, and the shepherd asked him
what he was doing there. He said that he had no work. The shepherd asked if he
would like to serve in his house, and the youth said that he would. His master,
the shepherd, told him that he should not go to Mount Sinai, because there was a
serpent there that would catch and eat him. Since this is what he was looking for,
he set off for Mount Sinai the following day. When he arrived at the mountain,
he released the sheep onto the green grass. When the sheep had filled their
stomachs, he began to drive them home, and came across the serpent. And he
said: 'Pray God, a lion!' And he became a lion. And they began to fight, and
when they were both worn out, the serpent said:

> 'If I had a warm loaf
> and a glass of eau-de-vie
> I would kill you,
> Brave lion!'

And the lion answered:

> 'If I had a warm loaf
> and a glass of eau-de-vie
> and the kiss of a maiden,
> I would kill you,
> Fierce serpent!'

And, tired from fighting so hard, each one withdrew. And he said: 'Pray God, a
man!' And he became a man once more. When he arrived home the shepherd
asked him where he'd been with the sheep. And the lad said that he'd taken the

Y ya al día siguiente por la mañana se fue otra vez al mismo sitio con las ovejas. Y el pastor tenía dos hijas. Y la dijo a una que se fuera detrás del chico a ver dónde las metía, que se escondiera entre los trigos y hierbas para que no la viera. Y después de estar por allí un rato el chico con las ovejas, ya se iba para casa cuando se encontró con la serpiente, y dijo: '¡Dios y león!' Se convirtió en león, y estuvieron luchando también como el día anterior. Y cansados ya de estar luchando, dijo la serpiente:

> Si yo tuviera un pan caliente
>
> y una copa de aguardiente
>
> ¡yo te daría a ti la muerte,
>
> león valiente!

Y contestó el león:

> Si yo tuviera un pan caliente
>
> y una copa de aguardiente
>
> y el beso de una doncella
>
> ¡yo te daría a ti la muerte,
>
> serpiente fiera!

Y ya, cansados de luchar, cada uno se retiró a un lado. Y dijo: '¡Dios y hombre!' Y se convirtió otra vez en hombre.

Y la chica, que lo estaba oyeno, fue corriendo y se lo contó a su padre, que el pastor que tenían se convertía en león y andaba peleando con la serpiente del Monte Sinaí, y que decía que:

> Si yo tuviera un pan caliente
>
> y una copa de aguardiente
>
> y el beso de una doncella
>
> ¡yo te daría a ti la muerte,
>
> serpiente fiera!

Y aquel día estaban cociendo y el padre la dijo a la hija: 'Pues, mañana, cuando estén en la pelea, vas, coge un pan de estos que estamos cociendo, le das a

sheep to the wheatfields, and that they ate the grass and left the wheat. Then, after locking them up, he went to bed.

The following morning he went to the same place again with the sheep. And the shepherd had two daughters. And he told one of them to follow the lad to see where he took the sheep, and that she should hide in the wheat and grass so that she wouldn't be seen. And when the lad had been there for some time with the sheep, he was on his way home when the serpent appeared again, and he said: 'Pray God, a lion!' He became a lion, and they fought again as on the previous day. And, tired of fighting so hard, the serpent said:

> 'If I had a warm loaf
> and a glass of eau-de-vie
> I would kill you,
> Brave lion!'

And the lion answered:

> 'If I had a warm loaf
> and a glass of eau-de-vie
> and the kiss of a maiden,
> I would kill you,
> Fierce serpent!'

And, tired of fighting, each one withdrew. And he said: 'Pray God, a man!' And he became a man once again.

The girl, who had been listening, ran home and told her father that their shepherd changed into a lion and fought with the Mount Sinai serpent and said:

> 'If I had a warm loaf
> and a glass of eau-de-vie
> and the kiss of a maiden,
> I would kill you,
> Fierce serpent!'

morder un cacho, le das una copa de aguardiente y le das tú un beso, a ver si es verdaz que la mata.'

Y al día siguiente vuelve el chico con las ovejas al Monte Sinaí. Y la chica se fue escondiendo entre los trigos. Cuando estaban otra vez en la pelea el león y la serpiente, dijo la serpiente:

> Si yo tuviera un pan caliente
>
> y una copa de aguardiente
>
> ¡yo te daría a ti la muerte,
>
> león valiente!

Y contestó el león:

> Si yo tuviera un pan caliente
>
> y una copa de aguardiente
>
> y el beso de una doncella
>
> ¡yo te daría a ti la muerte,
>
> serpiente fiera!

Llegó la chica por detrás, le dio a morder un cacho de pan caliente, la copa de aguardiente y le dio un beso. Y cayó la serpiente muerta. Y dijo entonces el león: '¡Dios y hombre!' Y se convirtió otra vez en hombre. Y dirigió a las ovejas hacia el pueblo. Y al llegar en casa del pastor le dijo: 'Me entrega ustez la cuenta, que yo mañana no puedo estar mas aquí . . ., que yo mañana me tengo que marchar a mi tierra.' Y le dijo el amo que no se fuera, que le casaría con la hija que más quisiera . . ., que le daría todas sus ovejas. Pero el chico le dijo que no podía ser. Y se marchó.

Y volvió al Monte Sinaí y abrió la serpiente, y salió una corza corriendo. Y dijo: '¡Dios y galgo!' Y se convirtió en galgo. Y, ¡venga a correr! . . . Y corrió detrás de ella hasta que la alcanzó. La cogió y la abrió, y salió una paloma blanca volando. Y dijo: '¡Dios y aguilica!' Y se convirtió en águila. Y empezó a volar detrás de la paloma hasta que la cogió y la abrió. Y la sacó un huevo de oro. Entonces empezó a volar hasta llegar al jardín donde había dejado a la princesa

That day they were baking and her father told the girl: 'Tomorrow, when they're fighting, take one of these loaves that we're baking and give him a piece, give him a glass of eau-de-vie and give him a kiss to see if he really does kill the serpent.'

The following day. the lad went back to Mount Sinai with the sheep, and the girl hid among the wheat. When the lion and the serpent were fighting once more, the serpent said:

> 'If I had a warm loaf
> and a glass of eau-de-vie
> I would kill you,
> brave lion!'

And the lion answered:

> 'If I had a warm loaf
> and a glass of eau-de-vie
> and the kiss of a maiden,
> I would kill you,
> Fierce serpent!'

The girl crept up behind him, gave him a piece of warm bread, a glass of eau-de-vie, and a kiss. And the serpent dropped down dead. Then the lion said: 'Pray God, a man!' And he became a man once more. And he drove the sheep back towards the village. And when he arrived at the shepherd's house, he said: 'Let's settle our accounts, because tomorrow I can't stay here any longer . . ., because tomorrow I must return home.' His master told him not to go and said that he could marry whichever of his daughters he preferred . . ., that he would give him all his sheep. But the lad said that it was impossible, and he left.

He went back to Mount Sinai and opened the serpent, and a doe ran out. He said: 'Pray God, a greyhound!' And he turned into a greyhound. What a chase! He chased the doe until he caught it. He grabbed it and cut it open, and a white dove flew out. And he said: 'Pray God, an eagle!' And he became an eagle,

encantada. Al llegar a un árbol, se puso allí encima. Y la princesa encantada, que estaba allí, al verla, dijo que sería él, porque allí no había aves de ninguna clase.

Y se hizo de noche, y se entraron el gigante y la princesa encantada dentro a dormir. Y dijo: '¡Dios y hombre!' Y se convirtió en un hombre. Y dijo: '¡Dios y hormiguica!' Y se convirtió en una hormiga y entró por las randijas de la casa. Y al llegar a la cama de la princesa, dijo: '¡Dios y hombre!' Y se convirtió en hombre. Y dijo: '¡María!' que así se llamaba la princesa. La princesa se asustó y empezó a gritar. Se levantó el gigante y la dijo: '¡Si me vuelves a llamar, te mato!' Y cuando se marchó, volvió a decir el chico: 'María, ¿pero no me conoces?' Y volvió otra vez a gritar la princesa. Y se levantó otra vez el gigante. Y empezó a mirar por todos los sitios, pero el chico se había convertido otra vez en hormiga, y el gigante no le veía por ninguna parte. Y la volvió a decir: '¡Si me vuelves a llamar, te corto el pescuezo!' Y se volvió a acostar otra vez el gigante. Y el chico dijo: '¡Dios y hombre!' Y se convirtió en hombre, y la dijo a la princesa: 'Pero María, ¿no me conoces? Si soy aquel del huevo de oro, que me encargaste que te le trajese.' Y dice la princesa: '¡Ah, sí! ¡Recuerdo!' Y dice: 'Mira: vas a subir allá arriba, y vas a mirar por aquella ventana. Si ves al gigante que está con los ojos abiertos, está dormido; si está con los ojos cerrados, está despierto. Y tienes que dejar caer el huevo sobre la frente. Si no le pegas en la frente, estamos perdidos los dos.'

Y el chico subió a la ventana y vio al gigante con los ojos abiertos. Y le dejó caer el huevo sobre la frente. Y el gigante dio un rugido y cayó muerto. Y el chico se lo fue a contar a la princesa, y la princesa dijo: 'Mañana saldremos de aquí y nos casaremos.'

Y así termina.

and began to fly after the dove until he caught it and cut it open. And he took out the golden egg. Then he began to fly until he reached the garden where he had left the enchanted princess. Coming to a tree, he perched there. When she saw the bird, the enchanted princess knew it was him because no birds ever came to that place.

Night came, and the giant and the enchanted princess went inside to sleep. And he said: 'Pray God, a man!' And he became a man. And then he said: 'Pray God, an ant!' And he turned into an ant an went in through the cracks in the house. When he came to the princess's bed, he said: 'Pray God, a man!' And he became a man. And he said: 'Maria!', because that was the princess's name. The princess was startled and began to shout. The giant got up and said to her: 'If you call for me again, I'll kill you!' And when he'd gone, the lad said again: 'Maria, don't you recognize me?' And the princess began to shout once more. The giant got up again and began to search everywhere, but the lad had turned himself into an ant again, and the giant couldn't see him anywhere. And again he said: 'If you call for me again, I'll slit your throat!' And the giant went back to bed. And the lad said: 'Pray God, a man!' And he became a man, and said to the princess: 'But, Maria, don't you recognize me? I'm the lad with the golden egg that you asked me to bring to you.' And the princess said: 'Ah, yes, I remember! Look, you must climb up there, and look through that window. If you see that the giant's eyes are open, he's asleep; if his eyes are closed, then he's awake. You must drop the egg on his forehead. If you don't hit him on his forehead, we're both doomed.' The lad climbed up to the window and saw that the giant's eyes were open, and he dropped the egg on his forehead. The giant gave a roar and dropped dead. The lad went to tell the princess, and she said: 'Tomorrow, we'll leave here and be married.'

And so it ends.

K. Las tres naranjas del amor [83]

Érase un príncipe que no se reía nunca. Y un día dijo una mujer: 'A este príncipe yo le haré reír y llorar.' Y la mujer se vistió con un traje de cacharros enhebrados en cuerdas, soltó el pelo sobre los hombros y, al son de un pandero, se puso a bailar frente al príncipe, que estaba asomado a un balcón de su palacio. Y bailaba dando grandes saltos, y en uno de estos rompiéronse las cuerdas que sostenían los cacharros y quedó desnuda en medio de la calle. Entonces el príncipe se rió de ella a carcajadas. La mujer no había contado con que le iba a caer el traje. Y cuando vio al príncipe reírse de ella, le dijo: 'Permita Dios que no se ría usted hasta que encuentre las tres naranjas del amor.' Desde entonces el príncipe comenzó a ponerse triste. Y un día dijo él: 'Necesito alegrarme y reír. Estoy dispuesto a ir a buscar las tres naranjas del amor adonde quiera que estén.'

Y marchó a buscarlas; iba a pie de pueblo en pueblo. Y una mañana se encontró con la mujer que le había echado la maldición, pero no la reconoció. '¿Adónde va?' le preguntó la mujer. 'A buscar las tres naranjas del amor.' 'Están muy lejos de aquí; están en una cueva, guardadas por tres perros. Camine usted hacia el norte y la encontrará en medio de un peñascal.' El príncipe compró tres panes y siguió andando. Y, por fin, llegó al peñascal donde estaba la cueva. Y cuando iba a entrar en ella, apareció a la puerta un perro refunfuñando. El píncipe le dio un pan y continuó su camino. A los pocos pasos plantóse delante de él otro perro; le dio un pan y le dejó pasar. Más allá salió el tercer perro. El príncipe le hizo el mismo regalo que a los otros dos y siguió adelante. Y mientras los perros se entretenían en comer los panes, llegó a una sala donde había una mesa de oro y encima de ella estaban tres cajas. Las cogió y echo a correr con ellas; cada caja contenía una naranja del amor.

---

[83] Llano Roza de Ampudia, *Cuentos asturianos*, 22-6.

K. The Three Oranges of Love

Once there was a prince who never laughed. One day a woman said: 'I'll make this prince laugh and cry.' And the woman put on a dress made of pots strung together, loosed her hair over her shoulders and, to the sound of a tambourine, she began to dance before the prince, who had gone out onto a balcony in his palace. She gave large leaps as she danced, and one of them made the strings that were holding the pots break, and she was left naked in the middle of the street. Then the prince roared with laughter at her. The woman hadn't bargained on her dress falling off, and when she saw the prince laughing at her, she said to him: 'May God not let you laugh until you find the three oranges of love.' From that moment the prince became sad, and one day he said: 'I must become happy and laugh. I'm prepared to go and search for the three oranges of love, wherever they may be.'

So he went to search for them; and walked from village to village. One morning he met the woman who had cursed him, but didn't recognize her. 'Where are you going?' asked the woman. 'In search of the three oranges of love.' 'They're a long way from here, in a cave guarded by three dogs. Head north and you'll find the cave in the middle of a rocky mountain.' The prince bought three loaves of bread and carried on his way. And, at last, he came to the mountain where the cave was. When he was about to go inside, a growling dog appeared. The prince gave it a loaf, and carried on. A few steps further on another dog appeared before him; he gave it a loaf and it let him pass. Further on the third dog appeared. The prince gave him the same reward as to the other two and carried on. While the dogs were busy eating the loaves, he came to a room with a golden table and on it were three boxes. He grabbed them and began to run; each box contained an orange of love.

Después de caminar algunas horas, sentóse bajo un fresno, y dijo: 'Voy a abrir una caja.' La abrió y dijo la naranja: '¡Agua, agua, que si no, me muero; agua, que me muero!' Y como el príncipe no tenía agua, la naranja murió. Emprendió de nuevo el camino y llegó a un mesón; allí pidió comida, una jarra de vino y otra de agua. Abrió la segunda caja, y dijo la naranja: '¡Agua, agua, que si no, me muero; agua, que me muero!' Y el príncipe, por coger la jarra de agua, cogió la de vino, lo echó en la caja y la naranja murió. Siguió andando, y al atravesar un monte encontró un río y allí abrió la tercera caja. Y dijo la naranja: '¡Agua, agua, que si no, me muero; agua, que me muero!' 'Por falta de agua' dijo el príncipe 'no te morirás.' Y metió la caja en el río. De pronto se formó sobre el agua un montón de espuma y por entre ella salió una princesa más guapa que el sol. El príncipe la llevó consigo y en el primer pueblo que encontró se casó con ella. Al año dio a luz a un hijo y esto aumentó la felicidad del matrimonio.

Y un día dijo el príncipe a su esposa: 'Vamos a ir a ver a mi familia; hace mucho tiempo que salí de casa, y desde entonces acá no he dado cuenta de mis actos al rey, mi padre.' Y se pusieron en camino, y cuando llegaron a la entrada de la ciudad donde vivía el padre del príncipe, este dijo a la princesa: 'Quédate aquí sentada al pie de este árbol, junto a esta fuente, mientras yo voy a comunicar al rey, mi padre, nuestra llegada. En seguida vuelvo por ti.' La princesa sentóse debajo del árbol, teniendo a su hijo dormido en el regazo. Entonces pasó por allí la mujer que había echado la maldición al príncipe. Y se acercó a la fuente para beber y vio reflejada en el agua una cara que resplandecía hermosura. La mujer se echó hacia atrás, y dijo: '¡Muy hermosa soy!' Volvió a acercarse a la fuente poco a poco y entonces la cara reflejada en el agua le pareció que resplandecía más que antes. Y otra vez se echó para atrás, repitiendo: 'Muy hermosa soy.' Se acercó por tercera vez a la fuente y entonces vio que la cara reflejada en el agua era la de la princesa, y le preguntó: '¿Qué hace usted aquí?' 'Estoy esperando al príncipe, mi marido.' '¡Qué niño más hermoso tiene usted! Tráigalo acá, yo tendré un rato por él para que usted descanse.' La princesa, aunque de mala gana,

After walking for a few hours, he sat under an ash tree, and said: 'I'll open a box.' He opened it and the orange said: 'Water, water, or I'll die!' Since the prince didn't have any water, the orange died. He set off on his way again and came to an inn: there he asked for food, one jug of wine and another of water. He opened the second box, and the orange said: 'Water, water, or I'll die!' Mistaking the jar of wine for the one of water, he poured its contents into the box and the orange died. He carried on his way, and while crossing the mountain he came to a river and opened the third box. And the orange said: 'Water, water, or I'll die; water, because I'm dying!' 'You won't die for want of water', said the prince, and put the box in the river. The water started to foam and a princess more lovely than the sun itself appeared. The prince took her with him and married her in the first village they came to. A year later she gave birth to a son and this made the couple even happier.

One day the prince said to his wife: 'Let's go and visit my family; it's been a long time since I left home, and I've not told my father the king about my adventures since that day.' So they set off and when they came to the gates of the city where the prince's father lived, the prince said to the princess: 'Sit here under this tree next to this fountain and wait while I go and tell the king, my father, that we've arrived. I'll come straight back for you.' The princess sat under the tree with her son asleep in her lap. Then the woman who had cursed the prince passed by. She went to the fountain to take a drink of water and saw a beautiful face reflected in it. The woman gave a start and said: 'How beautiful I am!' She slowly approached the fountain again and the face seemed even more beautiful than before. Again she gave a start and repeated: 'How beautiful I am.' She approached the fountain for a third time and then she realized that she was seeing the princess's face being reflected, and asked her: 'What are you doing here?' 'I'm waiting for the prince, my husband.' 'What a beautiful son you have! Bring him here, and I'll hold him for a while so that you can rest.' Although unwillingly, the princess let her have the child. Then the woman said 'What

le dio a tener el niño. Y después dijo la mujer: 'Qué pelo más bonito tiene usted, princesa; debe ser más fino que la seda; pero se le está despeinando.' Y, fingiendo que le iba a arreglar el moño, le clavó un alfiler en la cabeza y la princesa se convirtió en una paloma. La mujer, como era hechicera, tomó la figura de la princesa, puso el niño en el regazo y sentóse bajo el árbol a esperar al príncipe. Y cuando volvió dijo a la que creyó era su mujer: 'Parece que te encucntro algo desfigurada.' 'Tuvo la culpa el sol, que me ha tostado la cara, pero esto se quita en cuanto repose de las fatigas del viaje; ¡vámonos!' Y marcharon para el palacio real.

Al poco tiempo murió el rey y heredó el trono su hijo y la hechicera se encontró convertida en reina. Entre tanto, la paloma todas las mañanas volaba sobre la huerta del rey; posábase en un árbol a comer fruta y después decía:

'¡Hortelanero del rey!'

'¡Señora!'

'¿Qué hacen el rey y la reina mora?'

'Comer y beber y estar a la sombra.'

'Y el niño, ¿qué hace?'

'Unas veces canta y otras veces llora.'

'¡Pobrecita de su madre, que anda por el monte sola!'

Un día, el hortelanero le dijo al rey la conversación que tenía todas las mañanas con la paloma. Entonces el rey mandó cogerla para dársela al niño. Y cuando la cogieron, le reina quería matarla. El niño se entretenía jugando con la paloma. Y una tarde observó que no hacía más que rascarse la cabeza con una pata. Era que allí tenía un alfiler clavado. El niño se lo arrancó y la paloma convirtióse en reina. Entonces el niño comenzó a llorar y la reina le dijo: 'No llores, hijo mío, que yo soy tu madre.' Y cogió al niño y lo llenó de besos. En esto llegó el rey y se abrazó a la reina. Y ella le dijo cómo había sido encantada por la bruja a la orilla de la fuente. La bruja fue quemada en la plaza pública y los reyes vivieron felices.

beautiful hair you have, princess; it must be finer than silk; but it's coming undone.' And, pretending that she was going to rearrange her bun, she buried a hairpin in her head and the princess turned into a dove. Since she was a witch, the woman took the princess' form, took the child in her lap and sat under the tree to wait for the prince. When he came back he said to the woman he thought to be his wife: 'You look a little different.' 'It's because of the sun, which has burned my face, but that will soon go away once I've rested after our tiring journey; let's go!' And they headed for the royal palace.

Soon afterwards the king died and the prince inherited the throne and the witch found herself to be the queen. Meanwhile, the dove flew over the king's garden every day; it would perch on a tree to eat fruit and say:

> 'The king's gardener!'
>
> 'My lady!'
>
> 'What do the king and the Moorish queen do?'
>
> 'They eat and drink and stay in the shade.'
>
> 'And the child, what does it do?'
>
> 'Sometimes it sings and sometimes it cries.'
>
> 'Its poor mother wanders the mountains alone!'

One day, the gardener told the king about the conversation he had with the dove every morning. The king ordered that it be caught and given to his son. When they caught the bird, the queen wanted to kill it, but the child enjoyed playing with the dove, and one day he noticed that it was constantly scratching its head with a talon. That was where the hairpin was lodged. The child pulled it out and the dove became the queen. The child began to cry and the queen said: 'Don't cry, my son, because I'm your mother.' She took the child and smothered him with kisses. Then the king arrived and kissed the queen. She told him how the witch had cast a spell on her at the fountain, and the witch was burned in the public square and the monarchs lived happily ever after.

L. Los tres acertijos [84]

Una vez era un rey que tenía una hija muy lista. Y tan lista era, que su padre mandó publicar en un bando que su hija se casaría con el que le pusiera tres acertijos que ella no pudiera acertar. Iban y venían condes, marqueses y otros personajes a poner acertijos a la hija del rey, y todos los acertaba. Llegó esto a oídos de un pastor y le dijo a su madre: 'Prepáreme usted la merienda que voy a poner los tres acertijos a la hija del rey.' '¿Qué vas a poner tú acertijos, si eres hijo de un pastor, y además eres medio tonto? ¿No comprendes que te van a ahorcar?' El pastor se decidió a emprender el viaje. Y su madre le preparó para la merienda una torta envenenada con agua de sapos; prefería que su hijo se muriera por el camino, antes que el rey mandara ahorcarlo.

El pastor llevó consigo una perrina que se llamaba Adela, y como ladraba mucho, para que callara, le dio un pedazo de torta. Y en cuanto la comió, se cayó muerta. '¡Hola!' dijo el pastor. 'Veo que mi madre quiere más que yo muera envenenado que ahorcado.' Estaba el pastor echando sus cuentas, cuando en esto llegaron tres cuervos, comieron la perrina y se murieron. Y dijo él: 'Ya tengo un acertijo para la hija del rey:

> Torta mató a Adela,
>
> Adela mató a tres;
>
> adivíname lo que es.'

Continuó su camino y, al pasar por un monte nevado, encontró una liebre medio muerta de frío. La mató y sacó de su vientre dos lebratos, los cuales se comió asados, y dijo: 'Ya tengo otro acertijo para la hija del rey:

> Comí carne asada;
>
> no nacida,
>
> pero sí engendrada.'

---

[84] Llano Roza de Ampudia, *Cuentos asturianos*, 219-22.

L. The Three Riddles

Once, there was a king that had a very clever daughter. She was so clever, that her father ordered it to be proclaimed that his daughter would marry the man who could set her three riddles that she could not solve. Counts, marquises and other nobles came and went, setting riddles to the king's daughter, but she solved them all. A shepherd heard of this and said to his mother: 'Prepare some food for me because I am going to set three riddles to the king's daughter.' 'What business is it of yours to set her riddles, being the son of a shepherd, and an idiot to boot? Don't you realize that they will hang you?' But the shepherd decided to take the trip. His mother prepared a cake poisoned with toad's water for him, because she preferred for her son to die on the way, rather than be hanged by order of the king.

The shepherd took a small dog called Adela with him and, because she barked a lot, he gave her a piece of cake to keep her quiet. No sooner had she eaten it than she fell down dead. 'Well!' said the shepherd. 'I see that my mother prefers for me to be poisoned than hanged.' The shepherd was deep in thought when three ravens arrived, ate the dog and died. And he said: 'I now have one riddle for the king's daughter:

> 'A cake killed Adela,
>
> Adela killed three;
>
> Guess what this may be.'

He continued on his way and, going through a snowy mountain, he found a hare half dead of cold. He killed it and drew two leverets from its womb, which he then roasted and ate, and said: 'Now I have another riddle for the king's daughter:

Siguió caminando y, cuando oscureció, refugióse en una capillina que encontró en lo alto del monte. La carne asada le había dado mucha sed y no tenía agua para beber. Y se fijo en la lámpara que alumbraba las ánimas, y bebió el agua que estaba debajo del aceite, y dijo: 'Otro acertijo para la hija del rey:

Bebí agua que no estaba

ni en el cielo ni en la tierra.'

Ya tengo los tres acertijos. Llegó el pastor al palacio real y, cuando le tocó su turno, le dijo la hija del rey: 'Ahora te toca a ti, pastor. Puede ser que traigas unos acertijos muy guapos. A ver cómo es el primero.' Y dijo el pastor: 'El primero es éste:

Torta mató a Adela,

Adela mató a tres;

adivíname lo que es.'

La hija del rey estuvo discurriendo mucho tiempo y acabó por decir que no entendía el significado del acertijo. Y dijo el pastor: '¡Va uno!' '¿Y cómo es el otro?' dijo la hija del rey. 'El otro es bien fácil de acertar:

Comí carne asada;

no nacida,

pero sí engendrada.'

'¡Qué acertijos más difíciles trae este pastor!' decía la hija del rey. Y ella discurrir, ella pensar en esto y en lo otro, y ¡nada!, no acertó. 'Van dos' dijo el pastor. 'A ver cómo es el último' dijo la hija del rey. 'El último es cosa fácil; veá usted:

Bebí agua que no estaba

ni en el cielo ni en la tierra.'

'Eso no puede ser.' 'Piénselo usted bien.' 'Está pensado; no acierto.' '¡Van tres! Me caso con usted.'

La hija del rey dijo a su padre que no se casaba con el pastor. Entonces el rey llamó a sus consejeros para consultarles el caso y ver de qué manera podrían

'I ate roast meat;

it wasn't born,

but had been begotten.'

He continued walking and, when night came, he took shelter in a little chapel that he found on top of the mountain. The roast meat had made him very thirsty and he didn't have any water to drink. And he noticed the lamp that burned for people's souls, and drank the water that was under the oil, and said: 'I have another riddle for the king's daughter:

'I drank water that was neither

in heaven nor on earth.'

I now have the three riddles. The shepherd arrived at the royal palace and, when his turn came, the king's daughter said: 'Now it's your turn, shepherd. You may have some very fine riddles. Let's hear the first one.' And the shepherd said: 'Here's the first one:

'A cake killed Adela,

Adela killed three;

Guess what this may be.'

The king's daughter thought long and hard and finally said that she did not understand the meaning of the riddle. And the shepherd said: 'That's one down!' 'What's the next one?' said the king's daughter. 'The next one is quite easy to guess:

I ate roast meat;

it wasn't born,

but had been begotten.'

'This shepherd's riddles are so difficult!' said the king's daughter. And she pondered, and she thought about this and about that, and no!, she could not guess what it meant. 'That's two down', said the shepherd. 'Let's see what the last one is', said the king's daughter. 'The last one is easy, you'll see:

deshacerse del pastor. 'Esto es fácil de arreglar' dijo un consejero. 'Decidle al pastor que para casarse con la princesa tiene que irse al monte a cuidar doce conejos sueltos durante un año, al cabo del cual ha de traerlos todos al palacio. Y esto es imposible, porque los conejos, en cuanto se vean sueltos, se escapan.' Al rey le pareció bien esta proposición y se la comunicó al pastor. El cual se decidió a coger los doce conejos y marchar con ellos para el monte. Pero en cuanto los soltó, ¡pies, para qué os quiero!, desaparecieron en seguida. El pastor se puso muy triste: el caso no era para menos; pero en esto pasó por allí una señora y le preguntó que qué hacía allí. El pastor le contó lo que le había ocurrido y le dijo la señora: 'Yo te sacaré dél apuro; toma esta varita, toca con ella en el suelo y dices: '¡Todos aquí, al pastor!'' Lo hizo así, y todos los conejos aparecicron a su lado. 'Estamos bien, dijo el pastor.'

Ya faltaban pocos días para terminar el año y dijo el rey: 'Al pastor no se le escapa ningún conejo; hay que ir allá a comprarle uno, cueste lo que cueste.' Y mandó a la doncella de su hija que fuera a comprarlo. Fue y le dijo al pastor: 'Vengo a que me vendas un conejo; se necesita para una medicina para la princesa. Pide por él lo que quieras.' Y dijo el pastor: 'Por dinero no lo vendo, porque aquí no tengo en qué gastarlo; pero le doy el conejo si me deja dormir con usted.' '¡Calla, desvergonzado!' 'Pues no hay conejo.' Y dijo la doncella: 'Acepto; pero cuidadito que lo digas a nadie.' La doncella se llevó el conejo y, cuando iba llegando al palacio, el pastor tocó el suelo con la vara y dijo: '¡Todos aquí, al pastor!' Y el conejo volvió para con los otros. Entró la doncella en el palacio y le preguntó la reina: '¿Trae usted el conejo?' 'No, señora; no me lo quiso vender; dice que no necesita dinero, que allí no tiene en qué gastarlo.' 'No sirve usted para nada'; dijo la reina 'mañana voy yo a ver al pastor.'

La reina fue allí y le ocurrió lo mismo que a la doncella. Y cuando volvió para el palacio le preguntó la princesa: '¿Trae usted el conejo, madre?' 'No, hija; ese pastor desprecia el dinero.' '¡Ah! Pues mañana voy yo allí y verá usted como

I drank water that was neither

in heaven nor on earth.'

'That can't be.' 'Think about it.' 'I have thought about it and I can't guess what it means.' 'That's the third! Now I may marry you.'

The king's daughter told her father that she would not marry the shepherd. Then the king called his advisers to discuss the matter with them and see how they could get rid of the shepherd. 'This is easy to arrange', said a counsellor. 'Tell the shepherd that to marry the princess he must go to the mountain to look after twelve loose rabbits for a year, at the end of which he has to bring them all to the palace. And this is impossible, because rabbits run away as soon as they are released.' The king thought this was a good idea and told the shepherd. He decided to take the twelve rabbits and to set off for the mountain with them. But as soon as he released them, they showed him a clean pair of heels and they disappeared straight away. The shepherd became very sad: there was every reason for it; but just then a lady passed by and asked him what he was doing there. The shepherd told her what had happened and the lady said to him: 'I will get you out of trouble; take this wand, tap it on the ground and say: 'Come here all of you, to the shepherd!' He did as he had been told, and all the rabbits appeared at his side. 'Now we're alright', said the shepherd.

There were now just a few days to end the year and the king said: 'Not a single rabbit has got away from the shepherd; someone must go over there to buy one from him, no matter what the cost.' And he ordered his daughter's maid to go and buy one. She went as she was told and said to the shepherd: 'I've come to buy a rabbit from you; it's needed for a medicine for the princess. Ask whatever you want for it.' And the shepherd replied: 'I won't sell one for money, because here I don't have anything to spend it on; but I'll give you a rabbit if you let me sleep with you.' 'Don't be so impertinent!' 'Then you shall not have a rabbit.' And the maid said: 'Very well; but be careful not to tell anyone.' The maid took the rabbit with her and, as she was getting near the palace, the shepherd tapped

a mí me lo vende.' La princesa fue a ver al pastor y le ocurrió lo mismo que a su madre y a la doncella.

Venció el año. Y el pastor cogió sus conejos y fue a llevarlos al palacio. Entonces el rey llamó a uno de sus sonsejeros para consultarle la manera de deshacer el casamiento de la princesa con el pastor. 'Esto es fácil' dijo el consejero; 'vamos a mandarle que llene un saco de verdades.' El pastor dijo que llenaría. Y mandó tener por la boca del saco a la reina, a la princesa y a la doncella. Y dijo él a la doncella: '¿No es cierto que el día que fue usted a comprarme el conejo dormí con usted?' 'Sí.' 'Pues al saco.' Y dijo a la reina: '¿No es ciero que el día que fue usted a comprarme el conejo . . .' '¡Basta!' dijo el rey. 'Ya está el saco lleno.' Y el pastor se casó con la princesa y al poco tiempo fue rey.

the ground with his wand and said 'Come here all of you, to the shepherd!' And the rabbit returned to join the others. The maid entered the palace and the queen asked: 'Did you bring the rabbit?' 'No, ma'am; he didn't want to sell one; he says he doesn't need money, that he doesn't have anything to spend it on in the mountains.' 'You're useless', said the queen. 'Tomorrow I'll go to see the shepherd.'

The queen went and the same thing happened to her as to the maid. And when she returned to the palace the princess asked her: 'Did you bring the rabbit, mother?' 'No, daughter; that shepherd scorns money.' 'Ah! Tomorrow I'll go there and you'll see that he'll sell one to me.' The princess went to see the shepherd and the same happened to her as to her mother and to the maid.

The year was up. And the shepherd gathered his rabbits and took them to the palace. Then the king called one of his advisers to consult with him about how to prevent the princess' marriage with the shepherd. 'That's easy', said the advisor; 'we will order him to fill a sack full of truths.' The shepherd said that he would do this. And he ordered the queen, the princess and the maid to hold the sack open. And he said to the maid: 'Isn't it true that the day you came to buy a rabbit I slept with you?' 'Yes.' 'Into the sack with you, then.' And he said to the queen: 'Isn't it true that the day you came to buy a rabbit from me . . .' 'Enough!' said the king. 'The sack's full.' And the shepherd married the princess and very soon became king.

M. La mona encantada [85]

Éste era un rey que tenía tres hijos. Un día llamó a sus hijos y les dijo que, como ya era muy viejo, quería dejar su corona a uno de ellos. Y les dijo: 'Quiero que os marchéis por el mundo; y él que mejor regalo me presente, se gana la corona.' 'Pues, ¿qué regalo quiere usted que le traigamos?' le preguntaron. 'Una palangana. El que me presente la mejor palangana se gana la corona.' Y se marcharon los tres. Cada hijo cogió un caballo y se marchó cada uno por distinto camino. Los dos mayores la encontraron de seguía. Y el más pequeño se le hizo de noche. Y a fuerza de andar vio una luz a lo lejos. Y se acercó a ella, llamó a la puerta, y salió a recibirle una mona, que era la criada del caserío. Y la dijo: '¿Me podría hospedar aquí esta noche?' Y al mismo tiempo la mona llamó a la señorita: 'Señorita, que aquí hay un caballero, que si le podemos hospedar esta noche.' Y salieron unas cuantas de monas, porque en aquella casa todos eran monos y monas. '¡Que pase! ¡Que pase!' dijo la señorita. Llamó a los criados y dijo: '¡Recoger el caballo de ese caballero y lo arreglen ustedes!' Y a las criadas las dijo: 'Preparadle la cena.' Y pusieron una rica mesa, elegantemente vestida, con buenos manjares. Después de cenar, estuvieron jugando al tresillo. Y cuando terminaron de jugar, la señorita dijo a la criada: 'Conducirle a su habitación.'

A la mañana siguiente se levantó muy de temprano y le dijo la criada: 'Señorito, ¿Cómo se levanta usted tan pronto?' 'Porque traigo un encargo y tengo que andar el camino.' 'Espere usted que se levanten las señoritas. Señoritas! ¡Que se va el forastero!' '¡Ah! ¡Espere usted que se desayune, señorito! No se vaya usted.' 'Traigo un encargo que hacer y tengo que buscarlo. Y, ¿qué encargo tiene usted que hacer? Aquí se lo podremos dar.' 'Pues, soy el hijo del rey' dice. 'Somos tres hermanos. Y nos ha dicho mi padre que el que la mejor palangana le presentemos, que ganamos la corona.' Entonces la señorita llamó a

---

[85] Espinosa (hijo), *Cuentos populares de Castilla*, 120-4.

M. The Enchanted Monkey

There was a king who had three sons. One day he called his sons and said that, since he was now very old, he wanted to pass his crown on to one of them. And he told them: 'I want you to travel the world; and the one who brings me the best present will have the crown.' 'So, what present do you want us to bring you?' they asked. 'A washbasin. The one who gives me the best washbasin will have the crown.' And so the three went on their way. Each son took a horse and went in a different direction. The two oldest ones found a washbasin straight away, but night fell on the youngest one. By dint of walking he saw a light in the distance. He approached, knocked on the door, and a horrible monkey, who was the maid of the house, came to answer. He asked: 'Could you put me up for the night?' and instantly the monkey called for her mistress: 'Madam, there's a gentleman here asking if we can put him up for the night.' Several monkeys appeared, because they were all monkeys in that house. 'Let him come in!' said the mistress. She called for her servants and said: 'Take the gentleman's horse and see to it!' Then she told her maids: 'Prepare him some dinner.' They laid out a lavish table, richly adorned and full of delights. After dinner they played cards, and when they finished the mistress said to her maid: 'Take him to his room.'

The following morning he got up very early and the maid said to him: 'Sir, why have you got up so early?' 'Because I'm on an errand and I have to go on my way.' 'Wait for the ladies to get up. Ladies! The stranger is leaving!' 'Ah!, Wait and have breakfast, sir! Don't leave.' 'I'm on an errand and I must find what I'm looking for.' 'What are you looking for? We can give it to you here.' 'I'm the king's son', he said. 'We're three brothers, and my father has told us that the one who gives him the best washbasin shall have the crown.' Then the lady called her maid and said: 'Bring the oldest trough from the chicken run. Wrap it

la criada y la dijo: 'Trae el bebedero más viejo del corral de las gallinas. Y envuélvesele en unos papeles y dásele al señorito.' Lo trajo la criada, y la señorita se lo entregó al joven. 'Téngalo usted, caballero, y váyase usted a casa.' Y él, sin decir nada, lo cogió y se marchó.

Y marchaba muy triste, pensando en que llevaba el bebedero más viejo de las gallinas. Al llegar a una fuente, se bajó de su caballo y, pensando en que llevaba un bebedero tan malo, le desenvolvió. Y vio que era una palangana preciosa, llena de perlas, esmeraldas, rubís, topacios y brillantes Y al ver que era tan preciosa montó en su caballo y iba muy contento. Al llegar a su casa presentó su regalo a su padre y se encontró que sus hermanos habían presentado cada uno una palangana más inferior a la suya. Y le dijo su padre: 'La tuya es la mejor. Pero todavía no te has ganado la corona. Ahora tenéis que traerme una toalla. El que me presente la mejor toalla, se gana la corona.' Y montando de a caballo, como la vez anterior, cada uno se marchó por distinto camino. Y el menor se fue por el mismo camino que antes. Él, que no quería ir por aquel camino; pero el caballo no quería salir de él y siempre iba por el mismo. Y se le hizo de noche, y tuvo que volver por el mismo sitio que la vez anterior, porque el caballo no quería pasar de allí.

Llamó a la puerta, salió la misma criada, y dijo: '¡Señoritas, el señorito del otro día está aquí!' '¡Que pase! ¡Que pase! Y, ¡dile al criado que recoja el caballo y que lo arregle.' 'Perdonen ustedes, que el caballo no ha querido ir por otro camino. Y se me ha hecho de noche, y vengo a que me den ustedes posada como el otro día.' Le pusieron la cena como la noche anterior. Y dispués de cenar, estuvieron jugando al tresillo hasta acostarse. Al día siguiente se levantó muy temprano, y le dijo la crida: '¿Cómo se levanta usted tan pronto, señorito?' 'Porque tengo que hacer un encargo y tengo que buscarlo.' 'Pues aquí se lo darán las señoritas, como el otro día.' 'No, señora, no es cosa que ustedes me puedan dar. Es cosa más pesada.' '¡Señoritas, que se va el señorito!' Y salieron y le dijeron: 'Pues, ¿qué encargo tiene usted que hacer? ¿Qué desea usted? Aquí lo

in some paper and give it to the gentleman.' The maid brought it and her mistress gave it to the lad. He accepted it and left without saying a word.

He was very sad as he journeyed home, thinking that he had the oldest trough from the chicken run. When he arrived at a spring, he got off his horse and, thinking that he had such a horrible trough, unwrapped it. And he saw that it was a beautiful washbasin, covered in pearls, emeralds, rubies, topaz and other gems. Seeing that it was so beautiful, he got on his horse and continued on his way very happy. When he arrived home he gave the present to his father and found that his brothers had both given him a much poorer washbasin than his. His father said: 'Yours is the best. But you still haven't earned the crown. Now you must bring me a towel. The one who gives me the best towel shall have the crown.' Each one followed a different road on horseback, as they had done before. The youngest son went along the same road as before; he didn't want to follow this road, but his horse refused to leave it. Night fell and he had to go to the same place as before, since his horse refused to go any further.

He knocked on the door, the same maid appeared and she said: 'Ladies, the gentleman who was here the other day has come back!' 'Let him come in! And tell the servant to take his horse and see to it!' 'Forgive me, because my horse refused to go any other way. It got dark and I've come to ask you for shelter like the other day.' They gave him dinner as on the previous night, and after dinner they played cards until they went to bed. The following day he got up very early and the maid said: 'Why have you got up so early, sir?' 'Because I'm on an errand and I must seek it out.' 'The ladies here will give it to you as they did the other day.' 'No, madam, it's not something you can give me. It's a very tiresome thing.' 'Ladies, the gentleman is leaving!' They came out and said: 'What's your errand? What do you need? You'll find everything here.' 'A towel that we must give my father in order to win the crown. He's told us that the one who gives him the best towel shall have the crown.' They called the maid and the lady of the house told her: 'Bring the filthiest floorcloth from the kitchen.' They

encontrará usted todo.' 'Una toalla que le tenemos que presentar a mi padre para ganar la corona. Nos ha dicho que el que presente la mejor toalla se gana la corona.' Llamaron a la criada, y la dijo la señorita: 'Trae la rodilla más sucia que hay en la cocina.' Se la trajeron y se la envolvieron en unos papeles. Se la entregó la señorita, diciéndole: 'Téngala usted, señorito, y váyase para casa.' Y él, muy pensativo, se iba para casa.

Al llegar a la fuente, se bajó de su caballo y, pensando en que llevaba una rodilla sucia, desenvolvió los papeles. Y se encontró con que era una toalla de damasco preciosísima. Volvió a montarse a caballo y, al llegar a casa, enseñó la toalla a su padre. Y era mucho mejor que de los hermanos mayores. Y le dijo el padre: 'La tuya es la mejor. Pero todavía no te has ganado la corona. Ahora el que mejor novia traiga, se casará con ella y ganará la corona.' Montaron de a caballo al día siguiente, y cada uno se marchó por distinto camino. Y el menor se fue por el mismo camino que antes, porque . . . él no quería ir por allí, pero el caballo no quería salir de aquel camino. Al llegar al mismo sitio, llamó, y salió la criada: '¡Señoritas, el señorito del otro día!' '¡Dile que pase! ¡Y di al criado que recoja el caballo y que lo arregle! Y, ¡que pase!' Pusieron la mesa como noches anteriores. Cenaron, jugaron al tresillo y le recibieron en la misma habitación que las noches anteriores. En toda la noche no pudo dormir, pensando en que era cosa más pesada que las otras.

Al día siguiente se levantó más temprano que los días anteriores y le dijo la criada: '¿Por qué se levanta usted tan pronto, señorito?' 'Porque traigo hoy una cosa más pesada que las de los días anteriores.' 'Pues espere usted a que se levanten las señoritas. ¡Señoritas, que se va el señorito!' '¡Que espere un momento, que vamos ahora mismo!' Bajaron al poco tiempo. '¿Cómo se va usted tan pronto?' 'Porque traigo una cosa muy pesada y tengo que andar el camino.' 'Pues, nos diga usted, que aquí lo encontrará usted todo.' '¡Ay, no, señora! ¡No, señora! Usted perdone, pero eso no puede ser.' '¡Sí, sí! ¡Dígalo usted, que aquí lo encontrara usted todo! Pues, ¿qué? ¿No les han gustado a

brought it and wrapped it in some paper. The lady gave it to him, saying: 'Here you are, sir, go home.' So he went home deep in thought.

When he arrived at the spring, he got off his horse and, thinking that he had a filthy floorcloth, unwrapped the package. Inside he found a towel of beautiful damask. He got back on his horse and, when he arrived home, showed the towel to his father. It was much better than his older brothers' towels, and his father said: 'Yours is the best. But you still haven't earned the crown. Now, the one who brings the best bride will marry her and shall have the crown.' The following day they got on their horses and each one set off in a different direction. The youngest one followed the same road as before, because although he didn't want to go that way, his horse refused to go any other. Coming to the same place as before, he knocked, and the maid appeared: 'Ladies, the gentlemen from the other day is here!' 'Invite him in! And tell the servant to take his horse and see to it! Let him come in!' They laid the table as on the other nights. They had dinner, played cards, and put him in the same room as on the other nights. He couldn't sleep all night, thinking that his errand was more difficult than the others.

The following day he got up even earlier than on the other occasions and the maid said: 'Why are you getting up so early, sir?' 'Because today I have a more difficult task than on the other days.' 'Wait for the ladies to get up. Ladies, the gentleman is leaving!' 'Tell him to wait a moment, we're on our way!' They soon came down. 'Why are you leaving so early?' 'Because I'm on a very difficult errand and must be on my way.' 'Tell us, because you'll find everything here.' 'Ah, no, madam! No, madam! Forgive me, but that's impossible.' 'Yes, yes! Tell us, because you'll find everything here! So, what is it? Didn't you like the presents from the other days?' 'Yes, madam, they were the best. But this is very difficult.' 'Tell us, then!' 'Our, father', he said, 'has told us that whoever brings the best bride will marry her and shall have the crown!' The lady called the maid and said: 'Call the ugliest monkey in the house.' And the ugliest

ustedes los regalos de los días anteriores?' 'Sí, señora; han sido los mejores. Pero éste es muy pesado.' 'Pues, ¡dígalo usted!' 'Pues, nos ha dicho' dice 'que el que mejor novia llevemos, nos casaremos con ella y nos ganaremos la corona.' La señorita llamó a la criada y la dijo: 'Llama a la mona más fea que haya en la casa.' Y se presentó la más fea. Y dijo a los criados: 'Aparejar nuestros carruajes, y montarnos todos para ir a celebrar las bodas.' Todos eran monos y monas. El joven cogió su caballo y volvía con ellos. Y allí iba muy disgustado. Pero al llegar a la fuente, se pararon a merendar. Y se volvieron coches y señoritas, todos muy elegantes y muy majos, todos muy bonitos. Cuando llegaron a palacio, los dos hermanos mayores ya estaban allí. Y se creían que no las habría más bonitas que las suyas. Y al subir por las escaleras, el joven la subía del brazo, y, detrás, subían todas las señoritas muy elegantemente vestidas, muy majas, muy bonitas todas. Y cuando el rey vio a la princesa que venía con él, le dijo: 'Tú te has ganado la corona por haberme presentado los mejeres regalos y la mejor novia. Te casarás con ella, y ella será la reina.'

Se casaron, vivieron felices y comieron perdices, y a mi no me dieron porque no quisieron.

appeared. And she told the servants: 'Prepare our carts, and let's all set off to celebrate the wedding.' They were all monkeys. The young man took his horse and went home with them. He was very unhappy, but when they came to the spring they stopped to have tea, and the carts became carriages and all the monkeys became young ladies, all very elegant and nice, all very pretty. When they came to the palace, the two oldest brothers were already there, and thought that there would be no brides more beautiful than theirs. As they walked up the stairs, the young man took his bride by the arm while all the ladies came behind, very elegantly dressed and all very nice and pretty. When the king saw the princess that was with his son, he said: 'You have earned the crown for bringing me the best presents and the best bride. You shall marry her, and she shall be queen.'

They got married, lived happily and ate partridges, and they didn't give me any because they didn't want to.

N. El viaje maravilloso [86]

Éranse un padre y tres hijos; y él, viejo, fatigado, lastimado; y ellos, jóvenes y fuertes. Ellos iban a la escuela, y en los momentos de asueto dedicábanse a pedir; ellos iban a la escuela tan astrosos, que los niños les decían: '¿Por qué con el dinero que ganáis no os compráis un vestido?' Y el hermano mayor le dijo al padre: 'Padre, si no me compras un vestido me marcharé por el mundo.' El padre le respondió: 'Comeremos lo que ganen tus hermanos y ahorraremos lo que ganes tú.' Pero al hermano mayor le gustaban demasiado las aventuras, y como se cansaba en el lugar y no era buena su vida, resolvió partir de una vez. 'No, padre; yo me marcho.' Y se marchó.

Y se marchó y anduvo, anduvo . . . hasta que en un recodo del camino se le apareció un caballero. El caballero se enteró de sus propósitos, y le regaló una mula. 'Cuanto quieras de comer, de beber o de vestir, no tienes más que pedírselo' le dijo. Y el mozo le pidió inmediatamente: 'Mula, quiero comer a todo gusto.' Y la mula dio una coz, y el mozo se encontró con una mesa, de la que fueron brotando los manjares más sabrosos y los vinos más ricos. Cuando el mozo se hartó, pidió a la mula que le diera un traje. 'Mula, necesito un traje.' Y encontró de repente un traje riquísimo a sus pies, y se lo puso y partió. Pero a poco llegó a un río, la mula se metió en el agua, y él no quiso molestarse en perseguirla. La dejó, se volvió y encontró nuevamente al caballero. Este sonrió con pena, le entregó una barra de oro, y el mozo abrió un comercio a la entrada del lugar. Un día vio a sus hermanos, que venían a pedirle una limosna: '¡Una limosna por el amor de Dios!' Y les dijo con orgullo: '¡Yo soy solo!'

El hermano siguiente cayó también en la tentación de partir en busca de fortuna. Y dio con el caballero y recibió sus regalos. 'A la mula le pedirás de vestir, de comer y de beber.' Y él, en seguida: 'Mula, quiero vestir, quiero comer,

---

[86] Cabal, *Los cuentos tradicionales asturianos*, 148-55.

N. The Marvellous Journey

Once there was a father who had three sons. He was old, tired, worn out; they were young and strong. They went to school, and in times of hardship they went begging; they looked so shabby when they went to school that the children would say: 'Why don't you buy yourselves some clothes with the money you earn?' And the eldest brother said to his father: 'Father, if you don't buy me a suit of clothes I'll leave.' His father answered: 'We'll buy food with your brothers' earnings, and save yours.' But the eldest brother liked adventures too much, and since he was tired of his home and his life wasn't good, he decided to leave straight away: 'No, father; I'm leaving.' And he left.

He left and he walked and he walked . . ., until a gentleman appeared before him at a bend in the road. The gentleman found out his plans, and gave him a mule. 'You just have to ask the mule for whatever you want to eat, drink or wear', he said. And straight away the lad said: 'Mule, I want to eat heartily.' The mule gave a kick, and the lad found in front of him a table that produced the most tasty delicacies and delicious wines. When the lad had eaten his fill, he asked the mule to give him a suit of clothes. 'Mule, I need a suit of clothes.' Suddenly he found an exquisite suit at his feet, put it on and went on his way. Soon he came to a river, and the mule went into the water, but he couldn't be troubled to follow it. He left the mule, turned back and met the gentleman again. The latter smiled with pity, gave him a gold bar, and the youth set up a business at the entrance to the village. One day he saw his brothers, who had come to beg him for money: 'For the love of God, please give us some alms.' And he replied haughtily: 'I'm an only child!'

The middle brother was also tempted into leaving in search of his fortune. He met the gentleman and received his gifts: 'You can ask the mule for food, drink and clothes', and straight away he said: 'Mule, I want to have clothes, food

quiero beber a mi gusto.' Sucedió el milagro; pero comió también más de la cuenta, y cuando encontró el río, y vio que la mula se entraba en el agua, no quiso molestarse en detenerla. Se volvió y encontró nuevamente al caballero: éste le entregó una suma, y él se juntó al hermano comerciante. El hermano menor llegó a pedirles: '¡Una limosna por el amor de Dios!' 'Nosotros somos solos' le dijeron. Y le volvieron la espalda. El hermano menor se marchó llorando.

Y reunió los víveres, las telas y las monedas que pudo y se las llevó a su padre. 'Padre' le dijo, 'yo me voy también, pero volveré en seguida. En tanto, aquí tienes telas que vestir, víveres que comer y monedas que gastar. Se fue, encontró al caballero, y recibió la mula de regalo. 'Yo' dijo el niño 'necesito un traje, pero pídamelo usted.' Se lo pidió a la mula el caballero, y era un traje tan hermoso el que apareció, que el niño no quiso aceptarlo, porque se avergonzaba de que le viesen con prenda tan rica: la mula le dio entonces un sayal, y él se lo puso con gozo. Rogó luego al caballero que le proporcionara de comer, porque le apretaba el hambre; y rechazó manjares exquisitos, y sólo se comió los más humildes.

Después de cenar, rezó y luego se echó a llorar con desconsuelo. El caballero le preguntó: 'Hijo mío, ¿por qué lloras?' Porque me acuerdo de mi padre. Si usted me permitiera enviarle esta mula, yo iría por el mundo mucho más contento, porque él ya no tendría que tener apuros de miseria.' El caballero se lo permitió, y el niño mismo se la fue a llevar. La alegría de su padre fue infinita cuando le estrechó en sus brazos. Y él le suplicó a la mula que les levantara una choza, y la mula soltó una coz, y apareció un palacio colosal, todo mármol, oro y nácar. Los muebles eran verdaderas maravillas, y los jardines encanto de los ojos. En el palacio trabajaban numerosos sirvientes, y el sótano estaba lleno de cajas que contenían toda clase de piedras preciosas. Y el niño le dijo al padre: 'Padre, ya nada te falta; pero yo necesito marcharme por el mundo, porque estas cosas me demuestran que tengo que cumplir alguna misión.' Y se marchó por el mundo.

and drink to my satisfaction.' The miracle happened; but he also ate more than he realized, and when he came to the river and saw the mule go into the water he couldn't be troubled to stop it. He turned back and met the gentleman again: the latter gave him some money, and he joined his elder brother. The youngest brother came and asked them: 'For the love of God, please give me some alms!' 'We have no brother', they answered, and turned their backs. The youngest brother went away in tears.

He gathered all the food, clothes and money he could and took them to his father. 'Father', he said, 'I'm leaving, too, but I'll come back straight away. In the meantime, here are clothes to wear, food to eat and money to spend.' He left, met the man, and received the mule as a gift. 'I need a suit of clothes', said the boy, 'but you ask for it.' The man asked the mule for it, and it was such a handsome suit of clothes that appeared that the boy refused to accept it, because he was embarrassed to be seen wearing such an expensive garment: then the mule gave him a woollen suit, and he merrily put it on. Then he asked the man to give him some food, because he was hungry; he refused many exquisite delicacies, and only ate the simplest food.

After eating, he prayed and began to cry with sadness. The man asked: 'Why are you crying, my son?' 'Because I'm thinking of my father. If you permitted me to send him this mule, I'd be much happier on my travels, because he wouldn't be in the depths of misery any longer.' The man gave his permission, and the boy took the mule himself. His father was over the moon when he was able to hug him, and the boy asked the mule to provide them with a hut; the mule gave a kick and a huge palace appeared, all made of marble, gold and mother-of-pearl. Its furniture were truly marvels and its gardens were a delight to the eyes. There were many servants working in the palace, and its vaults were full of boxes of all sorts of precious jewels. The boy said to his father: 'You now want for nothing, father; but I must travel the world, because these things have shown me that I have a mission.' And he left to travel the world.

Llegó al río con la mula, y los dos pasaron sin mojarse. Se halló entonces en un prado muy extenso, de pasto dulce y vicioso, y notó que los animales que pacían en él eran sólo armazones esqueléticas, totalmente descarnadas. La hierba estaba en el prado salpicada de florecillas, y los pájaros las cortaban con el pico, las cogían e iban con ellas a perderse entre las nubes. El niño encontró después un río de sangre; después, otro de leche; después, un camino en cuesta, y en el camino dos enormes peñascos que se combatían con furor.

Iba montado en la mula y se apeó para evitar que los peñascos la aplastaran; instantáneamente se apartaron ellos, dejándole el paso libre. A poco llegó a un palacio y vio en él una hermosísima mujer, toda vestida de luto, que clamaba de continuo con angustia: '¡Ay, mi esposo! ¡Ay, hijo de mi alma!' El niño la miró con tristeza, deseoso de consolarla; pero no se determinó, y salió de este palacio, y llegó a otro; todas las personas que encontraba en él levantaban los puños, maldecían, blasfemaban sin cesar. En una habitación había dos camas; tocó una y en ella se le quedó un pedazo de dedo. Siguió luego su camino y hubo de pasar un puente de extraordinaria estrechez, a cuyo fin se tendía un arenal: los animales que por él andaban se apacentaban sólo de la arena, y sin embargo estaban gordos. Terminaba el arenal ante una puerta magnífica, y en ella se sentaba una señora de soberana hermosura, que a quienes se acercaban los preguntaba así: '¿Tenéis sed?' '¡Sí, señora!' '¿Y mi hijo?' 'Está esperándonos.'

El niño no pasó de este lugar. Desanduvo su camino y llegó nuevamente al caballero, que le recibió con amor. El niño le refirió las cosas que encontrara, y el caballero se ofreció a explicárselas. 'El río de agua que viste' le explicó 'está formado de lágrimas y separa esta vida de la otra. Las lágrimas son las tuyas y las de todos los hombres como tú; las que lloran las madres cuando se mueren sus hijos; las que vertió la Virgen cuando mataron al suyo.' '¿Y el prado que le seguía?' 'El prado de los avaros, que tienen mucho pasto que comer y sufren toda clase de miserias.' '¿Y los pájaros que vuelan junto a ellos?' 'Los niños que se mueren inocentes y que andan buscando flores para obsequiar a la Virgen.'

He came to the river with the mule, and the two crossed without getting wet. Then he found himself in a large meadow, full of sweet and luxuriant grass, and he noticed that the animals that grazed there were mere skeletons, without any meat on them. The grass in the meadow was dotted with flowers, and the birds picked them with their beaks and flew off with them into the clouds. Then the boy came to a river of blood; then, to a river of milk, and then to a path that led uphill with two huge boulders fighting furiously on it.

He got down from the mule so that the boulders wouldn't crush it; straight away they parted to let him pass freely. Soon he came to a palace and there he saw a beautiful woman who was dressed in mourning and who constantly cried with anguish: 'Ah, my husband! Ah, my darling son!' The boy looked at her sadly, wishing to console her, but he couldn't bring himself to do it and he left the palace and came to another one. Everyone he saw there shook their fists, swore and blasphemed continually. There were two beds in one of the rooms; he touched one and a piece of his finger came off. Then he continued on his way and had to cross an extraordinarily narrow bridge, with a sandy field on the other side: the animals in the field ate only sand, yet they were fat. The sandy field came to an end before a magnificent doorway, where the most beautiful woman sat and asked whoever approached: 'Are you thirsty?' 'Yes, madam!' 'And my son?' 'He's expecting us.'

The boy went no further. He retraced his steps and again came to the man, who greeted him lovingly. The boy told him what he'd seen, and the man offered to explain. 'The river of water that you saw', he said, 'is made of tears and separates this world from the next. The tears belong to you and to all men like you; the tears that mothers weep when their children die; the ones that the Virgin wept when her own son was killed.' 'And the meadow on the other side?' 'The meadow of the misers who have plenty to eat and nevertheless suffer hardship.' 'And the birds that fly nearby?' 'The innocent children who have died and who take flowers to give to the Virgin.' 'And the river of blood?' 'The blood

'¿Y el río de sangre?' 'El que lleva la sangre del Señor.' '¿Y el río de leche?' 'El que lleva la leche que maman las criaturas.' '¿Y las rocas que se batían en el camino?' 'Tus hermanos, que fueron como rocas. En vida los envenenaron las envidias, las disensiones y los odios; no tuvieron un momento de tranquilidad y murieron maldiciéndose. Cuando tú los encontraste iban los dos camino del infierno. Y han dejado sus tesoros enterrados para que ni tú ni tu padre los recogierais.'

Calló el niño con dolor y volvió al poco rato a preguntar: '¿Y el palacio donde todos maldecían?' 'El palacio del infierno. Las camas que tú tocaste estaban aguardando a tus hermanos.' '¿Y el puente?' 'El camino de la gloria.' '¿Y los animales que engordaban con arena?' 'Los obreros que ganaron en la vida un jornal de explotación.' '¿Y la señora hermosísima?' 'Mi madre . . . Tu madre . . . La Santísima Virgen.' Y continuó el caballero: 'Ya has cumplido tu destino y ya puedes regresar a tu pueblo.'

Regresó, llamó al palacio y salió un fraile a recibirle. El niño le miró con estrañeza y preguntó por su padre. Su padre hacía muchos años que se encontraba con Dios, y el palacio se había convertido en convento por su propia voluntad. El fraile contó la historia: se trataba de un anciano que había tenido tres hijos, y dos murieron odiándose, y nadie supiera del menor, que se fue por el mundo. Historia tradicional que narraban para ejemplo los libros de la casa y que en el decir del fraile ya era historia muy antigua, excesivamente antigua. '¿Tendrá doscientos años?' '¡Más aún!' Sólo en mirar a los pájaros, que le llevaban flores a la Virgen, había pasado el niño treinta y tres aunque le parecieran un instante. Y se metió en el convento, se hizo frailecito en él, y cuéntase que fue santo el frailecito.

of our Lord.' 'And the river of milk?' 'The milk that all creatures suckle.' 'And the rocks that were fighting on the road?' 'Your brothers, who were like rocks. Envy, discord and hate poisoned them in life; they didn't enjoy one moment's peace and they died cursing each other. When you came across them they were both on the way to Hell. And they left their treasures buried behind them so that neither you nor your father can find them.'

The boy fell silent with sadness, and then he asked: 'And the palace where everyone cursed each other?' 'The palace of Hell. The beds that you touched were ready for your brothers.' 'And the bridge?' 'The road to Heaven.' 'And the animals who got fat on sand?' 'The labourers who earned a pittance in life.' 'And the beautiful woman?' 'My mother . . . your mother . . . the Sacred Virgin.' And the man continued: 'Now you've fulfilled your destiny and you can go back to your village.'

He went back, knocked on the palace door and a friar came out to greet him. The boy looked at him strangely and asked for his father. His father had been with God for many years, and the palace had become a monastery on his instructions. The friar told him the story: it was about an old man who had three sons; two of them died hating each other, and no-one knew anything of the youngest, who had set off to travel the world. It was a traditional story from the household books and which according to the friar was now a very old story, too old. 'Two hundred years old?' 'More!' The boy had spent thirty-three years just watching the birds that took flowers to the Virgin, even though it had just seemed an instant to him. He entered the monastery, became a friar, and it's told that the young friar became a saint.

O. Los tres hijos del Sultán [87]

Pues, señor, esto eran tres hermanas mozas, que mientras cosían a la puerta de su casa sostenían esta conversación: 'Yo me casaría de buena gana con el panadero del rey, pues de esta manera ni a mí ni a mis hijos nos faltaría nunca el pan,' decía la mayor. 'Pues yo,' decía la mediana, 'me casaría con el pescador del rey, y de esta manera ni a mí ni a mis hijos nos faltará siempre buen pescado fresco y nunca pasaremos hambre.' 'Yo,' dijo la hermana pequeña, 'con quien me casaría de buena gana es con el Sultán, que es joven, gallardo y bueno.' El Sultán, que estaba paseando por allí, oyó las conversaciones y deseos de las tres hermanas, y acercándose a ellas, las dijo: 'Vuestros deseos se van a ver cumplidos. Vosotras os casaréis con el panadero y pescadero de mi palacio, y yo me casaré contigo,' dijo, dirigiéndose a la hermana pequeña. A los pocos días se casaron, celebrándose unas bodas fastuosas y grandes festejos, que duraron muchos días. Pero las hermanas mayores no podían olvidar que su hermana se había casado con el Sultán y ellas con el panadero y pescadero, y sentían no haber dicho también que deseaban casarse con el Sultán. Por esto, tenían envidia y odio grandes a su hermana pequeña, hoy convertida en Sultana.

Pasado el tiempo oportuno, tuvo ésta un hermoso niño. Sus hermanas cogieron a éste, le echaron al río y pusieron en su lugar un perro, marchando a decir al Sultán que su esposa había dado a luz un perro. El Sultán se enfadó mucho, pero reconoció que su esposa no era culpable. Al año siguiente tuvo la Sultana otro niño, al que las hermanas sustituyeron por un león, echando al río el niño, y diciendo al Sultán que esta vez había sido un león lo que la Sultana había dado a luz, cosa que sirvió también de disgusto al Sultán, pero perdonó a su esposa, coma la vez anterior. Pasó otro año, y fue una niña lo que tuvo la

---

[87] Told by Antonio Moríñigo Bernal from Madroñera in Cáceres. Curiel Merchán, *Cuentos extremeños*, 63-7.

O. The Sultan's Three Children

So, then, there were three young sisters, who had the following conversation as they were sewing in the doorway of their house: 'I'd gladly marry the king's baker, because neither I nor my children would ever go without bread if I did', said the eldest. 'I', said the middle sister, 'would marry the king's fisherman, because neither I nor my sons would ever want for good fresh fish if I did and we'd never be hungry.' 'I', said the youngest, 'would gladly marry the Sultan, because he's young, elegant and good.' The Sultan, who was passing by, heard the three sisters' conversation and desires and, going up to them, he said: 'Your wishes shall come true. You two will marry the baker and the fisherman from my palace, and I'll marry you', he said to the youngest sister. A few days later they were married in a magnificent wedding with a huge feast that lasted several days. But the older sisters couldn't forget that their sister had married the Sultan while they had married the baker and fisherman, and they regretted not having also said that they wanted to marry the Sultan. They therefore envied their younger sister, who was now the Sultaness, and hated her fiercely.

In due course, the Sultaness gave birth to a handsome son. Her sisters took him and threw him into the river, putting a dog in his place and telling the Sultan that his wife had given birth to a dog. The Sultan was very angry, but realized that his wife was not to blame. The following year the Sultaness gave birth to another son, who the sisters replaced with a lion, throwing the child into the river and telling the Sultan that this time the Sultaness had given birth to a lion, which also displeased him, but he forgave his wife as before. Another year passed, and this time the Sultaness gave birth to a girl, who was thrown into the river and replaced with a piece of rotten meat, which was also presented to the Sultan. In spite of his distress at not having an heir, he realized that his wife was

Sultana, niña que fue echada al río y sustituida por un pedazo de carne podrida, que también fue presentado al Sultán. Reconoció éste, dentro de su disgusto de no poder tener un heredero, que su inocente esposa era víctima de quienes la odiaban, sin poder suponer que sus propias hermanas eran las que tan mal la querían, y menos suponer lo que habían hecho.

Los dos niños y la niña hijos del Sultán, al ser arrojados al río, fueron recogidos por un caritativo matrimonio de molineros, que los crió con verdadero cariño de padres. Murió la buena molinera, y esto hizo gran mella en el anciano molinero, quien sintiéndose morir les llamó alrededor del lecho y les dijo: 'Voy a morir, hijos míos; pero antes voy a deciros lo que no sabéis. Aunque os he criado y querido como si fuerais hijos míos, y vosotros como hijos me queréis, habéis de saber que no sois mis hijos, sino hijos de un poderoso señor, y yo os recogí del río, donde fuisteis arrojados por enemigos de vuestros padres, que ignoran vuestra existencia. Si queréis conseguir vuestra felicidad, cuando yo muera, ir por el pájaro que habla, el árbol que canta y el agua que da limpieza al rostro.' Y dicho esto, murió el buen molinero. Enterráronle sus hijos adoptivos con mucho cariño, y pasados unos días, el hermano mayor se dispuso a cumplir las órdenes de su buen padre. Al marcharse cogió una brillante espada, se la dio a su hermana y la dijo: 'Toma esta espada. Si conserva su brillo, es señal que vivo y triunfo; pero si se empaña, quiere decir que he fracasado o he muerto.'

Marchó animoso en busca del pájaro, el árbol y el agua, y a poco se encontró con un anciano de grandísima barba blanca, a quien preguntó por esas cosas; pero el viejo no le contestó. El mozo entonces le cortó la barba, y el viejo, como castigo, le tiró una pelota, que fue agrandándose hasta convertirse en un monte, donde se encontró el mozo rodeado de multitud de piedras, pero instantáneamente quedó convertido en otra piedra negra.

Mientras su hermano ausente, miraba la hermana la espada todos los días, y al ver que había perdido su brillo comprendió que algo malo había pasado a su hermano, por lo que, llena de dolor, se echó a llorar. Su hermano menor quiso

the innocent victim of those who hated her, but didn't imagine that her own sisters were the ones who so disliked her, let alone what they had done.

After being thrown into the river, the Sultan's two sons and daughter were rescued by a kindly miller and his wife, who brought them up with the love of real parents. The miller's good wife died, which upset the old miller deeply and, feeling that he was dying, he called the children to his bed and said: 'I'm dying, my children; but first I want to tell you something you don't know. Although I've brought you up and loved you as though you were my own, and you love me as your father, you must know that you're not my children, but the children of a powerful lord, and I rescued you from the river where you were thrown by the enemies of your parents, who don't know that you're alive. If you want to find happiness, when I die go and find the talking bird, the singing tree and the water that purifies the face.' When he'd said this, the good miller died. His adopted children buried him with great affection, and after a few days the oldest brother prepared to carry out his good father's instructions. As he was leaving, he took a gleaming sword, gave it to his sister and said: 'Take this sword. If it continues to shine, it's a sign that I'm still alive and prospering; but if it becomes dull it means that I've failed or died.'

He set off eagerly in search of the bird, tree and water, and he soon met an old man with a long white beard and asked him about these things, but the old man didn't answer. The lad therefore cut off his beard and, by way of punishment, the old man threw a ball at him; and this ball grew quickly to the size of a mountain; the lad found himself surrounded by rocks and straight away he became a black rock himself.

While her brother was away, his sister checked the sword every day, and when she saw that it had lost its shine she knew that something bad had happened to her brother and so, grief-stricken, she began to cry. The younger brother tried to console her, telling her that he'd look for the bird, tree and water, and would also find their older brother. He gave his sister a rosary and said:

consolarla, diciéndola que él iría en busca del pájaro, el árbol y el agua y encontraría también a su hermano mayor. Dio un rosario a su hermana, y la dijo: 'Pasa todos los días las cuentas; si las pasas bien, es señal que vivo y triunfo; pero si no corren, señal es que me pasa algo malo o he muerto.' Se marchó y andar, andar, se encontró con el mismo viejo de la barba, a quien preguntó por lo que buscaba, sucediéndole en todo lo mismo que a su hermano, quedando convertido en piedra negra.

Su hermana, al ver un día que las cuentas sel rosario no corrían, supuso que algo malo sucedía a su hermano, y en busca de los dos, y del pájaro, el árbol y el agua, marchó valiente y animosa. Encontróse también al viejo de la barba, a quien hizo las mismas preguntas de sus hermanos, pero el viejo no hizo caso, tiró la pelota y ésta se convirtió en un monte lleno de las piedras negras, que sin cesar insultaban a la joven. Ella, valiente, no hizo caso de los insultos ni miró para atrás. Siempre con la vista hacia adelante, descubrió frente a ella y no muy lejos, un árbol frondodísimo, un pájaro en una rama y un vaso lleno de agua al pie del árbol. Suponiendo que fuera lo que ella buscaba, allá se fue. Quiso en seguida coger al pájaro, pero éste la dijo que no le cogiera, porque la mataría. No hizo caso, y le cogió, cortó una rama del árbol, cogió también el vaso de agua y con todo esto se marchó al monte de las piedras negras, que ya no la insultaban. Con el agua del vaso fue rociando todas las piedras, y éstas se fueron convirtiendo en jóvenes, encontrando entre ellos a sus hermanos, que locos de alegría la abrazaban y besaban. Contentos los tres hermanos, regresaron a su casa y allí vivieron felices durante algún tiempo. Echaron el agua del vaso en una pila y siempre tuvieron agua limpia y fresca, que limpiaba sus rostros, quedándoles que daba gusto verlos.

Un día pasó por allí el Sultán, que regresaba de caza. Venía sudoroso y lleno de polvo y quiso lavarse. Pidió agua y se le sacaron de aquella pila cristalina. Se lavó el Sultán y quedó limpio como nunca y mucho más joven. Le gustó esto, y desde entonces todos los días venía a lavarse con el agua de la pila y

'Count the beads every day; if they're all there, it's a sign that I'm alive and prospering. But if there are any missing, it's a sign that something bad has happened to me or I've died.' He set off and after walking for some time he met the same old man with the beard, and asked him about the things he was looking for, but exactly the same thing happened to him as to his brother and he was turned into a black rock.

When she saw one day that some of the rosary beads were missing, his sister guessed that something bad had happened to her brother and she bravely set off, eager to find her brothers, the bird, the tree and the water. She also met the old man with the beard, and she asked him the same questions as her brothers, but the old man ignored her, threw the ball at her and it became a mountain full of black rocks that constantly insulted her. She bravely ignored the abuse and didn't look back. With her eyes looking firmly ahead, she saw a luxuriant tree that was not too far away, with a bird on one of its branches and a glass full of water at the base of the tree. Guessing that this was what she was looking for, she approached the tree. She tried to grab the bird straight away, but it warned her that it would kill her. She ignored it, caught it, cut a branch from the tree, picked up the glass of water and set off for the mountain of black rocks, which had stopped insulting her. She sprinkled all the rocks with water from the glass, and each one became a young lad, and she found her brothers among them and they joyfully hugged and kissed her. The three returned home merrily and lived there happily for a while. They put the water in a font and always had clean fresh water to hand, which they used to clean their faces and which made them very handsome.

One day, the Sultan passed by on his way home from hunting. He was sweating and dusty, and wanted to wash. He asked for water and they gave him some from the crystalline font. The Sultan washed and was cleaner than he ever had been and much younger. He was pleased and from then on he came every day to wash at the font and spend some time in the company of the three siblings

a pasar un rato en compañía de los tres hermanos, a quienes tenía un verdadero afecto. Un día, mientras se lavaba, oyó cantar a la rama del árbol y que el pájaro le dijo: '¿Cómo has creído que tu buena esposa te diera como hijos un perro, un león y un pedazo de carne podrida? Tus verdaderos hijos son estos tres que tienes delante, los que, arrojados al río por tus perversas cuñadas, fueron salvados y criados como hijos por un buen molinero. Míralos bien y te convencerás que son tus hijos, pues los dos mayores se parecen a ti, y la joven, a su madre.' Los miró el Sultán fijamente y no dudó. Les reconoció como hijos, les abrazó y se los llevó a su palacio, junto con el pájaro, el árbol y el agua, que tan buen servicio les había dado.

¿Cómo decir la alegría de la buena madre, al ver a sus hijos hechos tres buenos mozos, y la tristeza y el odio de las malas hermanas, al ver fracasada su obra de odio y maldad? Fueron castigadas como merecían, es decir, arrojadas a lo más profundo del río, con una enorme piedra atada al cuello, para que sin salvación posible se fueran al fondo. El Sultán, la Sultana y sus buenos hijos vivieron contentos y felices por muchos años.

Y que tú lo veas también por muchos años, simpático lectorcito. Y colorín colorao . . .[88]

---

[88] As has already been explained, although the formulaic ending is incomplete, the audience understands what is meant and recognises this as a traditional means of bringing a tale to a close.

for whom he had great affection. One day, as he was washing, he heard the tree branch singing and the bird saying: 'How could you believe that your good wife could give you a dog, a lion and a piece of rotten meat for children? These are your real children that you see before you, who were saved and brought up by a good miller after your evil sisters-in-law had thrown them into the river. Look at them closely and you'll see that they are your children, since the two older ones look like you and the younger one looks like her mother.' The Sultan looked at them closely and was left in no doubt. He recognized them as his children, hugged them and took them to the palace, along with the bird, the tree and the water, which had served them so well.

How can we describe the joy of their good mother when she saw that her children had grown into three fine youths, or the sadness and hate of the evil sisters when they saw that their evil and hateful deed had failed? They were punished as they deserved, by being thrown into the deepest part of the river with an enormous rock tied to their necks so that they would sink to the bottom with no hope of escape. The Sultan, Sultaness and their good children lived happily for many years.

And may you too see happiness for many years, kind reader. And reddish red . . .

CONCLUSION

From a reading of the texts analysed in this study, it will be appreciated that folktales create a complex web of symbolic associations that may be interpreted in a variety of ways. The current study has chosen to adopt a predominantly Freudian approach to this analysis, but other psychoanalytical and structural techniques are equally valid, a fact which itself suggests that these tales appeal to the human subconscious on a variety of levels and in different ways in different contexts. The apparent simplicity of their style and explicit content masks their deeper resonances, the importance of which began to be recognized in Spain in the nineteenth century, but which only really came to the fore in the twentieth, somewhat later than in other parts of Europe, for reasons that have been suggested in Chapter 1. But the style of the tales is itself an additional source of great interest, as it highlights their oral background and, in particular, their nature as stories that are best absorbed through spoken delivery, rather than through reading. The performative dimension of these tales should not be forgotten, for this is another means of ensuring that their meaningful symbols and structures penetrate deep into the human psyche, bypassing the analytical and filtering processes that are characteristic of reading from the written page.

In many instances, this performative dimension is clearly in evidence in the tales' endings, with formulaic phrases such as:

Y se casaron y fueron muy felices y comieron perdices. Y a mí no me
dieron nada porque no les dio la gana.

[And they married and were very happy and ate partridges. But they
didn't give me anything, because they didn't want to.]

(*The Three Dresses*).

or:

En seguida se casaron y fueron felices, y a mí, que fue y vine, no me
dieron nada.

[They got married straight away and lived happily ever after, but they
gave me nothing, even though I went there and back.]

(*The Enchanted Forest*).

or, more simply:

... y colorín colorao, este cuento se ha acabao.

[... and reddish red, this story's ended.]

(*The Castle of Nevercomeback*).

Unlike the more neutral formula 'and they lived happily ever after', which is
commonly used in English, the Spanish endings either explicitly mention the
storyteller, so highlighting his or her role as a conduit for the tale, or,
alternatively, they indicate that the tale has ended. They do so by appealing to
the ear as well as to the mind's cognitive capacities through the use of rhyme and
assonance (*felices/perdices, nada/gana, colorao/acabao*), and in this way they
again show their desire to bypass conscious analysis, for the references to
partridges and reddish red are surely included primarily for their sound qualities
rather than for any rational meaning they may possess. The listeners are left in no
doubt that the performance is over, and that they are therefore free to react as
appropriate, perhaps by offering a reward for the entertainment. A hint to do
precisely this is given by the declaration that the storyteller received nothing
from the protagonists of the tale, the statement being an indirect invitation to the
current audience to make up for this.

These formulaic endings have their counterparts in the openings of the tales, where the English 'Once upon a time' is conveyed in expressions such as, 'Éste era un rey ...' [There was once a king ...] (*Seven Sunbeams*), or a variant thereof. Thus, the story itself is bracketed between clearly identified markers that define its opening and close in much the same way as the rise and fall of a curtain indicates the beginning and end of a play. These markers may help to universalize the tale by projecting it to a distant time and place, although this becomes problematic on those occasions when the storyteller associates him/herself with the protagonists at the end of the account. Equally importantly, however, they also help to define the telling of the story as a performance, the content of which is not meant to be believed on a literal level, whatever its deeper, psychological resonances. Folktales are meant to confirm social structures and provide reassurance to their audience, so it is important that they should not unsettle or confuse their listeners. By stressing the performative aspect of their delivery —a task which is also sometimes achieved when the storyteller makes his or her presence felt during the course of the tale, as when the listener is addressed directly with, '¿sabe?' ('you know?') in *The Castle of Nevercomeback*— the fictionality of their explicit plot is confirmed and the stories are free to weave their particular magic on the subconscious, unencumbered by the anxieties that might otherwise impose themselves via the conscious mind's desire for rational analysis and explanation. Disbelief is totally suspended as situations, actions and words are accepted without question. The listeners are invited to enter a marvellous world of make-believe, one which can be brought alive through all the performative techniques at the storyteller's disposal —gestures, changes of voice, changes of pace, etc.— but one which they know will deliver them safely back to reality when the tale has ended. The deadly serpents have been slain, the evil witches have been defeated, and all is well with the world. All can live happily ever after.

BIBLIOGRAPHY

The following bibliography will provide an introduction to the study of the folktale in general, and also a list of sources (primary and secondary) relating to the study of Spanish folktales in particular.

Aarne, Antti, & Thompson, Dean Stith, *The Types of the Folktale*, Folklore Fellows' Communications Nº 74 (Helsinki, 1928. 2nd edn, 1961).

Aguiló y Fuster, Mariano, *A la sombra del ciprés; cuentos y fantasías* (Palma: Imprenta de D.F. Guasp, 1863).

——, *Recull de eximplis e miracles, gestes e faules e altres ligendes ordenades per A-B-C, tretes de un manuscrit en pergami del començament del segle XV* (Barcelona: A. Vergaduer, 1881).

Aguilar Criado, Encarnación, *Cultura popular y folklore en Andalucía. (Los orígenes de la antropología)* (Sevilla: Diputación Provincial, 1990).

Barandiarán, José Miguel de, *Brujería y brujas en los relatos populares vascos* (San Sebastian: Txertoa, 1984).

Barandiarán Irizar, Luis, *A View from the Witch's Cave: Folktales of the Pyrenees*. Translated by Linda White (Reno, University of Nevada Press, 1991).

Barrio, Maruxa, and Harguindey, Enrique, *Contos populares*. Biblioteca Básica da Cultura Galega (Vigo: Galaxia, 1988).

Bauman, Richard, *Story, Performance and Event: Contextual Studies of Oral Narrative* (Cambridge: Cambridge University Press, 1986).

Ben-Amos, Dan, 'Are There Any Motifs in Folklore?', in Frank Trommler, ed., *Thematics Reconsidered* (Amsterdam: Rodopi, 1995), 71-85.

Berlioz, Jacques & Marie Anne Polo de Beaulieu (dir), *Les Exempla médiévaux. Introduction à la recherche. Suivie des tables critiques de l'"Index exemplorum" de Frederic C. Tubach* (Carcassone: GARAE/Hesiode, 1992).

——, *Formes médiévales du conte merveilleux* (Paris: Stock, 1989).

Bettelheim, Bruno, *The Uses of Enchntment: The Meaning and Importance of Fairy Tales* (Harmondsworth: Penguin, 1991).

Bigsby, C.W.E., ed., *Approaches to Popular Culture* (London: Edward Arnold, 1976).

Boggs Ralph S., *Index of Spanish Folktales*, Folklore Fellows' Communications Nº 90 (Helsinki, 1930).

Bottigheimer, Ruth B., *Grimm's Bad Girls & Bold Boys: the Moral and Social Vision of the Tales* (New Haven: Yale University Press, 1987).

Bouza Brey, Fermín, *La mitología del agua en el noroeste hispánico* (Vigo: Real Academia Gallega, 1973).

——, *Etnografía y folklore de Galicia*, 2 vols. (Vigo: Xerais, 1982).

Bravo-Villasante, Carmen, *Cien cuentos populares españoles* (Barcelona: Biblioteca de Cuentos Maravillosos, 1992).

Bremond, Claude, Jacques Le Goff and Jean-Claude Schmitt, *L'"Exemplum". (Typologie des Sources du Moyen Âge Occidental, fasc. 40)* (Turnhout: Brepols, 1982).

Cabal, Constantino, *Los cuentos tradicionales asturianos* (Madrid: Voluntad, 1924).

Caballero, Fernán, *Cuentos y poesías populares andaluces, coleccionados por Fernán Caballero* (Leipzig: F.A. Brockhaus, 1861).

——, *Air Built Castles. Stories from the Spanish of F. Caballero*. Translated by Mrs Pauli (London: London Literary Society, 1886).

——, *The Bird of Truth and Other Fairy Tales*. Translated by J.H. Ingram (London: W. Swan Sonnenschein & Co., [n.d.]).

Canellada, María Josefa, *Folklore de Asturias. Leyendas, cuentos y tradiciones* (Gijón: Ayalga Ediciones, 1983).

Caro Baroja, Julio, *Algunos mitos españoles* (2nd edn, Madrid, 1944).

——, *Ensayo sobre la literatura de cordel* (Madrid: Ediciones de la Revista de Occidente, 1961).

——, *El carnaval: análisis histórico-cultural* (Madrid: Taurus, 1965).

——, *Ritos y mitos equívocos* (Madrid, 1974).

——, *La estación de amor: fiestas populares de mayo a San Juan* (Madrid: Taurus, 1979).

——, *Ensayos sobre la cultura popular española* (Madrid: Dosbe, 1979).

——, *Del viejo folklore castellano. Páginas sueltas* (Valladolid: Ambito, 1988).

Castro y Fernández, Federico de, and Machado y Núñez, Antonio, eds., *Revista Mensual de Filosofía, Literatura y Ciencias de Sevilla* (Seville: Gironés y Orduña, 1869).

Chevalier, Maxime, *Cuentecillos tradicionales en la España del siglo de oro* (Madrid: Gredos, 1975).

——, *Folklore y literatura: el cuento oral en el Siglo de Oro* (Barcelona: Crítica, 1978).

——, *Cuentos españoles de los siglos XVI y XVII* (Madrid: Taurus, 1982).

——, *Cuentos folklóricos en la España del siglo de oro* (Madrid: Crítica, 1983).

——, 'Para una arqueología de los cuentos tradicionales en Castilla y León', in Luis Díaz Viana, ed., *Etnología y folklore en Castilla y León*, Colección

de estudios de etnología y folklore 2 (Salamanca: Junta de Castilla y León, 1986), 197-202.

——, *Catálogo tipológico del cuento folklórico español. Cuentos maravillosos* (Madrid: Gredos, 1995).

Childers, J. Wesley, *Tales from Spanish Picaresque Novels: A Motif-Index* (New York: State University of New York, 1977).

Childers, J. Wesley, and Reynolds, John J., 'A Guide to the Motif-Index of Timoneda's Prose Fiction', *Kentucky Romance Quarterly*, 25 (1978), 399-412.

Cooper, J.C., *Symbolic & Mythological Animals* (London: Aquarian Press, 1992)

Curiel Merchán, Marciano, *Cuentos extremeños* (Madrid: CSIC, 1944).

Deyermond, Alan, 'Folk-Motifs in the Medieval Spanish Epic', *Philological Quarterly*, 51, 1 (January, 1972), 36-53.

Díaz y Díaz, Manuel C., *Visiones del más allá en Galicia durante la alta edad media*. Biblioteca de Galicia 26 (Santiago de Compostela: Bibliofilos Gallegos, 1985).

Diego Cuscoy, Luis, *El folkore infantil y otros estudios etnográficos* (Santa Cruz de Tenerife: Publicaciones científicas del Cabildo de Tenerife, 1991).

Dundes, Alan (ed.), *Cinderella, A Folklore Casebook* (New York: Garland, 1982).

——, 'The Motif-Index and Tale Type Index: A Critique', *Journal of Folklore Research*, 34, no 3 (1997 Sept-Dec), 195-202.

Espinosa, Aurelio M., *Cuentos populares españoles*, 3 vols (Stanford University Pres, 1923; 2nd edn, Madrid: CSIC, 1946-47).

——, *Cuentos populares de España*, 3 vols (3rd edn, Madrid: CSIC, 1965).

Espinosa, Aurelio M. (hijo), *Cuentos populares de Castilla* (Buenos Aires: Espasa-Calpe, 1946).

——, *Cuentos populares de Castilla y León*, 2 vols, Biblioteca de Dialectología y Tradiciones Populares (Madrid: CSIC, 1988; reprinted 1996).

Fedorchek, Robert M., *Death and the Doctor: Three Nineteenth-century Spanish Tales*. Translated from the Spanish by Lou Charnon-Deutsch (Lewisburg, Pa: Bucknell University Press; London: Associated University Presses, 1997).

——, 'The Adventures of a Tailor', *Marvels & Tales*, 12, no 2 (1998), 351-63.

——, 'The Devil's Mother-in-Law', *Marvels & Tales*, 15, no 2 (2001), 192-201.

——, 'The King's Son-in-Law', *Marvels & Tales*, 15, no 2 (2001), 202-16.

——, 'The Bird of Truth', *Marvels & Tales*, 16, no 1 (2002), 73-83.

——, *Stories of Enchantment from Nineteenth-century Spain* (Lewisburg, Pa: Bucknell University Press, 2002).

——, 'The Souls in Purgatory', *Marvels & Tales*, 17, no 2 (2003), 258-61.

Foley, John Miles, *The Singer of Tales in Performance* (Bloomington: Indiana University Press, 1995).

Freud, Sigmund, *The Interpretation of Dreams* (Harmondsworth: Penguin, 1991).

Georges, Robert A., 'The Centrality in Folkloristics of Motif and Tale Type', *Journal of Folklore Research*, 34, no 3 (1997 Sept-Dec), 203-8.

Gillmor, Frances, 'Folklore Study in Spain', *Journal of American Folklore*, 74 (1961), 336-43.

Gissing, Vera (trans), *Spanish Fairy tales*. Illustrated by Michael Romberg (London: Hamlyn, 1973).

González Reboredo, X.M., *Lendas galegas de tradición oral*. Biblioteca Básica da Cultura Galega (Vigo: Galaxia, 1983).

Granch, H.C., *Cuentos maravillosos y de hadas españoles* (Barcelona: Maucci, 1945).

——, *Cuentos populares españoles* (Barcelona: Molino, 1962).

——, *Cuentos populares de animales* (Barcelona: Molino, 1963).

Guichot y Sierra, Alejandro, *Noticia histórica del folklore. Orígenes en todos los países hasta 1890. Desarrollo en España hasta 1921* (Seville, 1922; repr. Junta de Andalucía, 1984).

Haase, Donald (ed.), *Fairy Tales and Feminism: New Approaches*. Series in Fairy Tale Studies (Detroit: Wayne State University Press, 2004).

Haboucha, Reginetta, *Classification of Judeo-Spanish Folktales* (Baltimore: Johns Hopkins University Press, 1973).

——, *Types and Motifs of Judeo-Spanish Folktales* (New York: Garland, 1992).

——, 'The Judeo-Spanish Folktale: A Current Uppdate', *Jewish Folklore and Ethnology Review*, 15, no. 2 (1993), 32-58.

Hansen, William, 'Mythology and Folktale Typology: Chronicle of a Failed Scholarly Revolution', *Journal of Folklore Research*, 34, no 3 (1997 Sept-Dec), 275-80.

Haviland, Virginia, and Barbara Cooney *Favorite Fairy Tales Told in Spain* (Boston: Little, Brown, 1963).

Jung, Carl Gustav, *Collected Works* (Princeton: Princeton University Press, 1991).

Keller, John Esten, *Motif-Index of Mediaeval Spanish Exempla* (Knoxville: University of Tennessee Press, 1949).

——, 'Folklore in the *Cantigas* of Alfonso el Sabio', *Southern Folklore Quarterly* 23 (1959), 175-83.

Kolbenschlag, Madonna, *Kiss Sleeping Beauty Goodbye: Breaking the Spirit of Feminine Myths and Models* (New York: Doubleday, 1979).

Krekovicová, Eva, 'A Note in favor of Motif Indexes', *Journal of Folklore Research*, 34, no 3 (1997 Sept-Dec), 259-61.

Lacarra, Mª Jesús, *Cuentos de la Edad Media*, Odres Nuevos (Madrid: Castalia 1989).

Lévi-Strauss, Claude, *Structural Anthropology*, trans. By. Claire Jacobson and Brooke Schoepf (New York: Basic Books, 1963).

——, *Myth and Meaning* (London: Routledge, 1978)

Llano Roza de Ampudia, Aurelio de, *Cuentos asturianos. Recogidos de la tradición oral*. Archivo de Tradiciones Populares (Madrid: Caro Raggio, 1925).

Llinares, María del Mar, *Mouros, ánimas, demonios. El imaginario popular gallego* (Madrid: Akal Universitaria, 1990).

Lord, Albert Bates, *The Singer of Tales* (Cambridge, Mass.: Harvard University Press, 1960).

Lüthi, Max, *The European Folktale: Form and Nature* (Philadelphia: Institute for the Study of Human Issues, 1982).

Machado y Álvarez, Antonio, *Colección de enigmas y adivinanzas en forma de Diccionario* (Seville: Baldaraque, 1880).

——, *Estudios sobre literatura popular* (Seville: A. Guichot and Company, 1884).

——, ed., *Biblioteca de las Tradiciones Populares Españolas* 11 vols (Seville: A. Guichot and Company, and Madrid: Fernando Fé, 1883-1886).

Machado y Álvarez, Antonio, and Castro, Federico, *Cuentos, leyendas y costumbres populares* (Seville: Gaditana, 1872).

Marsan, Rameline E., *Itinérarire espagnol du conte médiéval (VIIIe-XVe siècles)*. Témoins de l'Espagne: Série historique, no. 4 (Paris: Klincksieck, 1974).

Maspóns y Labrós, Francisco, *Lo Rondallayre; quentos populars catalans* (Barcelona: Verdaguer, 1871-1872).

——, *Lo Rondallayre; segona série* (Barcelona: Verdaguer, 1872).

——, *Lo Rondallayre; tercera série* (Barcelona: Verdaguer, 1874).

Menéndez Pidal, Ramón, *Poesía popular y poesía tradicional en la literatura española; conferencia leída en All Sould College el lunes, 26 de junio de 1922* (Oxford: Clarendon Press, 1922).

Metmann, Walter (ed.), Alfonso X, *Cantigas de Santa María* 3 vols, (Madrid: Castalia, 1986-89).

Moutinho, José Viale, *Contos populares portugueses: antologia* (Porto: Familia 2000, 1978).

Pedrosa, José María, *El cuento tradicional en los Siglos de Oro* (Madrid: Arcadia de las letras, 2005).

Pelayo Briz, Francisco, *Endevinallas populars catalanas: accompanyadas de variants y confrontaments ab endevinallas francesas, lituanas, vascas, gallegas, italianas, ribagorzanas, provensalas, alamanyas, anglesas, portuguesas, nearnesas, castellanas y senegambesas, seguidas de un aplech de endevinallas modernas* (Barcelona: Librería d'Edualt Puig, 1882).

Pérez de Castro, José Luis, *Los estudios de folklore en Asturias* (Gijón: Ayalga Ediciones, 1983).

Perrault, Charles, and Angot, Christine, *Peau d'âne* (Paris: Stock, 2003).

——, *Complete Fairy Tailes*, translated from the French by A.E. Johnson and others (London: Constable, 1962).

Philip, Neil, *The Cinderella Story* (Harmondsworth: Penguin, 1989).

Propp, Vladimir, *The Morphology of the Folktale*. 2nd edn, revised and edited with a preface by Louis A. Wagner and a new Introduction by Alan Dundes (Austin, Texas: University of Texas Press, 1968).

——, *Theory and History of Folklore*, ed. with and Introduction and Notes by Anatoly Liberman (Manchester: Manchester University Press, 1984).

Rodríguez Muñoz, Javier., et al., *Folklore* (Gijón: Júcar, 1981).

Rodríguez Almodóvar, Antonio, *Los cuentos maravillosos españoles* (2nd edn, Barcelona: Crítica, 1987).

Rogers, E., 'The Hunt in the *Romancero* and Other Traditional Ballads', *Hispanic Review*, 42 (1974), 133-71.

——, 'The Perilous Hunt: Symbols in Hispanic and European Balladry', *Studies in Romance Languages*, 22 (Lexington: Kentucky University Press, 1980).

Salvador, Archiduque Luis, *Cuentos de Mallorca* (Barcelona: Biblioteca de Cuentos Maravillosos, 1995).

Sánchez Pérez, José A., *Cien cuentos populares españoles* (Madrid: Editorial Saeta, 1942; reprinted Barcelona: Biblioteca de Cuentos Maravillosos, 1992).

Santa Cruz de Dueñas, Melchor de, *Floresta española*, ed. with a prologue and notes by María Pilar Cuartero and Maxime Chevalier, with a preliminary study by Maxime Chevalier (Barcelona: Crítica, 1997).

Taggart, James M., *Enchanted Maidens: Gender relations in Spanish Folktales of Courtship and Marriage* (Princeton: Princeton University Press, 1990).

Thomas, Henry (trans.), *The Crafty Farmer. A Spanish Folk-tale Entitled How a Crafty Farmer with the Advice of his Wife Deceived Some Merchants*. Translated, with an Introduction, by Henry Thomas. Illustrated by Gregorio Prieto (London: Dolphin, 1938).

Thompson, Dean Stith, *Motif-Index of Folk Literature*, 6 vols (2nd edn, Copenhagen & Bloomington, 1955-58).

Timoneda, Juan de, *Obras de Juan Timoneda* (Madrid: Sociedad de bibliófilos españoles, 1947-1948).

——, *Buen aviso y portacuentos. El sobremesa y alivio de los cantares*, ed. by María Pilar Cuartero and Maxime Chevalier (Madrid: Espasa-Calpe, 1989).

——, *El patrañuelo* (Madrid: Espasa-Calpe, 1990).

Trueba y la Quintana, Antonio de (Antón de los Cantares), *Cuentos campesinos* (Leipzig: F.A. Brockhaus, 1865).

——, *Cuentos de varios colores* (Madrid: Centro general de administración, 1866).

——, *Cuentos populares* (Madrid, Romero, 1909).

Tubach, Frederic C., *Index Exemplorum: A Handbook of Medieval Religious Tales* (Helsinki: Suomalianen Tiedeakatemia, 1969).

Uther, Hans-Jörd, 'Indexing Folktales: A Critical Survey', *Journal of Folklore Research*, 34, no 3 (1997 Sept-Dec), 209-20.

Vasconcellos Pereira de Mello, José Leite de, *Contos populares e lendas* (Coimbra: Universidade de Coimbra, 1964).

Warner, Marina, *From the Beast to the Blonde. On Fairy Tales and their Tellers* (London: Chatto and Windus, 1994).

——, *No Go the Bogeyman: Scaring, Lulling, and Making Mock* (London, Chatto and Windus, 1998).

Zipes, Jack (ed.), *Oxford Companion to Fairy Tales* (Oxford: Oxford University Press, 2000).

Zorrilla, José, *Leyendas* (Madrid: Cátedra, 2000).

INDEX